SWARM THEORY

A MURDER-MYSTERY THRILLER

AWARD WINNING AUTHOR

E.W. SULLIVAN

ewsullivan.com

THIS IS A TEN TALENTS ® BOOK
1300 Old Highway 5 South
Ellijay, Georgia 30540

ISBN *(soft)*: 978-0-9887584-0-7
ISBN *(hard):* 978-0-9887584-1-4

Editor: Dennis De Rose, MoneySaver Editing

Manufactured in the United States of America
First Edition

To
my loving and supportive wife, Anita,
and the newest girl in my life, Paris.

And to
my late parents, George and Annie.
Put in a good word for me.

"...If there is no struggle there is no progress. Those who profess to favor freedom and yet depreciate agitation, are men who want crops without plowing up the ground, they want rain without thunder and lightening. They want the ocean without the awful roar of its many waters. This struggle may be a moral one, or it may be a physical one, and it may be both moral and physical, but it must be a struggle. Power concedes nothing without a demand. It never did and it never will."

—Frederick Douglass, *West India Emancipation Speech*, 1857

ONE

Puny Ass

ZONES HEARD THE SCREAMS, unsure if they came from man or beast. The whines of stray cats, when caught in a midsummer night's breeze, can sound like cries for help. *What woman would come here this time of night, other than whores?* He flipped up his collar and shoved dry hands inside his coat pockets. He stepped away from the entrance to Apple Massage and charged down a darkened street. Another scream followed the last one. Zones pushed the shrieks from his mind. This was Decatur not Atlanta—although it wanted to be. It had big dreams, just like every shithole town that surrounded that resurgent city.

Zones fought the wind, rushing through a stiff breeze. His coat made its own sharp noise while flapping in the wind. The screams grew stronger. He darted down another street, heading toward the sounds, no longer able to ignore them. Weak, inconsistent beams of light came from a flickering lamp that dangled from the side of a building. Around a corner, more light beamed from an alley hidden behind an abandoned restaurant. From the cover of darkness, he watched as a young woman struggled with a man twice her size.

The man shoved the woman hard to her knees. Zones watched as she tore the flesh-toned pantyhose that bronzed her long, pale legs. The man doubled her over on the ground. His hand was chocked-full of hair as he forced her head to the pavement. *That dirty, hard surface is no place for the soft, clean skin of a debutante.* She buried her hands deep into a puddle of water. It had rained earlier that day. The still wet pavement glistened beneath the light. The assailant grabbed the young women's arms and pinned them to the ground.

"What's this?" He lifted her hand. "Damn, girl, this is a big-ass rock." He ripped the ring from her finger. She cried, whimpering.

"Don't hurt me, please," she begged. Her assailant said nothing; he exuded heavy breaths full of torrid excitement.

The man tore the short, sequined dress she wore in half. He ripped away the black, laced lingerie and exposed her bare ass, the garment entangled in his fingers.

"Why the fuck you women wear this shit? Your man won't sniff these tonight." He chuckled with more grunt than laughter. He gripped the garment with his teeth and peeled it from his hand.

"Please don't kill me." She hugged the ground on her hands and knees, just like a praying mantis. "I won't tell. I just want to go home."

The man shoved his knee between her thighs, parting her legs. The woman screamed as the air burst from her lungs. He pulled her hair, still clenched in his hand, the stringy strands caught in his fingers like starchy spaghetti on a fork. He bowed her back and unzipped his pants. She flicked her wrist, spying the watch dangling from it, closed her eyes and covered her ears. Her elbows ground on the hard pavement.

"You're gonna get a treat, bitch; I feel lucky tonight." He moved up to her. She screamed again.

"Let *her* go," Zones said. His voice was calm but firm.

The man jumped to his feet. He turned toward Zones yet remained hidden.

"Who're you? Damn sure ain't no cop. They stopped coming here months ago. Come out where I can see you."

"I *said* let her go."

"You can have her puny ass when I'm finished with her, if there's anything left."

He dropped to his knees and pulled his victim close once again. She knelt there, head bowed, hands over her ears, crying.

"Why don't you just go away so he can finish!"

"You see, man, she wants it."

Zones charged toward the man from behind the shadow of darkness. He sprang to his feet again, pulled a large knife from his side and readied it. Zones drew closer. The man raised the knife. From out of nowhere, a loud explosion boomed disturbing the quiet night. Zones flew through the air and landed hard on the ground.

TWO

The Golden Buddha

"I'M DETECTIVE ROME FROM Major Crimes." Wearing her platform shoes, she strolled up to the officer all cool-like, as if she was too bad for her feet. "You called about a rape?"

"She was in that wagon you just passed."

"Where're they headed? Grady Hospital?"

"Yep."

"What's the victim's name?" Rome slipped a pad and pen from her coat.

"She didn't say, just told me someone raped her, then she fell into my arms. I couldn't wake her after that."

"Where did you find her?"

"I didn't, she found me. Came stumbling through that dustcloud over there, walking barefooted." He pointed toward a large plume that lingered in the distance.

"Wasn't the Golden Buddha over there once?"

"Damn shame it's gone, too. That was some good-ass yang food."

"Your mother know you talk that way?" The officer raised his brow. "Describe how she looked."

"...White, about so-high." He raised his hand to his chest. "She swayed from side to side. Her arms and legs went wherever the hell they wanted to, and her hair hung over her face. She looked a mess, like a zombie."

"Did she say who attacked her?"

"Just said someone raped her."

"Well, can't do much until they clear this mess. I'll go question our victim at the hospital."

Rome returned to her car. She glanced back at the blaring fire engines and flashing lights. *Won't find much evidence after they wash it all away.*

"Rome?" someone shouted. She turned to see Detective Marmaduke. "What're you doing here? I heard a call on an explosion, not a sex crime. Where're you coming from anyway, the club?"

Rome's hand shot to her hip. She posed; her long, lean legs were stuffed into skintight, bell-bottom jeans.

"Well, Marmaduke, I was just going to ask you the same. I don't see any dead bodies, and you're in Fulton County, not DeKalb."

"Heard the call and the sirens, thought I'd come by and lend a hand. The county line runs right through there you know." He pointed toward the fire.

"You...on the blotter? I'd have thought you'd be glued to your tube watching Congressman Stonewall. His rebuttal to the President's news conference on terrorism should be *must see TV* for you and the rest of your right-winged buddies."

"I'm a libertarian. What brings you out this time of night?"

"Rape victim. It happened in that haze right there."

"She could be a young co-ed and new to the area. They use the abandoned buildings for raves. We get those this time of year. You got a suspect?"

"I'm headed to Grady now to question my vic."

Rome and Marmaduke stood among the red fire engines and squad cars, staring at the fiery blaze. Firefighters dashed back and forth through the smoke and dust. They draped water hoses over their shoulders, dragging them into the haze. Helmet lights did little to pierce deep into the thick wall of billowing ash. They moved at a constant pace toward the wall with a chorus of barking dogs in the background. The two scenarios made for an eerie mix.

"Kecksburg, 1965," Rome said.

"What's that?"

"...A village in Mt. Pleasant Township, Pennsylvania and the sight of a crashed unidentified flying object."

"...A UFO?"

"Fire and police responded to a wooded area just outside town. Residents reported seeing smoldering wreckage. I image it looked like this, except with trees."

Marmaduke crossed his arms. He cut Rome a hard look. "...A UFO?"

The radio crackled. Marmaduke leaned in to a nearby squad car to hear the call.

> *We're going to need animal control on scene, over.*
> *...Animal control en route, copy.*
> *Make that animal control, homicide and the bomb squad, over.*

"...Homicide and the bomb squad?"

"Well, Marmaduke, I guess you're up after all. The crime gods are working overtime."

"You think your rape victim saw what happened?"

"I'll have more info for you once I talk to her." Rome wetted down her seventies-style Afro, pulled it into a ponytail and removed her doughnut-sized looped earrings.

"...Back to the club?"

"Funny, Marmaduke, just trying not to upset you white folk. Y'all see the Afro and next thing I've got an FBI escort."

"Let me know if you get something."

"I'll send you up a bat signal." She lowered herself into her car. "By the way, I'm an Independent."

* * *

Grady, the place had one name, like Cher or Madonna. Its fame came from poverty and anonymity, not wealth and celebrity. The hospital emergency room brimmed with the uninsured. The unhealthy loitered there, like mold on bread. People lay stretched over chairs and floors, mounds of blankets covered them. They propped themselves up against walls or wandered the halls and suffered through their pain. A strong odor lingered, a mixture of alcohol and antiseptic. You might get a hangover while you waited, but at least you wouldn't catch an infection.

Rome waded over through these huddled masses to a nurse sitting at her station. She flashed her badge.

"I'm looking for a rape victim that just came through here."

The nurse pointed down the hall. Rome headed that way. She came to another station and asked a nurse the same question.

"She's waiting for you," the nurse said, and she led Rome to a room where a young woman rested, tucked beneath clean white bed sheets.

"Hi, I'm Detective Rome." She forced out a smile. "Can you tell me what happened?" The woman nodded. Rome, with pad and pen in hand, pulled up a chair next to her bedside. "Okay, let's start with your name." The woman hesitated. Her words were stuck in her mouth. She opened it, but nothing came out. "Let me get you a drink, sweetie." Rome poured a cold cup of water from a pitcher that sat next to the bed. The woman sat up, grabbed the cup and took two big swallows. She coughed. Water spewed from her mouth. "Careful now." Rome took the cup and patted her back.

"Thank you," she said. Her trembling hand wiped across her mouth.

Rome hoped the water would provide the grease the girl needed to free up her tongue.

"Tell me your name, dear?"

"It's Kimble...Kimble Tyler."

Rome scribbled in her pad.

"Okay, Kimble, tell me what happened?"

"I was walking to my car and this guy attacked me. He dragged me into the alley and..." She cried. Her tears came slow at first, then harder.

"Do you need a minute?" Rome handed her a napkin and grabbed her hand.

"No...no, I'm fine."

"Okay. Let's start from the beginning. Why were you in that area?"

"Work...I dance at the Pink Pony."

"Why were you alone? Don't they give the girls an escort at night?"

"Sometimes they're no better than the creep who attacked me. You know, wanting to get broken off a piece for the protection."

"Where were you parked?"

"...Next to the club."

"Did the assault take place there?"

"No, he dragged me to an alley behind where the Golden Buddha used to be."

"Did you see him before that?"

"I think I saw him come out of the animal shelter."

"There was an explosion—"

"Yeah, when the other guy showed up."

"There were two guys?"

"No." Kimble shook her head. "He tried to stop him. That's when the explosion happened. I didn't see him after that."

Suddenly, the exam room door swung open.

"Hello, I'm Dr. Morgan. I'll be examining you." Two nurses and a uniformed officer carrying a camera followed her inside the room. The doctor reached out and touched Kimble on her shoulder. "How are you?" Kimble only nodded.

"I'm Detective Rome. I'm handling her case." She shook the doctor's hand. It was soft and cottony and different from the other doctors. Their hands always felt scratchy, like fine sandpaper.

"I need to do a full examination. I'll explain as we go. We'll take good care of you, okay?" The doctor washed and dried her hands at a nearby sink. She snapped on a pair of rubber gloves.

"I'll be right outside, Doctor." Rome left the room, stopping just on the other side of the door. She pulled her phone from her pant pocket and dialed. "Connect me to Detective Marmaduke."

"Please hold," the dispatcher said.

Before the call connected, one of the nurses exited the room carrying a bag. Rome hung up the phone.

"Excuse me, are those my victim's clothes?"

"I'm taking them to the lab now."

"I need these, her rape kit, and anything else of value sent to me. Here's my card. Give them to the desk officer." Rome stepped back inside the room and walked over to Kimble's bedside. She looked on as the doctor carried out her exam.

"I'll check your vitals first." Dr. Morgan wrapped a blood pressure cuff around Kimble's thin arm. She inflated it. "Do you have any medical conditions or any recent surgeries?"

"No."

"…And your last period was when?"

"Last month."

Dr. Morgan listened to her heart through the stethoscope. "Are you taking any contraception?"

"No."

"Okay, now, I understand the detective took your statement," she looked to Rome, "but I need to question you as well." Kimble nodded. "Was there penetration?"

"Yes, vaginal." Tears swelled in her eyes. Rome moved closer to comfort her.

"The nurse collected your clothing?"

"I gave her my card to have them sent to our office," Rome said.

"I'm going to ask you to undress so the officer can take photographs. The nurse will help you."

The nurse lowered the sheet that was wrapped around Kimble and removed her surgical gown. The officer readied the camera. She snapped shots of the bumps and bruises on her knees, elbows, hands and other body parts. Kimble flinched with every shutter snap. She lowered her eyes as the camera's flash struck them.

"Not my face," Kimble shouted. She threw up her hands. The officer lowered the camera.

"We're finished taking pictures." Rome stepped in front of the camera.

"What we need now, dear, is a urine sample," Dr. Morgan said. "It'll make you more comfortable during the exam, so please empty your bladder."

The nurse helped Kimble back into her robe and over to the bathroom door. "Use the container on the shelf. I'll be right here." Kimble entered and emerged with the sample a few minutes later, handing it to the nurse.

"Now, Kimble, I need to examine you," Dr. Morgan said. "I'll start at your head and work my way down your body." The doctor grabbed her head. She touched all over her face, her neck, and squeezed along her shoulders.

"Ouch." Kimble grimaced.

"Is that a tender spot?"

"It hurts."

"I don't think anything's broken, but we'll take x-rays to make sure." Dr Morgan worked her way along Kimble's left arm, wrist and hand. She placed her finger in her palm. "Squeeze please. Good." The doctor moved to her right hand and up her arm. "Lie back for me." She pressed on her torso. "...Any pain?"

"No."

"Okay, now, I'll do a pelvic exam." Dr. Morgan squeezed Kimble's legs. She raised them up and spread them apart. A sheet hung over them. "I'm going to check for any external injuries. If you sense any discomfort, let me know."

"Okay." Kimble tensed up and moaned. She fidgeted as the doctor probed gently around her vagina.

"I'm going to examine you inside using this speculum." She showed it to Kimble. "It should feel warm. Again, there may be discomfort. Are you ready?"

"Yeah, I'm ready."

Dr. Morgan slipped the stainless steel device inside Kimble. She probed her internally. Kimble was sweating, her body grew tense and her breathing shortened. Rome knew what this part of the examination meant. Often the victim relived the assault, living the trauma all over again. She grabbed hold of Kimble's arm and stroked it.

"Take deep breaths through your mouth," Dr. Morgan said. "Now I'm going to swab the inside of your vagina." Her head disappeared between Kimble's legs. She handed the nurse the samples she had collected. The nurse placed them into sample bags and labeled them.

"I'll get these to the lab for a baseline pregnancy test, Doctor."

"Thank you," Dr. Morgan nodded. She removed the speculum, greased her finger and inserted it into Kimble. "Does that hurt?" Kimble shook her head. "Sit up for me. I want to explain your medical options to you."

Detective Rome's phone rang. She let go of Kimble's hand and stepped from the room.

"Hello, Marmaduke...I can barely hear you...Can you hear me...Check the site...hello...Listen, I'll have to call you back." As she hung up, Dr. Morgan pushed through the door. "How is she, Doctor?"

"I gave her something to help her rest. But you know how these things go, Detective."

"I still need to question her."

"You better hurry. She'll be out of it soon."

Rome returned to the examination room to find her victim sound asleep. "Kimble," she called to her. She hated waking her. The only peace she might find may only come in her dreams. "Kimble," she nudged her. Kimble opened her eyes to see Rome with the same forced smile. "I need to question you a bit more. Can you tell me anything else about your attacker? Did you get a good look at him?"

"It was dark," her slurred speech slipped from quivering lips, "but he was white and over six feet tall. Oh yeah, he took my ring."

"Describe it for me, please."

"It looked like a huge diamond, but it was glass, a princess cut, with a white gold band."

"That'll help. Is there anyone I can call for you, like your mother or your father?"

"There's no one."

"You try to rest. I'll check in on you in the morning."

Rome left Kimble to wrestle with her thoughts. She made her way back down the hall, through the alcohol and antiseptic-filled air of the emergency room and out into the temperate Atlanta night. She hopped into her black '72 Corvette convertible, one of two she inherited from her father. She alternated the weeks she drove them, a habit he passed on to her.

A ball of untied hair barreled down the highway. The wind caught it and straightened out the curly spots. Rome thought back to the case. She had investigated many rapes since joining the Sexual Crimes Unit. Unlike other women who worked in the unit, she did not suffer some personal tragedy. She found sheer pleasure in punishing people who preyed on others. During her drive back to the crime scene, she hoped the smoke had cleared enough for her to find clues to do just that.

THREE

Southern Malcontents

MARMADUKE PULLED A HANDKERCHIEF from his pocket, unfurling it and placing it over his nose and mouth. He rubbed his eyes red. The smoke and dust soiled the freshly minted Marlboro Menthol he kept tucked behind his ear. He moved closer to the fire commander.

"Did I hear someone say they had a body?" Marmaduke shouted to the commander, trying to be heard above the engine noise.

"You from Homicide?"

Marmaduke nodded. He looked through the haze. He could see firefighters trying to wrestle the flames under control.

"Is it safe in there?"

The commander shot Marmaduke a hard stare. The oxygen mask was tilted on top his head. His arms were folded over his ample belly. His bushy, salt-and-pepper brows protruded from his face like porcupine needles. He tooted his top lip to his nose, to where it covered his nostrils. His squinty eyes shifted between the smoldering building and Marmaduke.

"If it ain't, I don't figure it'll take much time off your life."

Marmaduke shrugged off the commander's barbed comment and headed for the burned-out building. He donned the protective shoe covers and hardhat provided him by a nearby firefighter. Powerful, telescoping lights lit up the scene and showed the outcome of the battle between fire and water. Firefighters continued to focus their hoses on parts of the building that still smoldered, trying hard to keep the fire from spreading. They cut their way through the debris with axes and saws. Walls crashed to the ground as they weakened from the flames. Firefighters returned from deep within the burned-out structure. They carried soot-covered dogs and cats, caged and un-caged. Their constant piercing whines were hard to ignore.

Marmaduke stepped along the debris-covered floor. He lifted one leg and stretched his arms out to his sides to balance himself before he lifted the other.

"Careful, Detective," a voice called out.

Marmaduke looked up to see two men approaching. "I'm Detective Marmaduke. Someone called in a homicide?"

"I'm Inspector Siler from DCFD. This is Agent Thomas with ATF. Your body's over here."

"Is this DeKalb County? I thought the line between us and Fulton ran right through that road."

Inspector Siler nodded and led Marmaduke to the rear of the building where cages of dead or dying cats and dogs lay locked away. The stench of burning flesh permeated the space. He pressed the handkerchief tight to his face and took short breaths and long exhales. The body lay huddled near the cages. Another man was kneeling over it.

"Excuse me."

"Excuse yourself." The man stood and turned. "Detective Marmaduke, late as usual I see."

"...Detective DuBoise."

"What're you doing contaminating my crime scene, Marmaduke?"

"Oh, are you working for DeKalb County now?"

"You know damn well this is Fulton's jurisdiction."

"I'm afraid not, Detective. That side's yours," Marmaduke pointed to the street, "This side's mine."

"Bullshit."

"If you don't believe me, ask Inspector Siler." The inspector nodded.

"Fuck it." Detective DuBoise threw off the latex gloves he was wearing. "I don't need the work anyway." He stormed from the bombed-out building.

"Too-da-loo," Marmaduke sang, wiggling his fingers at him. He knelt beside the body and poked and prodded it with his pen. "It's a young white male, mid-twenties, six-feet tall, hair is blond and there're no visible tattoos and no signs of trauma." Marmaduke eased back up. "Until the ME takes a look, I'll have to say cause of death is smoke inhalation." He turned to Agent Thomas. "What evidence you have of a bomb?"

"Over here." Agent Thomas led Marmaduke back to the front of the building. He stopped where the door used to be. "The blast originated here. The fire destroyed much of the bomb, but we have blast patterns in that metal girder and that beam. We see a thirty degree bend in this stud. Shrapnel scarring throughout the building places the origin here as well. These signature marks on the floor, where they radiate out from this point, give us our plane of symmetry and third point of confirmation."

"You know what type of bomb it was?"

"We haven't found enough of it yet, just fragments. I'll say this, the device produced enough energy coupling to reach deep inside the building. We'll know more once we speak with the owners and analyze this stuff in the lab."

"Who runs this place?"

"It's a private organization, a real estate trust, PA Development. They lease the place to Urban Pet Rescue."

"Who'd want to bomb an animal shelter?"

"You'd be surprised, Detective. You have many animal rights crazies out there."

"Yeah, but they killed animals too."

"Have you heard of the A-L-F?"

"...The American Football League?" Marmaduke smiled.

"Funny, Detective. The A-L-F, it's the Animal Liberation Front. They're a radical animal rights group. They use destructive tactics like this to set animals free from places they believe are harmful."

"I could understand a testing lab or a fur farm, but why an animal shelter?"

"Some believe all animals should roam free, the same as people."

"I think we're getting ahead of ourselves. First, we don't know if they targeted the shelter or someone who worked here, our corpse for instance. Second, we don't know for sure what kind of bomb was used. This whole thing could be a prank gone wrong, not a terror plot by militants who don't like us cuddling with Fluffy."

"…Point taken, Detective."

"Now, Inspector, can I take over this crime scene? 'Cause I want to preserve as much evidence as I can."

"It's the agent's call."

"It's all yours, Detective."

Inspector Siler and Agent Thomas tramped through the building's charred remains. They vanished into the dark night, which was marred with streaks of fire engine red and blaring blue lights.

Marmaduke secured the scene and pondered the death of a young man caught in a bomb blast, nothing new in Georgia. Southern malcontents, those who resort to a chemist's brew of devises to express their displeasure with the world, littered the state's history. In 1958, the Hebrew Benevolent Congregation Temple was bombed in the early morning on a brisk fall Sunday in November. The rabbi's support of civil rights angered the perpetrator. In the eighties, bombs mailed to civil rights organizations killed an attorney in Savannah. During the 1996 Olympics, a bomb exploded in an Atlanta park dedicated to the games, killing two and wounding many others. Months later, two bombs, courtesy of the same Olympic Park bomber, exploded again in Atlanta. The targets were a gay nightclub and an abortion clinic. Bombings in Georgia seemed as common as the sound of an *Amen* on Sunday mornings.

"Detective," someone shouted, as Marmaduke searched where the body lay.

"Back here." He looked to see Dr. DeGlorious high stepping her way through the debris. He ran to help her. "Our body's in the back." He held the yellow police tape up for her to pass underneath. "Heels are no place for a crime scene, Doctor."

"I do everything in heels, Detective. And I do mean everything." She twisted past him. Her hips swayed. Her heels, muffled by shoe covers, tapped the concrete floor softly. She knelt beside the body, shined a penlight over it and slipped a wallet from its pocket. She opened it. "Your victim's name is Brandon Elerby, white male, blond hair, blue eyes, six feet tall. Here's his address." Dr. DeGlorious handed

Marmaduke the driver's license. He jotted down the number and the street and handed the license to an evidence technician who bagged it. "I don't see any trauma to the body. There's little rigor. What time did you get the call, Detective?"

"I heard it come in around nine."

"...Seems about right. Until I get him on the table, I'll say cause of death is possibly smoke inhalation."

"Yeah, that's what I thought. You okay here, Doc? Figured I'd handle the notification tonight, no need to keep his people worried."

"You're getting soft in your old age, Detective. Sure, go ahead, I'll finish here."

Marmaduke exited the burned-out building. He moved past the few officers and fire personnel that remained and headed to his car. The notification didn't have to be made now. He had waited longer on other cases. But he needed the work, like an old boxer in need of the extra rounds to get his legs under him. He would conclude the notification tonight and mix the anguish of the dead man's family with his own.

Marmaduke's phone rang as he drove. "Marmaduke, here."

"You're still on scene?" Detective Rome asked.

"Headed to my DB's family, why?"

"My rape victim said there were two men."

"Two...You think the other man was my DB?"

"Was he found in the alley behind the Golden Buddha?"

"...Inside a bombed-out building."

"You might have a second body."

"Oh shit! I'm turning around now."

FOUR

Interrupted the Quiet Night

"HELLO, DR. DEGLORIOUS. ARE you still at the animal shelter?" Marmaduke asked.

"I just finished up."

"Don't go anywhere. We may have another body."

"...Where?"

"The alley behind the Golden Buddha."

"Where's that?"

"Stay put; I'll be there in two minutes."

Marmaduke raced back to the crime scene. When he got there, the fire engines had gone. He pulled up to what remained of the building. The old Deuce added to the smoke that had scattered. A hinge squeaked as he opened his car door.

"Detective Marmaduke," Dr. DeGlorious called, "over here."

Marmaduke jogged over to her. He wheezed and coughed. He was back on the sticks of course. "Follow me, Doctor." He walked a short distance away from where the bomb blast had occurred. "So, you've never been to the Golden Buddha?"

"My taste is more uptown."

"You don't know what you missed."

"…From the looks of it, botulism."

They rounded the corner of the Golden Buddha. Debris littered the ground where they shined their lights. A screeching tire sounded nearby. Marmaduke turned to see Detective Rome pull up. She jumped from her car.

"What're you doing contaminating my crime scene?"

"…Your crime scene?" Marmaduke said. "You told me I had a body in here."

"Let's go."

Marmaduke shook his head. "Must be an Atlanta P.D. thing."

They walked shoulder to shoulder, flashed their lights on the ground, and combed for a body or whatever other evidence they could find.

"Why on Earth was she hanging out back here?" Detective Rome asked. "There ain't nothing here but rats, roaches and the stray cats that chase them."

"And whores," Marmaduke quipped.

"Sometimes I wonder if you had a mother." Detective Rome flicked her flashlight toward the building. "Surprised that light is still lit. They did shutdown this place, didn't they?"

"Damn shame too. That was some good ass yang—"

"Yeah, so I've heard."

"Don't get me wrong, it was a dump. It had seen its fair share of trouble. Made a few busts here myself back in the day. But you can't clean up every massage parlor and skin joint. You gotta leave something for the buzzards to eat or else they'll want the whole goddamn dinner."

"With this Bible toting crowd? Please. Even if they did stick *cuisine* on the sign out front, it couldn't hide the tacky neon lights or the smell of hot and sour pork from their snobby noses."

"Yeah, well, too bad for your vic. They packed the place back then. Someone may've noticed."

They walked a few more feet into the alley.

"Stop!"

"What is it?"

Detective Rome hushed him.

"Do you hear that?" A faint moan sounded. "Over there." Detective Rome raced to a spot nearby. The others followed. The moans got louder. They cleared piles of trash that covered the ground and uncovered a body. He lay face down, battered and bruised. "I'll call an ambulance."

Dr. DeGlorious dropped to her knees. She pressed against his neck. "His pulse is weak." She ran her hands over his body. "Sir, can you hear me? Can you tell me where you're hurt?" He continued to moan. "Help me roll him over." Marmaduke grabbed his feet while she stabilized his head. They rolled him over in small stages.

"Dr. Zones," Marmaduke said stunned.

Detective Rome returned. "An ambulance is coming."

"Dr. Zones." Marmaduke pressed his face close. He felt soft breaths.

Zones' eyes opened a slither. "If I'm dead, you're the ugliest angel I've ever seen."

"If you were dead, you'd be seeing demons, not angels."

"Are you going to kiss me or help me to my feet?"

"I don't think you should move," Dr. DeGlorious said. "We have an ambulance coming."

"If I lie here any longer, I'll sprout daisies. Help me up or we can stay here and discuss aberrant psychology."

"Not one of your brain-freezing speeches." Marmaduke wrapped his arms around Zones. He lifted him to a sitting position. He moaned. They rested. They knew the next move to his feet would hurt even more. "Okay, on three: One—Two—Three, up." Marmaduke pulled Zones to his feet, clutched him beneath his arms and wrapped them around his back. He steadied him, like balancing a penny on end. Zones wobbled between Marmaduke's outstretched arms. They walked to the end of the alley and out to the street. Just then, the ambulance pulled to the curb. They bandaged Zones' head and placed his arm in a sling.

"You need to go to the hospital," Dr. DeGlorious warned him.

"I'm fine."

"You may have a concussion."

"Nothing a strong drink won't cure."

"...Men."

"How in the world did you wind up face down in an alley, Doc?" Marmaduke asked.

"I walked by, ouch—" Zones grabbed his bandaged shoulder. "I heard screams. The next I know, I'm staring up at your ugly mug."

"You didn't witness a woman being raped here?" Detective Rome asked.

"…A rape? Yeah, that's what drew me here. What happened to her? Did they get the guy?"

"She's in the hospital and we're looking for her assailant. Did you get a look at him?"

"I'm sorry, but who are you?"

"Detective Rome, APD Major Crimes."

"What happened? How did I wind up on the ground? Feels like two Mack trucks hit me."

"A bomb blew up the animal shelter across the road," Marmaduke explained.

"…A bomb blast? Shit, that explains it. But who'd want to blow up an animal shelter? There're worse places."

"Right, so, why were you over here?"

Zones ignored Marmaduke's question. "I gather you want a statement, Detective Rome?"

"…If you're up to it."

"Can I catch a ride? I'm sure I shouldn't be driving."

Her eyes moved from Zones' head to his feet. "I may have to let the seat back, but you'll fit. Give me a minute to look for more evidence."

Marmaduke turned to leave. "I still have a notification to make. See y'all in the morning." He turned back. "Say, Rome, did your rape victim mention the explosion?"

"Said she thought her attacker came from the animal shelter. He also took her jewelry, a ring. I'm filing a stolen property report in case he pawns it."

"Sounds like our man."

"A bomber that sticks around to commit a rape?" Zones said. "That fits no psychological theory I've ever studied."

"It took us time to believe people would strap a bomb to their back and then blow themselves up, Doc, so it's possible."

"Possible, but it's not likely."

"But possible."

"…Yes, possible, Detective."

"Let's find this guy."

"I'll shake the bushes," Detective Rome said, "see what slithers out."

"I'm off to North Atlanta."

* * *

Marmaduke arrived at the address listed on Brandon Elerby's driver's license—a posh DeKalb County neighborhood at the western edge of Brookhaven. He parked under a light on the street and walked along a brick paved walkway. Steps led to the stoop of a large porch that dominated the front entry and whose only light came from the doorbell button. Marmaduke pressed it. Moments later, a single light flashed on inside that lit up the house, another followed that lit up the dark porch where he stood.

"Who is there?" a muffled voice carried through the closed door.

"Detective Marmaduke from DeKalb County."

The door opened a crack. A man stuck out an eye and nose.

"May I see ID, please?" his heavy accent combating his words. Marmaduke removed his badge and placed it up to the door crack. The man studied it from behind thick-rimmed spectacles. He peered back up at Marmaduke and closed the door. It swung open again a moment later, wider this time. "Come in, Detective." Marmaduke stepped through the door. The man, dressed in a bathrobe and slippers, greeted him. It was obvious that he had awakened him. "What can I do for you, Detective?"

"Do you know a Brandon Elerby?"

"Brandon Elerby? No."

"Mister….I'm sorry…your name?"

"…El-Arabi, Dr. Amal El-Arabi." Two women joined them, one much older than the other. The older woman spoke Arabic. She looked worried, not used to having law enforcement in their home this late at night, no doubt. "Excuse me, Detective, my wife, Badr, and my daughter, Aasima." Marmaduke nodded. "He is asking about a Brandon Elerby, and we do not know such a person," he confirmed with his wife.

"No such person lives here," she said in the same thick accent. Layers of clothes covered her rotund body. Black hair, pulled back tight on her round head, peeked from beneath a colorful scarf. Marmaduke looked over at Aasima who said nothing. She stuffed her fluffy form beneath many layers of garments just like her mother.

"Do you have a son, Dr. El-Arabi?"

"Yes, Muhammad, why do you ask of my son?"

"May I see a picture of him, please?"

They looked puzzled. "What is this about, Detective?"

"…Perhaps nothing, sir. A photograph will help clear this up."

Mrs. El-Arabi disappeared into another room. She returned with a photograph and handed it to her husband, who in turn gave it to Marmaduke. The image was of a dark-haired, dark-eyed young man in his early to mid-twenties. The picture had the wrong hair and eyes, but the face matched his victim. Marmaduke wasn't certain, however, and he needed to be sure.

"When did you take this picture?"

"A year ago," Dr. El-Arabi answered.

"You saw your son last, when?"

"A year ago. He is a student at university in Washington, D.C. He came home briefly for spring break."

"So, you wouldn't expect him back in Georgia?"

"…No, of course not."

"Could you contact your son for me?"

"…Now? It is late, Detective."

"I would not ask you if it wasn't important, sir."

Dr. El-Arabi walked over to a phone on a table, the old rotary, gaudy type, and picked up the receiver. He pressed it to his ear and dialed. Marmaduke listened as the phone rang. No one answered right away. He expected the delay, given the late night. The tension in the room built as they waited. They watched one another before all eyes fell back to Marmaduke.

Dr. El-Arabi shouted in Arabic through the phone. He seemed relieved. "Muhammad," he said.

Aasima rushed to his side. She pulled back the colorful scarf that covered her round face, grabbed hold the receiver and pulled it to her ear.

"Who is this?" Dr. El-Arabi demanded. "I'm trying to reach my son, Muhammad—Detective Marmaduke is here." He turned to him. The blood left his face. His jowls and eyes sagged. He held out the phone to Marmaduke, his hand trembling.

Marmaduke grabbed the phone and raised it to his ear. "Marmaduke, here."

"Detective," Dr. DeGlorious said, "this cell phone was in your DB's pocket."

"I see."

"I'll start the autopsy in the morning."

"Okay, Doctor. Bye."

"Detective, what happened to my son?" Dr. El-Arabi asked without waiting. "Who answered his phone?"

"Sir, ma'am, please have a seat." They gathered on a sofa. "Earlier tonight there was an explosion at an animal shelter, and we believe your son was a victim in that explosion."

"…An explosion in DC?"

"No, sir. The explosion was in DeKalb County."

"But I do not understand. Muhammad is in DC, at university. Are you sure it is him?"

"The victim matches the picture you showed me, and the person who answered his phone was the medical examiner."

"Medical examiner…you mean my son is dead?"

"I'm afraid so."

Mrs. El-Arabi shrilled through the house; the loud scream interrupted the peace that the night gave. She slapped her face and stretched her hands to the heavens. Her sleeves fell from her arms to expose them up to her shoulders. Dr. El-Arabi motioned to Aasima. She wrapped her mother in her arms and led her away. Her screams, however, lingered but never abated.

"How can this be?" Dr. El-Arabi asked Marmaduke.

"Your son changed the way he looked and had ID in another name. Can you tell me why?"

"Why he changed his appearance and his name?"

"Why he dyed his hair blond and wore blue contact lenses and used the name Brandon Elerby."

"Perhaps he wanted to fit in with everyone else."

"What do you mean?"

"Life was difficult for him after 9-11. Most of his American friends stopped coming around…he avoided associating with his Arabic friends."

"So you have no idea why he'd be in Georgia? What about his friends? Could he have reconnected with them?"

"I have no idea. As for his friends, I did not know them."

"Your daughter—they look close in age—would she know his friends?"

"I will ask her. Aasima," Dr. El-Arabi called to her. She rushed back into the room.

"Yes, father."

"Can you tell the detective about your brother's friends?"

Aasima took a moment. Her eyes shifted between Marmaduke and her father. "They stopped visiting."

"Give me their names, please. One of them may know what happened to your brother."

"I will write them down for you." She pulled a sheet of paper and a pen from a table drawer and began writing. "I think his friends have moved away though."

"What school did he attend?"

"George Washington University. He was a junior electrical engineering major."

"Engineering, so he knew how to build things?"

"Is this important, Detective?" Dr. El-Arabi asked. "You said an explosion killed Muhammad."

"I'm sorry, Dr. El-Arabi, but we have to follow up on deaths like these."

"Here you are, Detective." Aasima handed him the paper. "These are his friends, those that I know."

Marmaduke scanned the names. He folded the paper and placed it inside his coat pocket as he rose to leave.

"Thank you, sir, ma'am, sorry for your loss."

"Thank you, Detective," Dr. El-Arabi said, now standing.

"We'll need you to identify the body."

"I will come later in the morning."

"…One last question, sir, if I may? What do you do for a living?"

"I am an assistant professor of electrical engineering at Georgia Tech. My specialty is nanoscience. Why?"

"…Just in case we need to reach you. Good night, sir."

Marmaduke left the El-Arabi family to their misery. He knew he had no answer yet as to why this young man had died, but he had, instead, stumbled onto a person of interest for the bombing.

FIVE

The Wall

IT WAS EARLY THE next morning. Marmaduke, Inspector Siler and Agent Thomas met in Captain Franklin's office. Since they had found a dead body at the bomb site, Marmaduke took the lead in the investigation. So far, this new case had not felt the singe of the media's bright lights. *An explosion of unknown origin has occurred and the investigation continues,* was the only comment given. It wasn't far from the truth. They were still awaiting confirmation of a bomb.

The captain sported his new regalia—a pressed new uniform with sharp creases and additional bars for solving the Mormon murders. He did not sit from the time Marmaduke entered the room.

"Let's make this quick," the captain said. "I've got a luncheon."

"Where at, Cracker Barrel?" Marmaduke quipped.

"No, smart ass, The Marriott in downtown Atlanta. It's in my honor." He touched his chest.

"Who's giving it?"

"Some crime prevention organization, but I'm expecting more." Captain Franklin straightened his tie using a mirror that hung on the wall.

"Sounds like you're moving from underneath the shadow of the big boys in Atlanta," Agent Thomas said.

"Yeah, and it's about damn time. But I digress. You have anything more on the explosives used, Agent?"

"The blast destroyed the device. The fragments, if you can call them that, were too small to analyze. We don't even have enough for a chemical signature, not to mention a bomb signature—no fusing, no wiring, no timing mechanism, nothing."

"Have you ever run across this before, Agent, no bomb material residue at the scene?"

"Never this refined."

"You sure it was a bomb?"

"I thought about that, too, so I swept the area a second time using an entire crew. There're bomb signatures, just not the physical evidence of one."

"I hope you have better news, Marmaduke."

"I just might. I met with the family of my DB, the El-Arabi family. They're from Saudi Arabia. The old man is a professor of electrical engineering over at Tech, a researcher in nanoscience, whatever the hell that is. Now, when we found the kid, he was all Nordic-looking, just the opposite of his swarthy parents. There was an FBI working paper issued about al-Qaida trying to recruit Anglo-looking Muslims to carry out attacks. The kid had ID on him with the name Brandon Elerby. You can't get any whiter than that. Also, Elerby sounds phonetically similar to El-Arabi. I don't think that's a coincidence. One more point, he was a student in electrical engineering in DC. So, both he and his father knew their way around electronics."

"Any of this makes sense to either of you?" Captain Franklin asked Agent Thomas and Inspector Siler.

"Nanoscience deals with microscopic particles," Agent Thomas said.

"Well, there you go," Marmaduke said. "They made the bomb from this nano stuff. It explains why you can't find fragments."

"Nanobombs are sophisticated shit, Detective. No one but the DOD boys have that technology."

"Suppose they're not the only ones? Perhaps the good professor has been doing a little side work on his own?"

"Have you spoken to Georgia Tech about this egghead's research?" the captain asked.

"That's my next stop. We might want to check out his comings and goings in DC as well."

"Start at Tech. Do your shoe work here by phone for DC. You shot my budget to shit on your last case."

"You mean the one that got you those new bars and that fancy lunch?"

"'And where were you when I laid the foundation of the Earth, Job?'" The captain continued to fuss with his suit. "Had shit gone sideways, whose ass would've been in a sling, Detective?" Marmaduke said nothing. "Exactly. There's an order to things. If your head wasn't so far up your ass, you'd know that. In the words of that great philosopher Yogi Berra, 'You can observe a lot by just watching.' Now, what's the word on how this kid died?"

Marmaduke rolled his eyes. "Bomb exploded before he escaped. The blast and the fire trapped him."

"That's the word from the ME?"

"Wouldn't be the first time a bomber has tasted his own cooking. Isn't that right, Agent?"

"It's possible."

"The DA is gonna need more than, 'It's possible,'" the captain said. "Can you get us anything on this nanotechnology, Agent Thomas? If this stuff is real, a college professor's involvement could mean something much bigger."

"I'll bring Detective Marmaduke up to speed."

Captain Franklin glanced at his watch. "I gotta go. Call me if you find anything at the college, Detective."

* * *

Marmaduke headed for the campus of The Georgia Institute of Technology. It sat on the outskirts of downtown Atlanta, a distance from the City's ivory towers and away from local politicking. The campus loomed beneath the shadows of the Coca-Cola Company. The college suffered and benefited from these two juxtapositions. He wound his way through the tree-lined streets, made narrow by cars jammed on both sides. They tilled these grounds for those who sought to unlock the mysteries of the universe. All others, except for the occasional visitor with mundane pursuits, should tread lightly.

Marmaduke paid them a visit, death being an ordinary pursuit for him. He headed for the school of engineering to meet the dean and the director of their Nanoscience Research Group. A glass and brick facade greeted him. He made his way to the office of Professor Uza Landrosky, a Freudian-looking man dressed in a white lab coat. The professor stroked the pointed cut goatee he sported, as if to make sure it was still there.

"Detective Marmaduke, I presume," Professor Landrosky greeted him. He folded his arms across his chest. Marmaduke extended his hand. The professor ignored it. Surprised, Marmaduke examined his own hand. He saw nothing then stuck it inside his pocket. "Have a seat. You have questions about one of our faculty members, I understand."

"Yes, Dr. Amal El-Arabi."

"What would you like to know in particular?"

"In particular, Professor, I'm interested in the research he does here."

"His work is classified. Our investors have paid good money to keep our research proprietary. What I can say is that nothing Dr. El-Arabi works on at this facility is criminal."

"I understand that his specialty is nanotechnology. Could you at least explain that to me?"

"Nanoscience manipulates systems at the atomic level to develop technologies useful in our daily life."

"Atomic level, you mean small?"

"To one-billionth of a unit scale."

"How exactly can you use this technology?"

"Oh, it's used in many ways, Detective, from the tires on your car to lifesaving medicines. There's nothing this technology can't reach." He grinned as he explained, as if he had just discovered the fountain of youth.

"What about bombs?"

Professor Landrosky's schoolgirl smile disappeared from his face. Suddenly, he looked more worried than elated. For the first time, he stopped stroking his goatee.

"The making of bombs is the job of the Department of Defense, Detective."

"But the technology you're researching has an application for bomb making, does it not?"

"Are you implying that Dr. El-Arabi is making bombs using nanotechnology?"

"You tell me, Professor."

"Would your questioning have anything to do with him being Middle Eastern, Detective? I've known Dr. El-Arabi for many years. He has never displayed any anti-American sentiments."

"People said the same thing about the nineteen 9-11 hijackers. The proof of the pudding is in the eating, Professor. Now, back to my question, are you making bombs here?"

"If we were, I couldn't tell you. You are wasting your time here."

"Don't let there be more deaths. If I found out you could've helped prevent them, I'll see to it you're sitting next to your friend in handcuffs."

"...Deaths? You didn't say anything about any deaths."

"Well, your friend, Dr. El-Arabi, may have gotten his own son killed when a bomb he made blew up on him."

"Oh my God, he called to ask for a few days of sick leave, but he didn't say why."

"That's all you have to say?"

Professor Landrosky got up from his chair, walked to the half-opened office door and stuck his head out. He looked right, then left, moved back inside the room and closed the door behind him. He returned to his seat and stared Marmaduke in the eyes.

"You won't find the way out of this predicament by looking at my face, Professor."

Professor Landrosky leaned across his desk. "Dr. El-Arabi attends prayer at the Fourteenth Street Mosque. Investors got a little nervous about him working on our more...sensitive research. So I moved him to a lesser high-profile project."

"How did he react to that?"

"Not well. He threatened to file an EEOC complaint."

"Did he follow through?"

"Not after I reminded him he was up for tenure. He accepted the new position. I thought all was well."

"Well, it wasn't. Your colleague might be facing terrorist charges."

"Damn shame, he is a brilliant researcher. Too bad I'll have to get rid of him."

"No, don't do that. Keep him in his present position."

"Why? You just said he was making bombs and perhaps using our lab to do it."

"You kick him to the wind now, who knows where he'll land. No, the best thing to do is to keep him where he is, where we can watch him. Do you have surveillance cameras in the labs?"

"Not inside the labs, just cameras near the doors to and from the labs."

"We may have to set up surveillance in the lab and office where he works. Tell me the best time I can get the FBI's technical team in here?"

"We are due for an ISO9000 inspection. I could close the labs then. I'll need to inform the president of this."

"Okay, but only him. I'll see you soon." Marmaduke got up to leave, assured he was on the right track.

Outside Professor Landrosky's office, Marmaduke dialed Captain Franklin. James, his assistant, answered. She quickly transferred his call.

"Hey, Marmaduke, what do a theology major and an evolutionary biologist say to each other when they cross paths?"

"Captain—"

"Nothing." He burst into laughter. "You get it, Marmaduke? Theology and Biology, just a little egghead humor. Speaking of which, did you get anything from your visit to Tech?"

"That's why I called. Do our friends in DC have ears inside the Fourteenth Street Mosque?"

"Now, you do understand that's some sensitive shit, Marmaduke."

"I got a suspect in the bombing."

"I'll call you back."

Marmaduke pushed through the door of the Nanoscience Research building. His phone rang. "Hello." No one answered. The display showed a message. He answered it. Dr. DeGlorious had finished her autopsy on the body of Muhammad El-Arabi, also known as Brandon Elerby.

Marmaduke hopped in his car and merged onto North Avenue. He followed it all the way past the Krispy Kreme. The *Hot* sign was lit, tempting him to stop. The department's new physical restrictions tempered that desire. Doughnuts were not his only tempter. The drive took him through the old Fourth Ward and past Mama's; it was his favorite drinking hole. He drove fast, running a red light, fearing to even give it a glimpse. The neon signs and drawings of dancing Martini glasses drew him like a bare leg drew a male puppy. It didn't take much for him to want a drink. He followed a program and it worked. For now, staying busy was the key. He could not allow his mind to conjure up ways to justify him taking a drink.

* * *

Marmaduke arrived at the medical examiner's office and donned protective coverings and booties. He slipped through the door and into the exam room.

"Detective Marmaduke, over here," Dr. DeGlorious called to him.

Marmaduke walked to the stainless steel table where she stood over a corpse.

"Is this my vic?"

"The one and only. I met with the father earlier. Had a hard time understanding why he couldn't take the body for burial. You didn't tell me they were Muslims."

"I didn't know my damn self until I made the notification. I'm thinking the father looks good for the bombing though. So, Doc, what do you have for me?"

"...Not what I expected, Detective."

"What do you mean?"

"What I mean is this—" She flipped open the flaps of the corpse's chest cavity and pulled out a lung. She spread it out over the table like a fillet. "Your victim, Mr. El-Arabi, did not die of smoke inhalation. There's no soot in the lungs. There's no upper-airway edema or erythema, and blood hemoglobin is normal."

"Any trauma?"

"Some, but it's not the cause of death."

"What then, poison?"

"Toxicology was negative."

"You're killing me, Doc. What sent our boy to hajji heaven?"

"You know that's a slur, right?"

"What, 'Boy'?" Marmaduke shrugged. "He's not African-American."

Dr. DeGlorious shook her head. "When I opened the cranium, I noticed inflammation—"

"Meningitis."

"You've been listening, Detective. That's what I thought at first, except there were no inflamed meninges."

"Again, what caused his death?"

"It gets much better, Detective." Dr. DeGlorious pulled an infrared lamp and glasses from a storage cabinet. "Plug that in for me." She handed Marmaduke the cord. "Here, you'll need these." She handed him a pair of glasses and turned to her assistant. "Okay, Donny, hit the lights." The room went dark. She passed the infrared light over the brain of their victim, and it glowed.

"What the fuck?"

"More like, what the *fluorescent*, Detective."

"What is it?"

"Not sure. If I was to hazard a guess, I'd say it's a bioluminescent material that's penetrated the blood-brain barrier, with relative ease I might add."

"Is it contagious?"

"I've sent samples to the Centers for Disease Control."

"Have you ever seen anything like this before, Doctor?"

"Not on this side of the wall."

"What do you mean?"

"I'll call you if I have anything more, Detective."

Dr. DeGlorious ended their discussion. She walked across the room and flipped the switch. Lights flickered back on to bright. She placed the brain of the corpse into a glass jar containing a solution, screwed the lid back on and placed the jar on a shelf inside a large refrigerator.

Marmaduke watched Dr. DeGlorious progress through her routine. He wondered what she was keeping from him. Her reaction was puzzling, but he couldn't dwell on it. More questions needed answering. Marmaduke shed the protective clothes and headed for the door. He looked back. Dr. DeGlorious continued her work. He passed through the door, pulled his phone from his coat pocket and dialed the captain's office. James answered.

"Marmaduke, how come I still see red on the wall for your Mr. El-Arabi? This case is two days old now. I'll be glad when they get rid of affirmative action around here." She laughed. "Just busting your balls, child. What can I do for you, baby?"

"I need a contact in DC to do leg work on our Mr. El-Arabi. You have anyone on file?"

"Hold on, let me see." Marmaduke heard her peck at the keyboard. "DC," she muttered. "I have a Detective Baker in the Third District. We've worked with him in the past. I'll send you his contact info."

"Good."

He hung up, not waiting for James to deliver another jab. He still stood outside the medical examiner's exam room. Seconds later, his phone beeped. The information James sent popped up with a note. *You're welcome, asshole.* He laughed, happy to see their feud continuing. He dialed the number.

"Third District," a woman answered.

"Detective Baker, please."

"Hold."

The phone went silent. Seconds later, "Homicide," a man answered.

"Detective George Baker?"

"Who's calling?"

"Detective Marmaduke from DeKalb County, Georgia."

"DeKalb County…Yeah, I worked with y'all back in the day…a kidnapping case. Skip was the lead investigator."

"I'm sorry, Skip?"

"Skip Franklin. He's no longer there?"

"Oh, you mean Captain Franklin."

"We knew him as Skip, been seeing him make the talk show rounds after that Mormon case. What can I do for you, Detective?"

"I have a young man found dead at the scene of a bombing. He was a student at George Washington University. I need a little bird-dogging on his comings and goings in DC."

"Sure, I can do that for you. What's the name?"

"Muhammad El-Arabi, but he may also go by the name Brandon Elerby."

"Brandon Elerby?"

"Yeah, you got something?"

"Just had a missing persons come across my desk for a Brandon Elerby: male, six-feet, black on black, nationality unknown."

"Who filed the report?"

"Let me see…Okay, here we are. Amal El-Arabi filed the report."

"When?"

"Looks like three days ago."

"That's one day before we discovered the body. Do you have any information on Amal El-Arabi?"

"They took the report over the phone."

"And you're sure he reported his name as Brandon Elerby?"

"That's the name on the report."

"Why would his father report him missing under his alias, one he told me he knew nothing about?"

"You've already spoken with the father?"

"Yes, and he seemed as shocked by his son's presence in Georgia and his new identity as he would be seeing a boy with tits."

"Looks to me you have a mystery on your hands, Detective. I'll check out your victim on my end and get back to you."

"Great. Thank you."

For the second time, the case puzzled Marmaduke. Why would Dr. El-Arabi report his son missing a day before we found his body and not mention it to me when I showed up at his door? He smelled a lie and wanted the truth. He gave one last quick peek at Dr. DeGlorious through the glass in the exam room door before he ducked into the restroom a few doors down on the same side. Seconds later, Marmaduke pushed back through the door but stopped short. The doctor stood outside her lab on the phone. He decided to eavesdrop.

"Is my clearance still good—we need to talk, that's why—there's a man with his hair on fire. Is that urgent enough for you—that's all I can say over the phone—okay, I'll call you when I land." Dr. DeGlorious hung up and disappeared down the hall, walking in the opposite direction.

SIX

The Queen

ROME HIT THE STREETS hard to look for the man who assaulted her rape victim. Finding him would be difficult. He was faceless, formless and nameless—a ghost. To catch him, she needed resources and street intelligence, a snitch. She had cultivated many informers over the years. She gave them breaks on minor offenses or helped them get into programs for whatever they needed. She was fair but tough. On the street they knew her as *Queen*. Nobody crossed the Queen, not even the pimps and gangsters who strolled her beat. For those who stepped to her the wrong way, she came on strong, quick and hard with the beat down. When the johns, pimps, gangsters and hustlers saw that black or red convertible tear down the street, they knew a bad way was coming for them. They made themselves as scarce as possible.

This day, however, Rome was looking for answers, not trouble. She returned to the crime scene. It looked nicer at night. The wheels of the black Corvette squealed outside the Tri-City Pawn. Moments later, the doors to the cluttered shop flew open, letting in a gust of wind. The souls milling about turned to face a charging Detective Olga Rome.

"Skinner," she called to the owner. "Get your ass out here. I saw you running." Rome scanned the space, crammed with everything imaginable. She looked to a picture that hung on the wall, one of a UFO that hovered over a city. She lowered her eyes to see a sorry-looking figure emerge from behind a door. His shoulders slumped. His feet dragged. "What you scared for? You still running numbers out of here? 'Cause I'll shut you down if I have to."

Skinner braced his wiry body against the counter, shoving a large, brown paper bag to the side.

"Now come on, Queen, you know the Jamaicans took over the game. Ain't no honor in it now. They pay or don't pay. That shit's bad for business."

"Save the drama for y'momma. You know anything about what happened here last night?"

"What, the fire? All I know is I'm glad they stopped it before it got to me. I ain't got no insurance. Can't get it 'round here no more, at least not for cheap."

"Did you get the stolen property report this morning?"

"I haven't checked…I'll do it now."

Skinner stuttered and fumbled his way over to his fax machine. He thumbed through a stack of papers piled next to it. Rome waited. He placed a paper on the counter in front of her and rummaged through a drawer. The noise irritated her. Skinner pulled out a pair of glasses. He slipped them on over his bug eyes and read the paper.

"If you see that," Rome pointed to the description of the ring, "I need to be the first call you make."

Skinner nodded, trembling. "Is this good stuff?" he asked. "Cause if so, your man will likely take it to Cisneros on Ponce. He handles all the good stuff now."

"Cisneros on Ponce," she confirmed. "How come you're so free with the information? What happened to the Ten Commandments of thievery all you crooks follow?"

"…Just trying to help, Queen." Skinner held his bony hands in the air, palms up. His nervous smile revealed a mouthful of bad teeth. "But don't tell him I sent you."

"Put your veiny-ass hands down."

"Okay, Queen. Are you going to Cisneros now because he deals the good stuff?"

"I heard you the first time."

Rome knew the ring was junk, at least that's what her victim said. The perp didn't know it was junk though. Maybe he would pay Cisneros a visit, so would she. Rome gave the place one last look. "When're you gonna clean this mess up? It's a fire hazard."

"Yes, Queen." Sweat poured from Skinner's face. His hands trembled.

"Don't 'Yes, Queen' me. Why're you so nervous?" He said nothing as Rome eyed him hard. Skinner's gaze kept drifting to the left, down at the counter. "What's in the bag?"

"Nothing...I mean...I don't know."

"Which is it, fool?"

"It was here when I got here."

Rome punched at the bag, turning it over. Bricks of a white substance wrapped in clear plastic spilled onto the counter. She pulled her sidearm and aimed it at Skinner. His hands shot into the air. Another man stood frozen at the counter.

"Out of the way, fool. Don't you see this gun?" she yelled at the man.

Skinner ducked through a door. Rome holstered her weapon, leapt over the counter and gave chase. As she pushed through the door, a large concrete block fell from the ceiling, landing next to her. Skinner hurled objects at her or overturned them in her path. The low light made it difficult to see all that she dodged. He bolted through a steel door. An alarm blared as he breached it. Light flooded the stale-smelling space.

Rome charged through the same door, into an alley and onto a side street. She shortened the distance between them. Skinner glanced over his shoulder. Just as he turned again, a door from one of the shops opened in his path. He hit it, cracked the glass and crashed to the ground.

"Get up, chump." Rome grabbed Skinner by the scruff of his collar. He stumbled to his feet. She jacked him up against a wall. His thin frame bounced off the hard blocks like rattling bones being dropped into a tin can. With one hand, she latched onto his throat and with the other she gripped her gun. "I hope your old lady knows the pawn game 'cause your boys are about to become orphans."

"Please, Queen, please! I didn't know—"

"Save it, fool, for your maker 'cause there ain't no way you didn't know about that dope or that concrete block."

"The block yes. The dope no."

"And Cisneros, why're you selling them out?"

"They're in the dope game. All I wanted was for you to shut them down, that's all. Them wetbacks have been undercutting me for months. I figured if you caught them, it would end their low-balling me. I just wanted to do my civic duty, that's all."

"Then join the Red Cross, asshole." She pulled her weapon. "Now, I'm gonna do something for you that you didn't do for me. Tell me where you want it."

"Help, somebody help me!"

"Shut your bitch ass up." She struck him in the head with the butt of her gun. People walking by stopped and stared. Rome pulled her badge. She flashed it to the gathering crowd. "Y'all move on, now. Nothing to see here." She flipped Skinner around, pressed his face into the stone wall and handcuffed him. She marched him back through the streets, hands secured behind his back, blood dripping from his forehead.

"This ain't right, Queen." His voice cracked as if talking through tears. "You'll hear from my attorney."

"I reckon so since dead men can't talk."

"There're witnesses...People saw you...They'll know you did it...Your DNA."

"Tell that to O.J. Now save your whining." She snatched up his collar as they neared the pawnshop. People tore through the door, loaded down with all kinds of items.

"Hey," Skinner shouted. He turned to Rome. "You see what they're doing, Queen? Bring me my shit back here." He lunged after a young man carrying a large speaker. Rome held his arm tight. "They're stealing my goods. Are you gonna let them do that?"

"Would you like me to call the robbery boys for you to file a report? They can take an inventory of all your shit. And I mean *ALL* your shit." Skinner scowled. He turned to see the last of those running from his shop, stealing whatever they saw fit. Rome kicked the door open and shoved Skinner inside. Just then, the door swung back open. A young man tried to reenter. "Hey, let's not be greedy," Rome shouted. The young man turned and ran off down the street.

Rome pulled Skinner behind the counter. She dragged him to his office in the rear of the shop, flicking a switch, and lighting up a space over a desk. She hauled him over to a chair and plopped him down hard. She leaned against the desk, pulled the .44 caliber revolver backup weapon from her ankle holster, pushed out the cylinder and emptied the bullets. They pelted the desktop and bounced in the air, like Hoppin' Johns on New Year's Day. She picked up one bullet, slid it back inside the cylinder, closed and spun it around. Rome leaned in close to the chair and inches away from Skinner's face.

"Are you trying to kill me?" She moved the gun to his head.

"No...No, Queen," he stuttered.

Sweat and blood mixed as both poured from Skinner's face. His eyes swiveled over to the far corners of their sockets. They watched the cold, hard barrel of the gun hover close to his head. Rome pulled the trigger. A loud click sounded.

"Shit, Queen." Skinner jumped in his seat.

Rome sniffed the air. "What's that smell?" She looked down at his crotch. "Damn shame." She picked up a second bullet and loaded it into the gun. "As a bookie, you understand statistical odds, right?" She looked at him. His eyes locked onto the gun. She snapped her wrist, and the cylinder popped back into place. "So you understand that with each bullet your chance of living goes down." Rome spun the cylinder as before. "So the question you have to ask yourself is, 'Do I feel lucky?'" She moved the gun back to his head. "Who's my rapist?"

"I don't know." Another click of the trigger sounded. Skinner jumped and screamed. "Please, Queen, I don't know anything. I'm sorry."

A muffled ring sounded. Rome shoved her hand into her pocket and pulled out her phone. "Not a word," she warned Skinner. "Detective Rome, here."

"Detective, this is dispatch. I got Dr. Zones—"

"Good, put him in one. I'll be right there."

"He's not here, Detective, but I have an address."

"...Oh, okay, text me the directions." She squeezed the phone back into her pocket and turned to Skinner. "I gotta run." She loaded three more bullets. "Who's my rapist?" Skinner said nothing. Rome squeezed the trigger. Instead of a click, a loud bang filled the air. Smoke spewed from the gun's barrel. Rome looked to see Skinner's head on the desk. He screamed and cried, having ducked just in time to avoid the bullet.

"Get your ass up." She yanked him by the collar and propped him up in the chair. "Damn it, you're gonna pay for that bullet if you live." She loaded two more bullets. "My rapist. Give me a name, damn it."

"They'll kill me."

"You can die now or later, makes no difference to me." Rome placed the barrel tight to Skinner's forehead. She squeezed the trigger. The gun's hammer inched away from the strike plate.

Skinner watched as it reached the end. Just before the gun fired, he yelled, "The Jamaicans did it!"

Rome released the trigger. "Who, the whole fucking island? You better give me specifics."

"I don't know his name. He just showed up and tried to muscle me out of my shop. They're working with the Mexicans, moving White Girl and African Black through Atlanta to up north. Those are their bricks out on the counter."

"The Jamaicans—getting into the hard game?"

"Times is hard Queen. Everybody is forming alliances. Hell, even the Brotherhood and the Zulus I hear are talking. You didn't hear any of this from me though."

"What does this asshole look like?"

"I don't know…black with dreads."

"He's black?"

"…As a witch's heart."

"What else?"

"That's all I got, Queen."

"You mean to tell me some dreadheaded motherfucka came in here to jack your shit and you didn't get so much as a name?" She cocked the gun and aimed it at his head again.

"Okay." He tapped his foot and squeezed his eyes shut.

"I don't have all day."

"He had a lazy eye…the right one…and he wore a lion's head ring."

"A lazy eye, you're sure?"

Skinner nodded. Rome lowered her gun and turned to leave.

"You're not gonna leave me like this, Queen?" Skinner asked. Rome continued to walk. "Queen, I gave you what I know." She stopped short of the door, turned back and walked over to where Skinner sat. "Thank you, Queen. I sure am sorry for—"

"Shut up, fool." She circled behind him. "Lean forward." Skinner bent close to the desk. "You're right. I can't leave you like this." She raised her gun.

"Queen, please."

Rome spun the gun around and struck Skinner on the back of his head. He hit the desk with a loud thump, out cold. She uncuffed him and walked cool-like from the pawnshop. On the way out, she snatched the dope from the counter and the picture of the UFO from the wall.

"For my troubles."

* * *

Rome arrived at Grady Hospital and made her way to Kimble Tyler's room. It was empty. She went to the nurses' station, flashing her badge.

"Where did you move the patient in that room? Her name is Kimble Tyler."

The nurse checked through her computer. "We don't show a Kimble Tyler in our system. Are you sure that's her name?"

"They brought her in late last night. Could you reference that?"

The nurse tapped away at her keyboard. "The only rape victim from last night was a Stacey Knight."

"Do you have a description on her?"

"A white female, five-nine, blonde hair, weight one hundred twenty-five pounds."

"Sounds like my victim. Where is she?"

"…Says here she checked herself out early this morning."

"Did she leave an address?"

"Don't see one here."

"Do you have photographs?"

"…Just of the injuries. She didn't want any taken of her face."

"So I remember." Why would she give two different names? Why would she disappear?

"Don't worry, Detective. Sometimes the experience embarrasses these girls, or they don't want to suffer through a trial, so they give everyone bogus information, comes with the territory."

Rome headed back to her car. Her victim was more of a mystery than her assailant. The information she had on her was phony. There was still one place she needed to check out. Kimble or Stacey, or whatever her name was, said she worked at one of the local skin joints near the crime scene. *Who would make up a story like that?*

* * *

The Pink Pony sign was lit up. Even in the daylight you couldn't miss it. Rome rolled onto the parking lot; it was still early and only peppered with a few cars. She entered the dark space. Light flooded in. They kept it dark on purpose. Anonymity was important here. Men sat around the bar and at tables. For a moment, they turned away from the young women who pranced around naked, or nearly naked. Their gazes landed on her as she entered but quickly snapped back to the young women with paper bills tucked around their thighs.

The place oozed an upscale illusion with its shiny surfaces and the fancy-sounding names for the women who danced. There were no whales here, however, only guppies. Those with more refined tastes in the skin game spent their hard-earned cash at The Cheetah or treated themselves to a private party. The blue-collar crowd visited this place. They lived out fantasies that eluded them in their real lives.

"Barkeep," Rome called to the man behind the bar. He turned to show his flat, crooked boxer's nose as he continued to mix drinks as if he had Parkinson's.

"You'd wanna try Magic City downtown. We've browned out here, sweetie."

"Do I look like I want to shake my ass up in here?" She flashed him her badge but not a smile. "Get me your manager."

"Sorry, Detective. Jimmy," he called to another attendant, "takeover here." He left his station and returned with another man—a dwarf in a three-piece suit.

"May I help you, Detective?"

"I'm looking for one of your girls; she's blonde, thin."

"Take your pick, Detective." He stretched his arms out. "We specialize in thin blondes."

"This one goes by Kimble Tyler or Stacey Knight."

"There's no one by those names working here."

"You don't need to check your roster or something?"

"I know every piece of ass...girl who works here, Detective. Those names aren't on our rotation."

"Do you have photos of all your girls?"

"Sure," he nodded.

The bartender pulled a photo album from beneath the bar. He dropped it on the counter. Rome flipped through the album pages but didn't see her victim. Before she turned to leave, she asked,

"Say, what went on around here the other night?"

"You mean other than that explosion and the fire? Nothing much."

Rome headed for her car. She knew her case would be difficult to solve without her victim—for the rape and for the bombing. Kimble said she saw her attacker come from the animal shelter right before the bomb went off. If Rome was able to link the two cases, finding her rapist would become priority one.

SEVEN
The Muslims

MARMADUKE WAITED AND LISTENED from within the cramped quarters of the nondescript van parked a block away from the Al-Farooq Masjid. He and FBI agents eavesdropped on conversations between the imam and the directors of the mosque. The FBI had started their surveillance soon after the attacks of 9-11. An informant had infiltrated the mosque leadership as well. They were meeting with Dr. El-Arabi, a meeting that was arranged by their informant.

"I am sorry for your loss, Brother. Do you know when they will release the body?"

"That's Imam Khalid," the agent told Marmaduke.

"They say they have not completed the autopsy."

"That's my suspect," Marmaduke said. The agent nodded.

"I will speak with the authorities to remind them of our burial traditions. Do they know anything, how he died?"

"They have not told me much. I have not shared information with them either."

"This is good, Brother. We must ensure the secrecy of our plans. Do you know if they will reinstate you in the lab at work?"

"I am trying, but it does not look promising."

"We must try. Our brothers back home are depending on us. We must do our best to wipe this plague, this great scourge, from the world."

Marmaduke continued to listen through the headphones inside the dark van. The only light came from the electronic equipment they huddled over. Although he heard nothing incriminating, he knew they kept secrets. D*r. El-Arabi's research and his access to university labs can interest the imam for one reason only.*

"Make sure that I get a copy of this recording," Marmaduke told the agent. He hopped out of the van and headed to the home of April White. She was one of the names on the list of friends given to him by the sister of the deceased.

* * *

"April White? I'm Detective Marmaduke. I called earlier about Muhammad El-Arabi."

"Come in, please. April is my daughter. I must say, you surprised me with your call. April didn't know this El-Arabi boy well."

"Is your daughter here?"

"Oh…Okay…One moment." She gave Marmaduke the once-over and called her daughter's name from the bottom of the stairs. Moments later, a young, pimple-faced girl descended the stairs. She skipped to a rhythm only she heard. Her two pigtails flopped up and down as she made sure to not miss any steps. Her pace slowed as she neared the bottom and saw Marmaduke standing there. "This detective wants to speak with you about the El-Arabi boy." She took a sip from the cup she held. Mrs. White had that fake, Betty Crocker facade going. She looked to have slaved all day in the kitchen but probably hadn't.

"April, I understand you and Muhammad were friends. Had he been in contact with you recently?"

"I'm afraid you're mistaken, Detective," her mother said. "April only knew him from school. He was three grades ahead of her, for goodness sake. Tell him April."

The girl hung her head. She kept company with the floor more than Marmaduke. She twisted back and forth in place; her eyes shifted between the floor, Marmaduke and her mother. She was obviously nervous and reluctant to talk. Marmaduke sensed tension.

"Mrs. White, would it be okay if I spoke with your daughter alone?"

"Alone? What's this about, Detective?" She dropped the cup on a table top. It rattled. She stepped closer to April, gave her a quick look and put her body in between her daughter and Marmaduke.

"Mrs. White, we found Muhammad El-Arabi dead."

"...Oh, no."

April cried. She fell to her knees and sobbed. Her mother turned to grab her. She wrapped April in her arms and helped her from the floor and over to a sofa. Her cries were for someone more than a mere acquaintance. Her relationship with Muhammad was much deeper, apparently.

"April, can you tell me if you had spoken to Muhammad recently," Marmaduke sat down next to her on the sofa.

"He called me on Friday," she said through her tears. "We met earlier that day."

Marmaduke looked over to see her mother's mouth agape and eyes wide.

"What did he want?"

"He just said he wanted to meet. It surprised me since he was in town and away from school."

Mrs. White's hands shot to her mouth, but not before a loud gasp escaped.

"Did he say why he was here?"

"He was working on a project but couldn't talk about it."

"Did he say with whom?" She shook her head. "How did he look, appearance-wise?"

"You mean the blond hair and blue contacts?" April played nervously with her fingers. "I asked him about that; he said it was a class project."

"How did he say he got here?"

"I picked him up from the airport." She turned toward her mother who grew even more distressed. "I took him straight to the Mosque."

"To the Fourteenth Street Mosque? Do you know who he met with?"

"He just got out and walked inside. I left and returned home. I didn't hear from him after that."

"Okay April and Mrs. White." Marmaduke stood and headed for the door. "Thank you."

"Detective, how did he die?" April asked.

"We're still trying to find out."

Marmaduke returned to his car. He found it suspicious that Dr. El-Arabi did not know his son was in town since Muhammad had visited the Mosque where he was a member. Before he confronted him, he knew he needed to follow up on this latest clue. He would need help.

Marmaduke called Detective Chennault. "Chennault, who's our contact at Hartsfield-Jackson security?" he asked.

"Charles Duncan."

"Call him. I need the security footage pulled from three days ago. I'm looking for flights coming in from DC. The passenger's name is Muhammad El-Arabi, but he could have been traveling under the name Brandon Elerby. I'll meet you there in twenty minutes."

* * *

Marmaduke and Chennault reviewed video footage in the office of airport Security Director, Charles Duncan.

"There he is." Marmaduke pointed to the monitor. "We found him in those same clothes." They followed the footage as Muhammad El-Arabi boarded the train to the main terminal. They watched him as he stepped through the sliding glass doors to the outside where a line of cars stood idle to pick up and drop off passengers. Minutes later, a small car pulled up to the curb. Muhammad hopped inside.

"Who's that picking him up?" Chennault asked.

"That's the White girl's car. She told me she picked him up."

"We also pulled video from Dulles showing his departure," the security director said. He called up the footage. They saw another young man walking through the terminal close by.

"Who's that with him?" Marmaduke asked.

"Don't know."

"Look, they separated at the terminal. Who sat in the seat next to our vic?"

The security director loaded the seating assignment up on the system. "Robert McMillan," he read.

"He doesn't look Irish to me."

"Scottish," Chennault said.

"What?"

"McMillan, it's of Scottish origin, Gaelic to be exact. Same as Marmaduke, except you're Irish."

"Is that some fancy party trick to score girls?"

"He's on the prescreened list," the security director said. "Here's his picture."

"That's not the same person," Marmaduke said. "Can you ID this guy?"

"Let's see, we can ignore women, children and anyone transferring. He boards, it looks like, when they called rows thirty-five through fifty. That leaves us with ten possibilities."

"How did they pay? Perhaps we can eliminate business travelers."

"I'm with you. I'll filter out corporate paid travel. That gets us down to five names. That's as close as we can get."

"That's close enough. We'll need a copy of that and somewhere to work."

The director showed them to an area with two desks.

"Right here, this will do."

Marmaduke and Chennault divided the list between them and made the calls.

"I have one U.S. marine and a man traveling for a funeral," Chennault said.

"I'll raise your marine and funeral guy with a congressional intern and a retired cop." Marmaduke pushed his paper across the desk. "I can't reach this last name, a Mr. Chris Phillips."

"That guy didn't look like a Chris Phillips either."

"Perhaps that's the point. We need to find this guy. Have James run his name, maybe he's a local. Check with the FBI; see if that name came up on their recordings at the Fourteenth Street Mosque. I'll meet you back at the station."

* * *

City officials had recently approved the renovation of the DeKalb County Sheriff's offices. A fresh coat of paint would be good for crime solving, the city fathers hoped. Marmaduke's cluttered desk resembled a bag of shaken trail mix. It clashed with the new digs, which he didn't like anyway. He hated change; it cost too much mentally to keep up with. Give him the same-old-same-old anytime. He was an old-fashioned Tin Lizzie in a new Mustang world; he liked keeping it simple. This bombing case was panning out as a simple case of terrorism. He just needed to prove it.

His phone rang. "Marmaduke," he answered.

"Detective, this is Baker, Third District DC. I got some information for you on your victim, Mr. El-Arabi."

Marmaduke slung his coat over the back of his chair and loosened his tie.

"Something good, I hope." He plopped down.

"Well, most of this you may know already. Your victim was an electrical engineering major at GWU, a junior. His professors said he was a good student, carried a full credit load. He was a member of the I-S-A, that's the Islamic Student Alliance."

Marmaduke straightened his back and pressed the phone tighter to his ear.

"What do you know about them?"

"They're an outreach of The Islamic Center."

"What's that?"

"From what I can tell, it's a cultural and religious center."

"Do they have any affiliation with the Al-Farooq Mosque in Atlanta or an Imam Khalid?"

"I see an Imam Rashid Khalid as a board member. Is that important?"

"Not sure. Was Mr. El-Arabi working on any research, or did he have any special interests?"

"The Dean said that most research positions went to graduate students. But I did find an application he put in to the Defense Department. They wouldn't say if he worked for them or not. You know those cats, how they play the national security card."

"So that means he did work for them."

"They wouldn't confirm or deny it."

"You got any friends in DOD, Detective? I need to know if he worked there and, if so, what he was working on."

"Let me see what I can do…Can't promise you anything, though."

Marmaduke eased the phone down to its hook. He leaned back in his chair. The smell of paint thinner and the sound of ladders scraping against the cloth-draped floor invaded his senses. He looked off into the distance, drowning out the backdrop of noises and smells. He tried to piece together the common thread to all these parts. In his mind, this all reeked of a terrorist plot: Middle Eastern men—check. An Islamic mosque—check. A bombing and airport activity, including the lies and secrecy surrounding the victim's father—double-check. These factors all spelled terrorism.

Marmaduke's phone rang again. He snapped out of his daydream and answered it.

"Detective, this is Agent Rose. We're ready for you at Tech."

"We'll be right over." Marmaduke sprang to his feet, peeled his coat from the back of his chair and tightened his tie. "Let's roll, Chennault," he said, eager to see if the info they gathered from their surveillance of Dr. El-Arabi helped to fill in a few blanks.

* * *

Marmaduke and Chennault arrived on campus, heading for the Nanoscience Research Group minutes later. Professor Landrosky met them.

"This way, Detective." He still did not shake their hands. The professor led them to a secured room setup by the FBI. Monitors covered an entire wall. They watched Dr. El-Arabi as he fiddled and fretted with his work.

"Agent Rose, do these monitors cover the office and the lab?" Marmaduke asked.

"Every inch of them."

"What about his computer and his phone?"

"We've covered both. No warrant needed since the school gave approval."

"What about his cell phone?"

"It's covered. We ran his number through the NSA."

"A warrantless wiretap…That's impressive."

"It helps to know people, Detective."

Marmaduke's attention focused back on the monitors as Dr. El-Arabi went about his work. He watched him move between various lab instruments and items that sat on the tables. He was observed looking around and jumping at every knock and foot patter. This didn't seem the behavior of someone with nothing to hide. He was nervous, suspiciously so.

"Does anyone know what the hell he's doing?" Marmaduke asked. No one answered. "Chennault, get the professor." Moments later, Professor Landrosky entered the room. "Professor, explain what he's doing."

"I reassigned him to an electrical systems project." The professor stroked his goatee as he peered down at the monitors. "His work has nothing to do with nanotechnology."

"So there's nothing in this lab that he could use to make a bomb or bomb parts?"

"There are electrical parts in the lab, but I thought only nanotechnology concerned you."

"What can you tell me about bioluminescence, Professor?"

"Why do you ask?"

"Does any of your research involve using nanoscience to develop biological weapons? Before you answer, know this, I have Muhammad El-Arabi's autopsy report. It shows his brain was filled with something that made it glow in the dark under infrared light."

The professor whipped his head to Marmaduke. "You mean it breached the blood-brain barrier?"

"This research is yours?" The professor said nothing. He turned his attention back to the monitors. "I'll have Agent Rose shut this place down while we look for crime scene evidence, Professor. How would your investors like it if we closed your labs indefinitely while we combed slowly through all your research?" The professor remained quiet. "Agent Rose, shut this place down."

"It's not part of our research." the professor answered.

"But you are familiar with it…Professor, you are familiar with it?"

"Not on this side of the wall."

"What did you say?"

"I said that it wasn't a part of our research."

"Yeah, I got that. I mean, *'Not on this side of the wall.'* What does that phrase mean?" Marmaduke remembered hearing Dr. DeGlorious use the same term when she discussed finding the bioluminescence in the victim's brain.

"It's an old Defense Department term; it means in the civilian world."

"So you're former DOD?"

"I've done my time. And I've only seen what you've described in their labs." Professor Landrosky turned back to the monitors. Dr. El-Arabi still worked. "Wait. What's that?" He pointed to the screen.

"What is it, Professor?" Marmaduke stared at it as well.

"You're recording this, right? Play back the last minute," the professor demanded. The technician rewound the video as they all hovered around the monitor. They replayed the last minute of Dr. El-Arabi's lab work activity. "...Right there." The professor poked at the screen with his finger.

"I don't see anything," Marmaduke said. "Roll it back."

"Slowly—you see, right there? He pulled a vial from his coat pocket, smeared a solution onto a slide and viewed it under the microscope."

"What's strange about that?"

"The research I assigned him has no organic or inorganic chemical application—"

"In English, please."

The professor broke his focus on the screen. He stopped his hand gestures and cut to Marmaduke. "His research involves only wires and circuits, nothing solution based…no liquids."

"He ain't supposed to have that; is that what you're saying?"

"Correct."

Marmaduke gestured to Chennault.

"I'm on him." He and two uniformed officers pushed through the door. Minutes later, they appeared on the screen, all three surrounding Dr. El-Arabi. They placed him in handcuffs and led him from the lab.

"Thanks, Professor," Marmaduke said.

"What now, Detective?"

"I get our lab boys here to collect whatever's in that vial. Then we question the good doctor." Marmaduke broke for the door. He stopped short and turned to Professor Landrosky. "We'll continue our talk later."

EIGHT

"…get me Dr. Zones."

LIGHT FLICKERED FROM A lamp that lit up a huddled figure sitting alone in a police interrogation room. Dr. El-Arabi buried his face in his hands. He rubbed the top of his smooth head and pulled at the few hairs circling its edges. The door to the room flung open. Marmaduke strolled up to the table, plopped in a chair and flipped open a folder. He ignored his subject for the moment. He preferred to let him seethe instead. Marmaduke grabbed a pen tucked between his ears and tapped it on the table as he read through the file. He sighed, expelling a rush of air. The lids of his eyes sprung wide open as he gazed at his subject for the first time.

"Dr. Amal El-Arabi, graduate of Umm Al-Qura University, Saudi Arabia. Bachelor and Masters in Electrical Engineering, PhD in Electrical Engineering, MIT research interest in nanoscience." Marmaduke flipped the page and continued to read. "…Associate professor at several universities before your present position as associate professor at Georgia Tech." He closed the file, leaned forward across the table and asked, "Why no full professorship after all these positions and so many years?"

"Why am I here? Why have you taken me from my work, Detective?"

"It's Marmaduke. And I don't know how things work over in sand land, but in these good ol' United States of America, the law asks the questions, not the terrorist."

"Terrorist? May I remind you, Detective, it was my son who died in the bombing."

"You people sacrifice your young all the time. Isn't that what Allah calls you to do so you can get your seventy virgins and grapes? Besides, he could have been the bomber, just blew his damn self up by mistake."

"What reason would I have to do that?"

"Jihad, hatred of the West, someone drew a funny cartoon of your prophet. Take your pick."

Dr. El-Arabi spoke something in Arabic. He flailed and pounded the table.

"In English, Doctor."

"I want to speak with your superior. Now, I demand it!"

"I'm all you get. Now, tell me about your research at the university."

"My research is classified." He took a good look at Marmaduke, crossing his arms and legs. "You wouldn't understand it anyway." He smirked and turned his head.

"You mean it used to be classified. Now they got you building radios, something any seventh grader can do."

"I have a PhD. I graduated top of my class." He thrust his finger at Marmaduke. "With you Americans, anyone different, anyone smarter intimidates you. You throw your money away trying to educate women, taking money away from true research."

"What's in the vial?"

Dr. El-Arabi's eyes grew narrow. He stopped talking and leaned back in his chair. He hung his head, crossed his arms again and closed his eyes.

Marmaduke pounded the table. "The vial, what's in it?" The doctor's head popped up, and his eyes popped open. "Listen, our lab boys are analyzing that solution we took from you as we speak. It won't be long before we know what that stuff is. If they find a biohazard, we ship you to Homeland Security and then to NSA where you'll disappear into a black hole. No more contact with your family. You'll be using that PhD to make jailhouse tattoo guns and powering up scrub brushes."

"I demand to see a lawyer."

"Suit yourself." Marmaduke rose to leave. He reached for the doorknob, but then turned back to his suspect. "By the way, the bomb blast didn't kill your boy. The ME said a bioluminescent material infected his brain." Dr. El-Arabi sat up. His eyes bulged and his mouth hung open. "Lit up like a Christmas tree in the dark. Nice way to treat your own." Marmaduke pulled the door open.

"How did it break the blood-brain barrier?"

"Are you revoking?"

Dr. El-Arabi slumped back in his chair. Marmaduke squeezed through the cracked door and closed it behind him.

* * *

The door to Captain Franklin's office was closed—a sign to Marmaduke to prepare for an audience.

"Go on in. They're waiting on you," James said.

"They?"

"You know when things get blown up around here it attracts the multitude."

Marmaduke eased open the door and stuck his head in. "You wanted to see me, Captain?"

"Come in, Marmaduke." The captain sat at a conference table with three other men. "You know Inspector Siler and Agent Thomas." Marmaduke nodded. "And this is Byrnes Maximus, aide to Congressman Stonewall. Your bombing happened in his district."

Byrnes Maximus rose to shake Marmaduke's hand. "As I was telling Captain Franklin, this investigation has the full backing of the congressman. He sits on the Security Council and he takes these matters seriously."

"Have a seat, Detective," Captain Franklin said. "Inspector Siler and Agent Thomas are about to update us on their analysis of the crime scene."

Agent Thomas pulled a large envelope from his case. He slipped a folder from it filled with pictures and passed them around.

"The detonation device was pretty sophisticated. We gathered very little trace, and what we did find was severely damaged in either the explosion or the ensuing fire. The picture you're looking at is a fragment we suspect came from the bomb. In our interview of the building's tenants, there was nothing in the facility that would have contained that fragment."

"What is it?" Marmaduke asked.

"From what we can tell, it appears to be part of a Voice-over IP device."

"English, please, Agent Thomas."

"Sorry, Detective. It's a device that allows for verbal communication over the internet."

"You mean, like Skype?"

"Exactly."

"And the people from the animal shelter didn't have anything like that in their shop?" The agent shook his head. "What about any threats or run-ins? You mentioned at the crime scene something about the A-F-L."

"That's A-L-F, the Animal Liberation Front. Yes, we asked about them and other groups. All they said was they had run-ins with many different groups, and none of them left a business card."

"Where can I reach the owners? Sometimes you Washington boys are afraid to dip your fingers in the locals' tea. I would like to have a little talk with them."

"Sure." Agent Thomas slid a paper from the folder. "Here's their contact information."

Marmaduke studied the number. He folded the paper and tucked it inside his coat pocket. "You got any other evidence from the scene, anything related to nanotechnology?"

"As I told you before, Detective, you've been watching too much of the sci-fi channel. No one outside of DOD has those mental chops."

"It would explain the lack of trace evidence—might be there, just can't see it."

"What're you thinking, Marmaduke?" Captain Franklin asked.

"The ME found some strange things when she cracked open the head of our DB found at the scene."

"Strange, like what?" The captain sat straight in his chair.

"His brain glowed in the dark...well...sort of. It lit up when she waved an infrared light over it."

"And she said this was from the bomb?"

"…Not exactly. We're trying to figure that out now. The boy's father is a researcher over at Tech. His specialty is nanoscience." Marmaduke turned to Agent Thomas. "So you see, Agent, the technology may not be as proprietary as you think."

"Their research is mostly medical and industrial, none of the hard DOD stuff."

"So we were led to believe. Seems the good doctor was doing side work, got him on the wire discussing some grand scheme with the imam of the Fourteenth Street Mosque. We also caught him in Georgia Tech's lab with some kind of unauthorized liquid. Your eggheads are analyzing it now."

"If you're so sure of this guy, why bother with the animal rights nuts?"

"No stone, Agent, no stone. Besides, it seems that the in thing to do now for expensive, slick-talking defense attorneys is to represent hajjis."

"Hajjis, you do know that's an offensive term, don't you?"

"Shit, they come over here to fly planes into our buildings and blow up bombs. They deserve every goddamn slur made for 'um, plus some."

Agent Thomas cut Captain Franklin a look. He smirked, turned his head and tapped his thumbs together as he laced his fingers. Agent Thomas turned back to Marmaduke.

"I'm sure the good people of DeKalb County will rest better knowing they have Dirty Harry's finger on the trigger."

"John Wayne, damn it. I roll old school."

Agent Thomas took a deep breath. He turned to Byrnes Maximus. "Is this the kind of investigation the congressman wants?"

"I'm not here to tell the local authorities how to conduct their investigation, Agent, only to gather information and report back to the congressman." Byrnes Maximus pulled back the sleeve to his coat and shirt and turned the watch on his wrist around. "He has a news conference in—about now. I would very much like to have something good to report to him."

"You tell Congressman Stonewall that we are pursuing every lead and hope to have a suspect soon," Captain Franklin said.

"Well, gentlemen," the aide scanned each of them, "I look forward to our next meeting." Byrnes Maximus grabbed the arms of his chair and pushed himself to his feet. He saluted, strolled across the room and disappeared behind the closed office door.

"You think this Dr. El-Arabi is good for this, Marmaduke?" the captain asked.

"We caught him in a bunch of lies, and his son was the dead body found at the scene. He was exposed to something that his old man was working on, and he was probably the one who detonated the bomb. He's all we got right now."

"Okay then, you keep—"

"Captain?" James barged through the door. "A call came in. There's been another bombing." She grabbed the remote to the TV mounted on the wall and turned it on. Breaking news showed the wreckage of a toppled communication tower.

"When did this happen?"

"Minutes ago. It interrupted the congressman's news conference."

"This ain't good."

"No kidding. When the networks cut into the congressman's speechifying for Hurricane Katrina, he pulled all his campaign advertisement."

"That's not what I meant."

"Oh."

"Where is this?"

"The Georgia State University Language Research Center and Nature Preserve out in South DeKalb County. Apparently, they blew up a cell phone transmission tower."

"Isn't that where the primate research center is?"

"The animal crazies and the tree huggers got into it last year when they both protested there. Seems they couldn't agree on which living thing was more important."

"Marmaduke, are you sure of this Dr. El-Arabi? 'Cause I'm finding it hard to see the connection between Islamic terrorists bombing an animal shelter and now blowing up a transmission tower. The only boom those guys like hearing are the car, plane and big building kind. These bombings seem small potatoes to me."

"Perhaps they're trial runs for something bigger, wouldn't be the first time."

"We don't have the resources to track down all these different players. We need a profile."

The captain rose from the table, walked over to his desk and picked up the phone.

"Who're you calling?"

The captain flicked his eyes up from dialing but said nothing. He raised the phone to his ear. "Hello, Daphne, what do we have left in special projects?—That's all? What about discretionary?—Okay, thanks."

"What was that all about?"

"James, cancel this year's Christmas party, and get me Dr. Zones."

NINE

Headshrinking Scumbags

"DETECTIVE ROME TO SEE Dr. Zones." She flashed her badge to the guard at the desk.

"Down the hall to the right. But you'll have to leave that here."

Rome glanced at her sidearm then back at the guard. She unclipped her holster, slid the gun across the desk and turned to leave.

"And your backup too." The guard held his hand out and wiggled his fingers inward. "Makes you feel naked don't it? How do you think I feel in here with these animals all day?"

Rome huffed. She placed her leg up on top of his desk. Her platform heels landed with a loud thump. The guard jumped back in his chair as she rolled her pant leg up to expose her weapon. She unstrapped it. The Velcro made a ripping sound. Rome dropped the gun onto the desk and strolled down the sterile prison corridor. A guard standing outside a door directed her to a room. It overlooked another room where she observed Dr. Zones sitting with an inmate. Rome turned the volume on the speaker up and listened.

"And you say that you've been having these thoughts ever since—"

"Ever since they fucking started giving us motherfucking fruit cups instead of goddamn motherfucking oatmeal-raisin cookies, yeah. Goddamn it. Shit."

"I see." Zones stared at the inmate. He reached for a legal pad lying on the table next to him. "Well, Mr....um...Polite, I'll let the warden know how much distress this change in the menu has caused you." He scribbled in his pad. "Now, in the meantime, is there anything, culinary-wise, that would make up for the absence of oatmeal-raisin cookies and decrease your desire to cut off the genitalia of your fellow inmates, batter them up and fry them?"

"Culinary? Now, Doc, I didn't say shit about pleasing a female sexually. That's what got me locked up. But motherfucking chocolate milk would be a fucking nice substitute for now."

"No, I don't mean cunnilingus...so chocolate milk it is." Zones scribbled in his pad again. "Is there anything else, Mr. Polite?"

The inmate looked off to the side. He raised his chin in the air. "No, just the cookies. That's it." He smiled at Zones and winked.

"Guard," Zones called to him through the door. It swung open. "Mr. Polite is ready to return to his cell."

The guard grabbed the inmate by the collar of his jumpsuit and snatched him from the chair.

"Let's go, Mrs. Manners."

"The name is Polite, Mr. Polite. Tell him, Doc."

Zones smiled as the guard led the inmate from the room. He snatched the legal pad from the table and shoved it and a recorder into his briefcase.

Rome appeared at the door. She leaned against the jamb and crossed her arms. "Hell, if I knew headshrinking scumbags was that easy, I might've paid more attention in psych class." Zones' head snapped up, eyeing her. Rome strolled over to the table and plopped down in the chair across from him. She crossed her long legs and swung one back and forth. "You're a hard man to track down, Doctor." She looked around the room. "I see you like cold, dreary places."

"Detective Rome, how may I help you?"

"I'm still trying to catch the son of a bitch who raped that girl in the alley. You were supposed to call me to set up a meeting with our sketch artist."

"Yeah...sorry...I've been a little busy." Zones shoved a pen and some files inside his case. "Besides, it was dark. I really didn't get a good look at him."

"Word is that he's Jamaican."

"Possibly. I do recall an accent but that's about it. Can't the girl give you a description?"

"Can't find her. She disappeared from the hospital, and all her contact information was bogus."

"A rape victim that doesn't want to be found wouldn't be the strangest thing in the world."

"Well, we need to find her. Her story proves her attacker may have also been the bomber."

"Yeah, you said that before."

"But you still don't buy it."

Zones stopped packing. He looked Rome straight in the eyes. "Isn't Detective Marmaduke working the bombing?" She nodded. "And he's working the same angle?"

"Don't know; I haven't spoken with him."

Zones shoved the last of his things inside his briefcase. He stood and pushed his chair back. "Save yourself some time, Detective. Focus on this guy being guilty of only the rape." Zones grabbed a stack of folders from the table. He dropped one on the floor as he walked to the door.

Rome picked up the file. She read the name on it. "Cleopatra Zones, is she a relative?"

"My mother," Zones took the file from her.

"Why would you—"

"Detective, anything else you want to tell me? I have a plane to catch."

Rome stared at him, her mouth agape. She stood and said, "I guess not, Doctor." She marched to the door and turned back to him. "I'm sure your mother would be proud. I hope you find her killer."

"What do you know about my mother's death?"

"You have a good day, Doctor." Rome disappeared down the hall.

TEN

"'Sup Nigga?"

THE SMOKY ROOM OVERFLOWED with people—men mostly. Half-naked women carried drinks and scampered back and forth. Loud music shook the thinly made walls, rattling them. The scent of cheap cigars and expensive cologne clashed. The smell rocked the senses to full consciousness. Zones sat in the deep cut of this darkened space. He spied the naked women who gestured and gyrated on stage for the pleasure of men and tempted them into who knows what. He sipped on a half-filled glass of fake spirits, chilled by a few cubes of ice. The stingy, brown concoction of burnt sugar, Sprite and almond extract tasted horrid as it rolled down his throat. Although, it did relieve the large knot in it and helped to rid his mouth of the place's gritty taste. The strobe lights pulsated. They tranquilized his senses. This was how he drowned out the noises ringing in his head. Seedy places, those low in spirit like this New York haunt, gave him comfort.

"How are you, sweetie?" A young woman in lingerie interrupted his concentration. "You want a dance?"

Zones gawked as she twisted back and forth in front of him. She smiled a young school girl smile, batted her long, false eyelashes and flicked her false hair over her shoulder. The drinks weren't the only fake things in this joint.

"How long have you worked here?"

"Conversation cost y' just the same as a dance."

Zones huffed, "…How much?"

"Ten dollars and that includes the conversation." Zones counted two fives out. He placed them into her outstretched hand. She folded the bills and stuffed them between her breasts. She danced and removed pieces of her clothing slowly. "Two years, I've worked here two years."

"You know the playa in the black Kangol?"

She looked over her shoulder but did not break her rhythm. "Who, you mean Slim Man?"

"I guess so, he looks husky to me."

"No, that's his name, Slim Man. That's what they call him, at least. I don't know his gov'ment name. The girls here call his old, cheap ass Busta."

"What's his game?"

She stopped dancing. "You the popo? 'Cause I ain't no snitch—at least not for ten dollars." She snapped her hands to her hips and frowned. "Or is you gay or something? 'Cause I been shaking this ass and these tits in your face for the past five minutes, and all you want is to know about another man."

"Now would I be paying for a dance and for a piece of that ass if I was five-o or gay?" She smiled, sucked her teeth and continued her dance. "So, what's his game: drugs, girls or numbers?"

"You haven't even asked me my name, and y' keep pumping me for information, too."

"I already know your name, baby. It has got to be Ms. Fine."

Her smile grew larger. It covered most of her face. She straddled Zones and leaned in close to his ear. "I don't know for sure, but he bragged to some of the girls that he worked for some big shot in the gov'ment. He was drunk though, probably bullshit."

"He was drunk up in this place?"

"They keep the real stuff hidden in back for their VIPs."

"The government…Did he say who or what branch?"

"No, but stick around, he usually meets some white guy at that table over there in the corner."

"Over there?"

"Yeah, all secretive-like. They only order drinks, rum and coke for Slim Man and a scotch for his friend, but no dances." Zones stared at her, puzzled. "I bartend sometimes for extra money—to pay for classes, you know."

"Yeah, I know." Zones pulled a hundred dollar bill from his wallet. He shoved it between her breasts.

"That'll get you more than just a dance, sweetie."

"...For those...classes."

She kissed Zones on the cheek. "My name is Diamond," she whispered in his ear. "I get off at midnight." She stroked his chin with her finger, gathered her things and disappeared into the darkness of the strip club.

Slim Man stayed parked at the bar. He tossed back drinks, and he tossed money onto the stage at a tall blonde who danced in front of him. She was Puerto Rican, but the brothers paid a premium for the illusion. The door to the club swung open and let in a gush of cold air. A white man dressed in a gray trenchcoat strolled in. Slim Man eased from his seat, his eyes still locked onto the blonde. He chugged the last of his drink and moved to a corner table where he joined the man wearing the trenchcoat. They gestured back and forth. The white man in the trenchcoat rose from his seat. He dropped an envelope onto the table before darting through the club and out the door.

Zones grabbed his case, eased from his seat and followed the man. He hid behind a corner of the building and pulled a camera from his case. He snapped pictures of the trenchcoat wearing man as he entered a black sedan. Soon, Slim Man pushed through the same door. He hurried down the sidewalk beneath the *Mr. Wedge* sign that hung from the side of the club's brick facade. Zones followed him down the gritty streets of Hunts Point, past worn-out buildings and crumbled walkways. He kept within the shadows to stay hidden from the man he pursued.

They neared the waterways that spilled onto the Hudson. The slight smell of raw sewage and Mercaptan filled the air. Slim Man ducked into one of the warehouse buildings and disappeared inside a door off a darkened hallway. Zones followed him, stopping short of the door. He stuck a penlight in his mouth and clenched it between his teeth. He whipped out his mother's Bible, the one his father had given him, and rifled through its pages, stopping near the end. The light followed his finger down a list of addresses. He stopped at one and compared it to the address on the door; it matched. This was the second address that matched one from the list, the first being where he initially ran into Slim Man. Zones tried to piece together the significance of this. *Why would my mother have these addresses written in her Bible?*

Zones' phone rang; the sound echoed through the hall. He hurried to silence it. Suddenly, he heard the unlatching of the door, and he looked for a place to hide, ducking around a corner. The door opened. Zones took a peek. Slim Man poked his head out of the door. His phone rang again. It drew Slim Man down the hall, heading toward him. Zones raced from the building, heart pounding. He darted down the street, running away from the warehouse. When he glanced over his shoulder, Slim Man was charging toward him.

"Stop, you motherfucka," Slim Man shouted.

Zones picked up his pace, pulling away. Seconds later, the sound of gunfire filled the air. Bullets whizzed past him.

"Shit!" He ducked and covered his head with his hands as he turned down a dark alley littered with old car parts and house trash. He yanked on doors to buildings he passed, hoping one would open but none did. He reached the end of the alley. A block wall stood in front of him. A deadend was not good. He turned back and headed down the way he had come.

"I saw you come down here," Slim Man shouted. "I'm gonna fuck you up, whoever you are."

Zones scrambled for a place to hide. He ducked behind a trash dumpster and covered himself with a large cardboard box. The sound of footsteps and of things being tossed around moved down the alley. Zones remained hidden away, crouched behind the dumpster. He listened to the footsteps getting closer and closer. They stopped in front of him for what seemed a long time. Finally, he heard them heading away from him and back out to the street. Zones stayed hidden a while longer. Just as he was about to come out from hiding, his phone rang once again. He snatched it from his pocket, switching it to vibrate.

Zones searched along the ground next to him in the dark. He found a pipe and grabbed hold of it. He pushed the cardboard box away and emerged from hiding. Zones crept down the alley. He held the pipe like a Louisville Slugger, ready to swing. He looked both ways when he reached the street. It was clear, so he continued back toward the strip club. Two blocks down, he heard the cock of a gun and the feel of hard steel pressed against his head.

"'Sup, nigga. You looking for me?"

ELEVEN
The Dread

REGGAE MUSIC BLARED FROM speakers mounted outside the Patty Palace. Rome stepped inside the eatery; it was decorated with bright colors. The smell of curry smacked her square in the face. She knew one thing: Jamaicans loved their own home cooking. This was the fourth restaurant on her list. The others hadn't panned out. No one knew the Jamaican she was looking for. Rome headed toward the counter. A handful of customers sat scattered throughout the place.

"May I take your order?" A young girl, barely taller than the counter, asked in a thick accent. Her dreadlocks covered her face and her breasts, both the size of two sufficiently threatened blowfish, covered the keys of the cash register. "We have a special on beef patties."

Rome flashed her badge. "Get your manager for me, sweetie." The girl's eyes widened. She stood there frozen. "Sometime today, baby."

The girl eased back behind a wall. Rome reached over the counter and plucked a spicy fry from a basket. She moved it up to her mouth but tossed it back into the basket after she saw the sixty-eight health inspection score mounted on the wall behind the counter.

"May I help you?" A man appeared behind the counter, his hair covered in a colorful headdress similar to the painted walls.

"I'm looking for the Rastas who're running White Girl and African Black out of Decatur."

"…Can't help y', man. Why don't y' check with your own in Vice. Ain't that why we pay our taxes?"

"Vice says Jamaicans aren't into the hard game. I heard different."

"What'll you have me to do, man? If your own don't know, what makes you think I do?"

Rome looked around the restaurant. "What does a spot like this cost you—two, three grand a month? You must be pulling in some serious ducats to keep this going. I sure would love to have a place like this."

"I ain't looking for no investors."

"Explain this to me. How can a place with as few customers as I see here afford to stay in business?" She leaned over the counter. "What do you think I would find if I checked behind that wall, maybe a little ganja…A lot of ganja?" She stared him straight in the eyes. "'Cause your little order taker got mighty wide eyed when I flashed her my badge."

"You don't have cause to search my place, man, no warrant either."

Rome chuckled. "No cause, aye. Who're you now, Johnnie Cochran?" She turned to the young order taker. "Go behind that wall and scream."

"What?" the girl asked.

"Did I stutter? Go behind the wall and scream *now*." She whipped out her gun. The young girl scurried behind the wall and let out a loud scream. "There's my probable cause."

"You can't do this, man."

Rome charged around the counter and headed behind the wall. The manager stepped in front of her.

"You want to get shot, fool?"

"Okay. Okay." He threw his hands up and stepped aside.

Rome moved past the manager. She disappeared behind the wall and entered a space cluttered with boxes and bags stacked to the ceiling. A desk and chair sat in a corner of the room. The desk overflowed with papers and other stuff. Rome lifted the lids of some boxes. She rummaged through and overturned them onto the floor. She flung open desk drawers, she tossed things out onto the floor, she thumbed through the papers on the desk and flung some in the air after she read them.

"You're tearing up my place," the manager protested. She ignored him, pulled a box from the bottom of a stack and watched them tumble to the floor. "You see, nothing," he said. "These are all packing boxes for my place."

Rome stood in the middle of the room, looking at the things strewn around the floor. Before turning to leave she gave one last swipe at a stack of boxes. They did not fall like the others. She hit them again. Still, they did not move. Rome cut a look over at the manager. He stared back and swallowed hard. She leaned in closer and saw a handle hidden within the stack of boxes. She pulled on it. *It's locked.*

"Open it."

"This ain't right, man."

Rome pulled her Glock and pointed it at the handle. "You have three seconds. One, two—"

"Okay. Okay." He walked over to the desk and reached beneath it.

Rome locked her gun on him. "Easy now." There was a clicking sound behind her. She turned to see an opening in the wall. "You, come around here." She motioned the manager over from the desk, her weapon still trained on him. "What's your name?"

"…Yabba."

"Okay, Yabba, you're going to open it nice and slow. If there are any surprises, I *will* give you a third eye."

Yabba gripped the handle. He inched the door open. Rome braced and readied herself to fire. He swung the door all the way open. She stared into the room. Nothing but darkness stared back.

"Hit the light."

Yabba walked into the room. He felt for the light switch on the wall and flicked it on. The space lit up. More boxes filled the room.

"Now what?"

"Pull one out."

Yabba pulled a box. It hit the floor.

"Open it."

He flipped off the lid. "It's empty."

"Move back." Rome pulled a box from the bottom. The wall of boxes crashed to the floor to reveal a blocked passageway. "Where does this lead?" Yabba said nothing. "Both of you, let's go." She pushed

Yabba and the young girl along the passageway. "If there's something you want to tell me before we reach the end of this, now would be the time."

"Why don't you just leave us be, man?"

"'Cause you want to do this the hard way. Keep moving." They came to a set of double doors. "Go on, open them." Rome readied herself as before. Yabba cracked open the doors. A strong stench rushed out to assail her nose. "What on Earth is that smell?" She covered her nose and mouth. The doors flung open, and screams rang out. Young women packed the small space. Rome shot Yabba a nasty look.

"I can explain."

"Explain? Explain what, that you're in the skin game?"

"No, it's not that at all, man. I—"

"I nothing, motherfucka. Put your hands behind your back." She cuffed him. "You, order taker, get them out of there. Line them up along this wall."

"Please, let me explain."

"Save it, shit for brains. I'm no DA, but I see ten years on each count. You'll get enough prison time to leave to your great-grandchildren."

"Okay. Okay. What if I told you what you want to know?"

"So now you're Encyclopaedia Britannica, full of information. I can't help you on the slave trade charges." She pulled another door open. "But I might be able to help you out on the trafficking charge for this weed." Marijuana filled the shelves of a small closet. Yabba looked surprised. "The nose never lies. Now, what do you have?"

"Not here, man."

Rome ushered him back down the hall and into the office. "This is about as private as we're gonna get. Now what crew is running the hard stuff out of Decatur?"

"The Montego Bay Posse, they've teamed up with the Yardies."

"The Yardies? Who the fuck are they?"

"Jamaican posse out of Great Britain. They run cocaine between the island and England."

"Who runs the Montego Bay crew?"

"I don't know."

"Bullshit. You're supplying them with the skin."

"No. I mean...I don't ask any questions."

"Bullshit."

"I'm telling you the truth, man."

"Okay then, who's the dread shaking down pawn stores in Decatur?"

"Pawn stores in Decatur? That sounds like Jah-Boy. Those girls are his. He came in six months ago to pitch the skin business to me. Said it was low risk, 'No problems, man,' he said."

"You could have said no."

"Do you know what a lead enema is, Detective? They ram a chopper up your ass and empty the clip."

"You got a government name for this Jah-Boy?"

"Francis Dixon, but he gets angry if you call him Francis."

"I can see why. Does Mr. Dixon sport a lazy right eye and wear a lion's head ring?"

"Yeah, man. That's him."

"Where can I find this Mr. Dixon?"

"He and his posse hang out at club Intrigue in Stone Mountain."

"The old Aquarium night club?"

"Yeah, man."

"This better not be bullshit to deflect those trafficking charges."

"No bullshit, man. But you can't just roll up there with an army. They have lookouts all over the place. They'll be gone before you get there."

"We'll see about that." Rome called the precinct. "Send Vice and a wagon to the Patty Palace on Memorial, have someone from ICE meet it at the station."

"What about me, man? Are you going to talk to the DA?"

"You better hope I find Jah-Boy."

* * *

The sound of "Buffalo Soldier" pounded inside the half-filled club. Jamaican celebrations started late and ended late. Young men and women danced. They ground and gyrated against each other or by themselves. Others lounged around, their bodies plopped on chairs and sofas like a tossed away rag. They blew plumes of smoke in the air; it filled the club with the distinctive aroma of marijuana.

"Barkeep," Rome called him over. She hopped onto a stool at the bar.

"'Sup, baby, what can I get for you?"

"A Ciroc Grapevine on the rocks, no salt, no sugar."

"Coming right up."

Rome pulled out her phone. She pretended to dial. "Jah-Boy, where the fuck are you? I've been sitting here waiting on your ass—where?" She spun in her chair and looked around the club. "I don't see you."

"He's over there," the bartender said. He dropped a napkin and her drink on the counter. "You mind taking him this?" He handed her a bottle of Riesling. "Tell him, Happy Birthday, from Zack."

"Sure, sweetie, and thanks." She slid a twenty-dollar bill across the counter. "Keep the change."

Rome unbuttoned her blouse at the top. She walked across the club's dance floor and weaved her way between the mesh of bodies that moved about. The space was dark. Flashing lights pulsated to the beat of the music. She broke through the dance floor and walked over to a section of booth seats.

"Which one of you dreads is Jah-Boy?" She placed her hand on her cocked hip. The young men sitting at the table looked her up and down.

"Who wants to know, man?"

"You must be him. He said to look for the ugliest motherfucka in the place. I guess that's why all that hair is covering your face." She plopped the bottle of Riesling down hard on the table. "From Zack."

"Bitch, watch your mouth," one said. "Jah-Boy, you want me to check this skank, man?" Gun handles stuck out from his pant waist bands.

"Hold on, aye." Jah-Boy turned toward the bar. Zack, the bartender, waved from across the now cleared dance floor. He nodded back.

"Can we get this over with?" Rome said. "Your cheap-ass friend only paid for five minutes. Said that's all you'll need."

Jah-Boy turned back to Rome. He got up from his seat, walked over and sat on the edge of the table in front of her. His eyes moved the length of her body. "Hazel eyes, mocha skin, tight little ass, you must have some Indian in you." He took a drag from a blunt and blew the smoke in her face. He ran his hand up her leg to the crotch of her pants. Rome didn't flinch. She gripped the handle of the Glock she kept hidden in her waistband. He unsnapped her pants and pulled at her zipper.

She grabbed his hand. "Are you sure you want your boys to see…your skills?"

"Jah-Boy, take my car keys man and teach this bitch a lesson," one of them said. He flipped him his keys.

Jah-Boy grabbed Rome's arm. He pulled her toward the entrance. She turned to see one of the young men headed for the bar. Jah-Boy pushed through the door to the club. He pulled at her zipper again as soon as they got to the car door.

"Baby, don't you want that thing greased first?"

"Shit, yeah, I thought you said five minutes." Jah-Boy unbuttoned his already sagging pants.

"Let me do that for you, baby." Rome unloosened Jah-Boy's pants. They dropped to his ankles. She took one step back, pulled her Glock and pointed it at him.

"Crazy bitch. You trying to jack me?"

"Get your hands up, Francis." He lifted his hands above his head. "Now, turn around, slowly."

He turned. "I'll gut you like a goat."

"Well, we'll just have to add threatening a law enforcement officer to your rape charge, now move." Rome shoved Jah-Boy. He took baby steps forward.

"You five-o?"

"Go figure." She led him over to her car.

"Hold it, bitch," someone shouted. Gunfire rang out.

Rome pushed Jah-Boy to the hard pavement. "Don't move." She ducked behind a car and dialed. "This is Detective Rome, I need backup at the club Intrigue on Memorial Drive...officer under fire...I repeat, officer under fire." She stuffed her phone back inside her pocket and crouched behind the rear of the car. Her gun drawn, she ripped off a few rounds. The scene quieted. Rome turned to the sound of footsteps scraping against pavement. Jah-Boy scurried across the parking lot, his pants dragging on the ground. Rome raced after him. She tackled Jah-Boy to the blacktop. A hail of bullets whizzed past her crashing into car windows that shattered upon impact.

"Get off me, bitch."

"I got your bitch right here." Rome head-butted him. "I told you not to move."

"You broke my nose. My boys are gonna fuck you up."

"Oh yeah, I'll make sure you won't be here to see that." She tied his hands behind him with his belt. "Now, get up."

"Jah-Boy, where are you man?"

"I'm over here."

Bullets flew in their direction. The crackle of gunfire filled the air. Rome hid behind another car, dragging Jah-Boy with her and returning fire. Through the darkness, she could see human forms moving to her left and right. They weaved in and out between the cars, closing in around her. She fired at them, emptying her clip. She pulled her backup revolver and pivoted left and then right. Now, only a few feet away, Jah-Boy's posse moved in. Rome fired. She held them back until her gun fired dry.

"She's out," Jah-Boy yelled. "Fuck her up."

Rome pulled out a knife that was hidden beneath her pant leg. She pressed it to Jah-Boy's throat. "If I go, you go, slowly and painfully." He swallowed hard and began to sweat.

"We gotcha, Jah-Boy."

"Hurry the fuck up," he demanded. Rome pressed the knife tighter against his throat.

Sirens sounded in the distance.

"You hear that?" Rome shouted to them. "My posse is on its way. I hope this piece of shit is worth the time you're gonna get. You're already looking at twenty-five years for attempted murder of a police officer." The sirens grew louder. "They'll be here in a minute."

"Shit. She's five-o. Let's bounce." They pulled back.

"Where the fuck you going, man?" Jah-Boy shouted.

"Looks like your crew ain't ready to do time for you, Francis."

Backup arrived. Squad cars and blue suits filled the parking lot. Rome yanked Jah-Boy up from the pavement by the scruff of his collar. She marched him to an awaiting squad car and stuffed him inside.

"What're we charging him with, Detective," another detective asked.

"Rape and attempted murder, to start. We need to get a bead on his crew. They're the ones who shot up this place. Take a couple of your boys and hit the club. Start with Zack, the barkeep."

"Detective, the barkeeper said your perp and his crew run a trap house not too far from here."

"You get an address?" The detective handed Rome his notepad.

"Barkeep also said he has an old lady over in Dunwoody."

"So, he doesn't eat and sleep where he shits."

"Looks that way."

"You take the trap house; I'll take the girlfriend."

"What about warrants?"

Rome whipped two forms out of her car's glove compartment. "All they need are the addresses." She handed one to the detective.

"Wow, with signatures too. You sure this is legit?"

"Detective, I'm appalled."

"Your name and *by the book* ain't exactly synonymous, Detective."

"You just round up his crew, and let me worry about the paperwork."

* * *

Rome rang the doorbell to a suburban townhouse. The door opened to reveal a young white woman dressed in a house robe.

"May I help you?" the woman asked.

"Are you the owner of this house?"

"I live here…how may I help you?"

"Do you know a Francis Dixon, Miss, uh…?"

"Bonyet, Margot Bonyet. He's my fiancé…actually my boyfriend…but…" She looped her blonde hair behind her ears.

"Good for you. I'm Detective Rome. I have a warrant to search your home." She shoved the paper at her.

"A warrant? What's this all about?"

"This officer will explain it to you." She pushed passed the woman and entered the house. "Is there anyone else in here with you?"

"…No, just me."

Rome turned to another officer. "Start at the rear. You know what we're looking for."

"What is it that you're looking for?" Margot asked. "Is Francis okay?"

"When was the last time you saw Jah-Boy?"

"Francis, please. I hate that name. It sounds so…well, you know…"

"What, ghetto?"

"I'm not prejudice."

"Obviously not. Now, the last time you saw Francis…"

"Sunday night."

"Early or late?"

She sighed, "Oh, I don't know. He came in, changed clothes and left."

"Changed clothes? Do you still have them?"

"His clothes? I guess so; the wash is in here." Margot led Rome down a hall to a washroom. She opened a small hamper. "I haven't had a chance to do the wash yet."

"Let me get that." Rome moved Margot to the side. She snapped on a pair of latex gloves and fished the soiled items from the bottom of the hamper. "I need a bag," she shouted.

"Please tell me what this is all about."

"What does this smell like?" Rome raised a shirt up to the nose of the crime scene technician who held open a bag.

"Gunpowder, I'll get this to the lab."

Rome dropped the shirt into the bag. "Check for biologicals on all of these as well." The technician bagged a pair of pants and undergarments. He carried them away. Rome followed him back to the front of the house. "Ms. Bonyet, what do you know about your fiancé's business dealings?"

"Only that he owns a personal reclamation company, and he's a restaurateur."

"By personal reclamation, you mean pawnshop, and by restaurant, you mean the Patty Palace."

"Yes." She smiled nervously.

"What about his friends? You know the crew he hangs with?"

"Francis never lets me meet any of his friends. He said they're too uncouth."

"Uncouth, that's the term he used?"

"Are there any more questions, Detective?"

"That's all for now."

"Do you want me to have Francis call you?"

"I'm sure we'll be seeing each other soon."

Rome, the other officers and the crime scene technicians filed out of the townhouse. They gathered near the cars parked on the street. She looked back toward the house and hoped they hadn't overlooked anything.

"Talk to me." She turned to an officer. "Did you find the ring?"

"No ring, but I have a call for you from the detective at the other location. You can take it here." He reached through the open window of a squad car and lifted the receiver from the hook, handing it to her.

"This is Detective Rome. Tell me something good."

"Didn't find much, Detective, accept your typical crack house. Did find some jewelry, probably stolen. We bagged it and hauled it over to Vice."

"Any rings? I'm looking for one with a large stone in it."

"We found one like that. You know the owner?"

"Yeah, all I have to do now is find her."

TWELVE

The Beat Down of Slim Man

"I SAID, 'SUP NIGGA. You looking for me?" Slim Man pressed the gun harder against Zones' head.

"Naw, black, just lost, that's all."

"You in the wrong goddamn place to be lost pot-na. What the fuck is in the bag?"

"…Nothing, just papers, man. I was trying to find this address." Zones stuck his hand inside his coat.

"Slow y' roll, nigga."

"I'm just reaching for the address. Perhaps you can help me out."

"What the fuck do I look like, 411? But I *will* have a look at what's in that bag." Slim Man snatched the briefcase from Zones' shoulder. He rummaged through it. "Bible…papers…flashlight, I know a mack like you got more than this." He patted Zones down and plucked his wallet from his coat pocket. "Here we go. This all the bread you got, chump? Let me see who I'm dealing with." He clicked the flashlight on and read Zones' driver's license. "Thelonious Zones…where have I heard that name before?" He looked back down at the license. "East 125th Street, that's in Harlem. Where do I know you from, nigga?" He shoved him hard.

"I don't know. Look, you got my money. Let me have my things, and I'll be on my way." Zones gripped the pipe he still held, only tighter now. He was surprised his assailant hadn't noticed it.

"Who's running this, you or me? I should smoke your ass right here. Tell me where I know you from." Zones said nothing. "Motherfucka, you got three seconds. One, two—"

Zones heard the gun cock. "Okay. It's my father. You know him; he has the same name as me."

"Zones...oh yeah, now I remember." He uncocked the gun. "Your old man doing time, ain't he?"

"Yes."

"He's a soldier, seeing as how he's holding it down for someone else. But I figure you already know that. It's why you're here, ain't it. Too bad for you that you found me."

Zones' phone rang again, vibrating this time. It distracted Slim Man.

"What kind of phone you got, nigga, an iPhone? I can get good money for one of those." He ripped the phone from Zones' pocket.

Quickly Zones spun around. He brought the pipe up swinging it in a tight arc, striking Slim Man on the arm. The gun he held fired before it fell to the ground and skidded along the pavement out of reach. Slim Man dove for it. Zones followed, landing hard on top of him. They wrestled for the weapon, rolling around in a fray on the ground and both holding a death grip on the gun. Zones gained advantage. He straddled Slim Man and pummeled him with a barrage of blows to the face. He screamed and covered his head with his arms. Zones worked his body. He sank his fists deep into his side. Muffled groans sounded with every strike. Without a warning, Zones felt the unmistakable hardness of the gun barrel pressed against his chest. He stopped, frozen with fear. *Is this how it ends, shot dead on a filthy street in Hunts Point?*

"You're gonna die tonight, nigga." Slim Man pulled the trigger. The gun clicked, but there was no sound, no blood and no pain. Zones grabbed the gun, ripped it from Slim Man's hand and tossed it away. He hopped up, grabbed the pipe he'd carried and pounded Slim Man with it until he stopped moving. Zones scrambled to collect his things, now strewn all over the ground and speckled with blood. He shoved them inside his briefcase, not sure if he had gathered them all. Zones backed out of the scene, turned and ran down the street, believing that he may have just killed a man.

THIRTEEN

"…I want you."

ZONES AWAKENED TO THE unmistakable crackle and smell of bacon frying. He threw back the covers and sprang to his feet. Pain shot through his body. It slowed his movement as he stumbled down a hall. His nose and ears led him to the kitchen. The place was small and ratty, something a low-dollar stripper could afford.

"Breakfast will be ready in a minute," Diamond said. "Your clothes are almost dry. I tried cleaning you up as much as possible last night. If you want to take a shower, there are fresh towels in the bathroom back down the hall."

"Thanks."

"I was surprised to see you waiting for me outside the club last night. What happened to you, anyway…I mean…with the bloody clothes and all?"

"Oh, I got mugged."

"That's funny 'cause I heard they found Slim Man bloodied and lying in the street last night too."

"He's not dead?"

"No, just busted up from the beat down."

"Yeah, must've been the same mugger."

"Yeah. Right."

"Have you seen my phone?"

"On the stand by the bed."

Zones trudged back down the hall, plopped down onto the bed, swiped his phone from the nightstand and checked his messages. They were all from his employer Sam Drake. He pressed redial. "Sam, you called?"

"Damn, boy, where the fuck you been? I called you all last night."

"I'm in New York."

"What's going on in New York?"

"Nothing. What do you want?"

"I need you back here."

"My flight isn't for a couple of hours. What's this all about?"

"Not over the phone; I'll see you when you get here."

Zones hung up the phone, got dressed, packed his things, and returned to the kitchen. "I'm leaving."

Diamond turned to see Zones standing at the door again. "Leaving, but I'm cooking breakfast." She sashayed over to him. Her high-heel shoes tapped the tile floor. "And I wanted to give you something to remember me by." She untied her house robe and it fell to the floor. Zones' eyes followed the curves of her naked body down to her feet.

"I'll have to take a rain check, baby. Thanks anyway. Here, let me give you something for your troubles." He pulled his wallet out. It was empty. "I forgot, the—"

"Mugger, yeah, I know. This was on the house anyway. You sure you have to leave? It would be fun."

"I think I better go."

* * *

Zones burst through the door to Sam's office. "Now, what's so secretive that you couldn't tell me over the phone?"

"Dr. Zones," Sam said formally, "you remember Captain Franklin and Detective Marmaduke."

"What?" Zones turned to see them sitting at a conference table. "Yes...Captain...Detective."

"It's about time, Doctor," Captain Franklin said. "We've been sitting here waiting on you all goddamn day."

"For what? What is this all about?"

"Where in the hell have you been, Doctor? We've got bombs going off everywhere."

"The captain here," Sam said, "would like to enlist our services on this case."

"Enlist *our* services, you mean mine. Sam, you promised me that I could work only twenty hours a week for the next two months. I'm right in the middle of something else. Besides, the Bureau has a staff of profilers; ask them to assign one of theirs to the case."

The captain stood and straightened his coat. "No, I want you." He shoved a finger at Zones. "Detective Marmaduke will fill you in on the details. I want a complete profile on my desk by the end of the week. Now, I'm late for a luncheon with the next congressman of the Fourth Congressional District. Good day, gentlemen." He put on his cap and left the room.

Marmaduke slipped a file from a briefcase. "Here's what we have so far." He held it out to Zones, but he wouldn't take it. Marmaduke looked at Sam. He pointed to his desk. Marmaduke dropped the file on top of it. "Don't worry, Doc. I got a suspect already wrapped and neatly bow tied for you. He's just waiting to be delivered." Zones said nothing. "Yeah, anyway, we're meeting with ATF in the morning to go over the second bomb site again. If you want, I can swing by." Again, Zones said nothing. "I guess I'll see you when I see you then." Marmaduke left the room.

Zones charged Sam's desk. "I'm not going to do it."

"Yes, you are because I pay you a hell of a lot more than what I should, and it's not because you're family either."

"I'm not."

"I'll remind Sheila of that the next time you put those size thirteens underneath our dining table and ask for seconds."

"Man, I'm out of here."

"Hey, aren't you forgetting something?" Sam pointed to the file.

Zones snatched the file from his desk. "This ain't right." He pointed at Sam and stomped from the room. He didn't need another case, didn't want another case. The last one he worked on with the Bureau had consumed all of his time. Sam wasn't so quick back then to agree to him freelancing. Now that he had signed a lucrative consulting contract with the FBI, they couldn't come quick enough for him.

Just when Zones finally got the time to look into his mother's murder, to answer the questions that rattled around in his head, to put to rest any doubt of his father's guilt, this new case had landed in his lap. He hopped in his car and tossed the case file over his shoulder into the backseat. His mind was still on New York and what he had uncovered. *What did Slim Man mean when he said his father was doing someone else's time? I need to find out who the man was that Slim Man met with.* He knew of only one person who may have had the answer.

FOURTEEN

"Prison money ain't what it used to be."

ZONES SAT AND WAITED inside a windowless room at the federal prison in Benteen Park. The door cracked and then fully opened. Guards walked in dragging a handcuffed inmate behind them. They sat him down at the table across from Zones and removed his shackles. The inmate rubbed his wrists where they had cuffed him, no doubt relieved. The guards left the room and closed the door behind them. Father and son sat there gawking at each other.

"I'm surprised to see you again, son." Zones said nothing. He looked his father straight in the eyes, disgusted that he found himself back here once again. "How's Sam? Is he with you? He said he was coming by to get a game of spades going. You know, it's hard to get a game going in here. All these cats want to play is poker. They see that World Series of Poker on the TV, and now they all think they're Greg Merson."

"You planted those addresses in that Bible didn't you, and you gave it to me knowing that I would find them and investigate."

"Hold on, now. Slow down. What addresses?"

"What addresses." Zones laughed. "You know a cat with a street name of Slim Man? He hangs out in Hunts Point back home."

"Now, son, you know I've been locked up for a minute. I'm not as plugged-in as I used to be."

"Bullshit. An O-G with as much street cred as you is never out of the loop.

"What's this all about? Why are you hanging out around The Point and looking for trouble? Does Sam know about this?"

Zones pulled a scrap of paper from his pocket. He slammed it onto the table. "You didn't write these addresses in the Bible you gave me, the one that belonged to my mother?"

"Your mother? You mean my wife. You seem to forget that. And no, I didn't write those addresses in there. That's your mother's handwriting."

Zones snatched the paper back. "You're sure?"

"Am I sure? Of course I'm sure. Your mother was the writer in the family. She sent out all the Christmas cards, wrote all the letters to the family, even to people on my side she didn't like. Let me see that." Zones pushed the paper back across the table. "You see how she made her o's all fancy." Zones leaned in to see. "She didn't start doing that until after you were born. She liked the way it looked in your name. Said it was regal—like you. Damn near named you that too. If it hadn't been for me, you'd be named after a theater." T.O. stroked the paper with his thumb as he stared at it.

"I better get going."

"...Chinatown?"

"What...no...back to the city."

"No...this address...it's in Chinatown, in New York. A restaurant...what was the name...The Midong. Your mother took me there for dinner a few times, said it was one of the only ones on her route that she would eat at."

"What do you mean by *on her route?*"

"I forget you were still young. Your mother was a building and environmental inspector for the city of New York. She was one of the first black women to be hired. This was one of the buildings she inspected."

"What about the other addresses?"

"I can't say; perhaps she inspected them too."

"You have no idea why she would have kept these addresses?"

"No, but I'm sure they still have those records at the city."

Zones reached inside his case and pulled out a picture of the man who had met with Slim Man. "Do you recognize this cat?"

"No, should I?"

Zones stuffed the picture back inside his bag. "Do you have any of her old papers or files?"

"All that stuff is still in storage at the house."

"You still own the house?"

"Yeah, I had Sam lock it up soon after my...you know. It stayed that way for years until the attorney fees ate up all my savings. I didn't want to sell the place, so I had Sam rent it out, except for basement storage. If worms, rot or mildew haven't destroyed them, her things should still be there. Sam has the keys."

"Do you know any of mom's colleagues or anyone she was particularly close to?"

T.O. took a deep breath. He leaned back in his chair. "From work—Belinda...Belinda Tuscolli. Sam and I called her Big Booty Belinda. If you find her, you'll see why. She may still be with the city. Last I heard, she lived in Queens."

"Great."

"Are you gonna tell me what this is all about?"

"Just something I'm working on. I better go." Zones eased from his seat and headed for the door.

"Son—" Zones stopped and turned back. "It was good to see you."

"...Yeah."

Zones hurried from the room.

"You finished, Doc?" a guard asked.

"Has he had any visitors in the last couple of months?"

"I don't know offhand. Let me check the visitors log; it's on your way out." They reached an office right off the main entrance to the prison. The guard stepped inside and returned with papers on a clipboard. He thumbed through them. "It seems his only visitors for the last two months have been his attorney and a Sam Drake."

"You're sure?"

"All visitors are required to sign in. No one gets in otherwise."

"Okay, thanks, officer."

Zones pushed through the doors of the prison to the outside. The meeting with his father left him with more questions than answers. He still wasn't convinced this wasn't some elaborate scheme by him to bolster his claim of innocence in his wife's murder. Zones' near-death run-in with Slim Man, however, was real and his words were real: *...your old man doing time...for someone else.* He needed to return to New York but knew Sam would pitch a fit.

Zones headed back to his office. He arrived at the brick storefront on Ralph McGill Boulevard and darted past Sam's office straight to his.

"I see you, Monk." Sam shouted.

Zones walked back to Sam's office and stood in the doorway. "...Yeah."

"Don't *yeah* me. How're you coming with that profile of this nut job that's blowing up the place?"

"I'm working on it."

"You're working on it?"

"That's what I said."

"Don't bullshit me, boy. Prison money ain't what it used to be. They're cutting back on locking niggas up all over the country. That FBI contract was a goddamn godsend. So if you're even thinking about fucking it up, you better call Dr. Phil for a motherfucking change of mind." Sam pointed at him and cocked one eye, just like Uncle Sam on the military recruitment posters.

"Your friend said you had the key to the basement of the brownstone in New York."

"By my friend, you mean your father. When did you speak to him?"

"I just left the prison."

"Shit, are you feeling okay?" Sam eased up from his chair. He walked to the door and touched Zones on the forehead. "'Cause the last time we were there, you swore that it would be your last visit."

"Do you have the key or not?"

"Yeah, I got it. What's going on? You just left New York?"

"I just thought I might get to know my mother a little better, that's all."

Sam squinted and walked back to his desk. "You were a little young. Why didn't you just ask me? Sheila and I were your parents' best friends *and* your godparents. Is that what the trip up north was all about?"

"Yeah, just thought I'd try to reconnect...catch up...you know."

"Aaha. Are you looking for something specific?"

"No."

"So, just all of a sudden you want to search through your mother's things?"

"Yeah…since…like you said, I was young. I think it would help me to know her a little better."

"I tell you what, Monk, after you knock out this case with the captain, I'll give you a guided tour of the place myself." Zones cursed beneath his breath. "You say something?"

"No."

"Oh, and my door, will you?"

Zones slammed the door, trudged down the hall to his own office and plopped in his chair. He didn't know where to start. He had no names except street names. He had addresses but didn't know what they meant, if anything. He knew there could be answers in his mother's stored papers at the old brownstone, but Sam was standing in the way of him seeing them. He sat for a moment, thinking. *Big shot with the government.* He recalled his conversation with Diamond about Slim Man. He plucked the phone from the receiver and dialed the receptionist.

"Candice, get me the number to the New York City Building and Environmental Inspection Department." All the while he had been thinking federal, but what if the *big shot* was a local government official.

FIFTEEN

A Pigeon Cooking

MARMADUKE LEFT SAM'S OFFICE at Drake and Associates, heading to the ME's office. Yesterday, her preliminary autopsy showed that a bioluminescent material had caused the death of his victim, Muhammad El-Arabi, aka Brandon Elerby. She didn't know what, how or why, at least not then. He did, at least he thought he did. The victim's father, Dr. Amal El-Arabi, was cooling his heels in a DeKalb County jail cell. He looked good for causing his son's death, and he looked good for the bombings too, at least the first one at the dog shelter. Marmaduke would meet with the ATF tomorrow to see if evidence from the second bomb site could be connected to the first one. Yesterday, the medical examiner had few answers; he hoped she had something more for him now.

"Dr. DeGlorious."

"Detective, I'm over here."

"Is this my vic's brain?"

"No, this unlucky soul died of a good old-fashioned gunshot wound. Yours is over here."

"I was surprised to hear from you, Doctor. I thought you had forgotten about me."

"I had additional research to do. You don't see this stuff every day, Detective."

"I bet they do at the DOD."

"Who...how did you..."

"Relax, Doctor. Your time with DARPA is safe with me."

"You're fishing, Detective."

"Just wanna know who I've been working with all this time, Doc."

"Do you want to know about what killed Mr. El-Arabi or not?"

"It's your show."

Dr. DeGlorious pulled a glass container from a refrigerator and sat it on the counter. "Tissue samples we analyzed didn't have any of the known markers we're used to seeing in the lab." She pulled two glass slides from the container, slid them beneath a microscope and focused it. "Take a look."

Marmaduke peered down through the lens. "Okay, Doc, now you know I flunked biology. What am I supposed to be looking at?"

"The slide on the left is a brain dissection from your victim. The one on the right is from a primate."

"Don't see much of a difference."

"Put these on." She handed him a pair of goggles and switched off the lights.

"They're both glowing as before. Doc, I've already seen this light show."

"Keep looking, Detective."

Marmaduke squinted, as if it would help him comprehend something he still did not understand. "Shit, the one on the right is changing colors. How did you do that?"

"It's a marker. I used this frequency generator to find the right level of sound. When I reached it, the color changed."

"I didn't hear anything."

"This marker is set at a frequency below anything audible to humans. When activated, the eye color changed. That's how we could readily determine which primate had been exposed to the agent."

"What about El-Arabi's brain?"

"It either doesn't have a marker or we haven't found the right activator."

"But the technology, it is DOD?"

"Yes, but your bomber hasn't perfected it."

"What do you mean? They've blown up a building already, for God's sake."

"Remove your goggles, Detective." Dr. DeGlorious flicked on the lights. She walked back to the table near Marmaduke. In a measured way, she asked, "What's the purpose of a bomb, Detective, to blow up buildings or to kill people?"

"Is this a trick question, Doctor?"

"Do you know how much it costs to rebuild damaged infrastructure caused by a bomb blast? The U.S. spent billions to rebuild Europe after the Second World War and billions more on Japan. Think of how much money it would save this country if the only destruction caused by war is human. It costs a hell of a lot less to bury a body than it does to rebuild a building."

"A real nanobomb would kill people but leave buildings in place; I get it. Just how does that work?"

"Update your life insurance, Detective. If I told you that, I'd have to kill you." Marmaduke smirked. "Loosen up. If I knew how any of this worked, I'd be sipping piña coladas on a sunny beach instead of breathing in disinfectant and staring down a microscope at brain matter."

"Is there any way to trace this to the lab where it was developed? I got the victim's father locked up. He looks good for this."

"His father? You can't cook this stuff up in the kitchen."

"He's a PhD at Tech. His specialty is nanoscience."

"I see. In that case, they certainly have all the equipment. But I can count on one hand the number of people with the knowhow to engineer this."

"That includes you?"

"No, Detective, I just necropsied the bodies and crunched the biologicals. The real work is credited to the eggheads."

"Got a name for me?"

"Everyone I know is still active, and their names are classified, except one."

"Professor Landrosky."

"Yes…how did you…if you're looking to lay these bombings on him, look someplace else."

"He and my prime suspect work in the same field, at the same university, in the same building. You just said there are only a handful of scientists capable of engineering this, and he's one of them. When he saw that I had my sights on El-Arabi, he was mighty quick to give him up."

"I think you're wrong, but suit yourself."

Marmaduke's phone rang. "Marmaduke, here."

"Where're you?" James asked.

"I'm at the ME's office."

"Captain wants you at CSU. And don't ask me why 'cause I don't know."

"I'll be right there."

"Good news?"

"This nanobio stuff, Doctor, can it be in liquid form?"

"Liquid, solid, gas or plasma, why do you ask?"

"That was James. The captain wants me at CSU. I believe they've finished analyzing a liquid we collected at Dr. El-Arabi's lab. They probably want to go over the results with me."

"I can tell you now that it's not the stuff we've been talking about, the stuff that caused the death of your victim."

"How can you be so sure?"

"There would be no results to go over."

* * *

The lab director, Dr. Bruno, stood over a contraption. Glass tubes filled with fluids shot from it and spun around. He ate his favorite, bologna and mayonnaise on white bread, and washed it down with grape kool-aid, drinking from a glass jar labeled *Smucker's*. The lab seemed emptier than usual. Marmaduke looked at his watch—twelve o'clock noon. *No wonder my stomach is growling.* Dr. Bruno looked up to see Marmaduke approaching. He waved him over.

"I see you're still eating the lunch of champions," Marmaduke said. The director stared at his sandwich and then back at Marmaduke. "What do you have for me?"

"The solution they collected from the lab was water."

"That's it?"

"Yep."

"Just water, nothing else?" Dr. Bruno nodded. "You called me all the way over here to tell me that?"

The director took a bite of his sandwich and flipped through the pages of the report. "They also found traces of petrochemicals." He handed Marmaduke the report. "Here's the analysis on that." He pointed on the paper.

"Is this it? This is all they found?"

"Yep."

"Shit." Marmaduke headed for the door.

"There's something they didn't put in the report, Detective."

"What's that?"

"The water sample is from the Middle East, most likely Saudi Arabia."

"How do you know that?"

"The chemical composition. Specifically, the water's API gravity and sulfur content are unique to the region."

"You just knew that."

"I ran the lab at Dow. We bought many petro products from the Saudis. Had to make sure they gave us quality stuff."

"My suspect is from Saudi Arabia, but I don't know what Middle Eastern water has to do with the bombings."

"Why not ask him, Detective?"

"Can't, he lawyered up."

"When has that ever stopped you?"

Marmaduke raced up the stairs to his desk. There was nothing in the vial other than water tainted by oil. He needed more than this, together with what he already had on Dr. El-Arabi, to make a case. After the second bombing, the captain had gotten antsy, like he always did when there was something he couldn't control. That was why he had called in Dr. Zones. Marmaduke had no problem with this; they had worked together before. It often started off choppy, but they always got the job done. This was about stopping the next bombing since he knew it was coming. He didn't need to be a psychological profiler to know that. There were only two things that stopped these killers: death and getting caught.

Marmaduke reached his cluttered desk, sank into his chair, drummed his fingers on the desktop and thought about his next move. He picked up his phone and dialed.

"Hello, Professor Landrosky, this is Detective Marmaduke. I need to see you down at the precinct."

"I thought you were finished with me, Detective."

"Murder investigations are like fishing, Professor. You're not finished unless you catch something big."

"Are you fishing now, Detective?"

"Should I send a squad car, Professor?"

There was silence on his end for a moment. "I'll see you in an hour."

Marmaduke hopped from his seat and headed for Captain Franklin's office. James sat in her usual place outside.

"Hello, beautiful," Marmaduke said.

James scowled. "Prick."

"What did you say? You liked it from Dr. Zones."

"It just doesn't sound right coming from your mouth. What do you want, Marmaduke?"

"I need everything you have on Professor Uza Landrosky, from the time he took his first piss."

"When do you need this?"

"He'll be here in an hour."

"...Of course." James typed away at her keypad. "Are you gonna stand there waiting? 'Cause I'z ain't gonna run away massa."

"Call me when you're finished." He started back to his desk.

Captain Franklin stepped from his office. "Detective Marmaduke, where are we on the bombings?"

"I'm meeting with ATF at the second bomb site later today, and I'm bringing in Professor Landrosky for questioning."

"...Landrosky, the egghead from Tech?"

"Turns out he may know a little more about our bomb than he first let on. He'll be here in an hour."

"I want Dr. Zones here when you question him."

* * *

An hour later, Marmaduke's phone rang. He sprang from his reclined position and snatched the receiver. It was the receptionist from the first floor. Professor Landrosky had arrived.

"Send him up." He turned to another detective. "Jackson, this guy on his way up, put him in room five." He ran back up the stairs. "You got that info for me?"

"I was just on my way to see you." James slipped a sheet of paper from the printer next to her desk and handed it to him.

He read through it. "Is this everything? One hour of looking and this is all you found?"

"What can I say? This guy disappeared from the grid after college and, like a ghost, reappeared five years ago. I had to search through every database in the system just to find that. His social and his driver's license all seem to be relatively new. Who is this guy anyway?"

"That's a good question." Marmaduke stared at the one page. He still could not believe this was all there was on Professor Landrosky. "Staple a few of those blank pages of paper to this one."

"The Matador again?"

"You got it; I have no choice."

"How long are you gonna keep using these dumb tricks?"

"Until they stop working or criminals get smarter."

Marmaduke raced back downstairs. He headed for the interrogation room, flung open the door and stepped inside. The room was empty. He bolted back down the hall.

"Jackson, where's my guy? I asked you to put him in five."

"I moved him over to interrogation room one in the corner, just like you asked me to."

"What? Room one has windows. I never interrogate in one."

Jackson threw up his hands. "Robison has five now, and the painters are in all the others."

"…Never mind." Marmaduke stormed back down the hall to room one. He pushed through the door. "Professor Landrosky, thank you for coming."

"Did I have a choice? I don't know what more I can tell you about Dr. El-Arabi, Detective."

Marmaduke pulled a chair from beneath the table and sat down. "Tell me again about your work at the Department of Defense."

"I never said what I did at the department, Detective."

Marmaduke flipped through the blank pages. "You went to MIT. Is that where you met Dr. El-Arabi?"

"We were classmates."

"And after college, is that when you joined the Defense Department?"

"I don't understand. Why do you want to know about my work with the government? I thought this was about Dr. El-Arabi?"

"I'm just trying to get a better understanding of your relationship with my prime suspect."

"Our relationship was purely professional, Detective."

"You didn't hang out, not even socially?"

"He didn't smoke, he didn't drink, he didn't chase women, all of which I do. So, no, we didn't socialize."

"If I told you that Dr. El-Arabi has made statements implicating you in these bombings, what would you say to that?"

"Implicate me, how?" Professor Landrosky cut Marmaduke a hard stare. He stroked his goatee. "Do I need an attorney, Detective?"

"I don't know, do you? I have the names of," Marmaduke pretended to count, "five individuals capable of engineering a nanodevice like the one that killed Muhammad El-Arabi, and yours is one of them. The others are still…behind the wall, to use your term." Marmaduke flipped through more blank pages. "Tell me, Professor, about the marker used with the agent."

Professor Landrosky's stare turned to one of surprise. "How did you…that's classified information…I think I need a—"

The door to the room flung open. Marmaduke turned. "Sorry I'm late, Detective." Zones barged through the door. "Please, continue." He took a seat.

"Who are you?" Professor Landrosky asked.

"This is Dr. Zones."

"…Doctor? Are you a physicist?" Zones said nothing. "…An engineer?" Again, no reply. "Aaaa, a profiler, sent here to read my mental tea leaves."

"The marker, Professor Landrosky, what trigger did you use?" Marmaduke asked again.

"Tell me, Dr. Zones, what does your profile say about the type of person who committed these bombings? Is he…or she—we must be fair now, mustn't we—a bumbling fool, a genius or something much, much more? Detective Marmaduke can't seem to make up his mind as to which one of us he wants to charge with these crimes. He has a perfectly good suspect behind bars now. But he's a fisherman that doesn't know when his net is full. And we all know what happens when there are too many fish in the net. It breaks and the entire catch swims away. Now you," Professor Landrosky shook his finger at Zones, "you look like the fly-fishing type. You know when to catch and keep or when to catch and release. Unlike the detective, a partial victory is victory enough for you. So, am I your bomber, Doctor?" He leaned forward over the table.

Zones leaned back in his chair. With his gaze fixed on Professor Landrosky, he asked him, "How long were you institutionalized, Professor?"

"What!" Marmaduke shouted. He seemed unaware of his volume.

Professor Landrosky slumped in his chair. He looked away from Zones. At times, he closed his eyes completely. He got up, walked to the window behind him and opened the blinds.

"More classified information, Dr. Zones?" The professor stood at the window. He tucked his hands inside his pants pocket and jiggled the coins inside them. "So, what else have they told you?"

"Who?" Marmaduke asked.

"Come now, Detective, I can smell a pigeon cooking. The two of you are full of classified information not even the President has access to." He turned to them and folded his arms across his chest. "You must be getting too close for them."

"Them? Who's them?"

"The—"

Professor Landrosky fell to the floor. A mist of blood and chunks of matter sprayed the room. Marmaduke jumped to his feet. He pulled his weapon and rushed over to him. He knelt next to the professor. Zones followed. A large front section of his face was gone. A pool of blood flowed from his head, covered the floor and spread like red lava spewing up from the earth. The blinds rattled as gusts of air blew through a small, round opening in the window. It made a howling sound as the wind passed through it. Zones ran from the room and called for help.

"Stay down, Doc," Marmaduke cautioned. He remained with the dying, or dead, Professor Landrosky; he didn't know which. Soon, officers and detectives poured into the room and crowded the space.

Dr. DeGlorious pushed her way through the mesh of law enforcement. "Okay, everybody clear the room!" she ordered them. They filed out. Marmaduke and Zones stayed next to the body.

"How did you know he had been in the nut house?" Marmaduke asked Zones.

"I didn't, really. James told me about the gaps in his life, so I had her track his parents' movements. About nine years ago, they began to make weekly visits to Newark, Delaware from their home in Delmar. That's a four-hour drive round-trip. They did this religiously for three years. We tracked them through their credit card usage. Many of their charges centered around shops and motels near the Rockford Center, a private mental hospital."

"I still don't see how you made the connection."

"Well, Detective, at their ages, only a child would garner that kind of devotion. And since he had no siblings, it could only have been him. This was probably why he left the DOD and cut a deal to have his institutionalization classified."

Dr. DeGlorious made her way over to them. "What happened, Detective? Did he try to escape?"

"The bullet came through there." Marmaduke pointed at the window.

"That's some shot, couldn't have been an accident. Who's the victim?"

"Professor Landrosky." She froze and stared at the body. The damage to his face made him unrecognizable. "You okay, Doctor?"

Dr. DeGlorious looked back at the window. "We're about fifty feet from the ground, wouldn't you say?"

"That's about right."

"And the next building or structure closest to us at this elevation is over a mile away." Marmaduke nodded. "That's some shot in this wind."

"Yeah, the kind of shot only big money can buy."

"…Or big governments," Zones added.

SIXTEEN

A Rapist and a Bomber

ROME DROPPED A FILE onto Marmaduke's desk. It smacked the wooden top and made a loud sound. She had rushed from the crime lab with the test results from Francis Dixon's, aka Jah-Boy's, clothing. The place still bustled. It was a crime scene. Marmaduke turned in his chair. Rome stood in front of his desk with a big, *I know something you don't know*, smile on her face.

"Detective Rome?" Marmaduke looked down at the file.

"You know what that is there?" she asked.

"Judging from that Cheshire Cat smile on your face, something good for you, I hope."

"For both of us, Detective." She opened the file and pulled out a report. "This is the trace analysis from the clothing of my rapist."

"You caught him?"

"May have caught your bomber as well. You see what it says?"

Marmaduke pulled a pair of reading glasses from his desk drawer. "The clothes were positive for explosives."

"Explosives that matched samples collected from the crime scene."

"He was caught in the blast; how do you know it wasn't castoff?"

"You see here?" she pointed to the report. "The lab guys say that the sample particles taken from my rapist's clothes had a higher energy level than the samples collected from the site after the explosion."

"Meaning they were transferred prior to the explosion."

"That's right."

"Who's your rapist?"

"Some dreadhead dope dealer."

"Jamaican?"

"You sound surprised."

"Have you ever heard of the Jamaicans and the jihadists doing business?"

"What do you mean?"

"I have a Dr. El-Arabi on lockdown for the first bombing. It was his son that died in the explosion."

"…A doctor?"

"A PhD in electrical engineering over at Georgia Tech. We believe he was working with the lab director, who, unfortunately, just ate a bullet."

"I heard someone had, didn't know it was yours." Detective Rome glanced over Marmaduke's shoulder at the crime scene investigators moving back and forth. "So we have an Arab engineer, a dead American scientist and a Jamaican drug dealer as bomb suspects."

"…Appears that way."

"Who's going to sort this all out?"

"That, Detective, we're going to leave to him." Marmaduke turned and pointed to Zones as he walked out of an interrogation room.

"Dr. Zones. How did you get him in here? Last time I saw his ass he was rushing to catch a plane and too busy to give a damn."

"Well, whether he likes it or not, he's involved now. The doctor was in the room with me when the professor's head exploded."

"I see. I thought the captain may have put the screws to him."

"That too."

"So, which do we hit up first, your guy or mine?"

"How about neither. I got a meeting with ATF at the second bomb site as soon as CSU wraps things up here."

"You mind if I tag along?"

"…If you want the extra work. What about APD?"

"I'll tell them I'm on loan." She cut her eyes back to Zones. "I got a feeling that if Dr. Zones has anything to say about it, my job is already done."

"How do you mean?"

"He seems to think that my rapist can't also be a bomber."

"For what it's worth, Detective, he's usually right."

SEVENTEEN

"I don't wear FUBU."

DRIVING UP TO THE language research center, the scenery appeared to be tropical. Tree-draped canopies gave cover from the rain that started to fall. The river, more like a creek that ran through the property, trickled with flowing water. The loud drip drowned out the cacophony of bird sounds that came from high in the trees. Marmaduke and Detective Rome pulled closer to the shanty-styled building. Smoke still smoldered in spite of the drizzle. The tangled wreckage of a communication tower lay toppled; its descent barely missed the structure.

They stopped just short of the crime scene, outside of the yellow *police line* tape that stretched across the driveway. Marmaduke and Detective Rome stepped from the old Deuce. The sun peeked through the rain. The clouds and trees cast shadows over the wreckage, camouflaging it.

"Detective Marmaduke, over here." He looked up to see Agent Thomas wave him over.

"What do we have here, Agent?"

"Other than a downed tower and a small hole in the ground, not much. This bomb was different and more powerful than the one used at the first bomb site. What they do have in common is that we recovered very little of the bomb. We did find fragments from a cell phone, but there wasn't enough left of it to identify a make or model."

"I see a blast pattern in this direction," Marmaduke pointed.

"The explosive device was placed over here at the base." They walked deeper into the site, stopping at a concrete pad with a hole in the ground at one corner.

"It's a miracle the research center wasn't hit," Detective Rome said.

"No miracle. I believe it was a strategic placement."

"Strategic, how?" Marmaduke asked.

"A shaped charge."

"Aren't those used in construction demolition?"

"Construction, military, quarrying, petroleum industry, it's a pretty utilitarian device that'll make it more difficult to track down."

"So, you believe the perpetrator directed the collapse of the tower to fall in the direction of the research center but not hit it? That takes some skill."

"That sounds more like a warning," Detective Rome said.

"A warning is right," Agent Thomas agreed. "You see that utility shed? It's ten feet from the main structure. The width of the tower at the point where it landed in between the main structure and the shed is eight feet; that leaves one foot on each side."

"So who's capable of pulling something like this off?"

"You don't get skills like these from jobs where you're serving fries and shakes. You're looking for ex-military, most likely Special Forces. They could even be working in one of the jobs I mentioned earlier."

"Thanks, Agent. That really narrows our search down."

"Well, Detective, I may have something to make your search a little easier. Follow me." They walked back to where the cars were parked. Agent Thomas reached inside the rear cab of his truck and pulled out a brown paper bag. "This was in the rubble." He opened the bag and Marmaduke looked inside. He snapped a latex glove from his pocket and used it to lift a pearl-handled pistol from the bag. "The groundskeeper had just cut this area the evening of the blast. He said it wasn't there at the time. No one who works here knew anything about it either."

"Now you're talking. I'll get this to the lab; let's see if we can get any latent prints from it."

"Is there anyone working here today that we can speak with?" Detective Rome asked.

"The director of the center, Karen Shipley, canceled work for all the employees. She came in to make sure the animals were okay."

"...Animals?" Marmaduke said. "I thought this was a language research center."

"It looked like Wild Kingdom in there to me, Detective."

* * *

A chorus of sounds filled the space. Ape calls bounced off the cold, concrete floors and drifted up into the exposed trusses. Animals jostled inside cages. They swung and banged on the steel bars that imprisoned them. Marmaduke and Detective Rome waited outside a laboratory. They took in the scene.

"Detectives, I'm Dr. Shipley." A woman in a white lab coat appeared behind them from out of nowhere. "You want to talk about the tower? I've told the FBI everything I know."

"We hoped you might recall something more," Marmaduke said. "Have you received any threats from anyone?"

"Not since we took over."

"What do you mean?"

"The lab used to conduct research for the CDC when Emory ran it. That, of course, attracted some unwanted attention. We've been running the lab for over a year now. I guess one of the ARGs didn't get the memo."

"ARGo?"

"Animal Rights Groups."

"What makes you so sure it was one of them?"

"Isn't it obvious? Most people don't even know we're back here."

"What about disgruntled employees?"

"We don't have any."

"We're going to need all of their names and addresses, nonetheless."

"Sure, I've got a copy over here."

They walked back toward the front of the building.

"What exactly do you do here?" Detective Rome asked.

"We study language, everything from how it develops to numeric cognition."

"Doesn't that still require using those apes as guinea pigs?"

"All of our research is noninvasive, Detective." She snatched a paper from a folder inside her desk drawer. "Here you go."

Marmaduke scanned the list. "Thank you, Doctor." He and Detective Rome headed for the door. "One more question, Dr. Shipley; what do you know about an organization named Urban Pet Rescue?"

"The name doesn't ring a bell. Are they related to this incident?"

"Not sure." Marmaduke gave the place a last once-over. The muffled sounds of wild animal calls drifted through the steel door.

"Is there anything else, Detective?"

"What…no, that'll be all. Thank you, Doctor."

Marmaduke and Detective Rome headed for the exit.

"You familiar with abduction phenomenon, Marmaduke?" Detective Rome asked.

"You mean kidnapping?"

"Yeah, only not by humans."

"Is this about UFOs again?"

"It's pertinent to the case."

Marmaduke chuckled. "UFOs?"

"The language research center takes monkeys out of their habitat and performs experiments on them, right?" Marmaduke sighed. "Same with alien abductions. Now, if we knew for a fact this was happening to humans, wouldn't we do everything possible to stop it? What if these bombers feel the same way about the puppies at scene one and the apes at this scene?"

"Except we've got evidence of these crimes. I haven't heard about any reports of anyone blowing up alien property."

"But we do hear things about abductions."

"Please, a few kooks…I mean…media-hungry zealots wanting attention."

"The Reed Family in 1960, the Hills in '61 and Betty Andreasson in '67, were they all media hungry?"

Marmaduke gave Detective Rome a wry smile. "How 'bout them Dogs?"

"I don't watch football." A few awkward moments passed. "What's our next move? We bird-dog the names on that list?"

Marmaduke glanced down at the paper in his hand. It flapped in the breeze. "I don't know. There are too many potential villains in this story. We need a profile on the perp, or we'll keep bumping our heads."

"Have you heard the song, 'Love the One You're With'? I say we question the ones we have in custody. You've already interrogated your guy. Let's jack up the Jamaican, see if he's made of curry or jerk."

"I'm with you on that. First, let me check on the status of that warrant for Professor Landrosky's office and home."

"I'll call James and have her rustle up the dread."

* * *

Within minutes, Marmaduke and Rome rolled onto the precinct parking lot. The old Deuce needed shocks; it bounced up and down at every rough spot in the road. Between child support, alimony and a drinking habit, there was little money left for Marmaduke to repair and maintain his car or himself.

"Don't you think it's time to retire Shirley?" Detective Rome asked.

"Shirley is going out with me. When I retire, she retires. That is, unless you're offering me one of those Vets."

"Only one man has driven my girls and that's my daddy. He knew how to handle a woman. From the looks of Shirley," Detective Rome scanned the car's crumbling interior, "you're pretty hard on a girl."

"It must be a black thing."

"What do you mean?"

"You sound just like Dr. Zones when he rides in here."

"Brothers do like a nice ride. I know some Hebrews who'd slap some chrome twenties on Shirley's ass, drape her up, lay a nice polish down, a nice leather skin, wangin in the trunk, make her a ghetto beauty queen."

"Yeah…well…nobody is touching Shirley. I like her just the way she is, warts and all." He ran his hand over the dashboard. "Why do I need oversized trunk speakers when I've got this wangin 8-track?"

"I'm just saying, a new ride might improve your love life."

"Aww, now you know what I want for Christmas."

They scurried up the precinct's stairs and headed for the interrogation room. James sat parked outside the captain's office. She pecked at her computer, shuffled papers and opened and closed drawers looking busy. She popped her head up to see Marmaduke and Detective Rome approaching.

"I got your ganja king in room one."

"In one...but that's where...."

"What's the matter, Detective? You look...piqued." James smirked.

"Have the lab boys finished in there already?"

"You bet, and not a speck of blood or brain matter anywhere, a new window in there too."

"I'm moving him."

"Can't, all the other rooms are taken or have a contractor in them."

"Shit."

"Don't worry, Marmaduke. Bullets don't strike twice in the same place...or is that lightening?"

Marmaduke rolled his eyes. He huffed. "The captain pay you extra for that sarcasm?"

"I save it all for you, baby, all for you."

Marmaduke reached inside his coat pocket and pulled out the bag that held the gun found at the language research center. "I need this dusted for prints." He handed the bag to James and disappeared down the hall with Detective Rome. They stopped outside the door to room one.

"How do you want to handle this?" Detective Rome asked.

"This is your suspect; he's all yours."

"He's a hardcore banger. I may have to twist him hard, in case you're the squeamish type."

"After seeing a man's brain splatter all over the place, not much can faze me."

"Great, I'll break out the whips and chains."

They entered the room. Marmaduke scanned the space looking for signs of the violence that had taken place only hours earlier. Sure enough, the new window was there, and the place sparkled just as James had said—not a hint of blood or matter anywhere. His eyes shot to their suspect, Jah-Boy, slouched in his chair. His neck hung down. It bobbed and weaved—he was asleep. Detective Rome slammed the door. Jah-Boy eased from his sleep. She kicked his chair.

"Wake the fuck up."

"Bitch, are you crazy?"

She reached across the table and grabbed him by his shirt. "I got your bitch. Now, the next time that word crosses your lips, I better see your dog or your mother sitting next to you. Do you understand me?"

Jah-Boy lowered his eyes to Detective Rome's hand; it was still clinched tight to his shirt. She snatched it and pulled him closer to her.

"Yeah, man, I hear you."

"Okay, make sure you do."

Someone knocked at the door. Marmaduke answered it. James shoved a file and evidence bag at him. "The sheets on your ganja king."

Marmaduke returned to the table. He slid the file and bag to Detective Rome.

"Listen," Jah-Boy said, "I didn't know you were five-o, man. You came in the club shaking your ass like a bit...a loose woman. What was I supposed to do, man?"

"Oh, is that why you told your boys to kill me out in the parking lot, because you didn't know I was law enforcement?" Jah-Boy sank in his chair. He looked away. "But you have bigger problems than rape and attempted murder."

"I ain't rape or attempt murder on nobody, man. I got witnesses."

"Oh yeah, what're their names?" Jah-Boy leaned back in his seat and folded his arms, saying nothing. "I thought so." Detective Rome flipped the file open and read. "Tell me, Francis, why were you in Decatur Sunday night?"

"I was with my lady Sunday night, nowhere near Decatur, man."

"Your lady? Would that be a Ms. Bonýet because she said she didn't see your black ass at all that day, except for late that night when you came over long enough to change clothes and leave."

"No, not her. I got more than one lady, man."

"What's her name?"

"I can't remember all those whores' names."

Detective Rome stared at him. She popped open the evidence bag, removed the clothing from inside it and placed each piece on the table.

"You recognize those?" Jah-Boy slowly rolled his eyes at the items spread out across the table. He looked back at her but said nothing. "We got those from your little Ms. Whitebread in Dunwoody. Too bad for you she's not the domestic type. The lab boys said we wouldn't have been able to find the traces of explosives on your clothing had she washed them."

"That shit ain't mine. I don't wear FUBU."

"*I don't wear FUBU,*" Detective Rome mocked him. She turned to Marmaduke, almost smiling. "Can you believe this motherfucka?" She whipped her head back to Jah-Boy. "Negro, this shit is yours." She ripped a sheet of paper from the file folder and pushed it across the table. "Pubic and other hair samples retrieved from these clothes matched specimens taken from you."

Jah-Boy read the paper. "Margot is a whore." He flicked the paper away. "She could have gotten my clothes mixed up with one of her other niggas…cross contaminated my things with whoever owns those clothes."

"So you're CSU now?" He said nothing. "And Ms. Bonyet, your fiancée, is a liar?"

"A whore, a liar, and not my fiancée."

"She's protecting someone else; is that what you're saying?"

"Yeah, man, that's what I'm saying."

Detective Rome noticed her suspect's arms; black ink marks were scrawled all over them. One evidently stood out. "Who's 'Lil Man'?" she asked him. Jah-Boy rolled his folded arm toward him. He looked down at the heart-shaped image with the words *My Lil Man* scribbled across it. He covered the tattoo with his other arm and said nothing. Detective Rome turned to Marmaduke. "Well, Detective, let's take out a warrant for Ms.

Bonyet's arrest."

"What's the charge?"

"Aiding and abetting and accessory to murder."

"That's right, go sweat her about this shit, man," Jah-Boy said. He seemed to sit a lot more comfortably in his chair.

"It's a damn shame that baby will be born in jail," Detective Rome added.

"Baby? What baby?"

"Oh, you didn't know? No matter, it probably belongs to the guy she's protecting. Sit tight, Francis, I'll have someone take you back to your cell." Detective Rome stuffed the clothes back inside the bag. She and Marmaduke headed for the door.

"Detective, is Margot pregnant for real?"

"I saw the positive test results myself when we searched her place. Why are you so interested? Bitch has been fucking you and some other dick on the side."

"Bitch, don't say that, damn you."

"What the fuck did you say?"

"I said…I mean…Don't say that. Margot isn't like that."

"Like what?"

"Listen—those are my things."

Detective Rome leaned over the table. "Let me make sure I hear you correctly. These are your clothes?" She dropped the evidence bag on top of the table.

"Yeah, man, but I don't know anything about explosives."

Detective Rome sat back down. Marmaduke joined her. "So where exactly did you pick up traces of explosives on your clothing?" Jah-Boy squirmed in his seat. His eyes locked on the bag. "You know what happened in this room earlier? A man died—murdered actually." Detective Rome rose from her seat, walked over to the window and raised the blinds. "A bullet, from all the way over there somewhere, came through this window and struck him in the head." Jah-Boy turned to see her demonstration. "Come here, Francis, and let me show you."

"No, that's okay. I'm good."

"I wasn't giving you a choice." He remained seated. "Detective, I believe Francis needs a little help."

"Get up." Marmaduke grabbed Jah-Boy by the collar and jacked him up from his seat. He hauled him over to the window and held him there.

"This ain't right, man. I want a—"

"Please, don't say you want a lawyer," Detective Rome said. "The dead guy connected to this case had a lawyer, and you see what good it did him. Seems to me they're cleaning house, lawyer or not. So we're gonna stand right here and have a little conversation."

"Okay. I was there."

"Do I look like a psychic? Where is there?"

"In Decatur…when the explosion happened."

"Now we're getting somewhere." She hauled him back to his chair and sat him down hard. "Now, explain how you got the explosive residue on you."

"It must've come from the blast."

"No." Detective Rome ripped another paper from the file. "This report says the explosive residue on your cloths was pre-detonation. That means you had to have handled the stuff before the explosion."

"I'm no bomber, man. Sure, I run a little weed and shake down some people, but this al-Qaida shit, no way."

"Where exactly were you when the explosion happened?"

"…Back in the cut, near the old Golden Buddha."

"Doing what?"

"Nothing, I was walking from a club."

"You see a white girl near there that night?"

"…No, man."

"So, if I put you in a lineup, she wouldn't say, that's the motherfucka right there; he's the one who raped me?"

"It was no rape. She…"

"She what? She asked for it?"

"Yeah, man, exactly."

"Not only do we have your dumb ass on the bombing, but we got you on rape too. Son, you've been sampling too much of your own product."

"No way, man, you can't pin those on me. I want a lawyer."

"Yeah, well, you're gonna need one." Detective Rome marched to the door. She yanked it open and stepped halfway out into the hall. She gestured with her hand, and an officer appeared at the door. "Take him back down to holding and add sexual assault, human trafficking and terroristic acts to his charges."

"This ain't right, man," Jah-Boy protested as the officer led him away. "That bitch is railroading me. She's using police brutality. She broke my nose." His shouts echoed from down the hall.

Marmaduke leaned in close to Detective Rome as he watched Jah-Boy being dragged away. "The baby momma thing, how did you know it would work? Most of these guys wouldn't give a damn if the child was born in chains."

"Little Ms. Whitebread isn't pregnant. That was all just bullshit I told him. He doesn't give a damn either. Romeo has a number of child support orders against him. He has a hearing before Judge Hatchet next week."

"Judge *hack you up and eat you* Hatchet? Shit, damn near lost my shield fucking with her."

"Exactly, wouldn't look good for Mr. Francis Dixon if the judge thought he had another one on the way and born behind bars."

"So he'd rather cop to being in the area?"

"I guess he didn't figure it would come with terrorism charges."

"Aren't you forgetting one thing?"

"What's that?"

"Dr. Zones and his theory about a bomber that sticks around long enough to rape."

"Killjoy."

Just then, James came barging down the hall. "Marmaduke, the lab got prints from the gun and a match."

"That was quick."

"The captain wants all evidence processing on this case expedited."

"Who's the match?"

"Some con and one other print they haven't identified yet." She opened the file and handed it to him.

"Marcus Tanks—seems he did time for armed robbery. But I don't see any military background or specialized explosives training."

"Let me see that." Detective Rome grabbed the file. "Says here he was a member of RAM back in the sixties."

"What's that?"

"The Revolutionary Action Movement."

"Isn't that Al Sharpton's organization?"

"That's National Action Network. RAM was sort of a precursor to the Black Panthers. Those cats could have gotten some underground special training, especially in bomb making."

"Hold on. We've gone from a Middle Eastern terrorist to a DOD cover-up, a Jamaican drug lord and now an ex-con with a connection to the Black Panthers?" Marmaduke whipped out his phone and dialed.

"Who're you calling?"

"Dr. Zones. I need that profile."

EIGHTEEN

Reverend Ike

THE SILKY-SMOOTH SOUND OF Ornette Coleman tickled Zones' ears through the radio. He pored over the case file for the bombings from his cramped office space at Drake and Associates. The sun inched its way behind a distant line. He did his best thinking at night—no distractions, no pesky inmates complaining about the injustices of the criminal justice system. As he read, he snatched papers from the folder and slammed them down hard on top his desk. When he found information that interested him, he copied it, enlarged the writing or image and pinned it to the wall. By the time Zones finished, the wall was a collage of field reports, lab reports and crime scene pictures, all color coded to a system only he understood.

Sam burst through the door to Zones' office. "What the fuck are you doing in here, Monk? The dead can't sleep with all your banging." He turned to see the wall plastered with papers. "Damn, boy. What's that?"

"You're still here?"

"Not for long with the racket you're making, can hardly hear myself think." Sam walked over to the wall. "This looks like your bombing case."

"Not mine, yours."

Sam shot him a hard stare. "What do you have on the profile so far?"

"Nothing much. Just started. I got a call from Detective Marmaduke. Apparently I don't have shit else to do except work on his case." Sam folded his arms, puckered his lips and shoe-tapped the floor. "Yeah, anyway, based on the type of crime and the lack of any viable evidence, we know the unidentified subject is highly organized with the intellect to match."

"How so?"

Zones walked over to the wall. He scanned it, plucked out two pins, took the papers and handed them to Sam. "According to the FBI analyst, this is a device for IP communications. They think it was a component of the first bomb; perhaps it was used to detonate it. This is the ME's report on the dead body found at the scene. The autopsy of the brain showed a bioluminescent infection but not from the bomb. According to Detective Marmaduke, some sort of nanotechnology may have been used."

"So the sand-heads have gotten this advanced?"

"I don't think terrorist are responsible for the bombings, at least not in the classical sense."

"How do you mean then? I thought they had some Georgia Tech professor from Saudi Arabia locked up."

"Take a look at this." Zones unfurled a roll of paper. He pinned it to the wall. "This is a list of all the major bombings and attempted bombings and who committed them within the continental United States over the last twenty-five years. What do you see?"

"Hell, I don't know, a bunch of whack jobs blowing shit up."

"Compare the perps to their targets."

"The Islamist targeted financial, governmental and Jewish sites. The homegrown militias and rednecks went after abortion clinics and other soft targets, the exception being Oklahoma City."

"Now look at the targets of these bombings: an animal shelter and a language research center."

"They reflect a homegrown profile."

"Exactly, but not only that." Zones snatched another image from the wall. "This is a photo of the second bomb site. You see how close the tower came to striking the language research center and this smaller building here? Detective Marmaduke says the ATF thinks it was a strategic collapse, meaning they meant to miss both structures."

"That required some real skill. Was the same type of bomb used?"

"They don't believe so. Detective Marmaduke also said, and I agree, the unsub seems to be sending a message."

"You and Marmaduke agreeing on something, that's a first. What's the message?"

"That is one thing I haven't figured out."

"What about victimology?"

"There is one connection between the two crime scenes; they both cater to animals. I'm still analyzing the data on the body found at the first bomb scene."

"So, some big-brained redneck that loves animals is running around the county blowing up shit?"

"Most homegrown terrorists are of average or below average intelligence. They may've learned some specialized training but so have monkeys in a circus. And you don't see us hanging degrees on them. The sophistication of these bombs says to me that the unsub isn't your run-of-the-mill yahoo. I think we're looking for someone with access to advanced explosives training, the kind you only get from the government and certain corporations."

"Has anyone contacted the media or the police?"

"There has been no Kaczynskian manifesto, if that's what you're asking."

"So, the unsub has no grand mission or fantasies?"

"None that I can see, but I haven't worked out a motive yet."

"Have you considered one of the animal rights groups? Those fucks like to blow shit up."

"The FBI thought so as well."

"See, now there you go. Good thing I came in here. What else you got?"

Zones rolled his eyes and shook his head. "I don't know of any animal rights groups with an expert sharpshooter in their ranks. But if a group or an organization is the perpetrator, we should be profiling the group and not individuals within the group."

"What suspects do you have? Perhaps we can get some idea of the organization based on its members."

Zones ripped another paper from the wall. "Here are the suspects they have so far."

"...Dr. El-Arabi and Muhammad El-Arabi."

"Father and son. The doctor is on lockdown and lawyered up. His son was found dead at the first crime scene."

"Landrosky, he's the professor at Tech that bought a bullet to the head."

"That's right."

"Who's Francis Dixon?"

"Some Jamaican drug lord, ran a crew out of the Intrigue, a night club in Stone Mountain."

"How's he connected?"

"He was picked up for a sexual assault that took place across the street from the first bombing. I got there in time to interrupt his little party when the blast went off. The lab found bomb residue on his clothing. They said it was pre-detonation."

"What the fuck were you doing there?" Zones ignored him. "Let's see where this explosion was—off Cheshire Bridge Rd? Boy, the only things open that time of the night over there are booty clubs and massage parlors." Again, Zones said nothing. "...Monk?"

"Can we move on?"

Sam cocked his head. "What're you doing paying for pussy, boy? Weren't you bangin' that big-ass waitress over at Brullinni's?"

"Move on, old man."

"Okay. Okay." Sam threw up his hands.

"I told Marmaduke and this Detective Rome that a bomber who stayed around for a rape doesn't match any profile I know."

"I agree. Did they find a connection between any of the suspects?"

"No, not yet at least."

"Let's start with this. We know, from the different bomb devices, the group is dynamic, capable of making adjustments and adapting to new experiences."

"And they have the resources to implement their objectives."

"What about other psychometrics?"

"There doesn't seem to be a singular personality for the group, but it must be organized and have highly educated members with military or corporate training in explosives. Socioeconomically, there is a wide range. It would recruit from within its ranks and restrict membership to a select few. The lowest in this group would be well compensated to keep and reinforce their loyalty. Members would also have a shared ideology, but not all of them. The murder of Professor Landrosky speaks to this. They may have feared he would reveal what he knew about them."

"Professor Landrosky may have been a contractor."

"Not only him, but those who actually carried out the attacks as well."

"If we found another contractor, would he be able to lead authorities to the person who is behind these bombings?"

"I doubt it. These are not your run-of-the-mill paramilitary types. Those at the top will be insulated."

"When will you be presenting the profile to Captain Franklin?"

"In a couple of days."

"I better let you finish then." Sam gave the wall a long last look. He took a step toward it and snatched an evidence report. "Marcus Tanks, what does he have to do with this case?"

"You know this cat?"

"Yeah, he ran with your father and me back in the day."

"You mean with the Panthers."

Sam nodded while scanning the report. "Why would a gun with his prints on it be found at the crime scene? It's been a while since I've seen Tanks, but I don't think he's ever set foot outside New York."

Zones took the report from Sam. "According to this, he's in the lockup over at Fulton County. He must've gotten tired of the cold weather."

"Let's take a ride."

"Where? To see this guy? *No way.*"

"Why?"

"Because that's investigative work; all I'm obligated to do is the profile. And, as you know, I don't even want to do that."

"Aren't you the least bit curious about this case, Monk, about how all these people and parts fit together? You're the one who wanted to be a big shot FBI profiler, and now that you have the opportunity, you're shitting all over it."

"You promised me I could have time off, and then you reneged by letting the captain dump this case in my lap." Zones shoved a finger at Sam.

"What's the big goddamn problem? I've called your black ass back from vacation plenty of times, even had you cancel at the last minute. Now you act like I broke into your place and pulled you away from a good piece of pussy right before you hit your nut."

"Yeah…well…this time it's different."

"Why? Is it because you can't get back to New York to work on your mother's case?"

"How did you—"

"Know? What other reason would you have for hanging out around The Point, wanting to get inside the old brownstone, and having Candice bird-dog shit on the New York building department for you?" Sam slammed the papers he held on the table. He pointed at Zones, "You know, I'm disappointed in you, Monk."

"Disappointed in me?"

"Yeah, because you're acting irrationally, like some young school girl on her period."

"Man, please."

"That's right. I've been telling you since you've been old enough to understand that your old man didn't have anything to do with your mother's murder. All I've gotten for it are mean stares and your opinion that I was full of shit. Now, all of a sudden, you're running around trying to dig up information on Cleo's murder even though you believe your father is justifiably locked up for committing the crime. If that's not irrational, I don't know what is."

Zones said nothing. He stared out the window with his back to Sam. He watched cars jockeying for position in the rush-hour traffic. The sounds of honking horns and screeching wheels drifted into his small office space. They drowned out and helped to spare him from hearing some of Sam's bluster.

Looking at the reflection in the window, Zones watched as Sam marched over to retrieve his coat and cap. He plucked them off the rack and tossed them over to him. They fell to the floor by his side. Sam tore from the room and returned holding his own coat and charcoal-gray fedora.

"Let's go."

"I'm not going."

Sam marched over to Zones, picked up his coat and cap from the floor, draped the coat over Zones' shoulders and fitted the cap on top his head. He swatted Sam's hand away, but the cap was firmly affixed.

"I'll see you in the car; you're driving." Sam disappeared down the hall and left Zones standing at the window.

"Shit!" Zones ripped his coat off, slung it over his arm and followed Sam down the hall.

* * *

It was close to the end of visitation when Zones and Sam arrived at the Fulton County Jail. Scuff marks covered the vinyl tile floor and all of the tables and chairs were in disarray, scattered and overturned onto the floor. The room was surrounded with glass walls, and they could see security cameras dotting the ceiling all around them. Guards stood at the ready, waiting for some unknown event to happen. The place smelled of strong disinfectant, the kind you experience at the old folk's home. It reminded Zones of death, which made him want to get up and leave. He didn't like being there. His posture said it all as he slumped in his chair with his arms folded tight across himself. Every so often, he would give Sam a mean look from the corner of his eye and mumble some unintelligible words.

"That's bad for your back," Sam said.

"What're you, a yoga master now?"

"No, I'm serious. You should sit up with your back straight, your feet planted firmly on the floor." Sam showed him. Zones slouched even more and propped his feet against the wall. "Alright, I'm trying to tell you, when you can't hit that down stroke like you want to, you're gonna remember what I told you today."

"Is that all you think about, *sex*?"

"Don't you? Oh, I forget; you're still a young buck. Pussy for you is like ordering hot wings. All you have to do is pick a sauce. When you get to be my age, you need those wings to marinate overnight, softens them up some. Then you want them pan seared in olive oil, allowed to rest in the oven at 350 degrees—not deep fried. As for the sauce, none of that hot shit. Give me the mildest you got, well-cured, un-spicy pussy; that's what I like."

Zones scowled, shaking his head. "Dirty old man."

"And I will be dirty for the next thirty."

"You better hope—"

The door to the room was flung open. A guard marched a man, dressed in an orange jumpsuit, over to the table and shoved him down into a chair. His puffy beard covered most of his face. His bloodshot eyes peered back at them. He scratched hard at his black, leathery-looking skin, leaving thin white streaks across it.

Sam opened his eyes wide at the sight of the man. His mouth hung open; his lips drooped near past his chin. The man stopped his scratching, but his hand still clawed at his face. He leaned forward and squinted.

"Boy, you look just like your motherfuckin daddy." Then he turned to face Sam. "Drake the Snake, man, I thought I'd never see you again, not after we popped those pigs over near Q's. Your ass got outta town so quick, you'd a thought big-ass Angela's daddy was after you for knockin up his daughter." He burst into a hearty laugh and showed several gaps of missing teeth spread throughout his mouth.

"How've you been, Tanks?"

"How've I been? Shit, how do I look? These crackas got me down here on some trumped-up-ass charges. I knew I should've kept my black ass in Harlem. They're still fuckin with niggas in Dixie."

"What're they pressing you with?"

"Said I whistled at some white woman."

"They can't arrest you for that," Zones said. "Are you sure that's all you did?"

Tanks cut his eyes over to him. He sucked his teeth and contorted his lips. He leaned back in his chair and stretched out his neck. "Her booty may have hit my hand, but I didn't squeeze hard." Tanks shook his finger at Zones.

"Man, this is a waste of time."

"Now hold on, Monk," Sam said.

"Yeah, hold on, Monk," Tanks repeated. He stared wildly at him. "What're you two down here for anyway? I know this ain't no social visit."

Sam cleared his throat and fidgeted in his seat. He scooted up to the table and leaned closer to Tanks. "You remember that pearl-handled piece you used to carry?"

"…Yeah, Reverend Ike, what about it?"

"Whoa," Zones said. "You named your gun Reverend Ike?" Tanks nodded. "May I ask why?"

"Because when I stuck that barrel in a motherfucka's face, he prayed and gave up the money, just like I was Reverend Ike."

"Um…yeah…what did you do with it?" Sam asked.

"Shit, man, I don't know. It's been how any years, damn near fifty?"

"You mean to tell me you haven't seen that piece in over fifty years?"

"Not since we popped those pigs that night. Got rid of it soon after."

"Do you remember where?"

"Man, the only things I remember from the sixties are beatdowns and pussy. Everything else is in a gumbo-filled haze of acid, LSD and herb." Tanks stared up at the ceiling. He smiled and stroked his nappy beard, perhaps remembering someone or something special. He snapped from his trance-like state and asked, "Why are you so interested in that piece?"

"Because it's been found at a crime scene with your prints still on it." Zones said.

"Reverend Ike, found at a crime scene?"

"Yeah and, unlike you, those prints look fresh, not fifty years old. So, if you got a story to tell, you better get it straight. It won't be long before the *pigs* are in here jacking you up."

Tanks looked worried. He wrung his hands; they moved in the air in unmatched patterns. His fingers wiggled in slow, shaky lines and fidgeted with some imaginary thing.

"Can you tell us how your gun wound up there?" Sam asked.

"No."

"Man, later for this waste of time," Zones said. "Let's go, Sam." They gathered their things to leave. Tanks sat there, looking into space.

"Take care of yourself, bro, and keep this conversation between us, okay?" Sam said. He placed a hand on Tanks' shoulder as he walked passed him. Zones held open the door as Sam walked through it.

"Wait." Tanks turned toward them. "The last person I recall with Reverend Ike was…his father." He pointed at Zones.

NINETEEN

"…a killer, a rapist and a terrorist."

MARMADUKE RIFLED THROUGH THE desk drawers of Professor Landrosky's home office. He pulled out folders and dropped them down hard on top of the desk. He and Detective Rome searched through the professor's things for quite some time; they found nothing.

"If there's a connection between your dreadhead, Alibaba—who ain't talking—and this egghead, it's gonna take Einstein to figure it out," Marmaduke said. "Hell, I don't understand half of this crap. I mean, look at these papers: molecular physics, advanced biometrics, nanoparticle design. Unless the good professor was also the biggest drug dealer in Atlanta, I don't get it. Didn't you say your boy was also in the skin game? And…"

Detective Rome cleared her throat. She motioned with her head and looked over Marmaduke's shoulder. He turned to see Mrs. Landrosky standing at the door to the study.

"There's another file cabinet over here." Mrs. Landrosky walked past Marmaduke over to a large built-in bookshelf with drawers. She took short, quick steps. Her black pumps tapped across the rough-hewn hardwood floors. She slid on a pair of ivory-framed, butterfly glasses and pulled open one drawer. She bent over, exposing her tree-trunk legs. The tight cigarette dress she wore kept her from falling completely over as she pulled a stack of files from the drawer and walked them over to the desk. "Here you go, Detective." She sat the files down gently.

"Thank you," Marmaduke said.

"Let me know if you need anything else." She turned to leave.

"Excuse me, Mrs. Landrosky, do you have time to answer a few questions?"

"That seems to be all I have, Detective."

"Yes, ma'am. Did you know any of your husband's friends?"

"You mean his colleagues at Tech? I knew some of them and their spouses. We attended most of the functions given by the university, private ones as well."

"What about Dr. El-Arabi, did they socialize outside of work?"

"He was a Muslim, why would they?"

"What do you mean?"

"They can't drink, they have to pray every five minutes and, worst of all, they don't eat pork. That's downright sacrilegious in the South."

"What about his other associates, those not from his job?"

"You mean...like drug dealers, Detective?"

Marmaduke grew quiet. He realized she had overheard his conversation with Detective Rome. "Yes, a Jamaican drug dealer, in fact."

"Don't be ridiculous. Uza would have never gotten caught up in something like that. He was a university researcher, for God's sake."

"I don't mean any disrespect, Mrs. Landrosky, but it wouldn't be the first time a college professor was caught up in the drug game."

"I'm afraid you're wrong, Detective. Now, if there's nothing else—"

"Actually there is. Did you know about your husband's prior work with the Department of Defense?"

"Of course, that's where we met. I was the administrative assistant to the lab director."

"But did you know about his research?"

"It was all numbers and equations; I'm not a scientist."

"But you did know about his little stay at the, *Johnny can't play with sharp things motel*, didn't you?"

"I don't understand, where?"

"…Your husband's stay at the treatment center in Delaware, Mrs. Landrosky," Rome interjected. "You were aware of it, were you not?"

"That was before we were married, but I helped make the arrangements and visited him during his hospitalization."

"Do you know of anyone that might have wanted your husband dead?"

"He had no enemies, to my knowledge."

"Did your husband do any private consulting?"

"You mean outside of his work at the university? None, his research took up most of his time."

"Okay, thank you, Mrs. Landrosky."

Her eyes swept over her husband's study. "Be sure to put this mess back the way you found it."

Marmaduke watched Mrs. Landrosky disappear behind the double wooden doors. She took her time closing them, allowing him another peek at her pillar-like legs.

"I wonder what she saw in that old geezer."

"A wallet full of money apparently."

"On a professor's salary?" Marmaduke looked around the room. He shook his head. "This furniture is imported—Roche. This shit ain't cheap. You got that background on the professor?"

"Yeah, right here." Detective Rome pulled a sheet of paper from a clipboard and handed it to Marmaduke. He read through it, his finger scrolling down the paper.

"Here we go, two hundred and fifty thousand dollars. That was his salary. You think the professor could afford imported custom furniture, Tiffany diamonds and first print Boteros on this salary?"

"I'm impressed, didn't know you were such a connoisseur, Detective."

"Two years at the L'Ermitage, a waste of good money as far as I'm concerned. My parents thought otherwise."

"What does that shi shi foo foo prep-school education tell you about this?" She shoved another sheet of paper at him.

"Shi shi foo foo? I believe you've got me confused with Dr. Zones. What do we have here?" Marmaduke whipped out a pair of reading glasses and slipped them on his nose. "This is an invoice for Euro-Arabia Oil, so what?"

"You see the company name on the invoice?"

"…Landrosky Consulting."

"I thought the professor didn't consult apart from the university?"

"It wouldn't be the first time an employee did a little somethin-somethin on the side, Detective. Perhaps that's how he could afford the upkeep on Little Miss Versace."

"An Arabian oil company and an Arab perp cooling his heels back at the station. You see where I'm going with this?"

"We should question someone at Euro-Arabia."

"And the Arab."

"We can't question him, remember. He lawyered up."

"He can't be questioned, but there's nothing that says he can't listen."

"How do you suggest we have a conversation with him without having our asses handed to us by the captain?"

"Damn, Marmaduke, Captain Franklin must have broken off a piece of his foot way too deep. You're paranoid as hell."

"I still haven't heard a plan." Marmaduke shot her steely eyes.

"Okay, get James on the phone."

"Why?"

"Will you just *trust* me and get her on the phone."

Marmaduke flipped out his phone and dialed. He gave Detective Rome a distrusting stare in between pressing the numbers, not certain what scheme she had in store for them. This was their first time working together. They had not yet established that partner thing—that feeling between two people that's forged over many years of being in the fight together. Thoughts had to be synchronized and actions flawlessly choreographed. Communication was a nod or a wink, a twitch of the brow or a blank stare. It was how to know what to say and when, without ever having to compare stories and always getting it just right.

"James—"

Detective Rome snatched the phone from Marmaduke's ear. "James, what block is Dr. El-Arabi held in—he's in D block. Isn't that where they keep the snitches—I see, for his protection. You got any openings on that block—because I want Francis Dixon moved there, a cell next to the doctor—cool, we'll be there soon." She tossed the phone back to Marmaduke.

"Francis Dixon, the Jamaican? He lawyered up as well. We can't question him either."

"Did he? My recollection is that he said, 'I may want a lawyer,' big damn difference."

"That's not what I heard."

"Trust me, Marmaduke, my ears are much younger."

"And if this doesn't work, then what?"

"We still have that gun found at the crime scene to follow up on. The lab found a couple of prints. One matched some wine-o crackhead. He's drying out over in Fulton County."

"I hope you know what you're doing."

"Trying to catch a killer, a rapist and a terrorist, Detective"

* * *

The clean white walls of the DeKalb County Jail contrasted with the dirty crimes of the men and women housed behind its barred doors. The halls were vacant, much like the cold, steely eyes of the orange jumpsuit-clad inmates who barked out insults and made wild gestures to attract attention.

"Is that your new boyfriend, Queen?" someone yelled. It drew a soul-piercing stare from Detective Rome.

The echo from their cage-banging rang throughout the jail. The sounds deafened the ears. Their shouts of, *I'm innocent,* and their constant cackling, drowned out the inner thoughts and reflections jail was meant to elicit.

Marmaduke and Detective Rome walked past rows of cells. They peered inside at the mesh of bodies stuffed into the confined spaces. The smell of unwashed flesh fought against the Pine-Sol washes and bleach scrubs. They passed the cell that held Dr. El-Arabi. He was sitting there and reading quietly. Suddenly, his head snapped up in time to see them walk by. He rushed to the door and pressed his face between the bars. He focused his eyes so far to one side, trying to see them, that mostly only the whites of his eyes were visible. They stopped at the cell next to his. Francis Dixon, aka Jah-Boy, was slumped on his cot with his dreads splashed across his head, almost touching the floor.

"Open five," the guard who escorted them shouted. A buzzer sounded, and the guard slid the door open. "Get up, Mr. Dixon. You have company."

Jah-Boy eased his head up, pulling his dreads with him. "What's going on, man?"

"You have company; I said get up."

"They are no company of mine, man." He slumped back to the bed and pulled the pillow over his head.

Detective Rome grabbed Jah-Boy by one of his feet and pushed it to the floor. "Get your ass up before I have them haul you back to gen pop, in with the Dominicans."

"You can't talk to me without my lawyer, man."

"Then I guess you don't want to hear that I'm dropping the terrorism charges against you. Let's go, Marmaduke."

"Wait, man, what does that mean?"

"It means, for one, that you're eligible for bail."

"This is no bullshit, is it?"

"That's all I can say without your lawyer being present."

"Fuck him. When can I post bail?"

"You're going to have to be a little clearer before I can say much else."

"Okay, tell me what I have to do."

"Tell me that you waive your rights to speak with me with your lawyer present."

"I waive them motherfuckas; now tell me."

Detective Rome looked back at Marmaduke. He nodded. "Well, Mr. Dixon, you can tell the judge at your bond hearing that we found evidence in the home office of Professor Landrosky."

"...Who the fuck is that, man?"

"He's the guy I told you about that was shot and killed in that interrogation room upstairs."

Jah-Boy nodded, "Right, I remember, right."

Marmaduke noticed Dr. El-Arabi was listening. He poked his ear between the bars with the side of his face pressed tight to them.

"Evidence that implicated another suspect, one we already have in custody." Detective Rome said.

"How do you know it will stick, man? I don't want you to come back looking for me."

"Oh, the evidence is solid. He would need a mighty good explanation to refute this. I'm just worried about his wife and daughter. They're not U.S. citizens, so they'll likely be sent back home. I hear that fatherless daughters in their country end up as prostitutes over in Europe."

"What?"

"And the wife, she'll probably end up begging in the streets or working in one of their brothels. And I wouldn't be surprised if they both became drunks, dope addicts or both."

"What the fuck do I care about that? Tell me what I need to do to get out of here."

"And worst of all, the family name will be tarnished forever, for those still living and those not yet born."

"NO!" a shout was heard above the jailhouse din.

Marmaduke looked over in the next cell. Dr. El-Arabi cried out and banged his head on the barred door. He screamed in Arabic. Tears and blood flowed down his face.

TWENTY
The Prick, Mouthpieces and Softball Questions

MARMADUKE AND ROME LEFT the DeKalb County lockup. They headed west toward downtown Atlanta. Pieces of the city poked through spaces between buildings and tall trees and peeked over the horizon, like a southern Oz. The golden dome of the capital building glistened against a blue-colored sky that was pillared by the Westin Hotel that was rising up to meet it. The interchange snaked passed the city, knotting up in places and bringing their steady pace to a crawl. Like a Queen Mary on wheels, Marmaduke whipped Shirley in and out of traffic. Cars swerved, sped up or slammed their brakes to escape her wake. He took the Andrew Young exit and wheeled the Deuce to world-famous Peachtree Street. He hung a right, wheels squealed. The body rattled. The sound of ass sliding across fake leather drowned out *Rhapsody on a Theme of Paganini* as it streamed from an 8-track tape.

Detective Rome clung to the grab handles mounted to the roof of the car. "Damn, Marmaduke, slow your roll." She tried to pull back to her side of the car.

A short way up Peachtree Street, Marmaduke pulled off the road and in front of the SunTrust Plaza. The building, crowned with a step pyramid, jetted skyward. They flung open the doors and stepped out into the rush-hour lunch crowd. A mass of people pushed against them as they fought their way toward the doors and the elevators. They rode up to the twenty-third floor. The doors opened into a large reception area. The name of the firm hung in large, silver letters on a wood-grain wall panel. A young woman sat at a desk wearing a big smile. Her black hair fled from her face, scrunched into a ponytail. She stood and extended her hand.

"Welcome to Ben-Jarvis, Green, and Ellis," she said through her plastered smile. "How may I help you?" She had that salesperson voice, the kind that held the last word as if it was a note on a scale.

"I'm Detective Marmaduke. This is Detective Rome. We're here to see Taufic al-Saud."

"One moment, please." She hit a button on a phone and spoke softly through a headset that stuck out from her ear. She hung up. Her smile still lingered, "Follow me, please." She led them down a long corridor and through two sets of large slabs of lumber posing as doors. "Please, make yourself comfortable. Refreshments are arrayed in the bar against the window. Mr. Ben-Jarvis and Mr. Ellis will be with you shortly."

"What about al-Saud?" Marmaduke asked. She said nothing and disappeared down the corridor.

Looking around, they noticed that the conference room was twice as long as it was wide. A large table dominated the space. A lectern stood at the farthest end from the door and a screen that almost covered the entire wall was situated behind it. The room overlooked Peachtree Street. The large windows gave them a bird's-eye view of the happenings below but with none of the noise.

Detective Rome joined Marmaduke at the window. "How much you think they drop a month for a view like this? I bet it's more than I make in a year."

"More than what both of us make, you mean."

"I thought you said your people were old, slave-money rich?"

"If they were, all their slaves must've run away 'cause we're poor as hell now."

"That's okay, Marmaduke." She patted his back. "We'll take you in and make you an honorary Seminole Indian."

"I hate the ACC."

The door to the conference room was shoved open. In walked three men dressed in expensive suits. Marmaduke looked himself over and then looked at Detective Rome. He pressed his hand downward over his wrinkled shirt and tightened his dangling tie.

"Sorry to keep you waiting, detectives." They walked over to them. "I'm Robert Ben-Jarvis. This is Joe Ellis, and this is Mr. al-Saud." They shook hands, yet al-Saud would not shake Detective Rome's. "Please, have a seat." They rolled two chairs out from the table and sat down. "Now, how may we help you?"

"We're investigating the death of Professor Uza Landrosky," Marmaduke said. "Mr. al-Saud, we understand that he worked as a consultant for your company."

"And what leads you to believe that?" Mr. Ellis asked.

"There was an invoice found at his home office addressed to Euro-Arabia." Marmaduke turned back to al-Saud. "Are you denying that he worked for you?"

"No." Again Mr. Ellis answered. "We just want to try to understand your question. Mr. al-Saud didn't know this consultant personally. Consultants are often hired by middle managers."

"May I have their names?"

"We'll make sure you get those, Detective."

"What was the nature of Professor Landrosky's work, Mr. al-Saud?"

"That would be proprietary knowledge," Mr. Ellis answered.

"What Mr. Ellis is trying to say, Detective," al-Saud spoke up for the first time, "is that there are many trade secrets our competition would like to get their hands on. We are an energy company, and I can assure you, his services had something to do with that."

"It wasn't related to his research at Georgia Tech?"

"We are not sponsoring any research at any American university."

"I see, well, thank you gentlemen. We'll see ourselves—"

"Do you know a Dr. Amal El-Arabi?" Detective Rome asked. Al-Saud looked straight ahead, not paying attention to her. "Hey, I'm over here."

Preferring not to glance at her, al-Saud shook his head. It was more like a flick.

"No, Detective." Mr. Ben-Jarvis stood. "He does not know this person. Now, if you'll excuse us, Mr. al-Saud has a flight to catch. Please see yourselves out." Ellis and al-Saud followed Ben-Jarvis out of the room. The door swung closed slowly.

"Can you believe that prick? And what's with the softball questions? I've heard you order lunch with more toughness."

"For one, I thought you liked the strong, silent type. And two, a man doesn't pay that much money for legal advice and not take it. Their advice to him was to say nothing."

"The only thing likeable about that guy was him leaving. What's next?"

"…A date with Dr. Zones."

TWENTY-ONE

Cleopatra Zones

THE DOOR TO THE holding room flew open. Two guards pushed a shackled, stubble-faced T.O. inside. He stumbled just clear of the doorway with his hands locked in front of him.

"What the fuck happened to you?" Sam saw the fat lip and swollen eye he donned. One of the guards shoved him again. "Is that necessary?" He ignored Sam and shoved T.O. once more, closer to the table where they sat. "And those cuffs aren't necessary either."

"The rules say they are."

"…Since when?"

"Since he went Mike Tyson on one of the guards."

"So you fucked him up like this to teach him a lesson?"

"This ain't kindergarten, and we ain't playing patty-cake."

"The warden will hear about this."

"I'm sure he already heard—when he was screaming like a bitch." The guard pulled out a chair and pushed T.O. down onto it.

T.O. snatched his shoulder away from the guard's hand. "Asshole."

"Pussy," the guard shot back before he turned to leave the room. "You got thirty minutes."

"That's no time. We get forty-five minutes at least."

"That's for attorneys." The guard flipped through a pad. "And you ain't one." He and the other guard tore from the room and slammed the door behind them.

Sam scampered over to the door and peered through the glass. One guard stood watch outside. "Someone ought to kick his motherfucking ass."

"I already tried." T.O. chuckled. "That's one tough white boy."

"I'm glad you find this shit funny."

"Why are you so uptight? I'm the one that took the ass whooping."

"If you saw how you looked, like a one-eyed mullet fish, you'd be angry too."

"Boy, you sure haven't changed, still the same old Sam. I take all the licks and you do all the hollering." T.O. wrestled with his chains. He tugged and yanked at them as they draped from his waist and wrist. "You remember that time when we robbed Coolio's?" Sam didn't answer. He still looked down the hall. "Say, Sam, you there?"

"We ain't here to go down memory lane."

T.O. turned to Zones. "Coolio's was this liquor store and night club down on 116th street. It used to be the spot back in the day. That is until the Nation came in and closed down all the drinking spots. Called themselves the Fruit of Islam and tried to regulate shit. You remember that, Sam?"

"Yeah, I remember."

"Anyway, we were broke as a motherfucka this one night...broke and thirsty, a bad combination. We waited for Coolio's to close then broke in through the roof. That was the first time anyone that I know of had tried that shit. Someone in the crew was a roofer and knew how to cut that shit open. Who was that, Sam, the guy that did roofing work?"

"...Tanks."

Zones locked eyes with Sam. He had heard a familiar name.

"That's right, Tanks. He had all the equipment and everything. Whatever happened to him?"

Sam walked back to the table and sat. "He's in Atlanta. That's what I want to talk with you about."

"...In Atlanta? I thought he said he'd never leave Harlem."

"Listen, T.O., you remember the gun Tanks carried with him?"

"You mean that pearl-handled piece of shit he gave me to pay off his gambling debt?"

"...Yeah."

"He cried when I took it, used to call it some name like it was a real person. What was that name?"

"Reverend Ike," Zones said.

"That's it. How do you know that, Junior? That must've been ten... fifteen years before you were born?"

"Don't call me Junior."

"We've just come from the county jail where Tanks is being held," Sam said.

"Tanks is locked up too? Damn, before long, the whole damn crew will be pushing time. What's he in for?"

"You know Tanks. Could be for any damn thing." Sam scooted his chair around to T.O.'s side of the table. He leaned in close to him. "Do you know what happened to that gun?"

"Reverend Ike? Shit, I don't know. It could be packed in with all the other stuff back at the old brownstone. Why?"

"So you haven't seen it since—"

"Since I was locked up, no. What is this all about? Why do you want to know about some old Saturday Night Special anyway?"

"Your gun was found at a crime scene," Zones said.

"What! No fucking way. I told you that I haven't seen that piece in damn near twenty something years. And if they find any bodies on it from back then, they belong to Tanks. For any time after that, I've had a rock solid alibi, courtesy of the Georgia Department of Corrections."

"So, you have no explanation about how the gun made its way from Harlem to Decatur?"

"Not a one."

T.O. slumped in his seat. He cocked his head back, and it dangled over the back of the chair. A weight seemed to be lifted from his shoulders. He snored, his chest heaved as he labored to breathe in air. The sounds that rushed from his open mouth mixed with fluids to form a gurgle. Life on the inside had taken its toll. A young man when he first entered the prison system, his middle-aged body now felt the years of hard time on the inside. Sam looked at Zones and shook his head.

The door to the room flew open, and the same two guards stormed inside. They stood there, legs spread, hands on their hips, a mean look on their faces.

"Time to go," one guard said. T.O. still slept.

"I need a few more minutes," Sam said.

"You've gotten all you're going to get." The guard walked up behind T.O. and kicked his chair. T.O. flew forward onto the table.

"What the fuck, man," Sam shouted. He jumped to his feet.

"That's okay, Sam." T.O. pushed himself up from the table. "Old Tom here is what we call a pineapple redneck. He's hard and prickly on the outside but sweet on the inside, if you know what I mean." The guard yanked him around. T.O. blew him a kiss with a loud smack.

"That's Officer Tom to you, faggot." He pushed T.O. from the room. "I'm sure you boys can find your way out." He closed the door behind him.

"So, what now?" Zones asked.

"Don't know, but all this profiling work has made me hungry."

"Sylvia's is on the way back to town."

* * *

Zones and Sam pulled into the parking lot of Sylvia's. The smell of collard greens, candied yams, barbeque and peach cobbler masked the car exhaust odor that rolled in from interstate twenty. The stream of cars sent a constant hum through the air. It stopped only when the rush-hour traffic came to a halt.

The place was packed, but it was thinning out. As far as soul food went, Sylvia's was the best game in town. Zones grabbed a table at the rear with a line of sight to the door and the checkout.

"You got a taste for some soul food or for that big-legged redbone behind the counter?" Sam asked.

"Get ready to order. You can't chase crazies on an empty stomach."

"Why am I doing your job for you anyway?"

"Because your name's on the door."

"Don't be surprised if you have to weigh your next paycheck down to keep it from blowing away."

"Then I'll have to steal from you to make up the difference."

Sam huffed, "Smart ass."

The waitress approached. "Hi, I'm Toni. I'll be your waitress today. What'll you gentlemen have?"

Sam gawked. "How 'bout a taste of those pretty wings, girl."

"Sure, when you start to look and sing like Maxwell, then they're all yours, sweetie. Until then, how about our special. We have fried chicken, collard greens, macaroni and cheese with cornbread."

"That sounds good."

"What'll you have to drink with that?"

"…Sweet tea."

"How about you, sweetie?" she asked Zones.

"I'll have the same."

"I'll be right back with your order."

"One more thing, what time do you get off?" Sam asked.

Toni ran her hand over Sam's bald head. "Smooth." She then tapped him on it with her knuckles. "…And hard." She scurried off behind a door to place their order.

"That's not the only head that's smooth and hard," Sam said underneath his breath. Zones shook his head, scowling. "What?"

"Dirty old man, that's what."

"I've told you about that. When I've stopped thinking about pussy, I'm either dead or I've come back as Samantha in another life with a pussy. Then I'll have one of my own, and I won't have to think about it as much."

Zones' phone rang. He plucked it from his inside coat pocket and shoved it to his ear. "Zones, here."

"Doctor, it's Marmaduke again. I need to see you."

"I'm working as fast as I can on your case, Detective. I'm about to have lunch. Can't this wait?"

"It's a little late for lunch, isn't it?"

Sam reached over the table and snatched the phone from Zones. "Detective Marmaduke, this is Sam Drake. Where're you—he'll be there in thirty minutes." He tossed the phone back to Zones.

"What the fuck, Sam? I haven't eaten all day."

"We'll get it to go. Grab your things."

* * *

The elevator doors opened onto the third floor of the Homicide Department. Zones stepped out into a scene that was dying with the day. The hustle and bustle of contractors and crime scene analysts had dissipated. The atmosphere was more like that of any downtown office building. The lights were dimmed. The air was left hot. Empty chairs were void of the warm bodies seated in them just moments earlier. Zones searched around the open space. Detective Marmaduke was not at his normal desk.

"Dr. Zones, over here," a voice called from behind him.

Zones turned to see Marmaduke standing in the doorway of an office. "Congratulations on your promotion, Detective. I see…oh, hello, Detective Rome."

"Hello, Dr. Zones. We meet again."

"Have you caught your rapist yet?"

"Actually, he's cooling his heels upstairs."

"Good." Zones' eyes moved between the two of them. "I can come back if you two need to finish up anything."

"Have a seat, Doc," Marmaduke said. "Detective Rome is helping with this case now."

Zones looked back at Detective Rome. She leaned against a wall. "What happened to Detective Chennault?"

"There're enough murders to go around for everyone, Doc." Marmaduke dropped in his seat. "Where's your uncle?"

"I dropped him off at the office. What is so urgent that it couldn't wait until tomorrow?" Marmaduke lifted a file from the desk and tossed it over to Zones. He opened it and read. "This is the ballistics and lab report on that gun you found at the language research center." Zones closed the file and tossed it back at Marmaduke. "I got this report already. It was in the file you gave me."

Marmaduke tossed the file back. "Take a look at the page I've marked."

"A print was found that matched an inmate locked up in Fulton County Jail, so what?"

"Mr. Marcus Tanks is his name." Marmaduke and Zones stared at each other but said nothing. "Is there anything you want to tell me, Doctor?"

"Like what?"

"Like you and your uncle paid him a visit."

"It was necessary to develop my profile, the one you're on my ass to finish, remember?"

"Aaha." Marmaduke tossed another file at Zones.

"What is this?"

"It's an addendum to that lab report." Marmaduke rose from his chair. He walked over to the window and looked out. "I'll spare you from having to read it, Doctor. It says that a partial fingerprint pulled from the gun matched someone with your last name."

"Okay, Tanks was supposed to keep that to himself. What did it take, a sticky bun and Coke? They don't make these cons like they used to. They give it up quicker than a teenage hood rat. If there are any bodies on that piece, T.O. said they were Tanks'."

"Who's T.O.?"

"My old man, you pulled his prints from the gun."

"The prints we pulled were from a Cleopatra Zones."

"...My mother?"

TWENTY-TWO

Thirty to Life

"YOU HAVE NO IDEA how your mother's prints got on that gun?" Marmaduke asked Zones.

"I barely remember her. She died when I was four years old. Why were my mother's prints in the system anyway? Did she have a record?"

"She worked for the City of New York. Her prints were on file with them, for the background check."

"But your father knew Marcus Tanks." Detective Rome said. "That's why you and Sam Drake visited him down at Fulton County, isn't it?"

"They grew up together in Harlem, but I reckon you already know that."

"When you say, *grew up together*, you mean they ran with the Panthers?"

"So what? The times called for it."

"Listen, I feel you, Doctor. Brothers and sisters back then had to get down with the get down. Everybody was fighting against the system;

Dr. King had his way, Malcolm had his and the dark knights had theirs."

"The dark knights?"

"Yeah, that's what my uncle used to call them. My father worked on the force. He's retired LAPD, so they obviously didn't see eye to eye on the Panthers." Detective Rome walked over to Zones and took a seat next to him. "You spoke to your father about the gun, why?"

"Because Tanks said he gave the gun to him."

"You think that's how your mother's prints got there almost fifty years ago?"

"It's possible."

"Does your father keep up with any of his old friends from back in the day?"

Zones chuckled, "I doubt it."

"What makes you so sure?"

"Listen, what is this about?" Zones turned to Marmaduke. "You suspect my old man of having something to do with these bombings?"

"...If not him, then his friends." Detective Rome said. "We found a gun at the crime scene with your mother's partial print on it, a gun you've just admitted was last seen in your father's possession."

"That was almost fifty years ago."

"Your old man was, or still is for all we know, a member of a 60's militant group known to have possessed specialized training in bomb making."

"What? You're out of your mind. None of the evidence points to the Panthers."

"The gun points to your father and Mr. Tanks who were, or still are, Panthers."

"Marmaduke, she can't be serious."

"Let's all calm down," Marmaduke said. "We have enough suspects to go around without rushing to add new ones."

"Yeah, well, you let him tell it; a terrorist won't stick around to commit a rape."

"So this is what it's all about. You know my profile is going to dispute your theory of your rapist being the bomber."

Detective Rome reached across the desk. She grabbed a pad and pen and slammed it down in front of Zones. "Address and phone number where we can reach your father."

"Are you co-signing this, Marmaduke?"

"Just give us the information so we can clear this up, Doc."

Zones grabbed the pen, scribbled on the pad and tossed it at Marmaduke. "Here you go."

Marmaduke picked the pad up and read. "Are you serious, Doc?"

"What is it?" Detective Rome asked. Marmaduke tossed the pad to her. "...Atlanta Penitentiary?"

"Yes, Detective, he's doing thirty to life for first degree murder." Zones grabbed his briefcase. "Now, may I go?"

Marmaduke nodded. Zones bolted from the office.

* * *

The next morning, an early call came in. Zones scrambled for his phone as it rang by the bed. He snatched it from the nightstand.

"Zones, here," he whispered.

"Get up, Sleeping Beauty. Time to go to work."

"Detective Marmaduke, what's going on?"

"There's been another bombing."

TWENTY-THREE

The Profile, Sticky Bun and Coke

A WHITE, DEWY MIST settled over the crime scene, draping it like a bride's dress on her wedding day. The haunting willow trees slumped over; their branches reached down and tickled the tops of the reed canary grass that sprouted up from the earth. Other trees stretched toward the sky and poked through the mist in a million places but did not burst it. A rambling creek cut through the area and left a liquid scar for the many detectives and investigators to avoid as they combed through the devastation.

"Detective Marmaduke," Zones called out to him. The lifting fog was still too thick for him to make out those milling about.

"Dr. Zones, I'm over here."

Zones peered through the mist. "Where are you? I can't see you."

"I'm over here. Follow my light." A pulsating light flashed in the distance. Zones followed it and almost ran into Marmaduke and Detective Rome.

"What is this place?"

"The Snapfinger Creek Mitigation Bank. It's a protected wetlands area."

"...Wetlands? You're sure this is connected to the other two bombings? I mean...where's the bomb site? This just looks like some old fishing hole."

"Follow me, Doc." They walked a short way and came to a collapsed bridge and a burned-out building. It was still smoldering from the fire. "ATF collected fragments at the base of the bridge, similar to those found at our other two sites."

"And was the building bombed too?"

"...Arson. That and the bridge were part of that new housing development you passed on your way here."

"First it was puppies and apes, now a housing development? It doesn't' compute, Detective."

"Maybe it does, Doctor," Detective Rome said. "They're all animal related. Wetlands are protected to preserve the habitat of animals. That's your connection."

"I don't understand, Detective. The other day you were ready to string up your Rastafarian friend. Now you're ready to pin this on vegans?"

"Who says he can't be both?"

Just then, Marmaduke's phone rang. "Yeah—we're still collecting evidence—when?"

"No one is saying that he can't be both," Zones said. "I read his jacket, and you have him up on human trafficking charges as well."

"What of it?" Detective Rome asked.

"Why would someone with such little regard for people go on a terroristic campaign in defense of animals? It just doesn't make sense."

"I'll tell you what doesn't make sense, Doctor, your refusal to seize the opportunity to slap a 'Go directly to jail' sticker on this guy and call it a day."

"That's not my job, Detective."

"Just what is your job 'cause I haven't seen you do shit, besides get in the fucking way?"

"Is that what you really think?"

"Yeah, that's what I think."

"I'll be right there." Marmaduke flipped his phone closed. "Okay, lovebirds, that was James. The captain is forming a task force. It seems that three is the universal limit to bombings before the brass has a conniption."

"That's good," Detective Rome quipped, "maybe now we'll get a *real* profiler on the case."

"Don't get too carried away. Congressman Stonewall and his aide, Byrnes Maximus, will be at the first meeting. This case could get political, and you know what that means. Where're you with that profile, Doc?"

"I'm still working on it, why?"

"I suggest you put a period on it. The captain wants you to present your profile this afternoon."

"He wants it this afternoon?" Zones slipped his phone from his pocket to check the time. "It's seven. That doesn't leave me much time."

"Then I suggest you get a move on it."

* * *

Zones raced across town and back to Atlanta. Moments later, he was darting up the steps to his building and down the hall to his office. He sat at his desk and snatched a legal pad from the drawer. He studied the wall collage of the crime scenes. The date and time of each bombing had been marked. He noted these on his pad and added the date and time from the bombing this morning. He continued to study it. *They are carried out in series not in a parallel fashion.* Zones wrote, *Singular unsub? Contractor? Lone Wolf? The targets all have a connection to animals or animal causes, but crime scenes are void of message.* He added to his notes, *Lack of message = Diversion? Misdirection?* Next, he considered the suspects in the case: Jamaican drug dealer, Muslim researcher and his dead colleague, and some unidentified animal rights group. He wrote, *No apparent connections = Possible Hive? No collective identity? Divergent socio-cultural context? Shows no 'sense-making' from leader's unifying message.* Finally, he considered motive. *If the bombings are a red herring, then the motive is hidden, and what is unseen must be considered.* Zones scribbled, *Hidden Motive + Diversion + Contractor + Resources to implement = Profit Motive.*

From these notes, Zones developed a profile of the unsub. He formulated a theory of the crimes and the motive governing them. Some hours later, he was ready to share his findings with the captain and the task force.

Zones grabbed his things and rushed to his car. His phone rang. "Zones here."

"Doctor, where're you?" James asked.

"I'm headed your way, to the precinct, to prepare for the task force meeting."

"There's been a change in plans. We got a hit from a print collected at this morning's crime scene. Marmaduke is on his way with Atlanta PD and SWAT to pick her up."

"Her? Your perp is a woman?"

"We don't discriminate, Doctor."

"No…I mean…"

"What, a girl doesn't fit into your profile? Never mind that, the captain wants you there when they take her down."

"What about the meeting?"

"It's been rescheduled for this evening. The captain wants to see what information can be gleaned from her interrogation. I'll text you the address."

Zones' phone beeped with a text message. He made a U-turn down Ralph McGill and headed for the address in Little Five Points. The area was a hangout for college students, artists, the occasional Hare Krishna and those who had dropped out of life all together. When Zones arrived, the streets were blocked off. He parked on the outskirt of the barricade, hopped from his car and made his way up the steep road. An officer stopped him.

"I'm with the FBI."

"Let's see some I.D."

"Listen, just call Detective Marmaduke; he'll vouch for me."

"Wait right here." The officer leaned into his cruiser. He plucked the radio receiver from its hook. Moments later, he popped the trunk of his car, pulled a bulletproof vest out and handed it to Zones. "Alright, Doctor, put this on and head that way."

Zones slipped the vest on. He marched up the hill and saw Marmaduke secreted behind a car. He waved Zones over. Other officers were surrounding a house and pointing high-powered rifles at it.

"Get down," Marmaduke whispered. He motioned his hand in the air. Zones crouched and duck-walked over to him. "You got here just in time, Doc. We got the place surrounded. Our boys are about to take it now."

"How did you get a bead on this place so fast?"

"The perp was in the system. Here we go."

A loud noise sounded. A puff of smoke appeared. The front door blew open, and armed, military-style dressed men invaded the house, shouting and barking orders. Minutes later, they reemerged from the house with three half-dressed individuals in tow, kicking and screaming.

"Secure," a SWAT commander shouted.

"Okay, let's go."

Marmaduke and Zones marched toward the house. They climbed the steps and entered the interior. Pizza boxes and beer cans littered the bungalow. Small dogs ran around, up and under bean-bag and wicker-styled furniture. They barked at the officers who rummaged through the place. A porno movie was playing on a TV mounted to a wall. Some stopped to watch.

"Turn that shit off," Marmaduke ordered. An officer snatched the cord from the outlet, and the TV went silent. "These fucks can afford a fifty-inch TV but can't clean up this pigsty?" Detective Rome entered from the rear of the house. "What do you have?" Marmaduke asked her.

"Nothing so far, just some pamphlets and books on the environment and animal rights. We still have a few more rooms and the basement to go through."

"You finish up here, I'll take the basement." Marmaduke headed for the stairs. "You coming, Doc?"

Zones lingered behind. He surveyed the space. "…The basement, right." He followed Marmaduke down the stairs. The dark, musty space was crawling with bugs and other creeping things. Boxes stacked to the ceiling blocked what little light came in through a small window. "You're going to need Hazmat in here, Detective."

"You're right, Doc. We'll let CSU handle this." Marmaduke climbed back up to the first floor. He turned to give the space one last look. "Hold it."

"What is it?"

Marmaduke pushed past Zones and headed back down the stairs. He waded through the debris and cobwebs and headed over to a stack of boxes that teetered on top a small table. He grabbed the end and pulled up on it. The table did not move.

"Doc, how about a little help?"

Zones sucked his teeth. "Shit," he said under his breath before he headed back down the stairs.

"Grab that end."

Zones grabbed the end of the table and heaved. The legs scraped the concrete floor and made a loud sound. The table moved just enough for Marmaduke to squeeze between it and another pile of things. He stretched out to reach something.

"What do you see, Detective?"

"I almost...got it."

Marmaduke squeezed himself back through the sliver of space. He rolled up a large paper and headed back up the stairs.

"Marmaduke," Detective Rome called to him, "we found a stash of drugs hidden in one of the rooms."

"What kind?"

"Only pot so far with traces of a white residue."

"Bag it up and tag it for Vice." Marmaduke unfurled the large paper he had pulled from the wall in the basement.

"What is that?" Zones asked.

"It's an anti-Euro-Arabia poster."

"Is that what the large circle with a line drawn through it means? I mean, what's so special about it that you would squeeze that size forty-eight-inch waist in between that small gap?"

"There was an invoice in Professor Landrosky's home office for Euro-Arabia Oil."

"You're thinking he was targeted by this group for his association with the oil company."

"You sound skeptical."

"Not at all. Some of these groups have resorted to militant actions in recent time."

"But..."

"But few have the sophistication for bomb making that we've seen in these crimes."

"You'll soon see."

"What do you mean?"

"Captain wants you to lead the questioning."

"Why me?"

"Don't know, but I'd watch out for the talons on the girl. She looks like a mean one." They turned toward the police cruiser that held her. "I'll meet you back at the station."

* * *

A mop of short, black hair lay on top of the table. Arms with elbows pointed and marred with colorful tattoos shot from both sides of her head. There was very little movement from their suspect as Zones and Marmaduke watched her from monitors in another room. The raid on their Little Five Points home earlier this morning had jolted her and the others from their sleep.

"You two better get in there," Captain Franklin said. "Let's see what Sleeping Beauty has to say."

Zones and Marmaduke left the observation room and entered the interrogation room. There was still no movement, no acknowledgement from the young woman that they were even there. Marmaduke slammed the door. The loud sound shook the small space and rattled the walls. She raised her head from the table, enough to expose the handcuffs shackled around her wrists. She dropped her head back to the table.

"Get up, Ms. Pirote," Marmaduke said. She didn't move. He and Zones took a seat. Marmaduke opened a folder. "Charlotte Pirote." She still did not respond. He got up, walked to her side of the table and pulled the chair out from underneath her. She smacked the floor hard.

"Hey, man, that's police brutality."

"Now that I have your attention, Dr. Zones would like to ask you a few questions. The only question is will you answer them from the floor or from this chair?" Marmaduke stood over her, the chair swinging in his hand.

Charlotte looked up at him and growled, "The chair." Marmaduke swung it back close to the table. He grabbed Charlotte by the collar and lifted her from the floor.

"Go on, Doc."

"Ms. Pirote—"

"Charlotte," she snapped.

"Okay then…Charlotte. Can you tell us how long you've lived at your present location?"

"Cut the crap, bluppy, and ask me what you really want to know so I can get the fuck up out of here. And the drugs ain't mine, no matter what anybody says." She jumped forward in her chair and thrust her finger at Zones.

"Whose are they, then?" Marmaduke asked.

"I thought he was asking the questions."

"Just answer the question."

Charlotte fell back in her chair. Her eyes shifted between the two of them. "What kind of joint is this? Y'all don't feed anybody around here?"

"You're hungry?"

"Hell yeah, I'm hungry. It's y'all fault that I missed breakfast anyway, busting into my home all early and shit."

"We'll get you something to eat." Marmaduke looked to the camera mounted in the corner of the ceiling. "Now, about those drugs, who owns them?"

"What's in it for me?"

"Me not hauling your bony ass out of here and down to a jail cell, for one. Now tell me about the drugs." Marmaduke pounded the table. Charlotte looked wide-eyed and startled.

"They—"

A knock came at the door. It cracked open. A head poked inside. "I got breakfast," a detective said.

Marmaduke waved him in. "I'll take that." He grabbed the bag and can of Coke from him. "You were saying?"

Charlotte beamed at the bag and the drink. She smacked her lips. "Um…the drugs…yes, they belong to Wheeter."

Marmaduke shoved the bag and can at her across the table. She ripped into it, pulled out a sticky bun, popped the can's top and chugged it.

"Who's Wheeter?" Charlotte continued to gulp down the drink. Marmaduke reached over the table and snatched the can away. "Which one of your friends is Wheeter?"

"…The one with the buzz cut and bucranium."

"The bu what?"

"The bucranium, the ox skull tattoo," Zones answered.

"Oh. Who's his supplier?"

"I don't know." Marmaduke reached to snatch the sticky bun away. Charlotte pulled back and took a huge bite from it.

"I'll ask you one more time before I haul you to a cell. Who's his supplier?"

"You're trying to get me killed? Those guys don't fuck around, man."

"Okay, let's go."

"Alright, he buys his shit from some Jamaican dude."

"Name?"

"Damn, man."

"Name."

She huffed and squirmed in her seat. "His name is Jay-Man or some shit like that."

"You mean Jah-Boy?"

"Yeah, that' it. Now can I go?"

"Not yet. Dr. Zones has some questions for you." Marmaduke shoved the Coke can across the table. He got up, walked out and left Zones and Charlotte in the room alone.

"Okay, Charlotte, tell me why your fingerprints were found at a bombing in South DeKalb County this morning."

TWENTY-FOUR

"...redneck, white trash accent."

"MAN, THIS IS BULLSHIT," Charlotte said. "You can't pin no bombing on me!"

Zones flipped through pages of her file. "Let's see. You were arrested in '04 for protesting outside the Yerkes Primate Center. That's why they had your prints on file."

"So what, that doesn't prove a thing."

"It proves you were at the crime scene."

"Prints don't have no dates on them. I go to those wetlands all the time."

"I never said the bomb was in the wetlands."

"I'm not stupid; I listen to the news."

"I bet you do." Zones thumbed through more pages. "How do you explain the fact that you have a connection to two of the places that were bombed."

"Of course I have a connection. I've protested Yerkes' animal experiments, and I've protested the development at the wetlands."

"You're making my point."

"I protested at the Pentagon *and* at the World Trade Center *before* 9-11. You gonna blame those on me too? Oh, sorry, someone else has already gone down for them."

Zones stared hard at her as she choked down her meal. "So, Charlotte, which one of those clowns arrested with you are you doing?"

"Doing…you mean sex?" She rolled her eyes.

"Let's see. Ol' Wheeter is a good-looking dude, but you gave him up too quickly." Zones pulled a paper from the file. "How about Mr. Jacobs, all six–feet-nine inches of him; you look like a size queen."

"Hah, shows what you know. He's a camp."

"What did you say?"

"I said he's a fucking bender."

Zones shoved the paper inside the folder and snapped it closed. "Sit tight." He bolted from the room and headed back to where the captain and others were monitoring his interrogation.

"I've got to say, Doctor, it doesn't look like you're making much progress with her." Captain Franklin was pacing the room. He wrung his hands and rubbed his clean-shaven head. The room was cool but he was sweating buckets. "I think I'll let Detective Marmaduke take over the questioning."

"Listen, Captain, is this all you have on her?" Zones shook the file in the air.

"Are you saying that it's our fault that we don't have any more information?"

"What I'm saying, Captain, is that her life had to have started prior to—" Zones flipped open the file, "2004."

"That's all we have, Doctor."

"Have you checked with Interpol?"

"…For what reason? We're not dealing with some international terrorist here. Besides, it's not cheap to do that shit." The captain marched back over to the monitors. "What makes you so sure everything we need to know about her isn't in that folder?"

"Something she said."

"I'm listening."

"She used the words *camp* and *bender* to describe one of the guys picked up with her."

"So, they sound like perfectly good English words to me."

"That's exactly my point." The captain shot Zones a look. "I mean, *camp,* it's a British word to describe someone, a man, who is…effeminate."

"Gay?" Zones nodded. "You think that our little Ms. Sticky Bun and Coke is a British National?"

"From the region, for sure."

"…With that thick-ass, redneck, white trash accent?"

"You did see Jessica Tandy in *Driving Miss Daisy,* right?"

"One of the best movies ever. Why do you ask?"

"She's British."

"Get the fuck out of here. That white woman grew up in South Georgia."

"Nope, try London, England."

"Damn." Captain Franklin shook his head. He looked off into the distance. "Wait until my wife hears about this."

"…Captain?"

"Huh?"

"Interpol—are we going to run a check?"

"Oh, yeah." He turned to one of the detectives. "Run her name and prints through the system." The detective scurried from the room. "In the meantime, Doctor, what's your plan?"

"I'd like to know whom I'm dealing with before I go back in there. How long will the search from Interpol take?"

"Don't know, but if your girl is in the system, it won't take long." Just then, Marmaduke walked back into the room. "Anything from the other two?" the captain asked him.

"Well, they didn't cop to the drugs, naturally, but did seem to take great pride in our thinking they had something to do with the bombings."

"That doesn't make sense," Zones said. "…Suspects who want to be suspects?"

Marmaduke's phone rang. "Marmaduke, here—okay—hold on, I'm putting you on speaker." He fiddled with his phone and moved it between them. "Okay, Detective Rome, I have the captain and Dr. Zones here. Go ahead."

"We're still here combing through the house in Little Five Points." Her voice boomed through the speaker of the phone.

"Anything that will give us an idea about who these people are or who we're dealing with, Detective?" the captain asked.

"Not yet, sir, just a bunch of boxes filled with junk and some old placards with writing on them. We're still looking. I did come across a few with the initials A-R-M on them. Any idea what it stands for?"

"Hold on, Detective." The captain dialed from an office phone. "James, what do we have in the system for the initials A-R-M, something to do with tree huggers or no-meat freaks—the Animal Rights Militia. Is that it—Okay."

Marmaduke opened up a Google search from one of the computers. "…Says here they are a militant group that started in England."

"Looks like you might be right, Doctor. She may be from across the pond. We've connected them to your Jamaican suspect, Detective Rome, and to two of the crime scenes."

"…To Jah-Boy? How?"

"Those drugs you found, he supplied them."

"I guess bombers do stick around for a little rape action after all."

"What do you mean, Detective?"

"I think that's directed at me, Captain," Zones said.

The captain raised his brow. "Is there something I need to know?"

"…Just that none of this jives with my profile."

"Oh holy hell, here we go again." The captain paced the room, the same thing he had done before. Zones caught the body language but decided not to feed the already big baby. "Look, before I listen to any more, Doctor, you and Marmaduke go back in there and see what you can squeeze out of her. We have about four hours before the meeting with Congressman Stonewall and the task force. And if you come across anything at the house, Detective Rome," Captain Franklin leaned into the phone, "you get it here the fastest way you know how. Call me when you have something." The captain stormed from the room.

* * *

Back in the interrogation room, Marmaduke took a seat next to Zones, sitting across from Charlotte as she finished her meal. The empty can of soda lay on its side rolling back and forth on top of the table. The bun wrapper, balled into an unrecognizable crumble, blew across the floor from the slightest breeze. Her head was back in its original position, rooted into the table top like a potted plant.

Marmaduke kicked Charlotte's chair. "Now, where were we?"

"Damn, man," she squealed.

"What is it with these young people? You feed them and they still fall asleep on the job."

"I don't work for you."

"Where do you work?"

"Nowhere. I'm in between jobs right now."

"How do you support yourself?"

"What're you, social services? Can I go now?"

"You sell drugs for the Jamaicans. Is that how you support yourself?"

"I told you the drugs weren't mine."

"Because if it is, I'm having a tough time reconciling your wanting to save Fido and a bunch of trees, with poisoning ninth graders with that junk."

"I'm through talking."

A knock came at the door. A detective entered and handed Zones a folder. He scanned it, nodded and slid the folder over to Marmaduke.

"So, Charlotte, you never told me you were such a popular girl. Now I'm jealous. I'm going to have to share you."

"What are you talking about?"

"It appears that the British Police, or do you prefer the word *Bobbies*, and the Saudis would like to have a little chat with you, something about the bombing of an oil pipeline." Marmaduke turned to Zones. "Which one should we hand her over to first? I say the Saudis; they would know what to do with a young, white, hot little thing like her. I hear they don't like tattoos though. They cut them out over there, sometimes down to the muscle."

"You can't send me there."

"Oh look, a British accent."

"And not a moment too soon." She wiped her mouth and spit as if to remove a bad taste. "I don't know how you can stand listening to that twang, let alone speak it. And you're not sending me to the hajjis either."

"Then you better start talking."

"I told you who owned the drugs."

"I'm not talking about the drugs. I want to know who's planting those bombs. Where're you getting the technology from; it sure as hell isn't coming from your two bozo friends?"

"We didn't have anything to do with those."

"Bullshit, we have your prints. We have your friend, Jah-Boy, at one of the scenes. You push drugs for him and possibly his Yardie friends in

Great Britain too. And you've blown up oil pipelines belonging to Euro-Arabia Oil. Should I go on?"

"I don't know anything about all that; the oil pipeline, yes, but not the other stuff."

"Well, that's too bad because, for you, that means a one-way ticket to sand land." Marmaduke pulled his phone from his coat pocket. He dialed. "James, get me the Saudi embassy in Washington. I'll wait."

"He can't do this," Charlotte looked to Zones. "You have to send me back to England. You can't send me to the hajjis; they'll torture me."

"Then you better start talking," Zones said. "Give him something."

"They have an Atlanta contact; that's even better," Marmaduke said. "I'll drop her off there." He hung up. "Get up and let's go." He pulled Charlotte up from the chair.

"This isn't legal, man. I know my rights."

"Good, explain them to Akbar." He shoved her toward the door.

"Okay."

"Okay what?"

"I don't know about those other places, but they may be planning something."

"…They, who? Wheeter and Jacobs?"

"No, those two duffers are a daft half-penny. They just hang around for the wacky backy."

Marmaduke pushed her back toward the chair. "Sit." Charlotte plopped down; her handcuffs bruised the table top.

"How about taking these off?" She held out her hands.

Marmaduke unlatched the cuffs. "Let's hear it." He sat on the edge of the table.

"Kenney and Brian, they live at the flat too."

"Where were they?"

"They left just before you Bobbies got there."

"Last names?"

"I don't know."

"You tell me their names, or I'll have you hauled out of here."

"I don't know." She stared straight at Marmaduke. "I'm not yanking your crank."

"What're they planning?"

"I don't know, exactly." Marmaduke grabbed her arm and pulled the handcuffs back out. "They don't tell us everything. That's how they make sure no one talks."

"Go on."

"There was a map. I believe it was marked with their next target."

"Where was this map?"

"I don't know. I only saw it once."

"Think."

"Don't get a stiffy."

Marmaduke dialed his phone. "Detective, have you seen a map there—I don't know where, anywhere—Okay, I'll hold—Yeah, I'm still here—Can you take a picture and send it to my phone—Great." Marmaduke turned to Zones. "Detective Rome found something. Don't know what it is though." Seconds later, his phone beeped. Marmaduke shoved it up to Charlotte's face. "Is this it?"

"Yes."

"Where does this look like to you, Doc?"

"…Hard to say. Can't see any streets, just dirt roads and trees." Zones looked closer at the map. "There're some numbers here along the edges. Can you blow this area up?"

"Sorry, Doc, this is as good as it gets."

"Forward it to this email address." Zones pulled his iPad from his case. He logged on and pulled up the map. He enlarged an area that ran along the border. "33…28…7 on this border and 84…37…5 on this border, these numbers mean anything to you?" he asked Charlotte.

"…No, just numbers."

"Let me see that." Marmaduke took the iPad and studied the numbers. "What did this Kenney and Brian have with them when they left this morning?"

"…Backpacks, something to eat."

"Backpacks, the schoolboy kind or the outdoors wilderness kind?"

"They were big is all I know."

"So they were looking to camp out somewhere."

"Campers need camping gear: tents, a compass," Zones said. "I got an idea." He whipped out his phone. "Read me those numbers, Detective, those on the left border first." Marmaduke read. Zones punched the numbers into his phone. "My guess is they are latitudinal and longitudinal coordinates for the location on that map…what's in Tyrone, Georgia?"

"Tyrone? Let me see that." Marmaduke took the phone. "This is all old farmland. Most of it has been sold off and subdivided into lots for new homes, that is, until the market went sour. You have no idea why your friends would be interested in this area?" Marmaduke asked Charlotte. "Think hard before you say no."

"I've given it a welly and I don't know, I told you."

"Can't you put together a team to check it out?" Zones asked Marmaduke.

"Not based on a few numbers that could mean any damn thing. The captain will have my ass if I put a team on a misadventure. We don't even know if this map has anything to do with this case."

"What do you suggest then?"

"We're gonna have to run lead on this one ourselves."

"Just the two of us?"

"What's the matter, Doc, gun shy?"

"You're damn straight. Why don't you take G.I. Jane with you? She seems to be gung ho about that dope dealing rapist and these bombings. You know that I'm not."

"...Outside, Doc." Marmaduke led Zones through the interrogation room door, securing it behind him. He stood nose to nose with Zones and thrust a finger into his chest. "Detective Rome is onsite, for one. Two, it's your lead. And three, I don't know how to work this thing to find the location." He pointed to Zones' phone.

"Then that's too bad."

"Too bad, huh?" Marmaduke's hands shot to his hips. He poked his tongue to his cheek, making it bulge out. "Let me see your FBI ID."

"Why?"

"Let me see it."

"I lost it. I haven't had time to get it replaced."

"Lost it, huh? Yeah, right." Marmaduke folded his arms across his chest. "You know, I got a call the other night from the 41st out of New York. A Detective Franco was investigating the beatdown of some street hustler in Hunts Point. You're from Harlem aren't you, Doc?"

"What does some pimp getting jacked have to do with me?"

"Pimp you say? I didn't say he was a pimp."

"Come now, Detective. Hunts Point...beatdown. Even I know a hustle rumble when I hear it."

"Anyway. He caught this case. The victim was busted up something good. Damn near killed him too. The guy claimed he had gotten mugged. Detective Franco didn't know what to make of it at first. It's like you said, Hunts Point ain't Buckhead. He ran the alleged victim through the system, found out he had a sheet for stickups. Figured that ol' boy had just gotten the worst end of a jacking that he'd initiated. Franco found the spot where the attack had taken place, found a gun too. It was tossed some distance to the side of the road."

"I don't mean to interrupt your little crime drama, Detective, but what does some mugging in Hunts Point have to do with me?"

"Funny you should ask, Dr. Zones. They found plenty of blood, two different types, in fact. It appears that the other...for now let's call him perp two, put up a pretty good fight."

"Again, Detective, what—"

"How did you say you got that cut on your head?"

"I didn't. Now if you'll excuse me, I have other work to—"

"They also found this." Marmaduke pulled a plastic bag from his coat. He dangled it out at Zones. It contained a bloodied, torn portion of his FBI identification with the name *Zones* clearly written.

"Shit." Zones dropped his head.

"Come now, Doc, you can explain it to me on the way."

TWENTY-FIVE

Crafty Little **Bastards**

THE GREEN PLAINS OF Tyrone, Georgia were gentle and wide; they rolled through Fayette County like waves at low tide. The border of the farm was marked by rusting chicken wire attached to an aging post; it had worked long past its usefulness, now unable to keep the wire upright and straight. A beaten trail—tire tracks with weeds growing between them—cut through a field. It led to an old farmhouse set back in the distance. Unruly weeds, which carpeted the expansive field, sprang up from the ground to kiss a weeping willow and some drooping pine trees. Everything seemed unattended to, left to the whims of nature or the malice of men.

Storm clouds brewed a torrent. They settled in, darkened the sky and hovered above the farm as if to mark its place. Rain beat down and pelted the windshield of Marmaduke's old Deuce and a Quarter as he and Zones sat, parked inside. The peeling pleather seats pinched Zones' body in places that made the wait uncomfortable. He scowled at Marmaduke.

"…Still with Shirley?"

"Yep."

"How much you put in her each year to keep her rolling?"

"Why, you looking to contribute?"

"Just figured she's worth more money scrapped than on the road."

"You can perish that fucking thought. Me and Shirley are going out at the same time. We've been together longer…."

"What, you mean longer than you've been with your three wives combined?" Zones chuckled.

Marmaduke reached for a bottle of water that rested in a cup holder. He took a swig. "Wait until it's your turn to hold it down. Shit won't be so funny then."

Zones stared at him with suspicion. "Ain't gonna happen. I love my life."

Marmaduke took another swig from the bottle. "Water, in case you're wondering."

"Yeah, I was. You still better slow up. At your age, that bad bladder or prostate can kick in at any time."

"At my age? I'll have you know that I can still get down."

"How come all you old cats sound alike?"

"What do you mean?"

"I mean—" Just then, the rear passenger door flung open. "Shit," Zones shouted as he turned in his seat. Detective Rome hopped inside.

"What's the matter, Doctor, I scare you?"

"Damn, woman, you can get shot sneaking up on a brother like that."

"With what, your finger gun?"

Zones looked to Marmaduke. "Oh," he said, "I guess I forgot to tell you that Detective Rome would be joining us."

"Looks like we've got some action." Detective Rome pointed in front of her. A stream of bodies was heading to the farmhouse. Some rode on the back of trucks with their dogs while others walked with their dogs tethered to the end of a leash. "What do you make of that?"

"Don't know," Marmaduke said. "…Could be anything."

"Awful lot of dogs."

"This is the country. Could be a hunting party."

"Well, we're not gonna find out by sitting here." Detective Rome parted her hair down the middle and plaited it into two pigtail braids. She unbuttoned the top of her shirt and tied its tails tight around her waist.

"What're you doing?"

"Someone has to go in there, and you two stick out like a black woman at an NBA wives' party."

"We stick out? Just in case you haven't noticed, this isn't southwest Atlanta. And try as you might, you ain't Elly May Clampett."

"The only things those good ol' boys will see are tits and ass." She pushed her breasts up through the tight fitting shirt. "How do I look?"

"Umm...how does she look, Doc?"

Zones gawked. "Fine as hell...I mean, great...You look great."

"You can close your mouth now, Dr. Zones."

"We don't have backup, so be careful," Marmaduke said. "I need to wire you up."

"I don't need a wire."

"Can't let you go in there without one." She sulked and then nodded.

Marmaduke eased from the car and walked back to the trunk. The rain had slacked up some but still came down hard. They could hear him rummaging through the trunk. Detective Rome waited patiently while Zones tried, and failed, to keep his eyes locked on the farmhouse instead of something much more enticing.

"If you keep staring like that, Doctor, I'm gonna have to charge you."

"Sorry." He turned to face the front of the car.

"So you still think that Jah-Boy has nothing to do with this?"

"With this," Zones pointed toward the farm, "I don't know. With these bombings, I still say no."

"Are you this bullheaded when you're not working?"

"Are you this myopic when you're not?"

"Myopic, a lack of understanding or foresight, I like that word."

"You should, it fits you perfectly."

Detective Rome grew quiet. Zones caught a glimpse of her in the rearview mirror. She smiled as if she knew his thoughts. The driver side front door popped open. Marmaduke flew back inside the car, dripping wet.

"That water is real wet. Alright, Detective, here, it's the smallest mic I have. This fits just under your lapel, and this fits inside your ear. Here's an umbrella."

"I've been wired before, Marmaduke." She took the devices and inserted them. "Sound check: testing, testing, one, two."

"You're good. Can you hear me?"

"...Gotcha." Detective Rome stepped from the car, popping up the umbrella. She trotted across the road and along the path that led to the farmhouse.

"Talk to me, Detective. What do you see?"

"Nothing so far," her voice whispered over the receiver. "I'm coming to a structure at the rear of the farm. Looks like where everyone is gathering."

"Update me every five minutes unless something changes, and be careful, Detective. I'm out."

Zones turned to Marmaduke. "You just said, 'That water is real wet.' You know that shit makes no sense, don't you?"

"It made sense to my Uncle Charles."

Zones shook his head. "What're we doing here, really? We don't even know what these guys look like. We don't even know what we're looking for. For all we know, those guys could actually be camping."

"Are you always this pessimistic? You need to spend more time outside of those prison walls you work in. They're rubbing off on you."

"That's not an answer."

"It's the only answer you're gonna get."

They watched as more people trekked up the long path to the farmhouse. The radio squealed, breaking their focus. Detective Rome's voice crackled over the airwaves.

"I'm at the structure; it looks like we have a dog fighting ring."

"Yeah, I hear them. Do you see anything else?" The radio crackled with static. "Come in, Detective."

"No, nothing else." The radio went silent.

"What's the story on ol' girl?" Zones asked Marmaduke.

"Who, Detective Rome? Are you interested?"

"Not my type."

"You have something against pussy? 'Cause that's the only type of woman there is."

"You know what I mean. She's the balls-breaking type."

"Yeah, we call women like her man-eaters." They both laughed.

"She had the nerve to call me bullheaded."

Marmaduke stopped laughing and faced him. "Well, you'll be happy to know you're not her type either."

"That's because I'm not a punk brother. I don't play that."

"She doesn't play either, not with balls and bats. She does like catcher's mitts though, if you know what I mean."

"She's butch? Damn, what a waste."

"And she believes in Aliens and UFOs and shit."

"It figures. Her mother is Scandinavian. They believe in that stuff."

The radio crackled. "I think I got something."

"What is it?"

"Two guys with back—" radio static increased.

"Detective…Come in, Detective." He tried a while more. She did not respond. "Let's go."

"Let's go? Go where?" Zones asked.

"I can't reach her on the radio. We need to go in."

"Then call for backup. I'm not law enforcement."

"Today you are." Marmaduke pulled his backup revolver from his ankle holster and held it out to Zones. "Here." Zones took it. They stepped from the car, guns drawn and at their sides. They ran up the trail to the farmhouse. The closer they got to it, the louder the noise grew. "That way," Marmaduke motioned for them to leave the trail. They circled around to the other side of the house where they came to a stall that overlooked a large pitted area. A crowd had gathered, and they were shouting and gesturing at dogs fighting in the pit. They looked on as the animals snarled and growled, bit and slashed at each other. Blood gushed from open wounds and dripped to the ground, tainting the muddy soil. As the animals howled in pain, the crowd cheered as one dog took the advantage over the other. "Look, there's Detective Rome," Marmaduke pointed. "You make your way around to her, Doc. I'll cover you from here. And Doc, try to blend in."

Zones slipped his gun inside his coat and trudged through the soft soil. He wove between the bodies in the crowd and moved closer to Detective Rome. He eased next to her.

"Doctor," she whispered.

"…Detective."

"I didn't know you played with the big boys."

"At least one of us does."

"What do you mean?"

"Nothing, what do you have? Your mic went out."

"Three o'clock, those two with the backpacks."

"I see them; what's the plan?"

"Where's Marmaduke?"

"Across the way. He's keeping an eye on us."

"You're packing?" Zones opened his coat to expose the gun. "Okay, this is what we're going to do. Let's move over behind them and stick our guns right in their sides, march their asses right out of here."

"That's your plan?"

"Yeah, you got a better one?" Zones shook his head. "Let's go. I'll take the blond."

They backed out of the crowd and moved toward their suspects. Detective Rome led the way, her Glock gripped tight in her hand, held down at her side. Halfway there, Zones locked eyes with the tall, dark-haired one first and then the blond. The suspects moved away from them.

"Police," one of them shouted, tearing through the crowd.

"We've been made," Detective Rome said. She shoved a large man to the side and bolted across the muddy ground. Zones followed her. People, some with their dogs in tow, scattered. "Where did they go?"

"There." Zones pointed across the field. They ran stiff-legged, trying to keep their balance. The blond-haired suspect hurled something toward them. Sparks sputtered from the object as it spun in the air. Zones grabbed Detective Rome and dove to the ground. His body covered hers as the device exploded. Fragments flew in the air, striking the structures around the farm and some of the people as they fled.

Marmaduke raced over to them. "Are you okay?"

"Yeah," Zones said, "but now I'm mad as hell." He helped Detective Rome up from the ground.

"Thank you, Doctor."

"Good thing we landed in the grass, Detective. Now let's go get these fools."

They all ran toward a wooded area in the distance. Zones led the way. He rushed over high grass and weeds and plowed his way forward. They came to the edge of the field and spread out, guns drawn, inching their way into the woods. Marmaduke took the left flank, Zones took the right and Detective Rome went down the middle. Marmaduke whistled. All three stopped in their tracks. He pointed to the left and waited.

"Over there."

Two people dashed from behind bushes in the distance. They gave chase, darting in and out between trees. Zones took the lead again. He outran Marmaduke and Detective Rome, gaining on one of the suspects. The man hurled another explosive device at him, forcing Zones to duck behind a large tree. The explosion felled leaves, filling the air with smoke and debris. He peered out from around the tree. Both suspects were still running.

Zones looked back to see Marmaduke slipping and sliding on wet leaves. He continued to give chase, closing the distance between him and the suspects once again. He watched them drop the large backpacks they were carrying. A train whistle sounded in the distance. As he raced to the top of a slight hill, Zones could see the engine lumber down the tracks as it crossed over a clearing. The two suspects headed for the train.

"Stop or I'll shoot," Zones shouted. He was now within reach of the dark-haired suspect. The man looked over his shoulder to see Zones running close behind. He dove at him and tackled the suspect to the ground. They rolled around in the grass with Zones landing on top, throwing a flurry of punches, bloodying the suspect's nose and bruising an eye. The suspect wailed, crying like a crackhead when his dope is all gone.

Detective Rome pushed Zones away from the man. "Get up. I got him."

Zones leapt to his feet and chased the other suspect; he had put some distance between them. The train's whistle sounded again. It still chugged down the tracks and picked up speed.

"Stop…police," Zones shouted.

The blond-haired man turned as he approached the train, stumbled, fell to the ground and disappeared in the tall grass. He popped up a few seconds later and ran along the side of the train, grabbed hold of a rail that stretched the length of a car and lifted himself onto it. Zones raced to catch up to the last car. He grabbed for a rung on a ladder, but the train sped up and put the ladder out of his reach. He stood there beside the train tracks and watched the blond-haired suspect ride off into the distance, hanging off the side of the car.

Zones slogged back to where Marmaduke and Detective Rome were standing. They had the other suspect handcuffed and lying on the ground.

"Where is he?" Detective Rome asked. "Did you get him?"

"He hopped on a train headed that way." Zones pointed. "Has this one said anything?"

"No, but he will. One of them dropped a bag over there."

"Are you alright, old man?" Zones asked Marmaduke as he was standing bent over, gasping for air. Marmaduke nodded. Zones walked over and picked up the army bag, unzipping it. "Holy crap, Marmaduke, I think you better come have a look at this."

Marmaduke staggered over, knelt beside Zones and peered inside the bag. "Spring activated detonation devices. Saw plenty of these in the military. Once pressure is applied, it engages the explosive. When it's released, BOOM. This one seems to have a timing mechanism as well. Even if the pressure remains, there is still a discharge."

"Crafty little bastards."

"Let's get back to the station. I want to question him before the task force meeting."

"What about the crime scene?" Detective Rome asked

Marmaduke stood up and looked around through gaps in the trees. Red lights pulsed and uniformed officers milled about. "We'll let the locals take care of it."

* * *

The captain's office shined with a fresh coat of paint; the new antique-gray walls gave off an elegance the space had lacked before. It was much larger after the renovations. The same old furniture remained, however, putting the wart back on the pretty face.

The members of the task force were gathered there. Some sat around a large table while others stood. The door to the office flung open, and Captain Franklin and two other men stepped through. They marched to the front of the room.

"Everybody, listen up," the captain said. "This is Congressman Stonewall and his aide, Byrnes Maximus. The congressman would like to say a few words to you." The captain stepped back and the congressman stepped forward.

"Ladies and gentlemen, first, I want to thank you for the work you've done so far trying to find and bring the perpetrators of these bombings to justice. I've already told the captain; now I want you to know that you will have whatever support is needed from my office." He cleared his raspy, smoker's throat and brushed the sides of his slick, silvery hair back with his left hand. His right hand stayed tucked inside his vest pocket. A pendant with the initials, *ZBT,* clung to the lapel of his pinstriped, navy blue vest. The congressman pulled on a silver chain rested inside his suit vest and plucked out a round timepiece. He flipped it open. "I have a meeting with the governor. Max will see to it that all resources on the federal level are expedited. Let's leave no stone unturned. Go get these sons of bitches." With that said, he and his deep southern drawl left the room. His high-priced cologne, however, lingered.

"Thank you, Congressman," the captain said. "Marmaduke, bring us up to date on the case."

Marmaduke pushed up from his chair and headed for the front of the room. The captain looked him over and followed his muddy footprints back to his chair. Other detectives huddled around the room snickered.

"Quiet," the captain shouted. "Go ahead, Marmaduke."

"Most of you already know what we have so far. I've handed out a synopsis for those of you who don't. Our latest development is that we have tied these bombings to a radical animal rights group, the A-R-M."

"What does that stand for?" someone asked.

"Animal Rights Militia, they started out in England in the early to mid-eighties, I believe."

"What evidence do you have?"

"A fingerprint from the bombing this morning led us to a suspect and a member of this group. When we questioned her, she gave us the names of two other suspects and helped us to foil another well-planned bomb plot. We determined the location, an old farm in Tyrone, and disrupted their plans before they could carry them out. We facilitated the arrest of one of the perpetrators and brought him back for questioning."

"We? Who is we?" Captain Franklin asked.

"…Doctor Zones, Detective Rome and myself. We arrested one suspect but another one got away. I've issued a BOLO for one Kenney Garrett. There's a picture of him in your packet. We ID'ed him from information collected from a sack he abandoned at the site."

"Any other evidence, Detective?"

"They left these explosive devices behind." Marmaduke picked one up. The congressman's aide jumped back. "Oh, don't worry. Our bomb guys disabled them already."

"So one of the guys who made these is still on the loose?"

"I'm afraid so, Captain."

"Did the one you arrested say anything?"

"Other than, 'We were going to pay,' no."

"What did he mean by that?" Marmaduke shrugged. The captain turned to Zones. "How does this group fit in with your profile, Doctor?"

"Which group, Captain? I understand you have a number of them tied to the bombings."

"Right now, I'm talking about these animal people."

Zones felt Detective Rome's eyes bearing down on him. He turned his head and there they were, like two almond-shaped pearls. He swiveled back to the captain. "The profile is...inconclusive with respect to these recent developments."

"Inconclusive? What the fuck does that mean?" The captain looked toward Byrnes Maximus. "Are these animal nuts or any of the suspects good for these bombings, Doctor?" Zones said nothing. "Are they within the realm of possibility?"

"Possibility, yes. Probability, no."

"Lord, here we go again."

"May I, Captain?" Byrnes Maximus asked.

The captain flipped his hand. "Go ahead. Why not."

"Dr. Zones, is it?" Zones nodded. "What makes you so sure none of the current suspects committed these bombings?"

"For one, Mr. Maximus, I see only one person behind these bombings."

"Only one?"

"Yes, although the unsub would like us to believe otherwise."

"So, he's a lone wolf?"

"I'm not saying that someone else isn't directing him, only that these bombings aren't the work of this ragtag group we've assembled."

"If that's the case, Mr. Garrett is no threat."

"He's obviously a dangerous man, sir, but not for these bombings, as I've said. Even the devices they used at the farm have nowhere near the same sophistication as the other bombings."

Byrnes Maximus pushed up from against the edge of Captain Franklin's desk. He took a folder from the top of it and shuffled through the papers inside. He paced back and forth, reading.

"It says here that a print collected from one of the crime scenes belonged to your mother, Doctor. How do you explain this?"

"I cannot. My mother's been dead over twenty-four years."

"...At the hands of your father, who's serving time for her murder."

An audible gasp spread throughout the room. Zones glanced over his shoulder. He had felt one pair of eyes on him; now he sensed many more. He straightened his back, pulled his hands from his pants pockets and folded his arms across his chest. He bit down on his lip and stared menacingly at the congressman's aide. Zones was about to spew a few choice words when he looked to the captain who shook his head and wagged his finger ever so slightly.

"I don't understand what that has to do with this case?"

"Some may say that it gives you the motive to steer this investigation in another direction."

"Oh, please."

"...Because of evidence that may point to your father's old associates from the '60's, if you know what I mean."

"Now, Max," the captain said, "I can personally vouch for Dr. Zones' professionalism."

"That's Mr. Maximus to you, Captain."

"I don't need any help with this prick." Zones said.

"That's grand, Dr. Zones, because we are no longer in need of your help."

"It's a good fucking thing you're not the one to make that call."

Byrnes Maximus pivoted back toward the captain, up on his toes like a ballerina. "Captain, you may tell Dr. Zones that his services will no longer be needed."

The captain's gaze alternated between Byrnes Maximus and Zones. "Listen, there's no need—"

"Captain, Congressman Stonewall has charged me to direct federal funds, not only for this case but for future cases. I would be careful of your next utterance." Captain Franklin stood still, frozen, saying nothing. "...Captain?"

"He doesn't have to say anything. I quit." Zones pulled a file from his case. He walked it over to Captain Franklin. "Here's my profile." He shoved the file at him.

"No need," Byrnes Maximus said. He pushed the file away. "I took the liberty of having the FBI work up a profile. Their findings are here." He held the folder out.

The captain took it and read. "It says here that the perpetrators are most likely a group of well-trained individuals." He snapped his head back to Zones. "You're saying they're wrong, Doctor?"

"Does it matter what I think? Mr. Metro-sexual seems to have all the answers."

"And since I do, there's no further need for you. So, take your diagrams and leave." Zones, once again, looked at the captain. Like before, he said nothing. "Good day, Dr. Zones."

"I'll leave this with James," Zones told the captain. He stuffed the folder back inside his case, slung the strap over his shoulder and darted for the door.

"Aren't you forgetting something?" Zones turned to see Byrnes Maximus holding out the rolled-up diagram of his analysis. He walked back and snatched it from his hand. "You can tell your murdering-ass father he can expect a visit." Zones stopped short of the door. He felt his hand ball up into a fist. He turned, walked back and, with a cobra's quickness, slugged Byrnes Maximus in the face. He fell to the floor. "Captain, I want him arrested." He grabbed his face, smirked and wiped away the blood dripping from his nose.

Two officers grabbed Zones, cuffed his hands and rushed him from the room.

* * *

Zones lay slumped on a hard, thin mattress. The light in the cell was bright and made it hard to sleep, but so did haranguing from a man in an adjacent cell. He closed his eyes regardless and laced his fingers across his chest. Zones had been locked up for over two hours when he heard the unmistakable sound of a key being slipped into a lock.

"Let's go, Doctor."

Zones' eyes sprang open. He popped up from the bed to see Captain Franklin standing at the door of his cell. "What's going on? I didn't post bail."

"No bail, let's go."

"Is this a trick your little weak-jawed Roman put you up to?"

"Are you gonna eat the baby in the King cake or do you what to spend more time jerking off or whatever you're doing in here?"

Zones grabbed his coat. The captain led him down the hall. "Where're we going?"

"I'm going home. You're going wherever you need to go to finish working on this case."

"But—"

"But nothing." They stopped. The captain got close to Zones. He poked him in the shoulder with his finger. "No little shit-pants, Low-country, cadet bureaucrat is gonna tell me how to run my department. I don't care who he thinks he is or who he works for."

"Does Mr. Maximus know I'm back on the case?"

"Fuck no, I ain't stupid. We'll keep this on the down-low. You run your thing, and ol' Max gets to keep thinking he's in charge."

"Isn't he? I mean, he's in charge of the money. Where're you gonna get the funds to run parallel investigations?"

"Let me worry about that. Those pricks in Washington aren't the only ones who can play three-card monte with a budget."

"You're sure you want to do this?"

"No, which is why you will keep me informed the second you get anything. None of that shit you pulled last time."

"What about access to evidence?"

"I'll make sure James gets you what you need." They continued down the hall. Zones stared at the captain. "What?"

"Nothing, just surprised, that's all."

"Surprised at what?"

"You pushing back, going against the grain. You know, if ol' boy finds out, he'll have you bussed back down to beating the streets."

"You just better make sure that doesn't happen, or I'll make sure those assault charges get pulled out of a dead pile and expedited." The captain led Zones through the security checkpoints and to the elevators. "Here're your things." He shoved a plastic bag at him. "Take the back stairs so no one sees you leaving."

The captain headed for another door down the hall. Before Zones scurried down the stairs, he watched him leave. He wasn't sure what to make of the captain's plan, but anything was better than rotting in a jail cell and listening to the verbal ruminations of those barely on the verge of sanity. His stomach growled, empty from a long day without food. He glimpsed the time from his phone. It was well past dinner. He knew just the place for a good meal.

TWENTY-SIX
The Bomber

MOONLIGHT DRIFTED IN THROUGH the small clerestory windows. Like a mist, it settled over the objects strewn about the floor and the work table. The parts, unrecognizable in their disarray, made for a deadly cocktail when assembled. The bomber took one of the objects, slid it in place and then grabbed another. He connected wires; each one was color-coded to its purpose. He turned a screw here and soldered a component there. Beethoven's *Sonata Pathetique* played over the radio. It softened the hard, deadly work.

A whistle sounded, and he rose to remove a metal teapot from the stove. He cut the fire, ripped a teabag from its packet and dangled it in the air. He pulled a cup from a shelf and dropped the bag into it. It fizzled from the hot water hitting it, boiling out the tea and coloring the water. Two teaspoons of honey, a quick stir, a taste and he went back to his work. He lowered a light over the device he was assembling and adjusted a magnifying glass over a tiny circuit board. His steady hands cut, spliced and soldered the components with the usual efficiency when a knock came at the door.

"Pizza!"

The bomber froze as he held a hot probe in one hand and a metal strand in the other. He was almost done with the job. He stood and stared down at the knob before snatching the door open. A bespectacled, young man stood there holding a pizza box. His dark, windblown hair poked out from beneath his yarmulke. "Your pizza, sir…I mean…Brother." He held the box out. The bomber had not ordered a pizza, but he pulled twenty dollars from his wallet and handed it to the young man. "It was a credit card order, Brother."

The bomber smiled. "Well, in that case, come in."

"We're *not* supposed to come inside."

"Oh, very well then. I'll be right back." He slipped a credit card from his wallet and a Taser from a desk drawer. He handed the card to the delivery man who took it. He held the card next to a slip of paper attached to the pizza box. His eyes moved between them.

The driver looked back up, "These numbers do not match."

"Are you sure? Please look again." The young man compared the numbers once more. The bomber looked to his left, down the hall, and then to his right.

"No, Brother, they don't match."

"That's too bad." The bomber whipped out the Taser he had kept secreted behind his back. He thrust it up to the neck of the delivery driver. The shock paralyzed him to the floor. The pizza box fell; its contents nearly spilled out. He grabbed the box, placed it on a table next to the door, and dragged the young man from the hall into his apartment, kicking the door shut behind him. The bomber grabbed a roll of duct tape from the table and wrapped it around his captive's mouth, feet and wrists. He dragged the unconscious man to a chair and secured him. He attached the final components of the bomb, placed it inside the pizza box and left.

* * *

A rusting, red 1992 Celica GT sat idling in the parking lot of The Virginia Highlands, a Midtown apartment complex. The illuminated *Pizza* sign sitting atop the car shone bright in the night. The car drew no undue attention; after all, college students lived on the stuff.

The driver-side door popped open. The bomber stepped out carrying the pizza box with him. He pulled a worn Atlanta Braves baseball cap down over his brow and scanned the area. Seeing no one, he marched up to one of the first floor apartments and knocked.

"Pizza," he said.

The bomber pulled a black Glock from his waistband and eased it up to the door—head height. He looked over his shoulder, whipping his head from side to side at every noise. When no one answered, he sat the pizza box on the ground and pulled out a pry bar from the Georgia Tech letterman's jacket he wore. He slipped it between the door and jamb, forced it open, and stepped inside the darkened apartment, gun drawn. He flashed a small penlight and moved between the bathroom and the main space. No one was home. He retrieved the pizza box and sat it on top a table that shared the room with a bed in the small efficiency apartment.

The bomber lifted the mattress, taking care not to disturb the neatly made bed too much. Slipping the bomb underneath it, midway down the bed's length, he lowered the mattress and smoothed out the wrinkles in the sheet. Silently, he eased out of the apartment and waited inside the pizza car.

TWENTY-SEVEN

I'd Like a Bomb with That Pizza

ZONES PULLED INTO A parking space just outside his apartment building. The food from Sylvia's filled his car with the scent of fried catfish, mashed potatoes, collard greens and cornbread. His stomach growled as he shifted the car into *Park*. It had barely come to rest when he hopped out and dashed for the door, slipping the key into the lock. He paused to run his hand over the damaged jamb before pushing through the door and flipping on a light over the dining table. Zones hung his briefcase over a chair and dropped the plastic bag of food on top the table. The foam lid of the container popped open as it collided with a pizza box, releasing even more of the soul food aroma. Zones stuck his nose over the steam rising from the plate and took a deep breath. In one smooth motion, he sat down, snagged a fork and stuck it into a load of greens.

Zones took a moment to grab the plate from the bag, clicked on the TV and moved over to his bed. Just as he was about to lie down, someone knocked. Dropping the plate onto the bed, he walked back to the door, peered through the peephole and spied Detective Rome standing there. *I wonder what she wants.* Zones opened the door.

"Detective, what're you doing here? If this is about me telling the captain that your perps didn't fit the profile of the bomber...." Detective Rome said nothing; she just stared at him. "Detective, are you okay?" She took one step forward, wrapped her arms around his neck and kissed him hard on the lips. Zones backed inside and closed the door behind him, carrying her with her legs wrapped around him. They rolled up against the wall, locked together as their kissing intensified. "Detective...I don't understand..." he muttered through the kissing.

Detective Rome released her lip-lock on Zones. "Shhhhh," she hushed him, pressing her index finger to his lips. "I thought you were the strong and silent type. You're talking more than a babbling baby wanting a snack. Now, are we gonna do this or not?"

"Sure...fine...but when was I no longer the dick you thought I was?"

"But I hope you are that dick, Dr. Zones." Their eyes now locked, a long pause passed between them. Detective Rome tried unsuccessfully to hold back a mischievous smile. She was puzzling to Zones. Her affection for him came seemingly out of nowhere. He would normally not give a damn, but she caught him off guard. "Okay, Doctor. If it helps you to get cranked up, I think I misjudged you."

"Misjudged?"

"Yeah. You know, I thought you where one thing when you were actually another."

"A dick like I said."

"More like a prick. There is a difference."

"What exactly is the difference?"

"One sticks the other pokes."

"Thanks for clearing that up."

Detective Rome moved in for another kiss before pulling back. "Oh yeah, I loved the way you punched out the congressman's aid. It turned me on."

"I see more fights in my future." Zones grabbed two handfuls of Detective Rome's ass. He walked toward the bed with her draped over him. He plopped her down at the foot of the bed, crawled on top of her and ripped away the jacket she wore.

"Wait a minute." She sniffed. "What is that smell?"

"I don't smell anything." Zones bent down for another kiss.

"Have you been eating onions?"

He held his cupped hands to his mouth, blowing into them. "They were in the greens."

"You're gonna have to do something about that." Zones looked at her, puzzled. "Go on, I'll be here when you get back."

Zones eased from the bed, backed out of the room and ran into the bathroom. He brushed his teeth and gargled in record time. When he returned to the bedroom, Detective Rome was sampling a slice of pizza.

"...AAGH, meat. And it's cold." She dropped the slice back into the box.

"Where did that come from?"

"The pizza? It isn't yours?"

Zones ran to the door and snatched it open, feeling along the jamb edge. He scanned the parking lot before shutting the door, raced back to the bedroom and searched the closet.

"What are you looking for?"

"Someone has been in here."

"How do you know that?"

"The pizza, it's not mine and there are marks on my door. I think it was pried open."

"Is there anything missing?"

"Not that I can see."

Detective Rome walked back to the bed and sat on the edge of it. "Come here." She unbuttoned her shirt. Zones smacked his lips and made his way over to her. She lay back on the bed. He leaned over her. "Shit, your bed is hard."

"That's not the only thing that is."

"...Feels like something is underneath this mattress. Get up."

"Get up?" Zones noticed the swell in the bed. "No, don't move. Stay very still." He eased up from the bed, slid his hand along the mattress and probed it, looking for something. He moved to the foot of the bed and raised the end of the mattress, seeing hard metal peeking out from underneath it. "Shit." He locked eyes with Detective Rome.

"What is it?"

"A bomb, I think. Keep still. I have to find something to use to maintain the pressure." Zones searched around his apartment.

"You? Hell no. Call the goddamn bomb squad."

"No time. The bomb might be connected to a timer. How much do you weigh?" She gave Zones a mean look. "...Never mind." He ducked into the bathroom and returned with a large pail filled with water. He sat it on the floor and dashed into the kitchen, returning with pots and pans of all sizes. Placing them on the bed around Detective Rome, Zones filled them with water from the pail.

"You sure you know what you're doing?"

"You wouldn't be asking me that if I were hitting it."

Detective Rome smiled. "You're not off the hook yet. You still got some proving to do. But right now I need you to focus."

"So I guess this makes you bi?"

"...Bi?"

"Bisexual, you know, women and men. Hey, it's cool with me. I ain't into dudes, but the more women the merrier, I always say."

"Dr. Zones, what in the world are you talking about?"

"I know this is Atlanta, the San Francisco of the south. I'm just saying—"

"Wait, you think that I'm a lesbian?"

"Yeah, that's what Marmaduke told me."

She laughed. The water in the pots splashed onto the bed. Zones added more water to the pans.

"Stop moving. Are you trying to get both of us killed?"

"Marmaduke told you that I was gay." She continued to laugh. "He probably said that because I ignored his advances many times."

"Marmaduke tried running game on you? That would've been worth seeing."

"In his own little white boy way, always talking about jungle boogie and jungle fever. How come it's always about the woods with them?"

"What about this UFO thing? Was he wrong about that too?"

"Now, that he had right."

"You believe in little green men, ETs?"

"How do you think we got here, evolution or some magic genie?"

"Speak for yourself, I was born a god."

"But are you hung like one?"

Zones shook his head. "Okay, I think we have enough." He grabbed his briefcase and strapped it over his shoulder. "Give me your hand. On the count of three, I'll pull you up and we run like hell. Are you with me?" Detective Rome nodded. "One—Two—Three."

Zones yanked her from the bed. They tore from the room and bolted for the front door. He reached it first and grabbed the handle, ripping the door open. They started through when a loud explosion sounded. It blew them off their feet, knocking them to the ground just outside the building. Glass and debris littered the air. Flames shot out from every opening and smoke billowed everywhere. Alarms from parked cars blared, rocked by the concussion. A dusty, dark cloud fell over them as they lay still on the ground.

Zones raised his head, now dripping with blood. He heard moaning near him. "Detective," he called out. The sounds continued. He pulled himself across the ground, following them. He came to Detective Rome; she was lying face down. He rolled her over. She coughed uncontrollably. Hearing the faint sound of sirens in the distance, he told her, "Help is on the way."

Through the haze, Zones glimpsed a pair of lights blinking on. A car cranked over, an engine revved, tires screeched and a crimson blur sped away from the parking lot.

TWENTY-EIGHT

Pig Frisky

"WHO BROUGHT ME HERE?" Zones asked as soon as he woke up. He smelled the sterile, antiseptic air of the Grady Hospital room and immediately got up from the bed and ripped away the wires and tubes that were connected to him. Alarms sounded from machines on either side of him. He struggled to his feet, stumbled over to where his clothes hung and plucked them from the hooks. He tore away the hospital gown. His aching, bandaged ribs caused him to double over in pain. He dressed himself and rushed from the room.

Marmaduke met Zones outside the entrance to the hospital. "Hope you got your beauty rest, Doc. We got another bomb. Hop in."

Zones snatched the car door open and eased inside. "Where is it?"

"At a real estate broker's office in downtown Decatur."

"What's the damage?"

"From the bomb? Nothing, it's live."

"You mean it hasn't detonated?"

"The secretary got in early this morning and saw it sitting on top of her desk. Shit is just crazy. Aside from someone trying to blow your ass up last night and the bomb this morning, someone robbed the Fifth Third Bank a block away from this broker's office."

"What's the matter, Detective, too much excitement for you?"

"I can do without it. Speaking of excitement, how did Detective Rome wind up at your place?"

"You know her; she came by to bust my balls about my profile."

"Yeah, she just won't give it up."

"How is she, by the way?"

"Oh, she was at the scene this morning, gave the doctors hell about releasing her. Just had a few scrapes and bruises, that's all. She rode with one of the uniforms. I waited for you." They slowed down. "We're almost there."

Police cruisers had blocked off roads. Traffic was backed up in all directions. Officers directed cars and people to go around the scene and warned off gathering spectators. Marmaduke hit his lights and his siren. He wove between cars and dodged in and out of traffic. He flashed his badge to an officer standing watch and was waved through.

"This is as far as you go, Doc." Marmaduke pulled to the side of the street, just short of the broker's office. "The captain filled me in on your little side investigation. Congressman Stonewall's aide, Mr. Maximus, is in that ATF bus ahead of us. I don't suspect he'll be happy to see you after the fiasco you created the other day."

"I guess not."

"Sit tight. You can watch from here, but keep out of sight. As soon as this case is over, Mr. Maximus and the congressman will be back to what they do best—speechifying."

Marmaduke patted Zones on the shoulder. He popped open his car door and hopped out. Zones watched as he took cover behind other cars and made his way closer to the building. Other officers and detectives crouched behind their cars or whatever else gave them protection.

The door to the ATF van was flung open, and a man burst out. He was dressed in an oversized suit that puffed him up to three times his girth. He moved toward the building like a sumo wrestler, and he carried a toolbox with him. Byrnes Maximus stepped out from the same van along with Captain Franklin. They watched as the man in the suit entered the building. Zones sank lower in his seat. Seconds passed, then minutes. The captain and the aide continued to watch from the safety of the van.

A TV, hung by the window of a recently vacated coffee shop, caught Zones' attention. Congressman Stonewall was holding a news conference outside the Capitol building. The Governor was at the podium.

"Get those people back."

Zones turned to see the captain fan his hands in the air above his head. Officers herded the gawkers and escorted them a safe distance away from the building. As he watched, the Deuce's rear passenger door was opening.

"Shit." Zones turned to see Detective Rome hop inside.

"If you're trying to hide, you suck at it."

"Do you ever let a brother know when you're coming?"

"No, and remember that." They stared at each other for a moment, saying nothing. "How are you?"

"Bruised, but nothing a little somethin-somethin won't cure."

"Two hard heads, one bigger and one smaller, a typical man."

"I would ask the same of you, but I see that you're Miss Thang."

"Can't stand hospitals, that's all."

"I feel you."

"You still think we're off-base with these guys?"

"I don't know what to think."

"How many people do you have trying to blow you up? That bomb at your place was obviously from the perp that got away at the dog fighting farm."

"Maybe...I don't know...but why me? Why not you or Detective Marmaduke? He's the lead investigator."

"Maybe they didn't know that. Maybe we're next."

"This whole case is just one big mystery." Zones turned back to the TV. The congressman was speaking at the podium now.

"Something's happening," Detective Rome said.

Zones cut away from the TV. The man in the blast suit burst through the door and ran from the building.

"IT'S GONNA BLOW!"

The captain and Byrnes Maximus scrambled back inside the van and slammed the door shut. Everyone else hit the ground. Some closed their eyes and covered their ears, elbows against the hard pavement.

Zones popped the car door open. He stepped out and surveyed the scene. He looked back into the car. Detective Rome shouted and waved her hands, but he heard nothing. He walked toward the building, out into the middle of the street. He turned full circle. Something about this bomb scene, the position of the officers on the ground, reminded him of the first one.

Zones turned around a second time. Detective Rome charged toward him, tackling him to the ground and landing on top. A loud blast sounded. Debris and smoke filled the air. Glass and other objects showered down, littering the ground around them. A thick haze blocked their vision as they coughed and gagged from the cloud of smoke.

Detective Rome pulled Zones from the pavement. "We need to get out of here before this clears and your government friend sees you."

They raced up East Ponce De Leon and hopped on MARTA headed east. Zones slumped down in his seat and grabbed his head and side. The bandages, once neatly wrapped, now dangled. The train clanked down the tracks, swaying and tossing them about. He moaned from the discomfort.

"What was that all about back there? Do you have a death wish or something?"

"We need to find your rape victim."

Detective Rome looked puzzled. "You're kidding me, right?"

He looked away. "Where are we going?"

"To my place. It's the only one still in one piece."

Zones closed his eyes and tossed his head back. The train continued along the tracks. He tried to sleep, but the conductor's voice announcing stops interrupted his rest. He sat there, piecing together the revelation he had formed only minutes ago—a victim that was not a victim.

> "Five Points, Five Points is your next station. Please exit to the right for all northbound trains and to the left for all southbound trains. Five Points is your next station," the conductor announced.

Detective Rome nudged Zones. His head popped up and his eyes sprang open. "This is our stop."

* * *

Detective Rome opened the door of her Colony Square condominium, and the light from the east-facing windows flooded the space immediately. Zones plopped on a sofa while she disappeared into the bathroom and returned with a soapy washcloth. She unwrapped the bandage from Zones' head and washed his wounds.

"Now tell me why," she asked, "after spending so much time denying my suspect, you want to find his victim?"

"I don't think she was a victim."

"Come again?"

"When I came across your victim, she was on her knees. Her hands were covering her ears; the officers outside the broker's office were doing the same thing when the bomb went off."

"You think she knew the bomb was going to go off, the one at the animal shelter?"

"That's what I think."

"...At the same time she was getting raped?"

"Was it rape?" Detective Rome rubbed Zones' wound harder. "Ouch," he yelled.

"Did that hurt?"

"Yes."

"Good."

"Before you rub away part of my brain, do you care to hear the rest of the story?"

"Go ahead...Paul Harvey."

"Funny. You got something to wash this grit out of my mouth?"

Detective Rome got up from the sofa and walked into the kitchen. "It's gonna have to be water; I'm out of everything else."

"Water's fine." Zones watched her reach for a glass high on a shelf. She stretched her long, toned legs, poking out from beneath an oversized T-shirt, as far as they would go. "I know the lab analysis of your suspect's clothing showed pre-detonation material. It could have come from your rape victim."

"You're thinking it was transferred?"

"It's a theory."

"How're you going to prove it?"

"We need to speak with someone from the lab. The director, a doctor, uh..."

"Bruno, I'll make the call."

* * *

Detective Rome wheeled her black Corvette onto the parking lot of the DeKalb County Sheriff's Department. She and Zones scurried down the stairs to the lab director's office. They found him peering down the lens of a microscope.

"Come in, Detective Rome."

"Director, you know Dr. Zones."

He nodded. "I got your message. Here are the items you wanted me to analyze."

"Did you find anything?"

"You wanted to know if your rape victim's clothing had any traces of high-energy explosives on them."

"Yes."

"And they do."

"Were you able to determine if they were from the source or were transferred?"

"That's what I was about to do. It's a little difficult, if not impossible, to determine using Locard's exchange principle. I can, however, run a density algorithm on both sets of clothing using a modified headspace analysis to give you my best guesstimate."

"Explain that, please, Director, in English."

"Let's say I'm a pig and I like wallowing in mud. It's my birthday, so I treat myself to a good romp in a mudhole. I'm sufficiently dirty. Now I come to you, Detective, and I get a little pig frisky. Some of the mud that's on me will be transferred to you. You're muddy; I'm muddy. To determine which one of us is the likely source of the mud, I can measure how dense it is on each of us. The one with the highest density should be the source, or it could be reasonably assumed."

"Is that what this equipment is for?"

"Yes, first, I'll take samples." Dr. Bruno cut away corresponding sections of cloth from the victim's and suspect's clothing. He placed the first samples inside collection cylinders. "I'll now heat up the samples." He turned dials on two heating ovens.

"Are those from my victim?"

"Victim and perp, I'm running a simultaneous analysis. Your victim's sample is here," he pointed to one of the metal cylinders, "and your suspect's sample is here."

Dr. Bruno removed the cylinders from the heaters and placed them inside a refrigerated barrel. Vapors escaped when he removed the lid. After some time, he removed the cylinders from refrigeration. He washed them out with a solution and poured the liquid inside glass flasks. The flasks were placed separately inside another device. Minutes later, data printed out across the room. He repeated this process for all the samples that had been collected.

"Okay, Director, what do we have?"

Dr. Bruno unfurled the printed data onto a table. "According to this, the highest concentration of particulates came from your victim."

Detective Rome turned to Zones. He winked. "Let me ask you, Dr. Bruno," as she turned back to him, "when the suspect's clothes were collected, they were found in a hamper with other soiled clothing. Could that have influenced the results?"

"It's possible that enough trace material could have been transferred to the other items to offset the samples. We can test those if you have them."

"We don't."

"Then this is the best I can do, Detective."

"What about DNA, Director?" Zones asked.

"DNA...DNA...DNA." Dr. Bruno walked to the other side of the lab and slid open a file drawer. "Here we are." He pulled out a folder.

"What about the victim's?"

"Why would we run her DNA?"

"She's missing. We need to see if she's in the system, for one. And after your analysis, we'll have to consider her a suspect in the bombing."

"You're okay with this, Detective?"

"Before we go completely off the rails, do we have the lab results from my victim's rape kit?"

"Sure, right here." Dr. Bruno handed the report to Detective Rome. Her fingers moved along the lines of text, her eyes followed.

"Well?" Zones asked. She shoved the report at him. He scanned it. "Says here there was no DNA of the suspect found on any of the vaginal swabs."

"I'll go see the captain about giving us a few blue suits to help find this woman, once we know who we're looking for."

"Can you drop me off at my office? Since I can't be at the crime scenes, I want to revisit the information I already have. Perhaps I've missed something."

TWENTY-NINE

An Ugly Scar

THE BUILDING WAS SMOLDERING. Firefighters hacked their way through the brokerage office's collapsed walls and ceilings. They held tight to hoses that gushed water. They scampered up and down ladders, loaded down with oxygen tanks. The flames lessened when drenched but reignited and engulfed the first floor again. The explosion blew pieces of building in every direction; debris littered the streets and parking lots. Pockmarks peppered cars and other surrounding structures, leaving an ugly scar on an otherwise beautiful morning.

Once the fire had been put out, crime scene analysts, dressed in white jumpsuits, moved between the makeshift command station and the section of burned-out building. They collected samples and tested items found at the scene. Dogs on leashes pranced through strewn pieces of wood, stone and office items. One sniffed its way to an area where a small crater had formed. The dog's handler marked the spot with a yellow cone and continued on.

Amid this bustle, uniformed and plainclothes law enforcement officers tried hard to look unaffected by all that had happened. They held back gawking onlookers and directed traffic away from the devastation. Detective Marmaduke and Captain Franklin were in charge, standing beside the ATF van, their makeshift command center.

"Two bombs in as many days," the captain said. "This world is going to hell; I can feel it."

"You're not getting religious on me now are you, Captain?" Marmaduke asked.

"If things keep going this way, I'm becoming a monk."

"You? No more pussy, *pleeeease.*"

"Yeah, I guess you're right."

"Detective Marmaduke," Agent Thomas called from within the building. "I got something you need to see." He and the captain waded through the debris.

"What do you have, Agent?" Marmaduke asked.

"It's your guy, alright. We found this." Agent Thomas opened a paper bag and lifted out a fragment.

"What is it?"

"It's a larger piece to an IP communication device, like the one we found at the first bomb site."

"Did you find these fragments at the bombing last night at Dr. Zones' apartment?"

"A different device was used there, like the ones we deactivated from the farm in Tyrone."

"Why would this son of a bitch use two different types of bombs?"

"Don't know. Perhaps there're two different bombers."

"Not according to somebody I know," the captain mumbled.

"What did you say, Captain?"

"Um…thank you, Agent. When will you be finished here?"

Agent Thomas looked around, "We'll be here a minute." He headed deeper into the interior of the building.

"Okay, Marmaduke, you got any idea why this guy would choose this place? I mean, the animal shelter, the language research center and the wetlands, I understand the connection there. But a real estate broker? It doesn't make any sense to me."

"It's unlikely we'll find anything in this mess, Captain. I asked Chennault to pick up the owner. She's waiting down at the station with the secretary."

"You get down there and take Dr. Zones with you."

"What about our friend? By the way, where is he?"

"Still inside the van wiping shit from his ass, probably. He hollered like my five year old when that bomb went off. Took every damn thing I had to keep from laughing afterwards."

"You got babies?"

"Shit, I got a young wife. I got to punch in. But I digress. Go get the doctor."

"Ol' boy ain't gonna like seeing the Doc back on this case again."

"You leave Mr. Maximus to me." The captain peeked at his watch. "It's almost lunchtime. With a slice of Scooby's sweet potato pie stuck between his lips, he won't know the doctor from a lineup of redheaded, white midgets. Besides, he's the least of my worries."

"What do you mean?"

"In a few days, this place will be crawling with a bunch of deadheads listening to loud, bad music. They'll be too damn smashed to notice Mike Tyson in a miniskirt, let alone a bomb-carrying psychopath."

"You're talking about the festival."

"The mayor wants to cancel, but he's being pressed by the patricians and the plebeians to allow it to continue." Marmaduke gave the captain a questioning look. "I'm taking this classical civilization course over at CAU. The wife's idea, says it's for our personal growth and enrichment." He shrugged.

"Let's hope our bomber isn't a music lover."

THIRTY

The Suspects

ZONES STOOD AT THE open door to Sam's office while his head was buried in a book. He watched a large magnifying glass being waved back and forth over the pages. Sam's head followed back and forth. Vanity kept him from wearing his bifocals. Zones cleared his throat. Sam's head popped up to see him standing at the doorway. He pushed back from his desk, pulled out a key from a drawer and held it out.

Zones walked across the room, "You must've heard."

"Just make sure you lock the place up. Them Hebrews will pick you clean if given the chance. What do you expect to find there anyway?"

"...Something that would explain how that gun got to the bomb scene, for one."

"And?"

"To see if anything connects these bombings to the Panthers, the sixties, or whatever."

"You sure this isn't about your mother's death?"

"You've made your point about that already."

"Yeah, but did you listen?"

"In case you haven't noticed, I'm no longer four years old."

Sam chuckled, "You know, you sound like you're four."

"Can I go now?" Sam flicked his wrist and returned to his reading. Zones bolted down the hall. He grabbed a file from his desk drawer and headed back past Sam's office. "Later."

Candice, their receptionist, sat at her desk. "Your boarding pass is printing out now." She pulled a sheet of paper from the printer tray, folded it and handed it to Zones. A horn sounded, "That's your cab." Zones winked and headed out the door.

* * *

The flight to JFK was boarding as Zones squeezed down the aisle, tossed his baggage inside the overhead compartment and took his seat in row forty-two. He threw back his head, took a deep breath, closed his eyes and prayed. This was habit, not a belief. The pilot announced their preparation to depart. Zones settled in for the two-hour flight. He couldn't wait to get there. He had lied to Sam. This trip was more about investigating his mother's murder than it was about investigating these bombings.

"Excuse me," a man said as he crossed in front of Zones, his eyes still shut.

"Sorry." Zones eased up from his seat to allow the man to pass by. He sat back down.

"Are we leaving on time?"

Zones' eyes sprang open. He turned to his left. "Are you kidding me?" Sam sat next to him, a big smile on his face. "What are you doing here?"

"What, you're the only negro that can fly on a plane?"

"I don't need a babysitter."

"I'm long passed wiping up shit and cleaning boo-boos. This is about protecting my business and that means keeping you focused."

"You? Keep me focused...with your Alzheimer's head?"

"Half of what's up here," Sam pointed to his head, "is still sharper than all that's up there." He poked at Zones' head. "Now, what's your plan?"

"Plan for what?"

"To take over the world." He paused. Zones took note of his sarcasm. "This case, damn it. What do you think I mean? What's your plan for this case?"

"I don't have one."

"That's a problem. For someone who almost had his nutsack blown off, you sure don't seem to mind much. Me, I would be out for blood."

"You can't fight what you can't see."

"The hell you can't. You think we knew what the hell we were shooting at in those jungles of Southeast Asia? Hell no, you just shot. This case is no different."

"This isn't Vietnam."

"If you've been in one jungle, you've been in them all. The faces hiding behind trees and in the bushes might be different, but the objective is still the same: get them before they get you. Now, who're your suspects?"

The plane filled up. The pilot announced preparation to depart. Zones pulled the seat belt strap tight across his waist. The plane inched backwards, away from the gate. It taxied onto the runway and waited. Shortly, the plane rumbled down the runway and lifted off.

"Monk, did you hear me?"

Zones' eyes sprang open. "What did you say?"

"Your suspects, let's hear them. Once we whittle down your list, we can develop a plan of attack."

"You want to do this now? Why didn't you just read the report?"

"You got somewhere to go for the next two hours?"

"But we've already done this."

"That was before your mother's prints showed up on that gun and before somebody tried to turn you into Humpty Dumpty, the easy way."

"Okay, fine. Let's see, there's Muhammad El-Arabi and Professor Landrosky, both dead, so I guess we can cross them off our list."

"Not so fast. We still need to look at them."

"We're profiling zombies now?"

"Humor me."

The light on the ceiling in front of them illuminated the *No Seatbelt* sign. Zones unfastened his seatbelt. He retrieved his briefcase from the overhead and pulled the file from it, wetting the tips of his fingers as he thumbed through the papers.

"Uza Landrosky, PhD: married, worked at DOD until he was institutionalized."

"He spent time in the loony? Where?"

"...Delaware, Rockford Center. He got married, took a position with Tech as a researcher in nanoscience. Marmaduke found out where he did some consulting for the oil industry. He needed the extra income too."

"Why, do you think?"

"The professor had expensive tastes, or at least his old lady did. I think he was a contractor for the bomber and took a headshot for his troubles."

"Anything on that?"

"It was professional; that's about all. That brings us to Muhammad El-Arabi: aka Brandon Elerby, parents, Amal and Badr El-Arabi. He was a junior, majoring in electrical engineering at George Washington University. The autopsy showed the cause of death to be some hi-tech, bioluminescent material developed with nanotechnology."

"The same shit Professor Landrosky researched?"

"Muhammad's father too."

"Well, there you go," Sam said matter-of-factly. "The boy planted the first bomb and died of this nano shit before he could get away."

"...Sounds too coincidental."

"Sounds like fucking karma to me."

"Great, you've solved it. I can go to sleep now."

"Who's next, damn it?"

"That would be Dr. Amal El-Arabi: wife Badr, daughter Aasima, studied in Saudi Arabia and the U.S. He's an assistant professor of engineering at Tech, also in nanoscience. According to Professor Landrosky, Dr. El-Arabi wasn't too pleased about having his research restricted due to his nationality."

"You mean because he's an Arab." Zones nodded. "Shit, I don't blame him. Today, he's a college researcher; tomorrow, he's strapping bombs to his ass and turning himself into a human grenade."

"His son died in the first bombing, as I said. When Marmaduke first questioned him about Muhammad's death, he lied about knowing anything. Come to find out, he had reported his son missing under his alias a couple of days before the bombing."

"The more you talk, the guiltier they sound."

"Then you're gonna love this. The FBI has a wire in the mosque where he worships. Overheard Dr. El-Arabi and the imam discuss some plot, but it wasn't clear about what. Later, the FBI confiscated a water solution tainted with oil from his lab at Tech. They didn't find anything, but according to Professor Landrosky, it wasn't a part of his research at the institute."

"This cat is done."

"Not so fast. You may think differently after hearing about the others."

A cart was rolled down the narrow aisle. The attendants handed out packets of peanuts, pretzels, Biscoff cookies and drinks.

"A snack, sir?"

Sam leaned across Zones. "How about I snack on those two plump—"

Zones pushed Sam back to his seat. "Nuts for both of us and apple juice."

The attendant handed two packs of nuts to Zones and two juices.

"I don't want no baby juice," Sam said. "I'll take a Vodka and Coke."

"Don't you think it's too early for that?"

"For what, feeling happy?"

"You know what I mean."

"…Party pooper." The attendant mixed his drink and handed it to Sam. He dunked his finger in it, stirred, stuck his finger in his mouth and sucked at the mix. Zones stared and shook his head. Sam gave him a look. "…Go on." He took a sip of his drink.

"We have Mr. Francis Dixon, aka Jah-Boy: small time Jamaican drug dealer. He may have some connection to a group in Great Britain, the Yardies. He ran a crew out of Stone Mountain. According to Detective Rome, he's also in the skin game."

"Didn't they find bomb residue on his clothes?"

"That's how they caught him on the sexual assault. It was either that, and he deal with the local boys, or terrorism charges and he disappear into the federal system."

"…Any connection between him and the Arabs?"

"None that I've found, but he did supply local A-R-M members with herb."

"ARM? What's that?"

"Next on our list of suspects. It stands for Animal Rights Militia. We rounded some of them up at a dog fighting ring; that's where they were about to plant a few bombs. Their record consists of various property damage violations related to animals or animal habitats. One of their members, Charlotte Pirote, was linked to the third bombing through a partial fingerprint found at the site."

"How does she explain that?"

"Said they had targeted the location in the past but not recently."

"Sounds like a Nomeonthda."

"What?"

"Not me on that day. What about the other A-R-M members?"

"Ragtag, can't see them having the sophistication."

"They could be contractors."

"I can't see these animal activists joining up with whoever made these bombs. My profile says these bombings are driven by profit. That means capitalists or governments. ARM would rather catch fleas than to be in bed with Wall Street or spooks."

"Then you've run out of suspects."

"Not quite. Congressman Stonewall's aide, Byrnes Maximus, seems to think T.O., Marcus Tanks, and some black militant group are in cahoots with the Islamist. He's using the gun found at the primate language center—"

"The one with your mother's prints on it."

"He's using it to make his argument."

"So he sees a connection between the Arabs, the animal freaks and the brothers?"

"He sees what he wants to see."

"And what about you? What do you see?"

"I see a young, white girl on her knees with her ears covered as if she expected the explosion."

Sam choked on his drink, coughing. "Say what?"

"You heard me."

Sam leaned closer to Zones. "This wouldn't be the same white girl you bumped into near the Golden Buddha, would it?"

"Why?"

"I thought she was a rape victim."

"Technically, there was no penetration according to the doctor."

"So how do you go from that to bomb suspect?"

"I think the rape was staged."

"Does Captain Franklin know about your theory?"

"Not yet."

"Not ever. You keep that shit to yourself. This firm will not be associated with a Barnwonkle."

"What's that?"

Sam leaned in even closer. "Twenty years ago, Elizabeth Barnwonkle—twenty-three-year-old, white coed from Plano, Texas—was raped while returning to her dorm room at NYU after a night of drinking. It was hot that summer, so she wore these hot pants."

"...Hot pants?"

"Daisy Dukes...Booty shorts. Anyway, when her attacker went unpunished, the local authorities were slammed by her family and friends, thanks to the media. In retaliation, someone got the bright idea to leak the victim's prior sexual habits, pictures of the way she was dressed on that night and the fact that she danced in one of the clubs to pay for tuition."

"I hear what you're saying, but this isn't that."

"Sure sounds like it."

A bell sounded. The *buckle your seatbelt* sign flicked on. The captain announced their final approach. Attendants trolled the aisles, flipping up trays and righting chairs, collecting trash and securing open overhead luggage compartments. The plane touched down. Zones and Sam disembarked. Once outside the terminal, they took a cab to the family brownstone and walked into the past.

THIRTY-ONE
The Old Brownstone

IF MANHATTAN WAS THE jewel of New York City, Harlem was its soul. Its heart beat in the streets: Honking horns barked as drivers pressed into them, irritated by some small thing. The hard-boiled, steel mill grit of the northeastern twang sounded like an argument even in friendly conversation. The area tasted of the briny Hudson and smelled of mechanic shop air. The people looked and dressed like everyone else, but you could sense they were different. They walked hard and fast to get to where they were going, unlike southerners who meandered and found home wherever they landed.

The cab pressed down East 124th. Cars flanked both sides of the one-way street. The brakes squealed and the cab came to a stop. Zones and Sam hopped out and squeezed between the parked cars to get to one of the many homes that lined the street. The four story, Ashlar veneered brownstone stood like a soldier at attention between the other similarly looking homes. It sat right at the sidewalk as did all the homes on this bustling New York street. Stairs led to a door recessed deeply into the facade, covered by a dark shadow. The sun struck the burnt-orange color of the stone and bathed the home in a warm light.

"Does someone live here?" Zones asked. "The place looks nothing like what I imagined."

"I'm renting out the downstairs; it helps to pay for the upkeep."

"What about the upstairs?"

"Your father wanted me to rent it out as well, but I didn't have the heart. I moved everything from the basement to the upstairs and kept the place as it was. I wanted it to look as he remembered it, for when he got out."

"You know, my apartment isn't too far from here."

"Yeah, I know. Let's go inside."

They tramped up the steps. Sam slipped a key inside the lock, turned it and pushed the door open. It squeaked a haunting sound. A strong, moldy odor rushed from the dark interior past them and to the outside. Zones covered his nose and followed Sam inside. He flicked on a flashlight, illuminating stairs ahead of them. Zones stared at a spot on a step as they climbed them. Memories of him sitting there and watching his mother's cold, dead body on the kitchen floor rushed back to him.

"I stored all their things in the attic." Sam huffed and puffed up the stairs. "They should be okay, provided the rats haven't gotten to them."

"Rats!"

"Calm down, boy. I'm just fucking with you. Rats still freak you out, I see. Good thing you had a little brains on you 'cause I can't see you working sanitation."

"It would've been a step up from this gig."

"See, can't be nice to some people." They reached the top of the stairs. "...This way."

They entered a room on the top floor. The flashlight caught the shimmering strings of cobwebs hanging from the ceiling. Sam ripped the blackout cloths from the windows. Light washed the room as small critters scrambled to escape being seen. Boxes, stacked almost to the ceiling, overran the space.

"You don't expect me to go through all this junk, do you?"

"You wanted to get to know your mother. Well, here she is."

Zones ran his hand along one of the stacks. "Where do we start? This is a mess."

"It may not look like it, but there is a system in place here. Over there are your father's case files and everything related to your peanut head. Those boxes over there contain Cleo's work-related papers and back behind those is miscellaneous stuff."

"I'll look through mom's papers; you go through T.O.'s. But first, let's open these windows. It's stuffier than the Queen of England in here."

"I feel you on the windows, but how about we both go through your father's boxes together first. I don't want to be here all day while you catch up on the last twenty-four years."

Zones slid a box across the floor, closer to a newly opened window that overlooked the street below. He had a clear view of Marcus Garvey Park. The sounds of children playing, dogs barking and cars streaming by drifted through it. Zones peeled off the lid and dove into the stack of papers that pushed up from it. He searched box after box until there were no more of his father's papers to look through.

"I don't see anything that would explain how that gun got from here to the second bomb scene."

"...Could've been stolen."

"Did you notice any break-ins?"

"Not that I could see."

"Perhaps T.O. sold or pawned it and doesn't remember. It wouldn't be out of character for a drunk."

"Or someone broke in here without leaving a trace, stole the gun and planted it at the crime scene. Have you considered that?"

"...For what reason?"

"To implicate your father."

"He's already doing thirty to life."

"But there is the appeals process. If he's implicated in these bombings, it'll definitely affect his chances of winning an appeal."

"I'm supposed to be the conspiracy theorist here." Zones dragged another box across the floor. "I don't buy all of this happening just to keep a killer behind bars. Let's keep digging; there's got to be something to tell us what's going on." Zones dug into another box. He peeled back layers of papers. This box held remnants from his mother's life, a life he knew nothing about. "She was an AKA."

"What's that you say?"

"Mom, she was in a sorority."

"Yeah, she and your father met at a step show."

"Let me guess, *Q*?"

Sam let out a loud, dog-barking sound. "Any dogs in the house?" he screamed and stomped around the floor.

"Must you?"

"You're too good to step now?"

"No, but you're kicking up all this dinosaur dust. Who knows what's in it?" Zones stopped rifling through the box when he spied a manila envelope. He opened it and pulled out the papers that were stuffed inside.

"What do you have there?"

"The police report from the night of mom's murder."

"How did it get in there?"

"...Says here T.O. had threatened one of the neighbors with a pearl-handled revolver that morning. Sam, you have a gun, right? How often do you clean it?"

"It depends on the use. If I shoot once every week, I clean it once a month."

"Did T.O. shoot?"

"...Back in the day. Why?"

"The DeKalb County lab report mentioned only two sets of prints, hers and Tanks'. If T.O. cleaned it and mom handled it afterwards, that would explain only her prints."

"And, your point is?"

"How can that be when she was dead and T.O. was the last person to handle the gun, according to this report?"

"Perhaps it was a different gun."

"Perhaps, but how many pearl-handled revolvers could one man have?" Zones stuffed the papers back inside the folder. "You don't think Tanks would've registered the gun, do you?"

"You're kidding, right? Back in the day, a brother registering a gun would've been like taking part in a picnic at a Klan rally. He would've been inviting the man to keep a foot up his ass. Tanks most likely got that piece off the street."

"Who's handling T.O.'s appeals?"

"Some Jew in Manhattan, why?"

"You think he could get us access to the evidence? I would like to see that gun."

"How do you know they have it?"

"According to this arrest report, the cops took it from T.O. when they found him passed out across the street in the park."

"I'll take you by there but—"

"What was that?" The floor creaked beneath the sound of footsteps. "You're expecting someone?" Sam shook his head. Zones moved behind the door. He waved Sam to the other side behind a wall. The creaking grew louder. A shadow appeared on the floor. It crept into the room ahead of the person who cast it. The footsteps paused at the entrance. The person entered. Zones jumped from behind the door and grabbed the man in a chokehold. The man swung the bat he was carrying, attempting to strike Zones while he was standing behind him. Zones dodged his swings. He wrestled the man against the wall; the man gasped for air. Zones cocked his fist and spun the man around, itching to punch him in the face.

"Monk, stop it," Sam shouted. "Let him go." He ran over to Zones and pulled his hand from the man's neck. The man dropped the bat and fell to the floor.

"What's your problem?"

"You're gonna kill him." Sam knelt next to the man. "Are you okay, Wisk?" He slapped him on the face lightly. He groaned.

"You know this dude? And why is he snooping around here? "

"He rents the basement unit and watches the place."

"You need to tell your boy to announce himself first. He almost got put to sleep for real."

"Wisk. Wisk, wake up." He groaned some more before opening his eyes. Sam propped him up against the wall. His arms were draped over his knees as he shook his head; it hung like a dead goose momentarily.

Wisk looked up at Sam. "What happened?"

"Um…you had a little accident."

"Accident, feels like someone choked me." He rubbed his neck.

"What're you doing here?"

"I heard footsteps. Thought someone had broken in again. What're you doing here?"

"What do you mean…again?" Zones asked.

"This is Monk, T.O.'s son."

"Oh, yeah, I haven't seen you since you damn near drowned out at Randall's Island." He squinted at Zones. "That was over twenty years ago. You're a big motherfucka now, boy. Help me up." Zones and Sam pulled him from the floor. "Where's Louie?"

"Who's Louie?" Sam asked.

"…My bat."

"Here it is." Sam picked the bat up and handed it to him. "What did you mean by again?"

"I caught some dude trying to jimmy the lock on the front door one night."

"How long ago was that?"

"About six months. It's been peaceful around here since then."

"Did you get a good look at this guy?"

"It was dark. I had floods put up out front and in the rear after that though. That reminds me, you owe me six hundred dollars."

"Six hundred…What are they, stadium lights?"

"Can we get going, Sam?" Zones asked. "I would like to speak with that attorney before the day is over."

"First, let's stop by the Red Rooster. I'm jonesing for some barbeque pulled pork."

* * *

The law office stood at the corner of Broadway and East 4th Street; it was small and cramped. Red mahogany paneling dominated the walls halfway up. The rest they cheated on using cheap wallpaper of an argyle design. A receptionist sat at her desk and paid little attention to those waiting except when called. She made frequent trips to another room to show off her Tina Turner legs and her Kim Kardashian ass. Zones picked up a brochure lying on a table next to him. He pretended to read but lusted after her from behind it. The letterhead on the brochure read, *Stanley Shapiro, Attorney at Law.* The s's in his name were formed using the runic symbol used by the Nazis.

"Those negroes at the Red Rooster sure can get down." Sam rubbed his stomach. "Damn, I'm sleepy."

Zones turned to Sam who was slumped in his chair. He shook his head.

"Sam Drake," the receptionist called.

Sam eased to his feet. "Right here."

"The door's straight ahead." She pointed.

Zones followed Sam to the door. He pushed through it and went into another room. A man sat behind a desk that overflowed with papers. He waved them in and dropped the phone onto its hook.

"Stan Shapiro." He popped the suspenders he wore, stood up and stuck out his hand.

"Sam Drake, and this is Thelonious Zones."

"You're T.O.'s son. He talks about you all the time. Said you were some hotshot criminal profiler. I'm surprised you haven't contacted me sooner."

"Why's that?".

"I could use your expertise on your father's case."

"Negative, I'm not here for that."

"I don't understand. I thought that's why you wanted to meet."

"We're working on another case," Sam said. "Evidence from T.O.'s case may have been involved."

"What evidence?"

"...A pearl-handled Saturday Night Special."

"Wait a minute." Stan brushed back his long, salt-and-pepper ponytail. "If it's evidence, then—"

"It's in police custody, yes."

"When did your crime take place?"

"...About a week ago."

"Then how can it be evidence in my twenty-four-year-old case?"

"That's what we need to find out," Zones said. "If the gun is still in evidence lockup, we move on."

"And if it isn't?"

"Then we may have a problem."

"You need me to gain access to the evidence." Zones nodded. "How do you know for sure they have the gun?"

"It's in your client's arrest report."

Stan got up and walked to a file cabinet in the corner of his office. He pulled out a file, returned to his chair and hung his feet from the corner of the desk. He flipped the glasses propped on top of his head down to his nose and read.

"I see." He closed the file. "What's your time frame?"

"Today if possible."

"Not possible. I have to clear my schedule. Meet me back here in the morning."

"In the morning it is." Zones and Sam got up to leave. "By the way, what's up with the Nazi SS symbol in your name? That can't go down well in Bensonhurst or at the temple."

"I live in Queens, not Bensonhurst. It pisses off the ADL. And I've been in more churches and stupas than synagogues. Any more questions?"

"No."

Zones and Sam left the office.

"Where to now, Monk?" Sam asked.

"Building Standards and Codes."

"Why? What's there?"

"You know a Belinda Tuscolli?"

"…Big booty Belinda, she worked with your mother. Why do you want to know about her?"

"I'm working on something. I'll meet you back at the house."

"The hell you will." Sam stuck his hand in the air to hail a cab.

"What're you doing? It's only a short ways from here. We'll walk there quicker before you can get a cab."

"A short walk for you is a Bataan Death March for me."

"Suit yourself." Zones slung his case across his shoulder and headed south on Broadway. He reached the end of the block and turned to see Sam with his hand still in the air.

"Monk, wait up." Zones turned again to see Sam huffing and puffing his way up the sidewalk. "Those motherfuckas wouldn't stop."

"You've been in Atlanta too long. You're losing your edge, old man."

Sam grabbed his crotch. "I got your old man right here. Now let's go, but walk slow."

The cavernous street they walked was void of any sun. What little light there was came filtered through a canopy of clouds covering the city. The overcast hid some of lower Manhattan's grittiness. In the dimness, one didn't mind the construction scaffolding blocking off sidewalks or the streets turned inside out as heavy equipment dug into the ground. Sam seemed to fare better without the threat of unrelenting rays beating down on his hairless head. He kept up with the pace Zones set, albeit a slow one. Sam had not demanded any of the particulars, only asking, "Why do you want to know about her?" in reference to Belinda Tuscolli. Zones figured he knew that it had something to do with his father's case or better, his mother's death. The distinction made a difference to him.

They strolled up to the Sun Building; it was known to the city's jaded as the Marble Palace. A forest of scaffolding covered the entrance.

They headed inside, through security and up to the sixth floor. They worried a woman walking toward them for directions. She pointed down the hall.

"We're here to see Big...I mean, Belinda Tuscolli," Sam said to a young woman who sat behind a glass-enclosed counter.

"Is she expecting you?"

"No."

"Then—"

"Tell her Sam Drake is here; she'll see me."

The young woman disappeared into one of the offices. Another door, located off to the side of where they waited, was flung open. A tall, statuesque, older lady with broad shoulders stepped out. She seemed normal enough, professionally dressed, cheesing from ear to ear. For her age, she was put together quite well. Her outstretched arms wrapped around Sam.

"Sam Drake, you old rascal. Where have you been? I heard you were on the West Coast then down South. Now here you are uglying up my office." She laughed with a toothy, Steve Harvey-like grin.

"You know me, baby. I get around. And from the men I've known you to date, I know I'm the best looking thing you and this office have seen in a long while."

"You're still full of it." She released her grip on Sam and fixed her eyes on Zones. "And who is this handsome young man? I know he can't be yours, or if he is, Sheila used a sperm donor."

"This is Cleo's boy."

Belinda's eyes grew wide and teary. Her mouth dropped open, and her hands flew up to cover it. As she had done with Sam, she engulfed Zones with her arms. She squeezed him as if he had been long lost.

"Oh my God." She stepped back. "Look at you." She squeezed him again. "You got those hazel eyes just like your mother." She patted Zones on the hand. "Come into my office. We've got some catching up to do." She turned back toward the door, and there it was—that ass that had made her famous all these years. Sam tapped Zones on the shoulder and pointed like a high school teen while Zones swatted his hand away and shook his head.

Sam stepped into Belinda's office. "Look at you, running things."

"In workload only, not pay. Have a seat. Can I get you something to drink?"

"We ate not too long ago."

"I didn't offer you anything to eat; I said to drink." She turned to Zones. "I have missed giving him the business. Where did you go for lunch, Sam?"

"The Red Rooster."

"You wrong bastard. You knew you were coming here and didn't bring me any?"

"I didn't want to mess up that svelte figure of yours."

"Svelte? You've gotten sophisticated with your words over the years." She turned to Zones again. "Your mother told me Sam and your father called me Big Booty Belinda behind my back." She cut Sam a look as he sank into his seat. "But enough about him. The last time I saw you, I was changing your diaper. I babysat you for Cleo. Your mother and I were good friends. So what're you doing now, besides keeping bad company? And what brings you here after all these years?"

"I'm a criminal psychologist. I work for Sam."

"A psychologist, don't you have to get a PhD to do that?"

"He graduated from NYU last fall.".

"Well, I should be calling you Dr. Zones. You married?"

"No."

"Got a girlfriend? If you do, is it serious? My youngest is a senior at Howard. She takes after me, in every way. And I do mean...*every* way." She winked.

Zones cleared his throat. "There is something I need your help with."

"Sure, darling, what is it?"

Zones pulled a slip of paper from his bag and slid it across her desk. "Is this my mother's handwriting?"

Belinda shoved a pair of glasses onto her face. She studied the writing. "It's been a very long time since...give me a minute." She pulled open a drawer and riffled through it. When her head came up, she placed an envelope on top of her desk. "Your mother sent me this card for my birthday right before she died. I've kept it ever since." Belinda peeled open the envelope and slipped out the card. Her eyes moved between it and the paper Zones had handed her. "They look the same to me." She pushed them over to him. "You take a look."

Zones compared the two. "These addresses were in a Bible she left me. Do they mean anything to you?"

"Should they?"

Zones moved closer to Belinda. "This address is a warehouse near the river in Hunts Point, and this one is a building in the meatpacking district."

"What about the others?"

"I haven't had a chance to bird-dog those yet. From what I understand, my mother was an inspector."

"A damn good one."

"I was hoping you could tell me if any of these were on her inspection route."

Belinda studied Zones. "What is this about?"

"...Nothing, just curious about these addresses."

"Sam?" she turned to him. He shrugged. "The two of you waltz in here after over twenty years asking questions about *nothing* and expect me to open up my files? Do I look like Boo Boo the Fool?"

Zones pulled his camera from his case. He called up two pictures and showed them to Belinda. "Do you know them?"

Her eyes dropped to the camera screen. "The brother, no."

"How about the other guy?"

Belinda crossed her arms and leaned back in her chair. "My mother always said that when old dogs come snooping around that meant no good news."

"Hey," Sam said, "I have nothing to do with this."

"What're you doing here then, babysitting?" She got up from her chair and walked to a window. She stared outside, arms still folded. "You know how long I've worked here?"

"Forty years?" Sam said.

Belinda whipped around to him. "Thirty-eight years, six months and," she glanced at a calendar on the wall, "ten days. I was hired as a clerk six months before your mother. I don't know which one of us was happier to see the other, her or me. When she walked through those doors, it was like seeing a long lost sister. This was back in the mid-seventies. There weren't too many of us working in offices back then, especially educated women like your mother. She was a hell of an engineer. She would've been running this whole place had she lived." Belinda sat on the oversized window sill. A large portion of her ass hung off the edge. "Yes, almost forty years...The other man in your picture is Jack Burroughs."

"Who's he?" Zones asked.

"...The outgoing Director of Building and Development. He was here long before I arrived."

"You said outgoing. Is he retiring?"

"If you want to call it that. I hear he's in DC working as a lobbyist." Belinda sat back at her desk and pulled out a computer keyboard. "Let me see that list." Zones handed it back to her. She typed. "If these properties were on your mother's route, the records would be over thirty years old. That would mean a trip to the tombs. You'd be retiring by the time we got those. Good thing for you, all records are being digitized, and they just finished the seventies files."

"You haven't asked me why I have a photo of Mr. Burroughs or why I'm interested in him."

"Because the less I know about whatever is going on, the better off I'll be." Belinda read from her computer screen. "Yes, all these addresses were assigned to your mother."

"Can I get copies of her reports?"

"All of them?"

"...Pretty please."

"You sure do ask for a lot on our first meeting. I'm thinking twice about introducing you to my baby. Ain't no telling what you'll be asking her for."

"I promise to be a gentleman."

"You be sure to do that 'cause her daddy is crazy, and she'll probably give it to you, the little slut." She continued to peck at the keyboard. "This can't be right."

"What can't be right?"

"It says the files have been locked."

"What does that mean?"

"It means I can't print you out a copy."

"...None of them?"

"...Seems that way."

"All her files or just those?"

"Let me see. I'll test a few of them." A printer across the room fired up and spit paper into a tray. "No, just these."

"Is that normal?"

"For some sensitive locations, yes, but there's nothing special about these addresses."

"How do we get them unlocked?"

"You'll have to put in a request to the director."

"Who might that be?"

"Dr. Shrapwawineshah, but he's out of the country."

"…One more thing, who put the lock on those files?"

"They've been offline for a while now. It looks like Director Burroughs put in the request to lock all of them."

"They were locked before the new computer system was installed. How's that possible?"

"The hard copies were moved to a vault, and only the director can grant access."

"And when was that?"

"December 20, 1989." Belinda slowly turned back to Zones.

"…The day of my mother's murder."

THIRTY-TWO

White Girl In the Trunk

"I DON'T UNDERSTAND," BELINDA said. "You think these properties have something to do with Cleo's death? Who put you up to this—your father, his attorney?"

"I don't know and no."

"For what it's worth, I never did believe T.O. had it in him to kill her. He was a drunk and got a little handsy with too much liquor in him, but the man couldn't fillet a fish, let alone stick a knife into your mother. But even if he didn't kill her, he's still responsible. If he had his ass home that morning and not out sleeping off a hangover...well...I'm sorry."

"No, I feel you."

"What're you going to do now?"

"I need those records."

"I'd love to help but, as I said, you have to go through the director. I'll make the request for you, but that's as far as I'll go."

"Thank you."

Zones and Sam got up to leave. Half way out the door, Belinda said, "I just remembered; Cleo kept copies of her files, some of them at least."

"How do you know?"

"Barbra, a redneck Sally Sue from upstate, always mixed up her files. Cleo thought she did it on purpose. She started keeping copies after that."

"We searched the storage at the brownstone but didn't see any work files."

"All I know is that she kept them someplace."

"Could she have thrown them away?"

"Your mother was a bit of a packrat. She fished that card I showed you from the trash, made me promise to keep it. If someone hasn't taken them, those files are somewhere."

Zones headed for the elevator. Sam kept pace beside him. He didn't say much during their meeting with Belinda. Zones did most of the talking which was fine by him, cathartic even. Being close to those who were close to his mother gave him some comfort. In a weird way, he felt a connection to her that he hadn't felt before. This fueled his pursuit. He wanted to know more. Zones pushed through the entrance of the Sun building, back out beneath the scaffolding that covered the sidewalk and into the bustle of Lower Manhattan.

"Where to now, Monk?" Sam rubbed his palms together and smiled. "We still have until tomorrow before our meeting with Shapiro."

Zones whipped out the list of addresses. "I still have three locations to check out."

"And here I am, expecting an invite to the Sapphire Club. What's the next address?"

"…Water Street, Brooklyn Heights."

* * *

From the backseat of a dark blue, two-door '76 Cutlass Supreme, Zones spied a brick warehouse that sat on the bank of the East River. The tinted windows gave them some anonymity, but the twenty-six-inch, chrome Lexani custom rims took it all back. The area was gritty and tightly packed. The buildings were old and long past their usefulness. Brooklyn Heights looked over to Manhattan with envy and jealousy, no doubt. If it was this way now, it couldn't have been much better twenty-plus years ago. *What would make this shitty piece of New York worth killing over?* Nothing from the outside told Zones anything about the nature of the business transacted inside. Large trucks moved in and out between the side streets. They dropped off or picked up heavy loads, as evidenced by their bulging tires.

"Did Drake tell you about the time him, me and your father got drunk and tried to swim across this bitch?" Johnny—last name, Caesar—leaned far back in his seat. He chewed on a half-smoked cigar as he told his story. Zones had heard it every July 4th when Johnny and his brothers, Julius and Hail, ate barbecue at Sam's house. "His brick-bone ass just sank. Damn near drowned halfway across before your father lifeguarded his ass back to shore." He chuckled.

"Carwreck," Sam called him, "you're a goddamn liar. It was your black ass that damn near drowned. And it was in five feet of water, not halfway. You drank so much East River water that you pissed it for five days."

"That's not how I remember it."

"Yeah, you seem to forget a lot of things."

"What's that suppose to mean?"

"...Nothing."

"Nothing, my ass. You just can't hang that out there to stink. Now if you got something to say, Drake, say it."

Sam huffed, "Since you're telling stories, tell the one about you wrecking my car and his father's car."

"Man, you're dreaming. I didn't wreck nothing."

"Negro, why do you think we call you Carwreck? I bet your brother doesn't know you have his car, does he?"

Carwreck turned to Zones. "How do you take this?"

Zones looked back toward the building whose address appeared on the list. A large truck, with a familiar name on its flanks, rumbled onto a side street.

"Monk, are you listening to me? I asked you how you can take this guy." Carwreck nodded toward Sam. "I could've left your ass stranded at the metro. And why are we out here watching a building for anyway? If you niggas gonna steal, then lets steal."

"Pop the door," Zones said. "I'm out."

"Where're you going?" Sam asked.

"To get a closer look at that Euro-Arabia Oil truck."

The door opened and as the seat folded forward, Zones hopped out from the back. He scampered across a side street and walked toward the graffiti-sprayed brick walls of the building. All the lower windows and doors were boarded. He pulled at one of them, but it didn't budge. Zones walked to the back corner of the building. He scanned the area. Scrawled across the white-painted wall of the building opposite it was, *St. Ann's Warehouse,* painted in faded red. A door was flung open, and a woman emptied trash into a dumpster.

Zones ran toward her. "Hello, Miss." She turned to him, raced back inside and slammed the door. He headed back across the street to the brick building and moved along a covered walk that stretched its entire length. The lower doors and windows were boarded on this side as well. Zones eased to the corner facing the river. Men were guarding the entrance where the trucks drove in. He ran back to the car and leaned next to the passenger-side window.

"What did you see?" Sam asked.

"Nothing. Everything is boarded up. Guards are on the other side."

"Now what?"

"Sure would like to know what's in that building."

"The night time is the right time."

Carwreck perked up. "Now we're talking. I know just the cat to move whatever is in there. If we need help, he has a crew too."

"What're you talking about?" Sam asked.

"I'm talking about what you're talking about—getting paid."

"No, what you're talking about is going to jail."

"Not if we're careful."

"Jesus."

"Let me in." Zones pulled the door open and hopped inside. "We'll come back when it's dark."

As soon as the door closed, lights flashed and sirens sounded. NYPD squad cars surrounded them. Uniformed officers leapt from their vehicles with guns drawn.

"Driver, open the door and exit the vehicle with your hands up."

"Fuck," Carwreck said.

"What?" Sam asked. "We haven't done anything wrong."

"I got warrants."

"…What for?"

Carwreck reached for the ignition, "I can't go back to jail, man."

"What're you doing, fool? Haven't you heard of Amadou Diallo?"

"I can make it, Drake. These cops can't keep up with me." He turned the ignition. The car cranked. The engine roared.

"Check your boy, Sam." Zones said.

The police asked again but with more urgency.

Sam reached over and turned the ignition off. "Your name is Carwreck, fool. You can't outrun the police, and you're not about to get me killed. Now, get your black ass out of this car."

He paused. "There's something else."

"Goddamn it, what?"

"I made a stop before I picked you up."

"…A stop? Shit, how much?"

"Six…maybe ten ounces."

"Ten ounces, whole or cut?"

"Cut."

"Motherfucka." Sam glanced over his shoulder. "Where?"

"…In the trunk."

"You two want to tell me what's going on?" Zones said.

"Brilliant here has ten ounces of cut white girl in the trunk."

"You didn't know this nigga was a drug dealer?"

"Look, we needed a ride, okay. He was all I had." Sam stuck his head out the window. "I'm coming out," he shouted. The police demanded he stay in the car.

"I can beat them, I tell you," Carwreck said.

The police shouted to the driver one more time.

"You're on your own, jack." Sam pulled the handle. The door latch popped. He kicked it open wide and stepped out with his hands in the air.

Zones folded down the back of the front passenger seat. The car started, and it sped off before he could fully exit the vehicle. The door slammed shut. He fell back in his seat.

"What the fuck are you doing?"

"Sit back and hold on."

The car swerved past flashing lights. Demands to "STOP" went ignored. Police unloaded on the Cutlass. Bullets pelted the exterior. Broken glass sprayed the interior, covering Zones as he ducked from the hail of gunfire. He shook the shards from him as Carwreck tore down Water Street and took a sharp left onto Cadman. Wheels screeched as Zones bounced around in the backseat. He grabbed for anything to keep him steady. Out of the rear window, he saw a convoy of black and whites trailing them. His heart pounded while the car zigzagged through traffic. A cruiser pulled up alongside of them. Carwreck gunned it. The right front wheel hit the curb and the Cutlass fishtailed far to the left, jumping across a hard surface medium and sliding into oncoming traffic. A large truck barreled toward them; its horn sounded and headlights pulsed. He cut the wheel just in time, and the car crossed back to the right, out of the oncoming traffic. The Cutlass sideswiped a few parked cars. Carwreck stuck his head out the window. He looked up, his foot still pressed on the gas. The twirl of helicopters sounded above them.

"Oh shit!" Zones said as a bus crossed the street in front of them.

Carwreck slammed the brakes and cut the wheel. The car spun. Zones flew across the front seat, crashed into the dashboard and fell head first to the floor. He righted himself, pushed up from the floor and plopped in the seat next to the door. They came to rest in the middle of the street. Zones grabbed the door handle, pushing and pressing against the door. It would not open. He put his shoulder into it but still it would not move. Zones turned to see the police fast approaching. He locked eyes with Carwreck. Zones dove on top of him and they wrestled for the steering wheel. Carwreck elbowed Zones in the chest. The blow knocked him back to the seat. Zones fisted him in the face and grabbed hold of the steering wheel. They tussled in the cramped front seat. Carwreck punched the gas, and the car lunged forward. Zones jammed his foot down on the brake, and the engine raced. Plumes of smoke covered them, leaving Zones gasping for air. Carwreck kicked his foot off the brake, and the car shot down the street. People hurried across the road in front of them, and other drivers were wary of the speeding vehicle. The traffic thickened. Their pace slowed and then sped up again. Zones glanced at the speedometer. The needle was pressed all the way against the right side of the indicator. He buckled his seatbelt and held on.

Carwreck glanced over his shoulder. The black and whites had almost faded from view. He smiled, and slowly the smile grew into a menacing laugh.

"I told you I could beat them," he shouted, pounding the dashboard and pumping his fist.

The Cutlass seemed to speed up. They had traveled only a short way when a loud bang was heard as the car shook violently. The ride grew rough. The car swerved all over the road. Carwreck struggled to control it as they careened into a curb. Wheel parts scattered, and the car soared into the air. It flipped, rolled and skidded along the ground. Sparks shot up from the street. They pelted Zones as he hung upside down while strapped in his seat, his face only inches away from the grinding pavement. The mangled Cutlass, now missing its stylish rims and other wheel parts, slid to a stop in the middle of the street.

Zones moaned, his heart pounded, and his head and body ached. He looked to his left. The driver's seat was empty, and the door was swung wide open. He feared Carwreck had been thrown free and was possibly dead. He took a minute to collect himself. Liquid dripped onto his face. Zones wiped it away. He smelled it—gas. Smoke streamed in from the rear, and then a flame appeared. It crept along a gas-soaked path toward him. He reached for the seatbelt buckle, pulling on the release. The belt was jammed. The fire and smoke grew intense. Flames had now enveloped the entire rear of the car. A light wind helped to hasten the fire's march in his direction. He felt the hot flames against his neck. Zones scrambled to find something to dislodge him from the belt. Pieces of glass were pooled on the underside of the roof. He grabbed one and sawed at the belt. It scarred but did not cut the strap. Part of his seat caught on fire; it spread to his coat. He swatted at the flames, but they did not go out. Zones ripped his jacket off and tossed it out the window. He reached for the glove compartment, but the belt restrained him. He kicked it open. Many items fell out, including a knife. He grabbed it, clinched the closed blade in his teeth and yanked on it until it opened. Again he sawed at the belt. He cut through it and fell free onto the roof's interior side. A small explosion blew away part of the rear door, knocking Zones back into the windshield. He gathered himself once more and crawled through the passenger-side window. He pushed up from the ground and ran. A loud explosion sounded a few seconds later, hurling him into the air. When he hit the ground, police surrounded him, their weapons drawn.

THIRTY-THREE

Pride Before the Fall

"DRAKE AND ZONES," THE officer shouted throughout the Seventh Precinct lockup. Zones sprang from the small cot; the cell was built like a bunker. It was the day after the chase and crash. The scrapes and bruises he had suffered had been patched or wrapped. His clothes, however, remained tattered. Sam slept on the cot next to him, snoring. Zones kicked him, making him toss in his sleep. "Are you Drake or Zones?"

"Zones. That's Drake."

"Get him up. Let's go."

A few minutes later, Zones and a groggy Sam followed the officer to a processing area. They stopped short of the entryway.

"This your lawyer?" the officer asked in a growl.

Zones turned to Sam. He nodded. "Yes." He looked across the room; Stanley Shapiro stood there, waiting. He waved.

"Follow me." The officer led them into the area.

"What's going on?" Zones asked Sam.

"I called him while you and Carwreck were on your little joyride."

"Joyride? I didn't see you strapping in."

"I thought you two might have wanted some time alone."

"Next time, if there is one, we *will* rent a car. Seems like all your crew is either locked up, dead, or still in the game."

"Here're your things." The officer shoved two plastic bags across the counter. "Sign here. The yellow copy is yours." He slammed a pen down on the countertop. Zones grabbed it, signed and Sam did the same. "Next time the NYPD might not extend hospitalities to the FBI. I recommend you boys find yourselves another stooge; Mr. Caesar will be out of commission for a while."

Zones and Sam grabbed their things and headed over to Stanley Shapiro.

"You two sure do know how to get a party started," Stanley said.

"How did the cops know we worked with the FBI?" Zones asked.

"A detail you conveniently left out of your conversation with me. The two of you waltzed into my office out of nowhere asking for my help. Do you think I wouldn't check you out? I told them you were with the Feds which, as you know, isn't exactly the truth, but it served its purpose."

"So what do we do now?"

"Now we try to locate that gun."

* * *

Six boxes lined one wall of a room at 1 Police Plaza's evidence storage. Stanley pulled the lid from three of them. Zones lifted one from the floor and sat down at a table located in the center of the room. Sam grabbed one as well. The boxes were deep and wide, just like the ones used to pack bulk meat. Zones dove in. He pulled a paper bag from the box and searched it for the gun. Bloodstained clothes, fingerprint cards, jewelry and a knife lay crammed in the boxes, resting undisturbed for over twenty years. He ran his hands over the items, still protected by plastic. Memories invaded him as they had back at the brownstone. He saw a young child—his small, cherub face pressed against the stair rails. He gazed down at what remained of his mother.

"Monk, find anything yet?" Sam asked.

"What?"

"Get'cha head out'cha ass, boy. Have you found anything?"

"I haven't found a gun."

"Well, Stanley," Sam dropped a box to the floor, "that was the last of the boxes. This is your bailiwick. How do you explain a gun going missing?"

Stanley reached inside his coat pocket. He pulled out a piece of newspaper. "Before you start thinking conspiracy, I brought this for you." He slid the paper across the table. The heading read, *Audit Faults Police Storage of Weapons.* "Missing firearm evidence has been a problem for years."

"You think this is just your run-of-the-mill thievery?" Zones asked.

"In my world, Doctor, the quickest way to have a judge throw your case out of court is to start offering up conspiracy theories."

"Conspiracy or not, it's still a theory, and it must be tested." Zones got up and walked to the door. "Officer, may I see you for a minute?"

The clerk followed him into the room. "Yeah, what do you need?"

"Before we could take a look at this evidence, we had to sign in and leave ID."

"What about it?"

"How long has that been the procedure?"

The clerk tilted his head back. His brow rose. "Who are you? You're not with IA or the media, are you? I should have your asses tossed out of here. You told me you were defense attorneys."

"Hold your horses there, champ. We are who we said we are. Now, about the procedure."

"It's been the same since I've been here."

"And how long has that been?"

"Ten years."

"…And before you?"

"Mac…John McGinnis, he ran evidence and property for thirty years."

"Those log files, are they still around from back then?"

"Thirty years' worth? If they are, you'll have to read them through mold and mildew. We had a flood years ago, wiped out a lot of evidence and just as many files."

"But you still have them."

"…Somewhere."

"We need to see them."

"I gotta run this past the brass."

"We'll wait." The clerk turned to leave.

"Hold it," Stanley said. He snatched the newspaper article from the table and wrapped his business card in it. "Show this to your sergeant. Tell him there'll be more where this came from." The clerk left.

"Wait a minute, Monk," Sam said. "You want us to go through twenty years' worth of log reports? That'll take forever."

"It's the only way we'll know when the gun went missing and who was the last person to check out the evidence before that time. We can start with the day the gun was discovered at the bomb scene and work our way backwards."

"There has got to be another way."

"I'm listening." Sam said nothing while Zones paced the floor.

"Say, Doctor Zones, you mentioned there were other files," Stanley said.

"...At the brownstone in Harlem."

"You mind if I take a peek?"

"Sam and I have already gone through them."

"Even so, how about letting these old eyes have a look-see?"

Zones looked to Sam. He nodded and ripped a sheet of paper from a legal pad. "Here's the address. Ask for Wisk; he lives in the basement apartment. The files are in the attic."

The door to the room was flung open. The clerk poked his head inside. "Follow me."

The clerk led them through locked, steel doors and a maze of shelves loaded with boxes similar to those they had just searched. As they moved deeper into the large space, the distinct odor of mildew grew stronger. Water stains skipped across the white ceiling tiles and the sound of pipes hammering disturbed the eerie, peaceful quiet of the dungeon-like space.

The clerk led them deep into the interior to a wall filled with file cabinets. "The logs start here and end here."

Zones scanned the dates written on the card that was jammed into a slot on the front of the drawers. "The year ends in 2008."

"We keep five years' worth up front."

"We'll start there." They headed back toward the front. A phone rang. "Zones, here."

"Doc, where've you been?" Marmaduke asked. "I've tried to reach you since late yesterday afternoon. I called once and some Spanish chick answered."

"You must've dialed the wrong number."

"…Right."

"What's up, Detective?"

"The Georgia Tech researcher, Dr. El-Arabi, his attorney called. They want to talk."

"When?"

"Now, if possible. We've been delaying them until you got back from swimming with the dolphins or whatever you've been doing."

"I can't get back until tomorrow."

"I'll tell the captain you'll be in as soon as you've finished living la vida loca."

"One more thing, Detective, what loosened Dr. El-Arabi's lips?"

"…Pride."

THIRTY-FOUR

A Vial of Water

ZONES AND MARMADUKE STROLLED up to James' desk. She sat pecking away at her keyboard, her eyes locked onto her computer screen. She threw up her hand when Marmaduke tried to speak. His mouth hung open, but no words came out. They had waited almost a week to speak with Dr. El-Arabi; a few more minutes wouldn't hurt. Marmaduke had tried to question him once before. He asked for a lawyer. This would be Zones' first crack at him. He had several questions for the Doctor. His son's death seemed to be at the center of most of them.

Some people in law enforcement and even in congress saw Islamic extremists written all over these bombings. Those guys loved to talk about their handiwork, like teenage boys getting some poontang on the regular. They, however, had heard nothing on the terrorist wire, no videos posted or self-aggrandizing speechifying. The doctor had asked to speak with them, according to Marmaduke, because of pride, whatever that meant. Zones hoped he had a very good story to tell.

James slipped the headphones off her ears and down around her neck. She pulled a file from her drawer and shoved it at Marmaduke. "They're in room one." He and Zones headed down the hall. "And gentlemen," they turned back toward James, "the captain said to get something this time."

Marmaduke gave her a salute, and they continued down the hall.

"Back in room one again," Zones said.

"Just our luck."

"How do you want to handle the questioning?"

"I've had a shot at him, pardon the pun. You may want to take point this time, Doc."

"Any help you can give me as an edge?"

"Only that he doesn't want his family's name shamed."

"That's what you meant by pride."

"We've all got it."

Marmaduke pushed through the door and Zones followed. They sat down. Dr. El-Arabi, dressed in an orange-colored jumpsuit, was seated across the table with his attorney. No one said anything for the first few seconds; they just stared at each other.

The attorney cleared his throat. "Peter Block," he snapped two business cards on the table. "I'm representing Dr. El-Arabi in this matter."

"Detective Marmaduke and this is Dr. Zones."

"My client has asked for this meeting to answer any questions you may have concerning the death of his son."

"What? Let's go, Doc. This is a waste of time." Marmaduke pushed back from the table.

"You can't hold my client indefinitely, Detective. I've prepared a motion to have him officially charged or otherwise released."

"Your client has lied to us and hindered our investigation into—"

"What Detective Marmaduke is trying to say is," Zones said, "that if Dr. El-Arabi could expound upon what he knows of his son's death, it would help us tremendously."

Attorney Block turned to Dr. El-Arabi and nodded. "I have told you all that I know."

"Okay, let's start with this; Muhammad worshipped at the Islamic Center in Washington, D.C. but had stopped attending, why?"

"He had protested the removal of Imam al-Wasi from the masjid. He asked that I speak with Imam Khalid—"

"Rashid Khalid?"

"He is on the board of the Islamic Center. Muhammad had asked that I speak with him regarding the matter."

"And did you?"

"Yes."

"Where did you meet?"

"...At the masjid on Fourteenth Street."

"When was this?"

"Six days ago."

"Did you know that Muhammad had also visited the Fourteenth Street Mosque?"

"Only after the fact. I did not even know he was in Atlanta." He turned to Marmaduke. "I have told you all this before."

Zones flipped open the file folder. He ruffled through papers and pulled one slip from the stack. His eyes shot up to Dr. El-Arabi. They dropped back to the file folder. "What was in the vial of water?"

"I do not know...I mean...I am not sure."

"Which is it, Doctor?" Marmaduke asked.

"What my client means is—"

"Let your client tell *us* what he means."

Attorney Block glanced over at Dr. El-Arabi and nodded.

"Muhammad had become involved with this group, but they are not terrorists." He wagged his finger. "They were...how do you say...tree huggers?"

"Do you mean environmentalists?" Zones asked.

"Yes, that's it, environmentalists. They were angry about something to do with the oil field and the water. Muhammad sent samples and asked if I could analyze them."

"Did he say what environmental group he was working with?"

"I did not want to know anything. I say to him, 'Muhammad, you must be careful. You should be on your studies.' But no, he no listen."

"What were you looking for?"

"I did not know."

"Did you find anything, Doctor?"

Dr. El-Arabi took a deep breath. "I don't know. When I first analyzed a sample, I thought I had, but I could not believe the results. I had Professor Landrosky confirm my findings. He came to me a few days later saying he did not find anything. I could not believe it, so I was going to run the analysis again. That is what I was doing when the FBI raided my lab."

"CSU took a look at the solution taken from your lab, and they came up blank as well, nothing but Middle Eastern tap water."

Dr. El-Arabi dropped his eyes. He looked at Attorney Block. "My client believes the sample was switched."

"Oh hell, here we go again," Marmaduke said. "Another damn conspiracy theory. You people are full of them."

"Detective, please." Zones tried to calm him.

"No, I'm going to say this. Maybe you thought we knocked down our own damn buildings. Then, when that wouldn't fly, you blamed 9-11 on some grand Zionist conspiracy. I say we haul your ass back to your cell and call Homeland Security to disappear you into some third world torture chamber until you give up the goods."

"No. I can prove it."

"Prove it, how?"

"Before he answers that," Attorney Block said, "I want assurances."

"What *kind* of assurances?"

"If what he says pans out, you will drop all charges against him."

"Hell no, our investigation hasn't even concluded."

Dr. El-Arabi leaned over to Attorney Block and they whispered. "Okay, at least no objection to bail."

"...For a non-citizen, no way."

"Then I'm afraid we have nothing more to say, Detective."

"Wait a minute," Zones said. He looked hard at Dr. El-Arabi. "You say you can prove that the sample was switched?" He nodded. "What is it that you thought you had found in the solution?"

Again, Dr. El-Arabi looked to his attorney. He nodded as before. "A nanoengineered protein."

Zones sat straight up in his chair. "Okay, you got a deal."

"What?" Marmaduke said. "You might as well gift wrap him back to Saudi Arabia."

Zones ignored Marmaduke. "Now, tell us about your proof, Doctor."

"Aren't we getting a little ahead of ourselves?" Attorney Block asked.

"I said we had a deal."

"I know you may have a lot of letters behind your name, Dr. Zones, but none of them says *DA*." Attorney Block crossed his arms and legs. "We'll wait."

Zones and Marmaduke left the room. They headed back up the hall to Captain Franklin's office.

"Was that *bad cop* enough for you, Doc?" Marmaduke smiled.

"It was a little melodramatic, especially the 9-11 reference."

"That was no act. Tell me again how we don't know this nanowater wasn't something the good doctor didn't cook up in his lab."

"We don't. But if he did, we'll need it as evidence against him."

"You *can* be a sneaky bastard."

"I've learned from the best."

They walked back to James' desk. "What now?"

"We need to see the captain," Marmaduke said. "Is he in?"

"He's in with the DA and—"

"Perfect."

Marmaduke barged through the door. The captain was sitting at his desk with the DA and Detective Rome seated in front of it. Their heads snapped around to the sound of the door opening.

Captain Franklin scowled. "Why, just come the fuck in, Marmaduke. You too, Dr. Zones. You both know DA Hannah and Detective Rome."

"Captain, Dr. El-Arabi's attorney wants bond for him in exchange for his cooperation."

"What does he have to trade?"

"Hopefully something that will trip him up."

"Trip him up? Are we back to looking at the Arab for these bombings? Detective Rome was just asking for more people to track down some white girl." There was dead silence. "Somebody, please explain to me what's going on."

"If I may, Captain," Zone said, "Dr. El-Arabi may possess evidence that explains why these bombings are happening. To give it to us, he wants bail."

"He's a fucking flight risk."

"I don't think he's the man in charge of these bombings, but I do think he can help us."

"What's the evidence?"

Zones swallowed hard. He tugged at his collar and licked his dry lips. "…Water."

"Come again?" The captain turned his good ear toward Zones.

"It's a water sample from Saudi Arabia."

"Good Lord." The captain rubbed his face and head with dry hands. "You want us to release a terror suspect in exchange for a sample of Middle Eastern water? I hate to break it to you, Doctor, but it's only the oil that's valuable."

"Listen, Captain, this could be our best chance to find out the root of these bombings."

"And this water is going to do that?" Zones nodded. Captain Franklin looked to the DA. "It's your call, Jack."

"If you're sure the information will help, Doctor," DA Hannah said, "you can tell Dr. El-Arabi that we won't challenge his petition for bail."

"His attorney wants it in writing."

"I'll have something drafted right away."

Zones and Marmaduke turned to leave.

"Hold it," Captain Franklin said, "what about this white girl and the perp that got away at the dog fighting farm?"

"We're still looking for both," Marmaduke said. He turned and exited the office. Zones followed close behind.

* * *

Marmaduke rang the doorbell of the El-Arabi home in Brookhaven. A team of uniformed officers and crime scene technicians dressed in hazmat suits backed him up. Dr. El-Arabi had gotten what he wanted, and in exchange, he told Marmaduke where to find the water samples. Zones waited out on the street until they cleared the house. He paced along the edge of the property. Dandelion seeds, growing wildly over the curb, clung to his pant legs. The lawn, like the lives of those living in the house, had grown in disarray. Neighbors came from their homes to witness the commotion. The newly formed city of Brookhaven had not seen this much excitement since their secession from the City of Atlanta.

A window curtain was pulled back and the front door was flung open. Marmaduke and a horde of officers piled into the home. Minutes later, he stepped back out onto the porch and waved. Zones donned a protective suit and entered the home. He went into the kitchen where a team was emptying out the refrigerator. Jars filled with food covered the counters.

Zones grabbed a jar, held it up, turned it around and then placed it back on top of the counter. "Have you found the vials?"

"We've found two, so far," a technician answered.

"Where are they?" The tech pointed to a jar filled with a clear solution. "I don't see anything." The technician waved a red light against the jar. A smaller container appeared inside. "How did he do that?"

"The refraction index of the liquid and the flask are the same."

"Right, pack all this up and take it over to Georgia Tech; they're expecting you."

"Not the lab?"

"You don't have the equipment needed for this stuff."

Marmaduke appeared next to Zones. "Did you find it?"

"They're taking everything over to Tech now. They'll sort it all out there." Zones looked Marmaduke up and down. "Where's your suit, Detective?"

"They said if you're handsome you're immune."

"Then my condolences to your family."

"You got jokes, Doc. Get out of that thing. The captain called; he wants us back at the station."

* * *

Zones rushed past James and reached for the door handle to Captain Franklin's office. Marmaduke followed him.

"He's not in," James said. "They're in—"

"Dr. Zones, down here." He turned to see Captain Franklin leaning in front of a doorway to an interrogation room down the hall. He and Marmaduke headed that way.

Zones reached the door first, pushing through it and into the room. Marmaduke followed. The captain sat in a chair at the table.

"We've found the vials, sir...*oh*." Zones looked to his left. Byrnes Maximus and two other men also sat at the table.

"Have a seat, Doctor," the captain said.

"What's this about?"

"Please, Doctor." Zones pulled out a chair. "You know Congressman Stonewall's aide, Mr. Maximus, and these are Agents Hill and Knight, both with the FBI."

"Yeah, the cheap polyester suits gave them away."

"This is no time to be cracking jokes, Dr. Zones," Byrnes Maximus said.

Zones rolled his eyes and gave him a blank stare. "What about a more serious topic: how's your jaw?"

"…Captain!" Byrnes Maximus shot to his feet.

"Get on with your questioning," Captain Franklin told him. He eased back down to his seat.

"He's questioning me? I'm not answering *his* questions."

"Fine then, Doctor, and that's why I've brought these two gentlemen with me. Agent Hill, he's all yours."

"What's going on here?"

The captain leaned over to Zones and whispered, "Listen, Doctor, the quicker you let this dick hit his nut, the quicker we can get back to finding out who set these bombs off." Byrnes Maximus stared hard at them. The captain smiled. "I'm only appeasing this asshole because, for the first time, we're getting every resource we need, plus some. I'm counting on you to not fuck that up. You feel me? Smile if you do." Zones squeezed out a smile. "Now, I want you to say real loud, 'Yes, sir, Captain' and then answer this prick's questions."

"Yes, sir, Captain."

Captain Franklin leaned back in his seat. "Go ahead, Agent."

Byrnes Maximus pushed a file over to Agent Hill. He collected the papers inside it. "Dr. Zones, can you explain how the weapon found at the second bombing had your mother's fingerprint on it?"

"You're kidding me, right?"

"No sir."

Zones looked over at the captain. He nodded. "As you already know, the gun belonged to my father's friend."

"…Marcus Tanks."

"He gave it to my father. Why? I don't know. Apparently, my mother handled it at some point."

"Your father is Thelonious O. Zones I, right?" Zones nodded. "I need you to answer, Doctor, for the record."

"He's my father."

"He's serving life in prison for the murder of your mother; is that correct?" Again, Zones nodded. "Please, Doctor—"

"Yes, can we get to the point?"

"Okay then, did you know that your father was a convert to Islam?"

"It wouldn't surprise me. Many brothers do that on the inside. It's called survival."

Agent Hill pulled a slip of paper from the file. He slid it across the table to Zones. "Do you know this person?"

Zones studied the image, a black man dressed in a dashiki and wearing a kufi. "I don't know this cat." He pushed the picture away.

"What about now?" Agent Hill slid another picture to him.

"Is this a joke?" It was the same image of the man only this time it included Zones' father. The two men were walking together.

"His name is Nebu Atal, aka Leroy Brown. That photograph was taken at the correctional facility where your father now resides. Mr. Atal is suspected of laundering funds destined for overseas terror groups. He slipped out of the country before his misdeeds came to light."

"And this has what to do with me?"

"Well, in light of the evidence found at the crime scene that links to your father, and now his association with Nebu Atal, we want to know if you've heard anything about these bombings from your father."

"Wait a minute, you think that a man who has been locked up for the past twenty-four years is responsible for these bombings? No wonder we fucked up on 9-11."

"It isn't like he's immune to violence," Byrnes Maximus said. "He was a Black Panther. The leap to radical Islam wouldn't be all that great."

"He was also a grunt in Nam, and he killed as many Viet Cong as Agent Orange could chase from the jungles. But I guess defending Uncle Sam is one thing and defending yourself is another."

"So you believe in this philosophy?"

"I don't believe in anything."

"Not even God?"

"My mother was murdered in front of me when I was a child, and my father is in prison for doing it. What do you think? Now, if you're through psychoanalyzing me, I'm done answering your questions." Zones pushed away from the table, got up and headed for the door.

"...One more thing, Dr. Zones." Byrnes Maximus pulled a sheet from the stack and moved it to the top. "I see you visited North Africa three years ago, when you were still a student. The unrest there was at its peak back then."

"So what, I'm African-American. Marmaduke went to Northern Ireland last year; you gonna give him the business?"

"He's Catholic, but according to you, you're not Muslim—or anything, for that matter. What was the purpose of your visit? And don't give me this work nonsense that's listed on your visa."

Zone scanned the room. He gazed at each man before looking back at Byrnes Maximus. With a wry smirk he answered, "I went to see the turkey take to water." Zones looked at the captain, who could barely contain himself. He bolted through the door and Marmaduke followed him.

"What does that mean?" Byrnes Maximus shouted. "Dr. Zones...what...Dr. Zones."

Zones raced down the hall. Marmaduke caught up to him. "You think that was smart, Doc? My old man used to say, if you want to get an old hound off your ass, you gotta give it another scent to follow. All you've given that hound in there is more ass."

"Fuck him." Zones' phone sounded. He pulled it from his coat pocket and read the text message.

"What is it?"

"The lab at Tech. They've found something."

THIRTY-FIVE

Nano Stuff

ZONES AND MARMADUKE EXITED the Deuce and headed for the entrance to the Georgia Tech Nanoscience Research Center. They took the elevator to the basement. It seemed there were as many floors below ground as there were above. A bell sounded, the doors slid open and they stepped out into a large, well-lighted space.

"Over here, Dr. Zones." Dr. DeGlorious, the medical examiner, waved to them.

They made their way over to her. "Thanks for meeting us here, Doctor," Zones said. "Detective Marmaduke told me you had some experience with whatever we're dealing with."

"It has been a while. I never thought I'd be seeing it on this side of the wall."

"That's DOD speak for civilian life," Marmaduke said.

"We better get going. The observation room is over here. We're meeting with Professor Wong."

"Sounds like you know your way around here, Doctor."

"You've been in one lab; you've been in them all, Detective. Follow me."

They walked along a corridor. The white walls bounced the bright ceiling lights into their faces. Zones squinted from the glare until his eyes made the adjustment. She was correct; all labs were the same— white and sterile, just like this one. Two large, double doors hung closed at the end of the corridor. Opening them, they noticed three men in white lab coats seated in the theater-style room. They were watching a series of monitors hanging from the ceiling. The door clicked shut. One of the men turned, rose from his chair and walked toward them.

"Dr. DeGlorious." He bowed.

"Professor Wong." She stuck out her hand. He grabbed it and shook it. "This is Dr. Zones and Detective Marmaduke." He bowed and shook their hands. "The professor and I met at a conference in Beijing a few years ago."

"Yes," Professor Wong said, "a very smart, beautiful lady."

"I got a text stating that you found something in the vials, Professor," Zones said.

"Yes, follow me, please." Professor Wong led them over to the large monitors. "Please focus screen three," he told one of the other men sitting at the table. The screen zoomed in and out until a sharper image appeared. "This is your sample."

"What're we looking at?"

"This is just nebulous material, Dr. Zones."

"Nebulous, I thought you found something significant?"

"Yes. Hold your horses, Doctor." His smile consumed most of his face. He turned to the same man. "Magnify to one nanometer, please." Once again, the screen zoomed in and out. A new image came into view. "These are nanoproteins, Dr. Zones."

"That's what Dr. El-Arabi called them."

"So the Arab was telling the truth for once," Marmaduke said. "But how do we know he didn't create them?"

"There is no place that I know of that can create this technology," Dr. Wong said. "Except…"

"No place, except one," Dr. DeGlorious added, "the DOD." They all looked at each other. "Do you have infrared on the scopes, Professor?"

"...Of course." The screen went black and seconds later it lit up. The nanoproteins were glowing.

Dr. DeGlorious turned to Marmaduke. "Just like Muhammad El-Arabi's brain specimen. Where did you get this solution, Detective?"

"Dr. El-Arabi said the water came from Saudi Arabia."

"Can we verify that, Professor?"

He lifted a stack of papers from the table and thumbed through them. "We ran a volatile organic and an inorganic chemical analysis. According to the results, the sample is consistent with that found in the region."

"Do you have any idea what this stuff is used for?" Zones asked.

"It was found in drinking water so..."

"Human consumption?" The professor nodded. "But we don't know what it does."

"I'm sorry, Dr. Zones."

"Thank you, Professor." They headed toward the door. Zones turned to Dr. DeGlorious. "As you've noted, this appears to be the same stuff found in the deceased, Mr. El-Arabi. How did technology developed by the Defense Department end up in the drinking water of Saudi Arabia and in our DB? And what purpose does it serve?"

"Those are all good questions. Unfortunately, they only pay for answers."

"I have at least one, Tuskegee."

"Careful, Dr. Zones, you're about to wade into the very, very deep end of the pool."

"Okay then, how would you explain it?"

"I can't, but I'm not ready to make a leap from that to the assumption that our government is secretly spiking the water of another country. Besides, who says this couldn't be something the Saudis engineered?"

"You heard the man and you even said it yourself; the U.S. is the only country with the know-how to make this stuff."

Dr. DeGlorious took a deep breath. "My initial theory was a bomb that, when detonated, would kill people but leave buildings intact. But since the medium is drinking water, I'm not so sure."

"Are you still plugged into the other side of the wall?"

"I checked with my contact the minute I discovered the bioluminescence in the brain. He said nothing got out on their end."

"He could've been lying. It wouldn't be the first time." Dr. DeGlorious scowled. "Don't tell me you never had to do it when you were there."

"...Yeah."

"I have a question, Doctor," Marmaduke said. "In your lab, you made the color of the substance change. What about this sample?"

"I'm going to stick around to work with Professor Wong on that. Perhaps if we find the marker, it'll tell us more." She walked back toward the professor and the others.

Marmaduke gawked as Dr. DeGlorious wiggled away. "My, my, my, a little dab'll do y'."

"Are you finished?" Zones said. "I'd like to follow up with Detective Rome on locating the alleged rape victim from the first bombing."

"Alleged? You mean she wasn't?"

"It's a working theory."

"You better have more than a theory if you're gonna claim that a rape victim is crying wolf. If you're wrong, the captain will have your ass for bringing on that kind of heat."

Zones and Marmaduke left the lab's pale-white walls and bright lights. They pushed through the outer doors of the research building and piled back into Shirley. She had been Marmaduke's longest relationship. Zones knew that he did his best and hardest thinking when he drove her. This case needed some hard thinking. The suspects and the evidence changed with every inquiry and had many variables. The path down which the evidence led them teamed with danger. Crime solving 101 said, if the suspect could have possessed the murder weapon, that suspect must have used it. In this case, Zones suspected the U.S. Government, particularly the Department of Defense.

Zones stared at Marmaduke as he lay way back in his seat, barely able to see over the peeling dashboard. He slung his arm over the steering wheel and leaned to one side, like a pimp on the stroll.

Marmaduke gave Zones side eyes, but his head stayed straight. "You're staring like you're in love," he said. Zones chuckled. "You're really gonna go down that road, Doc? 'Cause if you are, it'll be a bumpy one. You just can't investigate Uncle Sam and not think there won't be consequences and repercussions. If they're doing what you suspect they are, the next leap is that they're also behind the bombings."

"...One conspiracy at a time, Detective."

"What other conclusion can you come to? We're not talking about some shithole, third-world country. We're talking about the standard-bearer of democracy."

Zones pulled his phone out. He logged onto the internet and Googled: *Saudi Arabia + Nanotechnology + Water*. Nothing came up. He entered a few more combinations before coming across an article detailing the harm fracking has done to the environment in the American Midwest. Zones read:

> *Fracking is a dangerous way to extract oil and gas from the ground. It pollutes water and air. Residences in some fracking zones have reported a strong odor of gas coming from their drinking water. When one homeowner set a match to their running water, it ignited. Environmental groups have asked Congress to investigate...*

"Doc?"

Zones looked away from the article. "What?"

"I asked you how the kid could know about this nano stuff. It took millions of dollars' worth of equipment and an army of eggheads for us to detect it."

"I don't think he did." Zones logged off the internet. He dialed. "Dr. DeGlorious, this is Zones. The nebulous material Professor Wong found in the water specimen, was any of it petroleum-based?"

"I'm looking at the report now and yes, quite a bit of it. I'm no expert, but some of these levels look excessive. I'll have someone from the EPA take a look at it."

"No, I mean, let's wait until after our analysis before we involve others."

"Okay, you know where I'll be should you need anything else."

Zones ended the call. "We need to question that crew we picked up from the dog fighting farm again."

"...What for?"

"Dr. El-Arabi said his son took up with some environmental group, right?"

"Yeah, so what?"

"What if he collected those water samples in Saudi Arabia to have them analyzed for petrochemicals?"

"And you think that's what got him killed? Why would it have mattered to the Saudis? They're dictators, and they can do whatever the fuck they want."

"Not if there was a possibility of having their little nanoprotein discovered. Especially if they found out Dr. El-Arabi was a nanoscientist and could trace it right back to the good ol' U.S. of A."

"We don't even know what this stuff does. It could be a way of purifying the water. You know, like chlorine."

"That's exactly my point."

"What is?"

"Nothing, but what we do know is that it's killed at least one person."

THIRTY-SIX
Fucking with Ishmael

ZONES' PHONE RANG AND he ignored it. The wall collage of bombing evidence occupied his thoughts. He stood in his office, his eyes transfixed once again on the data in front of him. He searched for signs or symbols the unsub may have left behind. The bomb locations and their detonation times had been mapped. He raked his hands over the papers and pinned pictures of the suspects to the wall, adding them to the collage. Next, Zones added secondary information collected from the crime scenes. **The animal shelter**: the dead body of an Arabic college student with signs of a bioluminescent material in his brain and the fragments of a communications device. **The language center**: a collapsed tower and a gun once belonging to an ex-Panther with Zones' mother's fingerprints on it. **The wetlands**: a burned-out clubhouse. Finally, next to his apartment and the brokerage office, he wrote two big question marks.

Zones stood near his desk, back from the wall. He hoped the distance would help him to focus on something he was not seeing when standing right next to his collage, like trying to see the whole picture in a modern art gallery. He continued to study the evidence; a knock came at his door. It flung open as Zones grabbed a gun from his desk drawer.

Marmaduke burst through the door. "There you are, Doc. Not answering your phone?" Marmaduke threw up his hands, seeing the gun. "Whoa, Doc, it's just me. What's the matter, bomber got you running scared?"

Zones lowered the weapon. "How did you find me?"

"Where else would you be? You don't have any friends."

"What do you want, Detective?"

"Grab your things; I got the owner of that real estate company down at the station again. The captain wants you there this time when we question her."

"You're gonna have to do it without me. I'm trying to find what I missed in my profile."

"Is that what this is?" Marmaduke gestured at the wall. He walked over to it. "What're these question marks?"

"I don't have any evidence from the bomb at my apartment or from the brokerage office."

"According to Agent Thomas, the bomb that damn near killed you was different than all the others, including the one from the brokerage office. Your bomb matched the devices we found at the dog fighting farm."

"The bomb used at the language center was different as well."

"They all used some kind of communication device; your bomb didn't. Listen, Doc, is it so hard to believe that these guys had something to do with the bombings? It wouldn't be the first time."

"What do you mean?"

"The Weather Underground, for instance, was a group of white, middle-class college students that adopted militant black liberation rhetoric when carrying out their bombing campaign."

Zones walked back to the wall. His eyes gravitated toward the autopsy report for the body found at the first crime scene. "You're investigating the death of the young man found at the animal shelter, aren't you?"

"Muhammad El-Arabi, yes I am. We ran background on him in DC. Didn't have much though."

"Who was your contact?"

"...In DC? A Detective Baker. Why?"

Zones walked back to his desk. He plucked the phone receiver from the hook and dialed. "Candice, book me on the next flight to Washington, D.C., okay?"

Marmaduke looked on and shook his head. "Why are you going to DC, Doc?"

"I need you to call Detective Baker and let him know I'm on my way."

"Not until you tell me why you're going to Washington."

Zones took a deep breath and exhaled it all at once. "Okay, Detective, Gestalt psychology."

"Gay…what did you say?"

"…Not gay, I said *Gestalt*. It's a theory that proves psychological phenomena are arranged in gestalts or forms and are not just a summation of individual sensations."

"Do my eyes look glazed over, Dr. Zones?"

Zones opened his desk drawer and slipped out a folder. He pulled a black and white sketch from it and held it up to Marmaduke. "What do you see?"

"I see a pretty, young woman in a coat with her head turned away and a feather in her hair."

"Look again; do you see an old woman with a big nose who appears to be sleeping?"

Marmaduke concentrated on the picture. "Yeah, I see that too. Damn, that's some trick, Doc."

"No trick. Your mind will first see that which it wants to see, in your case, a young woman. These bombings are no different than this sketch, only in reverse. Someone wants us to see the ugly woman when in fact it's really a pretty girl."

"And you think the answer lies in DC?"

"The deceased, Mr. El-Arabi, spent most of his time there just before he ended up dead here, did he not?" Marmaduke nodded. "Do you hunt, Detective?"

"I get my kill on."

"Then you know why you never clean the carcass where you intend to store the meat." Zones grabbed his case and headed for the door. "Make that call, Detective."

"What about the interview with the broker?"

"You're gonna have to do it without me."

"And the captain, what do you want me to tell him this time? He's expecting you at the station. He's even getting ol' Byrnes Maximus drunk on pie for the second time, and who knows what else, to distract him."

"Tell him…'He went to see the turkey take to water.'"

"What the fuck does that mean?"

* * *

Adams-Morgan had not changed much since Zones had last visited. It occupied a spot in the District of Columbia's exact center. The neighborhood, a confused mix of row houses and hole-in-the-wall shops, bound many cultures together. The people's knarred language and their free spirit lent a bohemian texture to the capitol city's rigidity. The street leading to the Third District police precinct cut across other streets at odd angles and in unexpected places before finding its sanity on a grid. The same could be said of Adams-Morgan's people. By day, the business and political elites, with their starched collars and shiny shoes, kept their distance from the dreadheads wearing harem pants and beating drums in the park. At night, the many bars and clubs dotting the area gave them license to throw off their inhibitions and mix freely.

Zones stepped from a cab at the corner of Seventeenth and V. He scurried up the sidewalk, snatched open one of two blue double doors and darted inside the building. Detective Baker met him promptly.

"I'm Dr. Zones." He stuck out his hand.

"Detective Baker." His handshake was delayed but it snapped out once he recognized the gesture. "Here's the file on your DB, Doctor. Detective Marmaduke has most of this already."

"He mentioned something about Mr. El-Arabi's work with the Defense Department. Were you able to get anything more on that?"

"I'm afraid not. Those cats hand out information like it's enriched plutonium. When I started asking questions, the pricks called my sergeant, said I was harassing them."

"What did he do?"

"Said he didn't need the heat, told me to back off unless I had something solid, so I did."

"What about the school and the mosque he attended?"

"Other than what's in the report, there's nothing new."

"May I hang on to this?"

"He didn't die in my city; the file is yours."

"Thanks."

Zones walked back out to the street. He waved his hand in the air for a cab. When one stopped, he snatched the door open and hopped inside. "The Islamic Center," he told the driver.

The driver peered at Zones through the rearview mirror. "As-salaam a-laikum, my Brother."

"A-laikum salaam."

"Are you attending a prayer session?"

"No. I'm visiting."

"The Center is very nice." Zones gave him a glance and a quick smile before turning his attention back to the people walking down the sidewalk. "Do you know the chairman, Brother?"

"No."

"He is a powerful man, a great man." He scratched his scalp through his multicolored kufi.

"Where're you from?"

"I am from Djibouti. Do you know it?"

"...East Africa, next to Ethiopia."

"Yes, I will be studying at the university this fall."

"...Which one?"

"Howard."

"Good school."

"Yes, it is the Mecca," he sang. His smile widened, and he bounced in his seat. "The masjid is not far."

They traveled a short distance. A crowd had formed on the sidewalk outside of a large ornate building surrounded by a wrought iron fence. The people sat without speaking. A bearded man, dressed in a prophet's robe and headdress, stood before them and shouted at the top of his lungs.

"What is this?" Zones asked the cab driver.

"These are dogs doing what dogs do. I spit on them." He rolled down his window and spat onto the ground. He shouted at them in Arabic. Those sitting there stood up and shouted back. When they seemed to be approaching the car, the driver sped off. "See, they even chase cars like dogs."

"What're they protesting?"

"They protest the chairman. He is my countryman. They wish to have their snake back." Zones looked through the rear window at the men. They still stood and watched. "I let you out on the other side. It is best." The driver made a right turn. The cab stopped. Zones paid him and hopped out. "Shall I wait for you, Brother?"

"I don't know how long I'll be."

The cab driver flipped down the overhead visor and slipped out a card. "Here is my number. Call me when you are ready. I pick up you." Zones took the card. The cab pulled away.

Zones yanked on a gate. It was locked. He walked back to the crowd and entered an opening in the fence. At the top of some steps were arched openings leading to a large court. He crossed the court to a bank of doors and knocked. One of them opened and a young man poked his head out.

"I'm Dr. Zones, here to see the imam."

"You have an appointment?"

"No."

"The imam doesn't see anyone without an appointment."

"Tell him it's about Muhammad El-Arabi."

"Muhammad?" He looked Zones over. "Wait here." He ducked back inside. The heavy door inched closed. Zones looked around the large court; it was hard and overbearing like the religion. He sensed, from the cab driver's reaction to the group gathering out front, that the mosque was going through some turmoil.

Zones pulled his iPhone from a side pocket and logged onto the internet. At the search prompt, he typed, *Islamic Center, Washington, D.C.* He surfed through a number of sites. One, in particular, talked about the forceful removal of Imam Jaber al-Wasi and his family from the mosque. Zones continued to read. His eyes cut back and forth between his phone and the door. According to the article, the Saudi government orchestrated the imam's removal some thirty years ago. Ever since that time, Imam al-Wasi has held *Jumu'ah khutbas,* Friday prayers, out on the sidewalk next to the mosque. *Interesting.*

The door popped open again. The same young man stepped out. "The imam will see you now." He held the door open. Zones stepped through. "You must remove your shoes." Zones' eyes dropped to his feet. "I will take them until you return."

Zones slipped out of his shoes and handed them to the young man. "These are gators."

"This way, please."

The young man led Zones through the sanctuary. The space soared above with a large chandelier hanging at its center. They entered a room off a hall. Two men sat at a table in the middle. Zones stepped inside. The door closed behind him as the two men stood.

"Dr. Zones, I am Imam Rafiqi. This is Mr. Suleman, our attorney. I understand this is about Brother El-Arabi. How may we help you?" They shook hands and sat.

"Well, Imam, I was hoping to learn more about Muhammad's time here in Washington, his friends, his associations and his work here at the mosque."

"We have told Detective Baker all that we know. I'm afraid, Dr. Zones, that we have nothing more to add."

"You have no idea who would have wanted to harm him?"

"No."

"What about his work here at the mosque?"

"Unfortunately, his work was against the mosque."

"Against it…" Zones pulled the file from his case, "it says here that he was a member of the Islamic Student Association. Isn't that affiliated with the mosque?"

"Yes, ISA is a part of the mosque, but Brother El-Arabi joined the opposition."

"You mean Imam al-Wasi." He nodded. "Is that him out on the street?"

"Imam al-Wasi," Mr. Suleman said, "is free to use the public square, Dr. Zones."

"How did that make you feel when Muhammad joined the opposition?"

"It is a free country," the imam said.

"Speaking of countries, you get most of your funding from the Saudis; is that right?"

"Our funding comes from many charitable sources, Dr. Zones."

"How involved are they in the Islamic Center?"

"What is this about, Doctor?" Mr. Suleman asked. "I thought you were here about Muhammad? I'm afraid your questioning is out of line."

"No, I'll answer it. The Royal Family has members on our board of governance, and they are actively involved in the running of the Center. Now, Dr. Zones, if there is nothing else?" The imam and Mr. Suleman stood.

"*Actually...*there is one more question, Imam. Is one of your benefactors the Euro-Arabia Oil company?"

"As I said, we have many charitable sources."

Imam Rafiqi and Mr. Suleman disappeared through another door off the room. The young man who met Zones at the front door reappeared.

"Your gators." He held Zones' shoes out to him for his inspection. The young man led Zones back through the sanctuary, out the door and into the courtyard.

Zones slipped on his shoes and headed for the exit. The crowd out front had gone, along with the loud, fervent sermon. He stepped to the curb and stuck his hand in the air. A yellow streak zipped by him. He remembered passing a train station on the way to the mosque, so he started up the sidewalk.

Cars whisked by at speeds too fast for the road. Zones glanced over his shoulder at the oncoming cars. The narrow walkway gave little barrier to the Friday afternoon DC traffic. One car stood out—a black, four-door sedan with missing whitewalls and dark-tinted windows. The car followed behind him, in no hurry to pass by. He ignored it at first. *Perhaps the driver has car problems.*

Zones stopped a man and woman walking toward him. "How much farther is it to the metro?"

They pointed, "Dupont Circle Station is less than a mile away."

Zones glanced over his shoulder once again. The same car still followed, but now it was stopped on the side of the road. Two men in dark suits and dark shades jumped out. They leaned against the car. Zones continued to walk as they followed him. He picked up his pace and then broke into a full sprint. The men gave chase. Zones weaved between the growing crowds of people on the sidewalk, pushing and shoving some aside. He dashed across streets in the middle of traffic. Cars slammed on their brakes. Drivers yelled and cursed; horns honked. He looked back to see the two men pile back into their black sedan. It pulled into traffic and approached at speed. The traffic thickened. The sedan stopped just behind him. The doors were flung open, and the men, once again, hopped out. Another car, a cab, swerved in front of them just past Zones.

"Get in," the cab driver said.

Zones snatched the rear driver's side door open and jumped inside; it slammed shut as the cab sped off. He pushed up from the backseat in time to see the men scramble back inside their car. The traffic eased, and the cabbie raced down the street, cutting between lanes. Tires screeched and horns sounded. Cars slammed into one another, littering the street with car parts as the cab barreled through traffic. The black sedan continued to follow them.

Zones turned to the driver. "Where did you come from, um…?"

"My name is Ali. I see you running down the street, and then I see the men. I say to myself, 'Ali, he needs a ride.' So I picked you and here we are again."

"Can this thing move any faster?"

"We move as Allah allows."

Zones pulled a hundred-dollar bill from his wallet. He dangled it in front of Ali's face. "Will this help Allah move a little faster?"

Ali snatched the bill from Zones' hand. "Allah, no, but Ali's foot, yes." He punched the gas, and the cab shot down the street.

Zones turned to see the sedan fall farther behind. He pounded the backseat. "*That's* what I'm talking about."

"Why do those men chase you, Brother?"

"I don't know. But a dog that's hit will either holler or bite. I guess this one bites."

"I don't understand."

"How far are we from George Washington University?"

"Not far. It's straight away."

They came to a roundabout that circumvented a park. The sign read, *Sheridan Circle*. Traffic was stalled as cars inched their way forward.

Zones saw the black sedan weaving between lanes of traffic. "We have to go. We can't sit here."

"Where would you like for me to go, Brother? I am a cab driver, not a pilot."

Zones looked around. Cars boxed them in on one side, and the park was on the other. The sedan was only five car lengths behind them. The same two men got out and walked next to other cabs that lined the street. They peered inside them.

Zones slumped in his seat. "We have to get out of here." He peeked out the rear window to see the men approaching. "Go through the park," Zones told Ali.

"Are you crazy? I can't cut through the park. I lose my license. And with no license I can't work. And with no work I can't make money to feed my family back in Djibouti. And I have a very big family, Brother."

Gunfire shattered the air, and the right rear-door window disintegrated. Bullets whizzed past their heads.

"Shit," Ali shouted. Anything additional was a mixture of Arabic and French.

"Go!" Zones dove to the floor. Ali took a hard right and headed through the park. The cab surged forward and hit something. The ride grew bumpy. Bullets sprayed the outside of the car, sounding like tin cans exploding. Zones tossed around in the back. Ali drove on, still shouting in his language. When the gunfire stopped, Zones got up from the floor and Ali eased back into the traffic.

"What have you gotten me into?" Ali whipped his head from the road ahead of him to Zones. "Look at my cab. It is destroyed."

"Look, I don't know what's going on, but I do know insurance will take care of your cab."

Ali pulled out of traffic and slammed his foot on the brakes. The rear of the cab fishtailed. He shifted the car into park and snatched the hundred-dollar bill from his shirt pocket. "I give you back your money. You get out."

"Get out where, here? You can't put me out here. Take me to the university."

"Get out of my cab. Get out of my cab!"

Zones looked around; he didn't know the area that well. "Okay, you want to know what I was doing at the center?"

"I do not care your business."

Zones leaned in close over the seat. "I'm with the U.S. State Department. As you know, the center is governed by a board of Islamic countries that has to be accredited by our government. Djibouti's accreditation has expired. I was inspecting the center's records for renewal. Now, if I don't get to the university, I can't complete my work; your country will lose its accreditation, and your beloved countryman will lose his chairmanship. I can say that Ali was a great help, ensuring that the chairman kept his position, or I can say Ali's actions directly contributed to him losing it. Now, which will it be?"

Ali pulled back into traffic. His cab rattled down the street all the way to George Washington University. They rolled onto the Foggy

Bottom campus and up to Tompkins Hall; it housed the School of Engineering.

"We are here," Ali huffed, shifting the cab into *Park*.

"Give me a minute." Zones surveyed the bullet riddled van and shattered windows, evidence of the danger he had just faced. He checked himself hurriedly, disbelieving he had gone unscathed. His chest heaved. His mouth hung open, gulping air.

"Are you okay, brother?"

Zones noticed Ali studying him and he gathered himself. "Wait here."

He leapt from the cab and trotted up the steps to the granite-clad building. A young woman sat at a desk. Her big eyes flashed brightly, like headlights on a clear, late night.

"May I help you?"

"May I see your chairman, please?"

"Do you have an appointment?"

"Tell him I'm investigating the death of Muhammad El-Arabi."

"Oh." The young woman picked the phone up and dialed. She repeated what Zones had told her and hung up. "He'll be with you in just a few minutes." Zones paced and peered through the door to see if Ali was still waiting—he was. After some time, the phone rang. "Okay." She placed the phone down. "Dr. Kumani will see you now. His office is down at the end of the hall on the left."

Zones walked to a door with *Chairman* stenciled into the glass. He pushed through it and was greeted by a tall, thin gentleman and another seated nearby. "Hi, I'm—"

"Dr. Zones, yes I know. Detective Baker called and said you might stop by. Come in and have a seat. This is Professor Magbar. I asked him to join us. He was Muhammad's academic advisor, and he knows more about him. Now, what may we do for you?"

"I understand that you've spoken to the authorities already."

"We told Detective Baker all we know about Muhammad."

"Did you see any change in him?"

"How do you mean?"

"When they found his body, he had dyed his hair blond and wore blue contacts."

"I wouldn't know about that. He looked perfectly himself when I last saw him." Dr. Kumani turned to Professor Magbar, who nodded in agreement. "But give me a minute." He got up, went to the door and opened it. "Rebecca," he called down the hall. A moment later, the office assistant appeared at the door. "This is Rebacca; she knew Muhammad...socially. Dr. Zones has some questions for you." Dr. Kumani took his seat.

"Hi, Rebecca, how well did you know Muhammad?"

She smiled and flicked back her hair. "Yeah, we...um went to a few parties together and stuff," she said it in her valley-girl voice.

"When did you last see him?"

"Yeah, I, like, picked him up from the airport after he got back from Hajj."

"...Hajj?"

"Yeah, isn't that, like, where they go when they go home?" She looked at each of them.

"So, you hadn't seen Muhammad since last fall."

"No. This was a week before he died. That's when he started acting weird and changing his appearance."

"This started after he had returned from Saudi Arabia two weeks ago?" She nodded. "Did he say why?"

"No. He just, like, was acting weird."

"Okay, thanks, Rebecca." She flashed her big, brown eyes and left.

Zones threw his head back and closed his eyes. He took deep breathes and exhaled slowly. Both men called to him, but he did not answer. Everything that had happened this week was marinating in his mind.

"Dr. Zones, are you okay?"

Zones' eyes sprang open. He continued his questioning as if nothing had happened. "I know Muhammad applied for a job with the Defense Department but didn't get it."

"He was very disappointed by that," Professor Magbar said. "But I warned him that it would be difficult for a foreign national to work in such capacity, especially a young man from the Middle East."

"What position did he apply for?"

"It was an internship. Other than that, he didn't say."

"Was he involved in any research here at the university?"

"...Nothing significant. As I told the detective, most research positions are reserved for graduate students."

"What about research that might be considered insignificant?"

"Well, he did approach one of our professors in environmental engineering about doing some research."

"Do you know what it was about?"

"I asked, but he never mentioned it to me or the other professor again."

"What is the other professor's area of research?"

"Dr. Sun researches water related issues: reclamation, desalinization, especially in environmentally sensitive areas."

"Is he available? Perhaps he can shed more light on this."

"I'm afraid Dr. Sun is on sabbatical in China," Dr. Kumani said.

"Why don't you check with Muhammad's father? Dr. Sun mentioned to me that he had worked with him on something," Professor Magbar said.

"Do you know what?" Professor Magbar shook his head. Zones thought for a moment. He stroked his goatee. Water pelting the window distracted him while a light rain fell. He remembered the report prepared by the crime lab and Georgia Tech on the liquid confiscated from Dr. El-Arabi's lab and home. Zones ripped the folder from his case, thumbed through papers and pulled out the report. "Does this mean anything to you?" He shoved the paper at Dr. Kumani. He lifted a pair of glasses hanging from a chain around his neck and put them up to his eyes.

"These are water analyses."

"Yeah, but what do they mean?"

"According to the TPH test, the water shows traces of petrochemicals. From the chemical makeup, the sample is from the Middle East."

"Where *exactly*?"

"API gravity…sulfur content…I'd say Saudi Arabia."

"It's a big country, Doctor. Can you narrow it down to at least a town or city?"

Dr. Kumani got up from his chair and walked to a large bookcase against a wall. He stepped on a small ladder, plucked a binder from a shelf and returned to his seat. He flipped open the thick, blue binder stuffed with papers and snatched out a magazine article. He handed it to Zones. "You can start here."

Zones took it. The caption to the article read, *Qatif, Saudi Arabia: The price we pay for oil.*

* * *

Ali dropped Zones at the Howard Hotel. He stood in the lobby and waited his turn at check-in. He looked around—same ceiling, same walls, same ugly-ass carpet. He hadn't been back to the campus since writing his dissertation. The hotel had been convenient while working on his research. Being on a campus full of beautiful black women didn't hurt either. For now, more pressing matters needed his attention—how to get into Saudi Arabia for starters. Zones slipped his phone from his coat and dialed.

"Monk," Sam shouted through the phone. "Where're you, boy?"

"Listen, you know anyone in the State Department?"

"That's too high up the food chain for me. Why?"

"I need to get into Saudi Arabia, and they don't give out tourist visas."

"Now, why in the hell do you want to go to Saudi Arabia?"

"…The case."

"…The bombings? I guess coming close to dying at the hands of terrorists at home ain't good enough for you. Now you want to go where they make them sons of bitches."

"Don't you get all concerned now; you pushed this case on me. I'm just following the evidence."

"I didn't know it would mean you having to go and fuck with Ishmael."

"Well, it is what it is. I have to go." Zones moved up to the counter.

"Dr. Zones, I just found you a room." The desk clerk handed him his room key.

Zones made his way to the room. He hopped on the bed and thought hard about his predicament. He needed to go to Saudi Arabia if he was going to learn the truth behind the bombings. He had obviously gotten close. Someone had tried to kill him, but who? Only Marmaduke knew about his travels to DC. *The Islamic Center, someone from there must have called the gunmen*, Zones concluded. His theory, however, left room for only one perpetrator. It seemed the deeper he dug into this case, the more convoluted things got. He needed help and soon.

Zones pulled his iPad from his case and booted it up. He logged onto the Compiled Database of Religious Symbols stored at Howard's School of Theology. He'd helped develop the database for his dissertation. He searched for the names of his colleagues who compiled the data for the Asian continent. Ten names popped onto the screen, two for the Middle East. He checked the time, 6 P.M. *There's a seven hour difference so that makes it one in the morning* in *Riyadh.* He would call in the morning. Zones picked up the hotel phone and dialed, requesting a 4 A.M. wake-up call.

* * *

The alarm sounded an irritating noise. Zones rolled to the edge of the bed and slapped at the phone. The alarm still blared. He picked up the receiver and the sound stopped. He dropped it back down. The clock next to the phone read 4 A.M. on the dot. He turned toward the window. The night still lingered. He wanted more sleep but knew he had to get up.

Zones swung his legs to the edge of the bed and pushed up, flipped on a light, struggled to his feet and headed into the bathroom. He showered, dressed and then called Riyadh.

"As-salaam alaikum," the voice on the other end said.

"Alaikum salaam. Is this Dr. Ayad?"

"Who is this?"

"Doctor, this is Thelonious Zones calling from the United States."

"Dr. Zones the criminalist, yes, I was expecting your call."

"How is that?"

"Is there a number I can call you back on? The phones here at the university need a bit of exterminating. Do you understand, Dr. Zones?"

"Sure, the connection is quite bad." Zones called out his number and hung up. In no time, his phone rang.

"Dr. Zones, this should give us freedom to speak."

"Tell me why you were expecting my call."

"Ever since the government announced the study, we've been getting calls from many law enforcement and criminology professionals worldwide."

Zones said nothing. He ran to his case lying on the chair next to the window. He booted his iPad and logged onto the internet, the phone still to his ear. In Google search, he typed, *Saudi Arabia + criminal study.* A number of hits popped up. One stood out. He read it. He had no idea what the study meant but didn't want to lose this opportunity.

"You're referring to the Qatif study, are you not, Doctor?"

"Of course I am. If you ask me, something seems a little fishy, but I'm just a low-level administrator. The government will allow only a handpicked few to review the data. The Kingdom has not quite grasped the concept of unbiased peer review."

"So why all the calls if the kingdom won't release the data?"

"To quiet their international critics, a presentation is scheduled, the results being the main topic. I assume you will be visiting."

"I can't get a visa."

"Say no more. You are now the newest visiting professor of business psychology at Dar Al Uloom University. My brother works at the embassy in Washington. Your visa will be ready within the hour. Where should I have it delivered?

"I'm in Washington, staying at the Howard Hotel."

"I'll have it left at the front desk. Call me at this number when you are scheduled to arrive. I'll meet you at the airport. And, Dr. Zones, if it's not too much trouble, a bean pie from the brothers would be much appreciated."

Zones pressed *End* on his phone. He scanned through the short article on the Qatif study. The Saudi government had managed to eliminate an already low crime rate, or so it seemed. *If I was a dictator, I could reduce crime too.* Zones flipped his iPad closed. The study was now his entry into the country.

* * *

Zones collected his things and picked up the visa from the front desk. He entered one of the cabs parked outside the hotel. He stopped at a haberdashery for some new clothing, the Masjid Muhammad for a box of bean pies, and then headed to Dulles International.

Zones' phone rang. "Hello, gorgeous."

"Where're you and what've you done wrong?" James asked.

"Why must I've done something wrong just because I paid you a compliment?"

"'Cause, that's the same thing my first ol' man used to do right after he'd been with some skank whore. So again, where're you and what've you done?"

"You don't want to know is my answer to your first and second question. What's up?"

"The captain is looking for you. He wants to know why you missed the questioning of the owner and the secretary of the bombed-out brokerage."

"Just tell him Detective Marmaduke felt it best that I not be there."

"Marmaduke felt it best?"

"Don't need two hands in a one-hand pot my grandmother always said."

"Look at you, getting all countrified."

"What can I say? The South is rubbing off on me."

The cab driver turned to Zones as they approached the terminal. "What airline, sir?"

"Lufthansa."

"Airline…Lufthansa?" James said. "You're leaving the country? What goose chase are you off on now, Doctor?"

"You have access to the FAA database, don't you?"

"…Yeah I do, but why?"

"The victim from the animal shelter, Muhammad El-Arabi, visited Saudi Arabia a week before he died. I need to know what city."

"You're going to the Middle East."

"And it's best that the captain doesn't know."

"Oh, the captain will be the least of your worries if you fuck up over there."

"Tell me about it."

"This is Lufthansa, sir," the driver said. "Your fare is one hundred and twenty dollars."

Zones paid the driver and leapt from the cab.

"Now, James, about Mr. El-Arabi and his—"

"I got it. He flew into Riyadh and, according to his credit card, stayed in some hostel in Dammam—the Tulip Inn."

"Dammam? Where's that?"

"Do I look like National Geographic? I also see charges here from Qatif."

"Are those on the same day?"

"…The Dammam and Qatif charges? Some of them."

"Then they must be near each other."

"According to Google Earth, they're thirty minutes apart by car."

"Text me a few of the places he visited. Thanks, James."

"Hold on. What do I tell the captain?"

"That I went to see—"

"The turkey take to water. Yeah, yeah, Marmaduke told me you said that shit. My mother used to tell my sisters and me the same damn thing when she didn't want us to know about her pony playing."

"There you go."

Zones hung the phone up. He stopped at the flight departure board; International Flight LH9051 to Riyadh was on time.

THIRTY-SEVEN

Sand Land

THE PLANE JUDDERED IN the wind. Zones clamped his hand over a glass of sparkling water and fruit juice. Faux liquor, he called it. Muslims didn't tolerate alcohol or pork in their countries. Saudi Arabia had a particular aversion to both, it being their holy land.

The plane broke through the clouds and flew into a low altitude auburn-colored sky. Sand caught up by the wind swirled in the air and caused a haze to hover over the city. Zones pulled the window shade down. The same young sun that saw him off from Washington now greeted him on a new morning in Riyadh.

They landed hard and bounced around a little. He exited the plane and entered the terminal. Unlike Dulles, King Khalid International could use some business. Only a few men in long, white garments and head scarves milled about.

Zones made his way to customs. He carried his case and a carefully wrapped box of bean pies with him. A guard waved him forward. He shouted something in Arabic.

"As-salaam—" Zones started. The guarded shouted again before he could finish. He snatched the box of bean pies from him.

Someone called out from across the terminal. The guard's head snapped around. Zones turned to see Dr. Ayad fast approaching. He snatched the box from the guard. The two spoke quickly back and forth, hands gesturing in the air. Dr. Ayad whipped a card from his coat pocket and shoved it into the guard's face. He scanned it. The guard looked at Dr. Ayad and then at Zones. He mumbled something and waved him through.

"I am sorry, Dr. Zones. There are some who still do not like foreigners visiting our country."

"Thanks for meeting me at the terminal."

"It is the least I can do since you have come such a long way. Besides, I have a treat." He raised the box of bean pies.

"I hope they've fared better than I have from the plane ride."

"Bruised bean pie is better than no bean pie at all, Dr. Zones." Dr. Ayad laughed and led Zones through the airport. They passed signs in English saying *Baggage* and *Transportation*. Arrows pointed the way. "What was your flight number?"

"...9051, why?"

"You have no bags?"

"I hadn't planned on staying long." Dr. Ayad frowned. "I mean, reviewing the report shouldn't take too long, especially if your government has released incomplete data."

"I guess you are right. Then we shall go to my office. The meeting isn't for several hours."

"Actually, I was hoping to tour the area."

"Sure, Riyadh has a number of tourist places. There's the—"

"I was thinking more of Dammam and Qatif."

"Dr. Zones, I'm afraid that will not be possible."

"Why? Wasn't the study done there?"

"Yes, but—"

"...But, what? They've gotten rid of all the crime, according to your government. It should be the safest place in the world."

"The area is mostly Shiite. They wouldn't welcome a stranger."

"Even with a guide?"

"A guide...you mean me?"

They pushed through the doors of the terminal out into the hot desert air and grit-filled winds. They raced across a road and into a parking area. Doctor Ayad pressed one hand tight to his head and the other holding the box of bean pies. The tail of his headdress flapped wildly in the air. It whipped back and forth like the tail on a kite. Zones cupped his mouth with one hand and shielded his eyes with the other. His ears were left to fend for themselves. They rushed toward a silver Mercedes SUV, got inside and brushed the sand from their faces.

"I need a shower after that," Zones said.

Dr. Ayad looked over at him. "Now, what is this about me taking you to Qatif?"

"I just want to see the proof for myself, what they are claiming. It'll be too late for any questions after they give their presentation."

"I guess you're right, but let me do the talking. The last thing I need to explain is a dead American on my hands."

* * *

A dusty town sprang up from the horizon. The gray buildings had little hint of color anywhere. The people were varied—some light, others swarthy—but all were Muslim.

"Turn left right here," Zones said. He held his iPhone up and followed the GPS. They continued a distance down the road. "Pull in here."

"The Tulip Inn? Why are we stopping here? Is this where you are staying?" Zones rolled down the window and poked his head from the car. The smell of salty water rode on streams of air blowing off the Persian Gulf. The blue neon sign anchored to the wall was in Arabic and English; it flickered. Zones popped the door open and eased one foot out. "Hey, where are you going?" Dr. Ayad jumped from the car.

"I'm going inside."

"Is this where you are staying?"

"Are you coming?"

Dr. Ayad scurried to the other side of the car. "Dr. Zones, there are much better accommodations in Riyadh. Please, let me arrange for more pleasant surroundings."

Zones grabbed his case. He slid across the soft, leather seats and eased his body from the car. "This will do." He slammed the door behind him and headed for the hostel's entrance. Dr. Ayad walked lockstep with Zones as they entered through glass doors. A young, dark-haired man dressed in western clothes greeted them from behind a granite-topped counter. He said something in Arabic and pressed his right hand against his chest. Dr. Ayad replied in Arabic and gestured in kind.

"This is Dr. Zones. He would like one of your best rooms."

"Welcome to the Tulip Inn. My name is Ahmad." Zones sat his case down and stuck his hand out. Ahmad looked at it and then grabbed it. "For how long do you wish to stay?"

"I'm not sure, perhaps a few days."

"You are in luck, Dr. Zones. Come, I will show you our best rooms. This is not our busy season, so we have many to choose from and for only three hundred and fifty, U.S."

"Per night? That's pretty steep. A friend of mine stayed here two weeks ago and only paid a hundred and twenty-five dollars a night."

"Do you know which room he stayed in?"

"No, can't you check?"

"What is your friend's name?"

"...Muhammad El-Arabi."

Ahmad typed at the computer's keyboard. "Oh yes, Muhammad."

"Do you know him?"

"I checked him in. He stayed in room 105. It is one of our modestly priced rooms."

"He was here visiting family in Dammam."

"He was here but not to visit family."

"Oh, then why was he here?"

"If I recall correctly, he said he had business in Qatif."

"What's in Qatif?"

"A lot of our guests go there on business to the oil fields."

"...Euro-Arabia?"

"And others." Ahmad continued to peck away at the keyboard. "I can let you have that room for ninety-five dollars, U.S. It is our off-season price. Would you like to see it?"

"That won't be necessary. Here's my card." Ahmad took it. Zones turned to Dr. Ayad. "Let's go to Qatif?"

"I do not understand, Dr. Zones. Why would you want to stay here rather than in Riyadh? Do you not know that there has been unrest in the area?"

"According to the study, there is no more crime or unrest."

"As I have told you before, something smells fishy with that study."

"We shall see."

* * *

The silver Mercedes raced east and then north. The sign read, *Route 95.* Dr. Ayad barreled down the highway toward Qatif, kicking up dust from the road. The car's wiper blades scraped against the windshield, clearing a patch of glass on both sides. They drove for half an hour before they reached town.

"Where exactly are we going in Qatif?"

"There's a restaurant there, I bet."

"…A restaurant? But there were plenty of places to eat in Dammam." Zones looked at Dr. Ayad but said nothing. "Why do I get the feeling this has nothing to do with the study, Dr. Zones?"

"Turn right at the next street. I'm looking for the Al-Tanour."

"There it is." Dr. Ayad pointed ahead of him, pulled off the road and parked in front of the eatery. "What are we doing here, Dr. Zones? First, we went to the hostel and now this place. You seem to be following this Muhammad character. What has he done?"

"…Got himself killed, for one."

"Why are you following a dead man?"

"I'm helping his family find out who killed him. Muhammad had just returned from a trip to Saudi Arabia before he was killed."

"He was killed in America?"

"Yes."

"Then the murderer is in America, not here."

"It's a little more complicated than that."

"More complicated? You Americans complicate everything. With Arabs, things are black and white. You steal; we cut off your hand. You kill anyone and we kill you, quickly. Our heads are not filled with all the different shades of gray that you must keep up with."

"Now that you've analyzed the American psyche, can we go?"

"Yes, but this time let me do the talking. Qatif is not Dammam. The Shia are not happy these days. Saying the wrong word could cause us both to lose our heads."

Men eating sandwiches and sipping hot tea filled the small shop. They sat shoulder to shoulder and took long drags from pipes fashioned like gaudy lamp bases. Plumes of smoke clouded the air. Zones tugged at his collar as he coughed and sniffed. Well-worn, long faces and untrusting eyes locked on him, shifting only when two men were overheard arguing over a game they played.

Dr. Ayad wove through the tables and chairs—they were laid out in no particular order—and headed for the rear of the dark sandwich shop. Zones followed close behind. They found a table in the corner and sat. Music played; it was a mix of strumming guitars, tambourines and bongos. The only thing missing were the harem girls, dancing preferred.

A man stepped from behind a counter and headed toward their table. He cleared the empty cups and plates away and wiped the table down.

"You are American?" he whispered as he wiped. He looked off to the front of the shop. "You are either brave or foolish wandering this far from the city."

"We are neither," Dr. Ayad said.

"What are you doing here? It can't be the sandwiches that you seek."

"Where were you born, Liverpool, Birmingham?"

The man stopped wiping. He looked at Dr. Ayad. "…Sheffield."

"Ah, of course, you must be Yemeni."

"My mother is from Yemen, and my father is Saudi. You are very observant, like a spy."

"No, my friend, just—"

"We are friends of Muhammad El-Arabi," Zones said. The man froze. Dr. Ayad gave Zones a sharp look. "He was here two weeks ago. Why?"

"If he is your friend, you would not have to ask that question. Now, if you two gentlemen would excuse me, I have paying customers to attend to."

Zones grabbed the man's arm as he turned to leave. "Muhammad is dead." The man turned around; his eyes grew wide. "And I believe it has something to do with his visit here."

The man's gaze traveled from Zones to Dr. Ayad. "Follow me."

"Where to? How can we trust you?"

"If I wanted you dead, all I would need to do is shout that you are CIA."

They followed the man to a door at the rear of the shop.

"What is this all about?" Dr. Ayad whispered to Zones. "This sounds like more than just a simple homicide."

"It's best that you don't know, just in case something goes wrong."

"In case something goes wrong, like what?"

The man held the door open for them; they stepped through it and the door closed. Without notice, men jumped out from behind stacks of boxes. They grabbed Zones and Dr. Ayad.

"What the fuck? I'm gonna kill you," Zones snarled, immediately knowing he had been betrayed. He shoved one man off, sending him to the ground. Another man charged him, shouting unintelligible words. As he drew near, he swung. Zones stepped back, out of reach of his long arcing fist. The man stumbled forward. He gathered himself and lunged with a growl, his full weight behind him. His hands fisted, Zones sidestepped his charge, and he punched the man in the gut, sinking his fist deep into his flesh. The man doubled over and moaned. *Oh, it's on now motherfucka.* Next, Zones grabbed the man's head. He palmed it as he would a ball, raised his knee and with force drove it into his face. The man dropped to the floor, unmoving.

Zones reached for the door handle. Someone grabbed him in a bear hug from behind. He kicked off a wall. Both he and the man flew across the tight space and crashed into a stack of boxes. The man's grip loosened. Zones unleashed a torrent of blows with his elbow. He pivoted, now facing the man. The two of them squared off. Zones attacked first, seeing an opening, and landed a strike to the face. The man swung back but found no target. Zones eased backward, feeling caged. The man advanced, bobbing and weaving like an aged boxer. Zones measured him with a stiff jab to the forehead. The man continued to close the distance. Now within range, Zones raised his foot and kicked him in the head. The man's burly body fell back against another stack of boxes. Zones knew he had to finish him, and he charged the man, kicking him in the face and body. The man fell and slumped to the floor, out for the count. Zones turned to see Dr. Ayad pinned to the floor. He rushed over and shoved that man off him. He then raised his fist to strike him.

"Behind you, Dr. Zones!" Dr. Ayad shouted. Zones turned and just as quickly, the man from the sandwich shop slipped a small sack over his head. Everything went dark as Zones tugged at the sack. A few seconds later, he was bludgeoned with a heavy object; the pain was intense.

THIRTY-EIGHT

"...ain't no oil in Harlem."

THE SACK FLEW OFF and darkness turned into a flood of light. Zones squeezed his eyes tightly. His pain remained, and the light gave him no balm. He tried to rub his head, but his hand would not move. He was seated and tied to a chair; his hands secured behind his back.

Zones heard voices. He squinted, and through the slits of his eyes, he saw forms moving back and forth.

"Wake up, Dr. Zones, if that's your real name." Someone patted him on the face. Zones moaned. His left eye was forced open as he looked into the face of the man from the sandwich shop. "You hurt my friends very, very badly. They are quite angry at you."

"Looks to me like they need fighting lessons."

"You Americans are funny. Like...Eddies Murphys." Zones laughed. "You are in peril, yet you laugh."

"Listen...what's your name?"

"...Lateef."

"Listen, Lateef, tell me what this is about, and we can try to clear up this misunderstanding."

"A misunderstanding? Is that what you think this is?" Lateef paced around Zones. He stopped behind him and leaned close to his right ear while slurping the last of a Coke through a straw. Zones turned his head. "I understand the situation perfectly. You are CIA and now you are my captive. American spies fetch a considerable price in these parts." He stood straight, spoke something in Arabic and laughed with the others. They left Zones and Dr. Ayad in the room stacked with boxes.

"What did he say?" Zones asked Dr. Ayad, who was tied up next to him.

"He said that al-Qaida and Hezbollah will pay handsomely to have just half of you. We have to get out of here."

"No kidding." Zones scanned the room. "You wouldn't happen to have a knife, would you?"

"This is no time for jokes, Dr. Zones. When they return, we can both kiss our heads good-bye."

"Perhaps not. You see that empty Coke bottle?"

"Unless you are a magician, we are still tied up, and that bottle is a good fifteen feet away."

Zones scooted his chair, inch by inch. Its legs scraped the concrete, making a loud, irritating noise. He reached the bottle; it was sitting on the edge of a box five feet above the floor. He rocked his chair. The back side of it struck the boxes. The bottle teetered along the edge before it fell onto the floor, making a loud popping noise and shattering into small pieces at the same time.

There was a bang at the door. Zones froze and Dr. Ayad mimicked him as their eyes locked on the door. They waited, expecting someone to charge through. Seconds passed. Zones bit down on his bottom lip and lines of sweat streamed down his face. If only he had a little more time, he knew he could free himself.

Zones turned his chair around and rocked side to side. It balanced on two legs before tilting over, his shoulder hitting hard on the concrete floor. He grimaced, clenched his teeth but did not scream. Looking at the door, Zones felt around for a piece of glass. He grabbed at one and turned the sharp edge toward the rope. It could not reach; it was too small. He felt around the floor and grabbed at another—a larger piece this time. He fitted it into his right hand and sawed away at the rope binding his wrists. He felt the strands fray as he cut at the rope.

"Hurry, Dr. Zones," Dr. Ayad cheered him on in a whisper.

Zones continued to cut. The rope gave way and his hands slipped free. He cut the rope away from his legs and rolled from the chair. He grabbed his shoulder, massaged it and stood up slowly, aching in several places. Zones walked to the door, pressed his ear to it and listened. He rushed back to Dr. Ayad and cut him free.

"Are you okay?"

"It will take more than a few…how do you say…*sissies* to harm me. How do we get out of here? That seems to be the only exit." He nodded to the door.

"Who said we're going anywhere?"

"You are kidding, right?"

"Mr. Lateef knows something about why my victim was here, and I intend to find out what that is."

"Your victim? Are you CIA?"

"Not quite, I'm working a case for the FBI."

"That is no better. Why do you bring me into this?"

"I'm sorry, but I needed a cover."

"So you chose poor, dumb Baswan—me—to die with you." He rambled in Arabic.

Zones cut away the last of the rope. "I've got an idea."

"Is it one that will not get us killed, I hope?"

"We shall see. Don't move." Zones lifted the overturned chair and placed it just below the one light that hung from the ceiling. He stepped on top the chair and tapped the bulb with his fingers. "That's hot." He grabbed the sack used to cover his head and used it to unscrew the bulb from its socket. The room went dark. Zones hopped down from the chair.

"Dr. Zones, where are you?"

"Right here." Zones was standing next to him.

"What's the plan?"

"I'll hide behind the door and you call out to them. When they enter, I'll jump them. When I tell you to, screw the bulb back in."

"*That's* your plan?"

"Yeah, best I got."

"What if this plan doesn't work?"

"Then we pray they use a sharp knife." Zones walked to the other side of the room and hid behind the door. "Okay, go ahead and yell for them."

Dr. Ayad yelled in Arabic. Zones banged on the door and pressed his ear against it. As soon as he heard voices and footsteps, he stepped back. The knob turned, and the door was flung open. Zones peeked through the gap between it and the jamb. One of the men stood there with nothing but blackness before him. Zones heard the click of the light switch and more words in Arabic. Dr. Ayad spoke again. The man came inside the room. Zones slammed the door shut and grabbed him around the neck from behind. They struggled. Zones wrestled the man to the floor and choked him to unconsciousness.

"Now, Doctor."

The light flashed on. Zones dragged the man's body across the room, tied him to the chair and covered his head with the same sack used on him. They repeated their ruse, screaming and yelling, until Lateef answered their call. Like the other two before him, he entered the darkened room. He flicked the light switch on, but this time the room lit up.

"Hassan…Saddiq," he called out from the doorway. One of the two men moaned; his head was covered and his body slumped in the chair. Lateef stepped into the room. As before, Zones slammed the door shut behind him. Lateef turned. Zones stood with his hands fisted, ready for action.

"I will kill you," Lateef shouted. He charged Zones. They wrestled. Dr. Ayad eased up behind Lateef and struck him on the head. He fell to the floor, out cold. Dr. Ayad stood over him, a can of peas taken from one of the boxes in his hand.

Zones dragged Lateef over to the other two men, both seated and unconscious. He kicked one of them from the chair and onto the floor. "Grab his feet." They propped Lateef in the chair and used leftover rope to tie him up.

A knock came at the door. "Lateef," someone else called to him.

"I better go and divert him."

Zones nodded and then walked to a door hidden behind a stack of boxes, shoving them to the side just enough to open the door. He found a closet with a sink and a pail in it. He filled the pail with water, carried it, and sat it next to the unconscious Lateef. Zones raised the pail and doused him with water. Lateef's head snapped back. He moaned.

"Hey, wake up." Zones slapped at his face. Lateef's head bobbled. Zones filled the pail with more water, grabbed Lateef's head and dunked him in it. Water spilled from the pail while Zones yanked his hair and pulled his head up from it. "Are you awake now?"

Lateef huffed and his eyes bulged. "I will have your head for this."

"Yeah, I know. Take your time. I understand that you're a little...*tied* up." Zones laughed.

"How long do you think you can keep me here before someone knows I'm missing?"

"Not very long, which is why you will tell me *now* what Muhammad El-Arabi was doing in Qatif."

"Go to hell. I tell you nothing."

"That's too bad." Zones grabbed a shard from the floor. He lifted the long, white gown Lateef was wearing and sliced it. He parted the material and ripped the garment in two, up to his waist. "Do you know what operant conditioning is?" Lateef said nothing, scowling as he watched Zones slice strips of cloth from his clothing. "It simply means that behavior will be repeated if it is rewarded. For example, you will not answer my questions if I reward you by not punishing you. You understand?" Lateef still said nothing. "It doesn't matter. Because the real question is, what kind of punishment do I need to exact to change your behavior? And for that, you must know your subject."

"I am not afraid of you. We love death as much as you love life."

Next, Zones sliced one of Lateef's pant legs and ripped it apart up to his groin. "You think Americans are soft, that at the first sight of a threat we tuck tail and run. You think we are intolerant of pain, but you are wrong. Our psyche is much different than you think. The death sentence for many crimes is enacted swiftly in your country. Our system of justice is long and protracted. We tolerate slight and insult, but to you these are capital offenses. We question the acts of God. You ask nothing, following blindly." Zones tied a piece of rope around Lateef's thigh.

"What are you doing?"

"Do you know anything about the Inquisition?"

"I am not ignorant, you—"

"It was a rhetorical question." Zones slit Lateef's inner thigh with the shard of glass. Blood dripped from the wound and pooled on the floor below him. He screamed and shouted in Arabic.

The door to the room was flung open, and Dr. Ayad stuck his head inside. "What are you doing? What is taking you so long?"

"Close the door."

"I can't keep up this charade for very long, Dr. Zones."

"I'll be finished soon."

Dr. Ayad eased the door closed. Zones snatched the headdress from the man in the other chair and shoved it into Lateef's mouth. He wrapped a strip of cloth around his head to secure it. It muffled his screams.

Zones continued to cut strips of cloth from Lateef's clothing. "The inquisitors used *tortura rata* to extract confessions from those they suspected of apostasy. They made slits in the abdomen of the accused and inserted rats they had sufficiently starved. The rats ate their way through the intestines. Do you know that the human body has over twenty feet of intestines?" Zones held the strips of cloth beneath the dripping blood. He tied one around Lateef's thigh near the wound and stretched the others out along the floor over to a corner of the room. Zones cut another slit in Lateef's thigh. He squirmed in the chair as the blood flow increased. Rats began to crawl out from hiding. "The rat has a highly developed sense of smell, many times more sensitive than humans. They're also veracious eaters. A pack can devour a carcass in minutes." Zones walked to the door and cut the light. The room went dark. Within minutes, muffled moans grew louder. He flicked the light back on and noticed a pack of rats covering Lateef's leg. His eyes were stretched the size of an Arabian moon. He tried to shake the rats off, but they clung tight. Zones walked back behind the chair. "What was Muhammad doing here?" Lateef nodded and Zones snatched the gag from his mouth.

"Get them off. Get them off!" He gasped for air.

"Muhammad?"

"He was asking about the oil fields."

"...Which oil fields?"

"...Euro-Arabia."

"Who did he meet with?"

"I don't know. He came in, asked if he could have some water and left. I heard that he repeatedly asked the same thing at other shops as well."

"That's it? He just asked for water?"

"Yes, now get them off."

Zones fanned the rats away. They leapt from Lateef's leg and scattered back into their holes. Zones picked his coat and case up off the floor and headed for the door.

"Untie me!"

"And have you and your goons chase us down to decapitate us? Not a chance. I'll untie the big one. When he wakes up, he can untie you." Lateef yelled Arabic curses at the top of his voice. Zones grabbed the headdress and shoved it back into his mouth. He cut the light and closed the door behind him.

At the front of the shop, Dr. Ayad served sandwiches and poured drinks for the patrons. The shop still brimmed with people. Zones stopped just outside the storage room door. He eyed Dr. Ayad, nodded, and darted straight for the exit. The Doctor stepped from behind the counter and joined him. They both wove their way through the tables and headed out the door, walking at a fast pace toward the silver Mercedes SUV. Zones turned his head around and saw men running toward their car.

"Let's go." Zones slammed the car door shut. Dr. Ayad fished the key from his pocket and jammed it into the ignition. The car fired up. He shifted into reverse and hit the gas. They backed out of the parking space, reversed direction and tore down the street. Tires squealed and kicked up dust. The SUV fishtailed and nearly crashed. Gunfire sounded. Bullets pelted the outside of the vehicle as glass shattered and sprayed the interior of the car.

Dr. Ayad shook his finger at Zones, "You are going to get me killed."

"Don't you mean *us*?"

"Who gives a shit about you? If you don't give a damn about your own life, *brlahem el Allah,* may God have mercy; just keep me out of it."

They traveled south through the desert. The Mercedes rattled as they bounced around inside it. The wind picked up; sand devils twirled and danced in the distance. The wipers screeched back and forth to clear the grit from the windshield. The clouds parted as midday approached.

Zones pulled the passenger-side visor down in front of him. He glanced at the fuel gauge on the dashboard.

"You need gas."

"We are good."

"What do you mean good? You've got less than a quarter of a tank."

"I said we are good."

Zones threw up his hands and gazed out the window, seeing nothing but a sea of sand. In the distance, structures peeked above the horizon. "What is that?"

"…The Qatif oil fields."

"Who runs it?"

"Euro-Arabia."

"Stop the car!"

"What? No, no more. We are going back to Riyadh, to the presentation."

"A look, I just want to take a quick look."

"I am not listening." Dr. Ayad pressed a button on the dashboard. Music poured from speakers. Zones watched the structures get closer and then fade in the rearview mirror. He couldn't help but wonder what role the oil company had in this whole thing. *Did Muhammad discover a fracking mishap or something much more serious?*

The car jerked forward and sputtered, slowed to a crawl and stopped. "What's wrong?" Zones asked.

"I do not know. It just stopped."

"Pop the hood." Zones hopped out, walked to the front of the car and lifted the hood. He jumped back; the heat from the engine smacked him in the face. "Shit!"

"What do you see, Dr. Zones?"

"Nothing yet." Zones fanned at the heat. He eased back up over the engine and looked it over. He sniffed the air and then got down on one knee. Something was dripping from beneath the vehicle. Zones made his way to the rear of the SUV and stuck his finger in a large hole. "I think we took a bullet to the gas tank."

"That is not good. The closest station is over ten miles away. We will have to thumb it."

"What?"

"Thumb it, you know." Dr. Ayad fisted his right hand and stuck out his thumb.

"Oh yeah, thumb it. How long do you think before someone comes by?"

"It could be minutes or hours. Allah knows."

"What about calling AAA?"

"I do not have."

"I say we start walking." He collected his case from the car and they started down the long, vacant road. "My grandfather used to say, 'The rain will come when the well is already full.'So once we get going a bit, a car will come along."

"Let us hope that is not the case." Dr. Ayad opened the box of bean pies, unwrapped one and sank his teeth into it. A wide smile grew on his face. "Were it not for these, I would have left you back there with those mujahideen."

A truck approached and Zones ran to the middle of the road, waving his hands. The truck slowed to a stop just ahead of him. Dr. Ayad spoke to the driver from the passenger-side window. He gestured. "Come, Dr. Zones." They piled onto the back of the truck; it was filled with watermelons.

* * *

The truck pulled up to a high, masonry wall with security wire running along the top of it. A sign out front read, *Prince Mohammed bin Nayef Center for Counseling and Care.* Zones and Dr. Ayad hopped from the truck's bed, waving to the driver as the truck pulled away. They walked to a large gate that was partially ajar, squeezing through the opening. A short, bearded man with a potbelly met them.

"We are here for the presentation."

The man looked them over. "...Your names?"

"I am Dr. Ayad and this is Dr. Zones."

The man scanned a paper. "*He* is not on the list."

"He is new to our faculty."

The man stared hard at Zones before turning back to Dr. Ayad. They spoke in Arabic. All Zones made out was *Americana and Denzel Washington.* The man snatched open a door; he stepped to the side and allowed them to pass.

"What did you say to him?"

"He said they already had Americans here. I told him you were making a film. He wants Denzel Washington to play him."

"Don't we all."

Another man, dressed in a white gown and a checkerboard headdress, escorted them to a room filled with other people. They found seats to the rear of the darkened room. Light from a projector beamed onto a white backdrop. A man clicked through slides and addressed the gathered crowd.

"This line of the graph shows the number of jihadists before, and this line shows the number after implementing the protocol treatment." The man waved a red beam of light over the screen. "As you can see, the line is virtually flat, indicating no activity in Qatif and Dammam." He clicked to the next slide. "This represents the rate of recidivism prior to the protocol, this bar here. There is no indication of same after implementing the protocol because it is zero. We have had no lapse by any of the subjects who underwent the protocol."

A hand shot up at the front of the room. "Will the supporting documentation be made available for peer review?"

"You have all that you will receive in your packet...Lights please?" The room brightened. "We will now tour the facility. Please gather your things and follow me."

Zones and Dr. Ayad filed out of the room with the others. They toured a well-equipped gym; men ran on treadmills and lounged around in Jacuzzis. They visited the inmates' living and dining quarters and a volleyball court where they batted a ball around dressed in their long, white gowns.

"We will now visit one of our educational classes." The man led them back inside to another room. Men sat around at school desks and listened to a lecture. A man stood at a whiteboard.

Zones whispered to Dr. Ayad, "What is he saying?"

"He is explaining the definition of jihad and when it is permissible."

"Are these men terrorists?"

"It would seem so, Dr. Zones."

"So this is how your government deals with terrorists; they coddle them and send them to a spa? No wonder this war will last forever. Do they expect us to believe this shit?"

"I do not know."

"Ask him if they've killed anyone?"

"Why do you want to know that?"

"I want to know if they're going to release hardcore terrorists back out into the world." Dr. Ayad raised his hand and asked the question. The man replied. Those sitting at the desks laughed. "What did he say that's so fucking funny?"

"He said they have not killed any Muslims."

"That's comforting. I've seen enough." Zones checked the time on his phone. "If I hurry, I can catch a standby on the next flight back to the states. You got any place where I can clean up?"

* * *

Zones, fresh off his flight from Riyadh, poked his head through Sam's open door. "Hey."

"Monk, you back in one piece, boy? I done increased your insurance policy and everything." Sam laughed.

"Funny. I need a place to crash."

"Shit no, ain't somebody trying to kill you? I know we're family and all, but I can't afford to get my nuts blown off. I got more babymaking to do. You can't shack with some piece of ass for a minute?"

"Someone is trying to kill me because of you."

"Are you still tripping on that? You're worse than a woman when it comes to holding a grudge." Zones entered the office and took a seat. "Well, come in, what the fuck." Sam got up from his desk and walked to a counter; he poured two cups of coffee. "You still like it black?"

"Like my women."

"I feel you, although there's nothing wrong with adding a little cream to the mix every now and then." Sam carried the two cups back to his desk. "Tell me about your trip to Saudi Arabia. Did you find out anything related to the case?"

"I'm not sure. I retraced Muhammad El-Arabi's footsteps, but apparently all he did was collect water samples from merchants in Qatif."

"No one goes all that way to collect water."

"You do if you're an environmentalist and you suspect the oil industry there of contaminating the drinking water. The FBI *did* confiscate a water sample from the lab at Tech."

"But they didn't find anything."

"...At first, no. The sample had been switched, we presumed by Professor Landrosky. Dr. El-Arabi turned over other samples his son had given him. We had a professor at Tech, Dr. Wong, analyze those. He found a nanoprotein and petrochemical contamination in the water. He and Dr. DeGlorious are trying to find out what it does."

"Sounds to me like you're chasing your ass."

"...Could be." Zones sipped his coffee. He scanned Sam's spacious office. Books lined almost every wall, mostly the classics. Their spines looked new and unbroken. Photographs were scattered all over the walls—some old, some new. One, in particular, drew his attention.

Zones got up from the chair and walked over to it, pressing his face as close as he could to the picture.

"…Harlem, 1985." Sam stood next to Zones. "That's me and that's Sheila on the left. Your father is on the right, and your mother is in the middle. That little turd she's about to shit out is you."

"I've never seen this picture before."

"…Really? It must be one Sheila dug out of her stuff. She decorated this place, you know. We took that in Chinatown, in front of the Midong."

"Midong…didn't Mom inspect that place?"

"How did you know that?"

"Is it still there?"

"They shut it down about four years after this picture was taken, too many health violations, if I remember correctly."

"T.O. said it was one of the few places Mom would eat."

"Your father would know. All I know is that shortly after it closed, they built a gas station there."

"I see." Zones gave the picture one long last stare. "Well, thanks for the coffee." He shoved the mug into Sam's chest and headed for the door. "By the way, what do you know about a terrorist rehabilitation program in Saudi Arabia?"

"You mean the bullshit program those ragheads concocted to get their boys released from Gitmo?"

"So the U.S. Government knows about the program?"

"Sure they do. Stonewall was one of its biggest proponents."

"Congressman Stonewall? But he's a hawk in the war on terror?"

"Even hawks gotta eat."

"How do you mean?"

"Shit, Monk, do I have to draw you a picture? The congressman and the Saudis are dick in hand with each other."

"How do you know that? They don't usually advertise any deal-making with dictators."

"Because I tried to get funds for a similar program for the brothers after they've been released from the joint."

"Why were you denied?"

"…Because there ain't no oil in Harlem."

"So it's a money thing."

"No, we just put up with them manufacturing terrorists and blowing our shit up because it helps to keep the population in check. Of course, it's about the money. You let the Congo dispatch a bunch of niggas out to the world and they do some of the shit you see the Arabs doing. There would be a big-ass hole right in the middle of the African continent from the bombs we would drop on their heads. The country's name would be changed to *Co-go*."

"What about Somalia? They're hijacking boats and kidnapping people."

"No, they're hijacking and kidnapping stupid white people who think they can go to Africa like they're Jane Goodall in *Gorillas in the Mist* and cuddle up with them niggas."

"You mean Dian Fossey?"

"Who the fuck ever, the point is Somalis are too damn poor to buy a plane ticket to travel anywhere. I was in Mogadishu in the eighties before the Civil War, and they were shit poor back then too. But, the Arabs got the oil." Sam walked the empty mugs over to a sink, sat them down and turned the faucet on. He washed the cups, dried them and turned them over on the counter. "Why are you asking about this program anyway?"

"I visited a center in Riyadh. It was part of some study the Saudis were touting as a miraculous cure to crime."

"You think it has something to do with the case?"

"I don't see how. The place was a joke."

"Then, why go?"

"It was the only way I could get a visa to enter the country; I had to attend a presentation given by their government."

"Well, you're back in one piece."

"I still have my head." Zones walked to his office and the phone rang. "...Zones here."

"You're back," Marmaduke said. "It's about damn time. Let me know the next time you decide to take a vacation in the middle of a case."

"It was no vacation, believe me. What do you want, Detective?"

"The music festival starts in one hour. The captain wants all hands on deck as a show of force, that means you too."

"I'll be there in a minute."

"Nope, Captain wants me to escort you personally. I'll see you in twenty."

THIRTY-NINE
Chasing a Bomber

THE TORTUROUS SOUNDS OF young-folk songs and juvenile laughter escaped between the tight and wide-open spaces of downtown Decatur. The city was located on the site of the old Sandtown and Shallowford Indian trails, marked by a sign that declared its love of God, knowledge and family. Music drifted high and low, filtering through bistros, bars and eateries. A band's rendition of "Losing My Religion" settled on the surrounding neighborhood of bungalow-styled homes and high-spired churches. People hung from their balconies that overlooked the drum-beating, string-plucking and spirit-possessed dancing. They milled about the shops and vendor tents that landscaped the streets and sidewalks. Children tugged at their parents' arms and dragged them to every corner of the festival, hoping to experience all the wonderful things they saw.

Zones strolled down East Ponce, hands tucked in his pockets, Ray-Bans shielding his eyes. He scanned the crowd for anything or anyone that looked out of place. Between the hippie-looking types and the button-down stuffed shirts, everyone seemed normal. Red barricades stood at the entrance to streets around the square. Cars rolled along slowly on the outer streets and wound their way through the mesh of people crisscrossing in front of them. They honked their horns and raced their engines when the crowds grew thick, impeding their progress. Zones' radio squealed. A voice announced, "All clear in green." He took a left onto Church Street and crossed the old courthouse square. People stuffed themselves around a stage, like trying to put a too big foot into a small shoe. The band played and people danced. Music boomed from large speakers that flanked both sides of the raised platform. The noise drowned out any private thoughts he may have had.

Zones stopped at the cart of a street vendor and plucked one bottled water from a barrel filled with ice. "How much?"

"…Two dollars."

Zones raised the eight-ounce bottle to his eyes, lifted his shades and read the label. "I don't see Evian written here." He cut the vendor a long look.

"And you don't see free on it either, two dollars," the man and his straggly beard smiled. Zones pulled out his wallet and paid the man his last two dollars.

"Thank you kindly, sir."

Zones cracked open the cap and chugged the water. Someone shoved him from behind, causing him to spill some of it. Zones turned to see Marmaduke behind him.

"There you are, Doc."

"Damn, man, that was my last swallow."

Marmaduke reached over into the same barrel and pulled two bottled waters out. "Here you go, Doc." He tossed one to Zones; he twisted off the cap and raised the bottle to his lips.

"That'll be four dollars."

"What?" Marmaduke scowled.

"The water, they're two dollars each."

Marmaduke curled his lips. "Please." He took a swig of water.

"I'm calling the police," the vendor shouted.

"You see that?" Marmaduke whipped out his badge. "Now pipe down."

"Where were you five minutes ago?" Zones asked. He gulped the rest of his water.

"You seen or heard anything?"

"Other than bad music and bad dancing, no, I have not. What about you?"

"A lot of T and A, not that I'm complaining. I just don't like getting that horny feeling, you know?" Zones shook his head. Marmaduke cracked the cap from another bottle of water. A hand snatched it from him. "What the…"

"Thanks, Marmaduke." Detective Rome appeared beside him. "You two on the job or working on your tans?"

"This isn't your zone."

"You don't think I know my colors, Detective?" She took a swig of water. "I got my eyes on a little bird."

"…Where?"

"Three o'clock, coming up the stairs. Camouflage coat and hood carrying a backpack. I tailed her from East Trinity, coming out of Twain's."

"How can you tell it's a she underneath that hood and all those clothes?"

"I don't know too many men who wear fuchsia fingernail polish."

The suspect moved across the square, stopped, looked behind her, and then continued. She eased the backpack off her shoulders and lowered it on top of a planter next to the courthouse steps. It rested there for a moment. The crowd thickened.

Zones moved to another spot on the square and shoved people to the side, out of his line of sight. "Do you see her?" he asked Marmaduke. He, in turn, looked to Detective Rome. She shook her head. Zones climbed a nearby tree. He scanned the crowd, looking for the suspect.

"You see anything?" Marmaduke asked.

Zone leapt down from the tree. "She's removing something from the backpack."

"Let's go take a look."

They moved through the crowd, Marmaduke taking point with Zones and Detective Rome flanking his left and right respectively. Just as they broke through to the other side of the square, the suspect looked up. Zones froze. They locked eyes. Her head swiveled to Marmaduke and then to Detective Rome. She reached into the backpack and pulled out two canisters. Zones moved forward. She hurled a canister at him and the other at Marmaduke. Zones dove to the ground. Smoke engulfed the square.

"Do you see her?" Marmaduke shouted. He coughed and gasped for air.

Zones fanned at the smoke as people scattered. They stampeded each other and raced all around him. He pushed up from the ground and strained to see through the haze. A faint outline of someone in a hood caught his attention. The smoke cleared enough for him to see the camouflage jacket the suspect wore. "I got her." Zones dashed from the square and down a ramp, stopping at the bottom of it. His head snapped left toward a parking lot and then right to the Decatur MARTA station. A car pulled out of a space. Zones ran over to it. The black Toyota Celica screeched to a halt. The driver, an old woman, froze for a moment—bug-eyed, her mouth wide open—as she rolled down her window.

"I'm sorry. I didn't see you."

Zones backed away from the car and ran to the other end of the parking lot. He moved between the rows of parked vehicles and looked inside each one. The ground rumbled. He raced to the entrance of the station and hopped a fare gate. From the floor above, he watched a train pull up to the platform. The doors slid open and people poured out. Those waiting to board piled into the train. Zones studied them—*no camouflage coat.* A bell sounded, and the conductor announced the closing of the doors. Just as they slid closed, someone jumped from behind a pillar, grabbed the closing door and dashed onto the train. The doors popped back open.

"Hey!" Zones shouted. He tore down the steps and raced toward the train. The doors slid to a close again. He reached the last train car and managed to squeeze through a slither of open door. Passengers turned to see him stumble inside. He grabbed hold of a metal pole to steady himself. The train swayed and rumbled down the tracks as it pulled away from the station. Zones moved along the aisle. His head shifted left to right as he passed each seat. He reached out to remove a hood from the head of a passenger. The man turned and frowned. When he came to the last seat, he pushed through the door that connected to the next car. One car after the other, he made his way through the train, looking for the suspect.

Zones entered through the door of another car. The train slowed. *"Eastlake station next stop, Eastlake station..."* The brakes squealed and the car jerked. Passengers stood and clung to anything that would keep them upright. The train stopped, doors popped open, and passengers filed out. Zones stepped out onto the platform and trotted alongside the train, heading toward the engine. The familiar warning of the doors closing sounded. He hopped into another car and noticed one of the passengers sitting near the rear wearing a hooded, camouflaged coat. Fuchsia-colored nails poked from beneath its sleeve. Suddenly she jumped from her seat and bolted through the door before it was fully closed. Zones gave chase. She ran back onto the train and then off again, racing along the platform. Zones gained on her until he was close enough to tackle her hard to the granite floor, facedown. Zones rolled her over. She screamed and swung wildly at him. He pinned her arms and straddled her.

"I got you now. You're going to jail." Zones looked up to see two officers charging toward him. They wrestled him off of the suspect. "No! What're you doing?" They dragged him along the ground and pinned his arms behind him. The officers turned Zones flat on his stomach, one pressing a knee to his back. As his chin ground against the dirty floor, he looked up to see the suspect spring to her feet and race down the stairs. The officers lifted Zones from the floor and hauled him off, his hands cuffed behind him. As they led him away, he caught a glimpse of the subject running across the street below. "You two have just fucked up big time," he told them.

* * *

"We're sorry, Marmaduke," one of the MARTA officers said. "All we saw was a big guy and a little woman."

"Don't sweat it." Marmaduke patted him on the back. "All you've done is let the number one terrorist in the country get away." He turned to Zones as they removed the cuffs from him. "So, Doc, did you get a good look at her? Was she the same girl from the first bomb scene?"

"I don't know." Zones rubbed his wrists. "I didn't see much of anything that night, too dark. Didn't they take pictures of her that night at the hospital?"

"Got to ask Detective Rome. She processed her at the hospital."

"By the way, where is she?"

"...Back at the station with ATF. I'm on my way there now."

They left the MARTA and headed for Marmaduke's car.

"Did you get anything from the bag she dropped?"

"I don't know about you, Doc, but I like all of my fingers and toes. Those crazy assholes from the bomb squad did all the peeking."

"What about the tape from the station?"

"Got it right here," Marmaduke patted his coat pocket. They hopped into his car and headed to the station. A phone rang. "Marmaduke here—okay, we're on our way." He slipped the phone back inside his coat pocket. "Well, Doc, it looks like the crime gods are through fucking with you."

"What do you mean?"

"They picked up your bomber."

"…The girl?"

"No, the guy, the one from the dog fighting farm."

FORTY

"…I'm protected."

CAPTAIN FRANKLIN SPEWED VENOM; it oozed through the cracks of his office door, landing on the ears of those nearby. James sat at her desk, headphones on as usual, eyes locked onto her computer screen. She pecked away at her keyboard as papers shot from the printer. She snatched them from the bin, shuffled them and added them to others. James stapled the stack of papers together and shoved it at Marmaduke.

"What's this?"

"The file on the perp they brought in. They've charged him and—"

"Charged the one you just called me about? We haven't even questioned him yet."

"No need, he came in here singing his fives and claiming police brutality. CSU processed him. You have his pictures and priors in your hand."

Marmaduke thumbed through the file. "Is this it?" He shoved the file at Zones.

"That's all I got so far."

"He loves the ink," Zones said.

"Don't they all. Me, I hate needles."

"Says here they picked him up at the house they raided in Little Five Points."

"Damn fool must've gone back there afterwards. Good thing we still had eyes on the place."

Zones looked toward the captain's closed door. "What's that all about?"

"He's pissed that you lost the bomber."

"Who's he giving the business to?"

"No one, but he had me print out your picture."

"Funny." Zones turned to Marmaduke, "Where to now, Detective? We can't question this guy."

Marmaduke picked James' phone up and dialed. "Rome, you processed your girl at the hospital, right—did you take photos?—we need to take a look at them—okay, we'll meet you there." He dropped the phone back down on the hook. "Detective Rome will meet us down in evidence."

* * *

Zones stood in front of the evidence room, stuffed with boxes of cold cases decades old, layered with dust and smelling musty. He pledged to keep that from happening to this case. Someone had tried to kill him; his hunt for the bomber had turned personal.

Detective Rome stepped to a window where a clerk sat perched on a chair. She scribbled on a pad that was slid to her from behind a secured window. She shoved the pad back at the clerk; the girl disappeared behind another door. Detective Rome turned to Zones and scanned him from head to toe.

"What're you, about six-two, two hundred pounds? This girl was about five-nine, one twenty-five?"

"...Your point?"

"No point, only that a Mandingo like you shouldn't have had a problem holding on to Buffy, just saying."

"Don't you two lovebirds start," Marmaduke said. "It wasn't Dr. Zones' fault that she got away, Detective."

"Was she our girl from the first bombing?"

"As I told Detective Marmaduke, It was dark that night. That's why I need to see the photos taken of her at the hospital on the night of the alleged rape."

The door to another room flung open, and the clerk stood at the entrance. "It's ready."

Detective Rome stepped into the room. Zones and Marmaduke followed. A box sat in the middle of a table. She pulled it closer to her, flipped off the lid and removed a file folder from it. "Here are the photos." She tossed the folder to Zones.

He studied the images of a woman's tattooed body. "I don't see any headshots."

"She freaked out when the analyst tried to photograph her face. I didn't think much about it at the time. I figured it was the trauma."

"So we still got nothing," Marmaduke said.

"Maybe we do," Zones held up two photographs. "Take a look at this."

"I see skin and a lot of ink, Doc."

"Look closer." Zones pointed to a spot on one of the pictures. "You see this mark that looks like a bottle, and here, I see the same thing?" He pointed to a spot on another picture.

"What am I supposed to be seeing?"

"The tags," Detective Rome said. "Some artists tag their bodies, much like graffiti artists tag buildings."

"We see the same thing with prison tats," Zones added.

"So all we have to do is find the scratcher who did these," Marmaduke said. "That's impossible."

"Maybe not, this photograph is from our alleged rape victim. This one is from the bomber they picked up today in Little Five Points."

"I thought you said they weren't related."

"They're not, but nothing says they can't have a passion for the same tacky tattoos."

"You forget one thing, Doc, our boy lawyered up."

"But his friends are still talking."

The three of them left the room. "We're finished here," Detective Rome told the clerk. They rode the elevator to the ninth floor.

"Tell me, Detective Rome, did they find anything in the backpack?" Zones asked.

"ATF found components but no fully functioning bomb."

"Can they match them to any of the fragments found at the other bombings?"

"They're working on that now."

They all stepped from the elevator.

"Why would she show up without a complete device? It would be very risky to assemble a bomb onsite."

"Don't know. Perhaps this was a dry run, getting ready for the real thing."

They came to a security checkpoint and were cleared to continue. A guard led them down a corridor straight to Charlotte Pirote's cell. She leapt to her feet.

"Are you releasing me?"

"One question," Marmaduke said, "and I want the truth the first time." Zones handed him the picture of the tattoo. "Whose scratch work is this?" He slammed the picture against the bars.

"I don't understand."

"Who tags his tats like this?"

Charlotte moved closer to the door and pressed her face to the picture, looking at the image very closely. Her jaw tightened, and her eyes showed a look of surprise. "That looks like Kenney's tattoo." She gasped and turned to Marmaduke. Her hands shot to her mouth. "Is he dead?" She backed away.

"Don't worry yourself. Mr. Nordic is alive and well. Now give me a name."

"His name is Dorian Milkthistle."

"...The Milkman?" Detective Rome asked. Charlotte nodded.

"You *know* this guy?" Marmaduke asked.

"He runs with a crew out of Clayton County."

"Where can we find Mr. Milkthistle, Charlotte?"

"I don't know." Marmaduke raised his brow. "I don't, really. The last time I saw him was six months ago."

"Where was that?"

"He worked out of some pawnshop off Cheshire Bridge. Some skinny, pokey-eyed bloke owned it."

"Skinner," Detective Rome said. "I questioned him after the first bombing. His shop is a block or so away from the animal shelter."

"Let's track this guy down."

* * *

Marmaduke pulled to the curb. He parked a block away and across the street from Tri-City pawnshop. The name on the street sign read, *Wellbourne Drive*. Zones sat inside the Deuce and surveyed the area, watching people hustle through the doors of Alfredo's and Fat Matt's Rib Shack.

The first bombing had happened not too far from the pawnshop, within walking distance. They seemed to be going in circles on this case. For Zones, the same characters kept cropping up, no matter how much he tried to beat them out of his profile. He knew the so-called rape victim had something to do with the bombings. What, though, he did not know. He needed to find her, and so far staking out a pawnshop was his only lead.

"Skinner's office is in the back," Detective Rome said. "A door leads to an alley and out to the street."

"He's a runner?" Marmaduke asked.

"And a scary one at that. I'll take the alley."

"Wait a minute, you?"

"If Skinner sees me coming anywhere near his shop, he'll be like the wind."

"You two got history?"

"You can say that, in a scummy, disinfectant kind of way. Give me two minutes and then hit the front door." Detective Rome hopped from the car, cut across traffic and disappeared behind a building.

"Well, Doc, it's just you and me. Let's go see what falls from this tree."

They rushed from the car, dashed into traffic and reached the other side of the street. Marmaduke snatched open the pawnshop door. A bell chimed and heads behind the counter snapped up. They approached the counter that stretched along the back end of the shop. The space was overflowing with junk; old televisions, instruments and electronics clung to shelves and littered the floor like kudzu.

"What can I do for you, Detectives?" a man that matched Skinner's description asked.

Marmaduke handled a Charles Barkley bobblehead from the counter. He leaned into Skinner. "Any man who can sniff out a cop from across the room like that must have the nose of a canine or a record longer than *The chosen Priest and Apostle of Infinite Space*." Marmaduke winked at Zones. "We're looking for Dorian Milkthistle."

"Some call him the Milkman," Zones said.

"We hear you let him run illegal ink out of this place. And before you let that lie slip from your lips, know beforehand that I'll find half a dozen violations in here to shut you down."

Skinner licked his lips and swallowed hard. "I...I got his number in the back," he stuttered.

Marmaduke flicked his wrist. "Run along then." Skinner disappeared behind the door in the wall.

"You think she'll need any help?"

"No, but ol' boy may." Marmaduke stuck his hand into a bowl of nuts sitting on the counter. He tossed a few in his mouth and chomped on them. Zones gawked. "What?"

"You know how many hands have been in that bowl?"

"Do you know why the cockroach outlived the dinosaur, Doc?" He tossed back another nut. "...Dirt."

"What?"

"Dirt. Most germs are found in the ground. That's why your mother told you not to eat it as a child unless, that is, she wanted to build up your immune system. You see, while Godzilla breathed all that nice, clean air, the cockroach crawled under the ground. It bathed itself in germs. Its immune system developed right along with the germs, and it built up a resistance to them. So, when that meteor hit the Earth and kicked up all that dirt and germs in the air, the dinosaurs breathed them in and died."

"This must be your week with the kids and a National Geographic marathon."

"Three part series on the Jurassic Age."

The door that Skinner disappeared through opened, and he and another man stumbled through it. Detective Rome followed them out. "Look what I found crawling out from under a rock." She pointed her Glock 9 in the air. "This is Milkman, and I believe you've met my buddy Skinner here."

Milkman cowered on the floor against the wall. "What've I done, Queen?"

"Get up, fool." She kicked him and he eased himself up.

Marmaduke pulled a photo of the tattoos from a file. "Is this your work?" He thrust the picture at the Milkman. "Well, is it?"

"Yes, that's my tag."

"Who'd you do this for?"

"I've done plenty of dragons. Ever since that book came out—"

Detective Rome slapped him on the side of the head. "Focus, asshole."

"Now I remember." He jabbed the picture with his finger. "I did this for that skinny, little, white girl...what was her name? She had another tat...." Marmaduke whipped out the other pictures. He spread them on the counter. Milkman pressed his face close to the pictures, as if he had trouble seeing them. He moved from one end of the counter to the other, looking closely at each one. "Angela...Angela Hightower, that's her name."

"You got all that from a tattoo?" Marmaduke asked.

"You see this here?" Marmaduke and Zones moved closer. "This angel sitting on top of this tall building, Angela Hightower. You get it? That's what she told me."

"You're sure about that name?" Detective Rome asked. "She's given us two others already."

Marmaduke reached inside his coat. He pulled out his phone and dialed. "James, what do we have on an Angela Hightower—white—according to her hospital admittance, five-nine, one twenty-five—send it to my phone." He hung up. "James is sending me a picture." Seconds later, Marmaduke's phone buzzed. He held it up to Milkman. "Is this Angela?"

"That's her, yup. Now, can I go, Queen?"

Detective Rome looked to Marmaduke. He nodded. "Get out of here, but leave your shit. You don't have a license to be marking anybody up."

"But, Queen, that's how I eat."

"If you're worried about eating, I know where you can get three hots every day." She pulled out her handcuffs. Milkman ran around the counter and out the door. Detective Rome turned to Skinner. She gave him a hard stare. He tore back through the door in the wall.

"Do you have an address for Ms. Hightower?" Zones asked.

Marmaduke flipped through his phone. "An address in Atlanta. I'll have Atlanta SWAT meet us there."

* * *

The Spire Condominiums stood at the corner of Peachtree and Seventh. The glass and concrete behemoth jetted toward the sky like long legs in high-heeled shoes. It shimmered in the sun, a sapphire tone reflected from its glazing. Balconies clung to the building's edges like false eyelashes on a drag queen. It seemed more like a cathedral than a residence, a secular Notre Dame that housed a very bad soul.

A team of SWAT commandos and Detective Marmaduke stood outside the door of unit 2510. They readied their guns.

"Didn't think we could handle this by ourselves, DuBoise?" Marmaduke said.

"My city…My takedown. Besides, what's the tallest building y'all have in Decatur, ten feet max?"

"Ready when you are, Detective," the SWAT team commander said.

"Let's do it," Detective DuBoise ordered.

The building security guard slipped a key into the lock, turned it and cracked open the door. The point man moved the guard to the side. SWAT snaked their way into the space. Zones stuck his head inside as they moved around walls and though rooms. Marmaduke pulled him away from the door.

"You trying to get a buzz cut, Doc?"

"I didn't know you cared, Detective."

"I don't, it's just that blood is hell to get out of cotton."

Zones spied Marmaduke's crisp, white cotton shirt and pocket square. "Your mother must be in town."

"How did you know?"

A call came over the radio. "…One suspect in custody."

"Let's go." Marmaduke pushed through the door. Zones followed. They rounded a corner; a flood of light filled the space. Commandos stood at the ready, their MP5s pointed at a naked young woman, her hands locked behind her head. She sparkled as the sun reflected off beads of water that covered her body. Her mopped, blonde hair was splattered over her face. Colorful tattoos peeked out from parts of her body, the same tattoos that were in her pictures. "Get her some clothes." One of the commandos ducked inside a room and returned with a robe and flung it over her slight frame. "Is this her, Doc?"

Zones walked around the suspect. She hung her head but followed him with her eyes as he circled her. "Yes, that's her. She's the one I chased on the train."

"That's one down and one to go. Where's Detective Rome?"

"Right here." Detective Rome rounded the corner. "Hello Angela, or is it Kimble or Stacey? Girl, you've given us more names than God gave Israel." She walked up to her, grabbed her under the chin and pushed her head up. "Let me get a good look at you. You've gotten over being raped very well. But we both know that was just a lie."

"You don't know anything."

"Oh, no, here's what I do know. I know that your clothes had bomb residue on them and the little gift bag you left behind at the festival had components in it that matched those of the other bombings."

"You can't touch me; I'm protected."

"Protected? Protected by whom?"

Angela rolled her eyes. "I want a—"

A window marbled but did not break. Angela's head exploded. A crimson mist of blood and matter sprayed through the air. She fell limp to the floor, like fountain water when the pressure is cut. A pool of blood formed around her head, more oozed out. Detective Rome's face, clothes and hair glistened with blood spatter. She stood there, eyes wide. Zones tackled her to the floor. Everyone ducked and scrambled for cover. The SWAT commandos took up positions, but no more shots came. Zones crawled from the condominium with Detective Rome and back out into the hall where she ripped open her blouse.

Zones grabbed her. "No, CSU may need those."

Detective Rome pushed his hands away. "I don't give a damn." She tore off the rest of her clothes and stood in the hall dressed in nothing but panties and a bra. Her clothes lay in a pile at her feet. "It's no damn mystery whose blood it is."

Marmaduke rushed into the hall. "Is everyone okay?" Detective Rome grabbed the crisp, white pocket square from his coat and wiped the blood from her face. "What the...your clothes...CSU—"

Detective Rome stuck her finger in Marmaduke's face. "I don't want to hear it." A few more wipes with his handkerchief and she tossed it to the floor on the pile of clothes. She turned and barged toward the elevators.

"...Detective?" Zones ran to her, removed his coat and placed it over her. She smiled, batted her big doe eyes at him and moved in to kiss him. He pulled back, seeing Marmaduke staring at them. The elevator chimed. The doors opened and she stepped inside. As they slid closed, she blew him a kiss.

"So what now, Doc?" Zones turned to see Marmaduke at his side. "I'm thinking the same people who knocked off the egghead from Tech took this gal out as well."

"I guess ballistics will tell us that for sure." Zones pressed the down arrow button on the elevator.

"Where're you going?"

"Call me if you come up with anything on Ms. Hightower. I'm going to follow the money."

FORTY-ONE

The Seven Sisters

ZONES EXITED THE PEACHTREE Center MARTA station in downtown Atlanta. He slipped between cars that sat bumper to bumper in rush hour traffic and crossed the street to the Fulton County Library. He took the elevator to the fourth floor and logged into a computer, typing, *Euro-Arabia Oil Company,* in the search field and then clicked on one of the links. He read:

> *The company was founded in 1933 by two oil conglomerates, one American and one British, after the discovery of oil in Qatif, Saudi Arabia. The joint-venture built pipelines from the oil field to the Mediterranean Sea....*

Zones closed the page, opened another one and continued to read:

> *Oil shortages during World War I and the exclusion of American oil companies from the San Remo Agreement*

*helped lead to the formation of AMEURO, the precursor
to the Euro-Arabian Oil Company.*

Zones opened another search. He typed in, *San Remo Agreement.*
He clicked on a link to the U.S. Department of State, Office of the
Historian. It described the agreement as being a post-World War I
arrangement to determine the precise boundaries of territories captured
by the allies and, more importantly, to divide the oil exploration rights
of the former Ottoman Empire in the Middle East. The Royal Dutch
Shell, Deutsche Bank and the Turkish National Bank formed the
Turkish Petroleum Company to pursue oil exploration. American oil
companies protested their exclusion from the agreement. It was
eventually amended to include them.

Zones fell back in his chair. He felt that Euro-Arabia Oil had
something to do with his investigation, but he didn't know what. He
reached into his pocket, pulled out his phone and dialed.

"James, this is Zones."

"You don't think I know your sexy voice by now?"

"Sexy, hah."

"Yeah, like Barry White mixed with…who's that guy from Fantasy
Island?"

"You mean Ricardo Montalban?"

"…No, *De plane, De plane, the* one that says that."

"Funny."

James laughed. "What do you need, baby?"

"Who does the department use to consult on petroleum-related
issues?"

"You mean gas?"

"Yes, crude oil, in particular."

"This ain't Texas, baby, but hold on." The phone went dead.
Minutes later, James came back on the line. "I spoke to someone at the
EPA. She gave me a list of people. Do you need an engineer? Tell me
what you're looking for."

"No, not an engineer, unless he or she is familiar with policy or
history."

"I have one Dr. Hawkins with the Petroleum History Institute. He's
also a consultant for the industry."

Zones typed a search for the name. He scanned down the screen and clicked a link to the Petroleum History Institute. "I got him. Thanks, beautiful."

"And don't you forget it. By the way, the captain wants you to present your profile to the task force."

"Why? I left my report with him?"

"He said he didn't understand that psycho shit."

"...Psycho?"

"...His word, not mine."

"You know it didn't go very well the first time around."

"So I heard. Captain said he'd be sure to keep you and Mr. Maximus in separate corners this time. Besides, it was his idea."

"The Roman requested the meeting?" Zones took a breath. "Well, I'm working on something right now. When does he want to meet?"

"Within the next day or so. I'll give you a heads up."

Zones hung up. Contrary to what James had said, his report was not that difficult to understand, even for the captain. *Why would Congressman Stonewall's aide want to meet now? He probably wants another shot at me or at my crime theory.* The computer monitor went timeout black. Zones tapped the keyboard. The page to the Petroleum History Institute still covered the screen. He dialed their number.

"Dr. Hawkins, here."

"I'm Dr. Zones with the FBI. I'm investigating an energy options scheme. I was hoping you could answer a few questions for me. I'm trying to get a historical perspective."

"How may I help you?"

"What can you tell me about the San Remo Agreement? I understand it was amended to give U.S. companies access to oil explorations."

"Yes, that's correct. The Saudis, however, bought out all other interests in the venture back in the eighties."

"So, there are no foreign concerns holding an interest presently?"

"The Kingdom has purged itself of the infidel, Doctor."

"What about Euro-Arabia?"

"It's European in name only. They started out as a conglomeration of American oil companies."

"...American?" Zones pulled a pen from his pocket and grabbed a small slip of paper from a tray beside the computer. "Who were these companies?"

"Have you heard of the Seven Sisters, Doctor?"

"No." Zones searched the Seven Sisters.

"The Seven Sisters were the Standard Oil Companies of New Jersey, New York, and California, the Texas Oil Company, Gulf Oil, Anglo-Persian and Royal Dutch Shell."

"I've just run a Google search; it says that those companies are now Exxon, Chevron, Texaco, BP and Shell."

"That's correct. The Conglomerate disbanded after the Saudi government bought out their interests, but they still refine most of the crude oil that comes from the Middle East."

"So the Saudi government owns one hundred percent of Euro-Arabia?"

"That's correct."

"One more thing, Dr. Hawkins, do you know of any environmental issues pertaining to drilling in Saudi Arabia, Qatif, in particular?"

"I thought your investigation was about securities, Dr. Zones."

"From my experience, these kinds of cases can have many tentacles."

"I see. No, I don't know of any environmental issues but, then again, the Saudis aren't that open with information like we Americans are."

"Thank you for your—"

"Now that you mention it, there is something, but it's not related to the environment. A bill has been making its way through Congress on the QT; it would reduce the amount of oil imported from the Middle East."

"Congress has tried to pass a bill to curb oil imports from the region since the Carter administration, and yet the percentages keep growing."

"From my understanding, Dr. Zones, this one has a very good chance of passing. They're using the recent unrest from the Arab Spring to argue for the bill."

"But Saudi Arabia hasn't been affected by the uprising."

"It doesn't matter. If you're near the water when the splash comes, you get wet."

"Who's the sponsor?"

"Congressman Bulwark."

"The congressman from Texas. It's no secret he wants more domestic drilling. He has argued for it since his election to the seat over twenty years ago."

"...Looks like he's going to get it."

"Thank you, Dr. Hawkins."

Zones hung up. He wondered how this latest piece of information fit into this crime. A librarian was pushing a small cart between the stacks, restocking books on the shelves. Zones approached her.

"Excuse me."

"How may I help you?" The woman wore a big, bucktoothed smile. She batted her eyes and held her hands in a prayer-like position.

"What resources do you have for viewing impending congressional bills?"

"Have you tried Thomas?"

"What is that?"

The librarian led Zones back to the computer station. "Are you working here?" She pointed to a computer.

"Right here." Zones pulled the chair out.

The librarian tucked her sundress around her and sat. She pecked at the keyboard. "Thomas is the Library of Congress' legislative site." The website popped up on the screen. She grabbed the mouse, moved it to a place on the screen and clicked. "Here, you just enter your information in this box. Do you know the bill number?"

"No."

"Then you do a word or phrase search. Got it?"

"Thank you." She slid from the chair and returned to her filing. Zones eased back down into his seat and studied the screen for a minute. His fingers hovered over the keyboard, stroking the air momentarily without hitting the keys. He entered *oil* in the search box and pressed *Enter.* The results popped up on the screen. Fifty of the five hundred entries showed per page. He scrolled through pages of results. Midway through his search, he came to a bill that showed Representative Josiah Bulwark as the sponsor. He clicked the link; another page opened. He scanned the bill and came to a section that read:

> *...countries deemed as providing safe haven to terroristic organizations or with groups deemed to be terrorist organizations, will be targeted for restriction in oil imports. Likewise, countries with increasing sectarian unrest or those deemed to be pursuing nuclear weapons will be targeted for this restriction.*

Zones typed a search for Congressman Bulwark's website. He wrote down the number to his office. The librarian pushed her cart closer to the computer station. Zones stopped her again.

"Where would I find the newspapers?"

"Newspapers are kept on the second floor."

"Thank you." He took the stairs and descended to the second floor. A sign, *Periodicals*, marked a section of space where newspapers lay folded on a shelf. Zones walked down the aisle. One shelf held the Atlanta Journal Constitution; he reached out to pick it up. His eyes spied a magazine lying on a table, and he grabbed it instead. He moved to an isolated corner of the floor between the stacks and unfurled the Black Enterprise Magazine to the political column. Zones pulled out his phone and dialed.

"Congressman Bulwark's office, how may I help you?" the woman answered.

"My name is..." Zones turned the magazine around, flipped to a page and braced it against his knee "...Makkada Saleh, I'm with Black Enterprise Magazine. Is Congressman Bulwark available to answer questions regarding..." Zones pulled a piece of paper from his pocket and read it, "his bill, H.R. 150?"

"Hold please."

Country music blared through the phone as Zones yanked it away from his ear. Seconds later, a voice cut in. "Hello."

"Congressman Bulwark?"

"This is his Chief of Staff, Miles Collins. I understand you have questions about H.R. 150."

"Chief of Staff...oh...okay."

"If you care to meet here in my office, I would be happy to answer any questions I can."

"Can we talk now?"

"I don't give interviews to faceless voices, Mr. Saleh. Give your number to the secretary, and I'll be in touch."

"But...Hello...Hello."

"Please give me your number, sir," the secretary said. Zones gave it to her. "Thank you, sir." The phone went dead.

Zones headed for the stairs, reaching the first floor and pushing through the entrance of the library, out into a dark night. He hopped a train to Midtown and settled into a seat. His eyes drifted to a TV mounted on one wall of the train. He watched a news report on the bombings. Closed-captioning scrolled up the screen, it read:

>   *...11 Alive has learned the bombings that have plagued DeKalb County are thought to be the work of suspected terrorist, Nebu Atal, formerly known as Leroy Brown. Sources say that Mr. Atal left the country before money laundering charges, for supporting suspected terrorist, could be brought against him...*

"Shit."

The train slowed. "Arts Center station next stop," the conductor announced. "Exit here for Piedmont Park, Woodruff Arts Center, John Marshall Law School..."

Zones exited the station and arrived at the Colony Square Condominiums. The concierge let him up to Detective Rome's tenth floor unit. He knocked and the door opened immediately.

"I wondered what had happened to you," Detective Rome said. She grabbed Zones by his shirt and pulled him inside. She pushed the door closed and wrapped her arms around his neck. She kissed him. He lifted her up and she tied her long legs around him. Zones walked to the bedroom, his hands filled with her ass. He lowered Detective Rome onto the bed and hovered over her, his hands pressed into the mattress.

"Detective, we've got a problem."

"It's Olga and it can wait."

FORTY-TWO
Dropping Knowledge

ZONES HAD GROWN ACCUSTOMED to the dreary, rat-maze-like rooms of the Atlanta Federal Prison in Benteen Park. After this visit, he would have seen his father more times in the past ten days than he had in the past ten years and the sudden realization was really quite surprising. Although his investigation into his mother's death seemed fishy, he wasn't ready to exonerate his old man, not quite yet. That, however, would have to wait. Today he had questions for his father about another crime—the bombings.

Zones and Detective Rome sat at a table in an interrogation room. She reached over and stroked his hand. Taking his eyes off the door, he glanced over as she flashed those pearly whites. He had a thing for feet, nice ass and pretty teeth, found them to be damn near irresistible.

"About what I said concerning your mother's death…"

"Don't worry about it. I know you were just trying to find a way to get with this." He smiled and squeezed her hand. She smiled back and batted her cat-like, hazel eyes. He had a weakness for those too.

The door to the room was flung open; two burly guards and T.O. stepped inside. They shoved him down in a chair causing the chains shackled to his legs and wrapped around his waist to rattle. His eyes immediately locked on to Detective Rome.

"Hi, son." He didn't look at Zones when he asked, "Who is this?"

"I'm Detective Rome." She stuck out her hand. T.O. struggled to raise his arm, but the chains pulled it back. He let out a short laugh, "Don't worry yourself."

"I don't get to see anything as pretty as you around here. These two," he motioned to the guards, "are the best we get."

"She's not here looking for a date. Tell me about Nebu Atal."

"Nebu who?"

"Are we really going to do this?"

T.O. leaned back in his chair. His eyes bore down on Zones. "Son, do you know what my grandfather used to say? 'When the blackbird is singing, the rooster don't crow.'" T.O. glanced over his shoulder.

"Officers, can we have a minute alone?" They looked at each other and left the room. "Okay, now tell me about Nebu Atal and why the FBI thinks he's behind these bombings."

"First of all, what makes you think I know this cat?"

"Other than the picture I was shown of the two of you out on the yard, damn near locked hand in hand?"

"Oh, that."

"When did you last see him?"

"Listen, son, Brother Nebu was just dropping some knowledge on me, that's all. I haven't seen him in several months."

"...Knowledge, like what?"

"You know, about what the brothers are going through."

"Do you mean brothers-brothers or this new Muslim brotherhood you've gotten yourself into?"

"There you go again, down on all religion."

"Man, I don't care if you worship a stone; a snake; or a six-foot, big booty, black Amazon warrior princess. I just want to know what you know about Brother Nebu's," Zones emphasized with his fingers, "*terrorist activities.*"

"Terrorist? Shit, Brother Nebu ain't no terrorist. That's just some bullshit the man cooked up to silence his criticism of these wars in Muslim countries."

"Is that what you told them when they questioned you?"

"...When who questioned me?"

"The FBI."

"Ain't nobody come to ask me shit, especially the Feds. But if they do, I'll tell them the same damn thing." T.O. turned back to Detective Rome. "Now, does this pretty lady have any questions?"

Zones threw up his hand.

Detective Rome turned to T.O. "They say Atal fled the country. Any idea where he went?"

T.O.'s eyes followed some unseen thing around the room. They landed back on Detective Rome. "This room has ears."

"Stop stalling," Zones said.

T.O. ignored him. "Are you a fan of the classics, Detective?"

"As in stories of people long dead? No, can't say that I am."

"That's too bad because you'll find that which you seek where the Oracles come from."

There was a knock at the door. "Time's up." The same two guards barged in and grabbed T.O. They pulled him from the chair and rushed him away.

"Wait, what do you mean?"

"The origin of the Oracles, Detective," he shouted as they dragged him through the door and down the hall.

"Am I the only one who finds it strange," Zones said, "that the FBI hasn't questioned him if they believe he knows where this Atal guy is?"

"Perhaps they hoped you would do their work for them. What do you think your father meant by this Oracle stuff?"

"Crazy talk. He probably got hold of some jailhouse hooch before they brought him in here."

"I don't know; he seemed pretty lucid to me."

"If you want to believe him, go right ahead. I hear enough of these stories every day to know when my leg's being pissed on. Now, can we get out of here?"

* * *

The black Corvette pulled onto Interstate Twenty going west. Detective Rome wove between lanes until she reached the farthest to the left, and the V8 engine roared down the highway. She shifted gears and slowed down or sped up as desired, handling the machine the only way it could be—confidently. Handled by a lesser driver and the Vet might have bucked, like a thoroughbred whose wrangler has a heavy touch.

"Perhaps he's in Greece," Detective Rome said.

"Who is?"

"Nebu Atal. Perhaps he's sunning himself in the Greek Isles. Your father asked if I liked the classics and said something about the Oracles. It sounds Greek to me. Get it?"

"…If you say so."

"Sounds like you don't think he could've done these bombings either."

"No more than all the other suspects."

"You think the FBI's got it wrong?"

"I just don't like having evidence spoon-fed to me."

"What do you mean?"

"I had a little sit-down with the Roman, you know, that congressman's aide, the prick, Byrnes Maximus. He mentioned Nebu Atal and his…*association* with T.O. He even showed me pictures."

"You discount Atal's involvement based solely on who the information comes from?"

"That's right."

"You felt the same way about your father, even me. You see a pattern here?"

Zones sighed, "You need to slow down before you kiss that wall." Zones pointed to the concrete barrier that separated east and west-bound traffic.

"You have control issues—but I like that, especially the way you control that tongue." She smiled a sly smile. Her eyes eased toward Zones and back to the road. He said nothing. "You know, if you want to rule Atal out, you're gonna have to find him."

FORTY-THREE
The Oracles

DETECTIVE ROME SAT AT Zones' desk with her head close to his computer screen. The sound of rapid typing traveled to the other side of his office. The collage wall of the crime had his attention...Well, most of it. He glanced over his shoulder and saw a puff of hair sticking up above the monitor. He shook his head. *You're wasting your time.*

"According to Wikipedia, Pythia was the most important Oracle. She was the priestess of Apollo at Delphi." Rome poked her head up as she typed. "And Delphi is located on the south-western spur of Mount Parnassus in the valley of Phocis, wherever that is. Oh, here's a map. It's on the east coast, off the Aegean Sea. A black man would stick out like a vegetarian sumo wrestler there." She cleared her throat. "Anytime you want to contribute to this conversation is fine with me."

"You won't like what I have to say."

"What, that I'm wasting my time?"

"You said it, not me."

"Okay, but amuse me. I'm missing something. You're the PhD, put it to work."

Zones huffed, thinking out loud. "Delphi couldn't have been the only place the Oracles were found."

"Let's see, there were two Oracles to Gaia, one at Olympia—that's in the northwest Peloponnese in southern Greece—one to Zeus...it seems all of these are in Greece."

"Actually, T.O.'s exact words were to look, 'where the Oracles come from.' You've been looking where they went."

"I don't understand?"

"Here, let me." Zones marched over to his desk as Rome moved over. He typed, *Herodotus + Greek Oracles,* in the search field and hit *Enter.* He grabbed the mouse, clicked one of the results and scrolled down the page, stopping midway and highlighting a section. "You see what it says here?" Zones walked back across the room.

Detective Rome read:

> *This was what I heard from the priests at Thebes; at Dodona, however, the women who deliver the oracles relate the matter as follows: "Two black doves flew away from Egyptian Thebes, and while one directed its flight to Libya, the other came to them."*

"*The History of Herodotus.* It's says that the Oracles came from Egypt?"

"The Greeks called them doves because they were foreign and black for the obvious reason."

"And that's where Nebu Atal is hiding—Thebes?"

"Now that we've solved that riddle, can we focus on this?" Zones pointed to the collage.

Detective Rome joined him at the wall and smacked him on the ass. "What're you looking for?"

"Some sign, a pattern or a grand scheme."

"What makes you think there is one?"

"When I visited the Islamic Center, men chased me through the city and were shooting at me, why? You only garner that kind of attention when the stakes are high."

"You think there's a conspiracy? I thought it was a singular unsub?"

"It is, but he or she uses a highly compartmentalized network. I don't think any of them know the others exist or what the grand scheme is."

"And what looks like a fifth grader's art project tells you this?"

Zones continued to study the wall. "I'm missing something too."

Detective Rome stepped in front of him. "These are the locations of the bombings, and these are their times, right?"

"The first bomb at the animal clinic off Cheshire Bridge Road detonated late Sunday night or early Monday morning. The second bomb at the language research center off Panthersville Road detonated at six thirty at night. Bomb three at the Snapfinger Creek Mitigation Bank went off at about seven on Thursday morning, and the bomb at the real estate office detonated early Friday morning in downtown Decatur."

"What about the bombing at your apartment?"

"Something felt different about that. Why would the bomber target me?"

"To send you a message."

"…Or as a diversion."

"A diversion?"

"The Feds said the bomb at my apartment matched those recovered from the dog fighting farm but lacked the sophistication of the others."

"Someone tried to implicate the animal freaks is what you're saying."

"It's a theory."

"But only law enforcement knew the makeup of the bombs. I hope you're not thinking what I think you're thinking."

Zones folded one arm under the other, poked his chin with his finger and stared at the wall. "Wait a minute." Zones rushed to his desk and snatched open a drawer. He rummaged through it and pulled out a black marker. He ran back to the wall as he popped off the cap.

"What do you see?"

"The first bomb site, your phony rape victim, that was a sexual assault, right?"

"But I thought you said—"

"Hear me out." Zones wrote a large *S* next to *Animal Shelter*. "The language center, there was a weapon found belonging to an ex-con. What would the charge be?"

"An ex-con caught with a gun would be a weapons violation."

"…Right." He affixed a *W* next to *Language Center*. "Now, the burnt-out clubhouse at the wetlands, that's arson." He wrote an *A* next to *Wetlands*.

Detective Rome moved closer to the wall. "There was a bank robbery around the corner from the bombing at the real estate office," she said. Zones scribbled an *R* next to *Broker's Office*. "What's SWAR?"

"Not quite finished." Zones wrote *Next Bomb* on the sheet and next to it; he scribed an *M*. "S-W-A-R-M, SWARM."

"What is that and what does your *M* stand for?"

"To your first question, I don't know, at least not yet. The *M* is for Murder."

"But you got that from the death of Muhammad El-Arabi."

"I don't think that killing him was the initial plan. He must've stumbled onto something. I think we'll know more once Dr. DeGlorious finishes her analysis of the nanoprotein they found in that water sample."

"And this is the sign you've been looking for?"

Zones' phone rang, "Hello."

"…Time to come see momma, handsome."

"James, so soon?"

"If the captain tries to understand another word in your report, he'll be pissing stones."

"I'll see you in a shake." He hung up.

"Trouble?" Detective Rome asked.

"Captain Franklin needs a little hand-holding."

"Let's ride."

* * *

Zones pushed through the door of the conference room. Captain Franklin stood at the head, behind a podium, addressing members of the bomb task force.

"Ah, there you are, Dr. Zones." The captain waved him over. "Please, give us your profile of the bomber."

The captain stepped back and Zones stepped up to the podium. He took a minute to scan the crowd. Men and women were sitting in hard chairs or standing propped up against a wall. They all had writing pads and pens at the ready, waiting for him to say something profound. It was still early so well starched creases cut through crisp, white shirts and dark, striped suits. They thought he had the answer to the problem. He could feel it.

Zones cleared his throat, took the captain's copy of his profile and flipped it open.

"The perpetrator of these bombings is not your garden variety terrorist, although a social deviance is displayed. He or she follows no defined precept nor does he or she adhere to any religious dogma. The motivation for committing these crimes is strictly profit-driven." A hand shot up from the front. "Yes."

"Are you saying there is no Islamist, radical environmentalist or animal rights groups involved?" a female officer asked.

"The groups you've mentioned are motivated by one ideology: either religious dogma, protecting the Earth or creation. They fight for a cause and would eagerly make known their motive and involvement in the bombings. They make video tapes, scribble graffiti all over their targets or write manifestos. We see none of these things here."

"You used the term 'social deviance,' please explain."

"I simply meant that there is a lack of fit between what this society considers success and the proper means of achieving it and what the unsub perceives them to be."

"So the unsub is just a common criminal?" Marmaduke asked.

"He would not consider himself as such. In fact, he would not consider himself a deviant. The bombings are just a means to an end."

"What's he or she profiting from?"

"Of that, I'm not certain, but there's always money."

"What about this guy's personality, Dr. Zones," the captain asked.

"No single terrorist personality trait exists, Captain, but the unsub may suffer from Machiavellianism."

"Mack, what did you say?"

"Machiavellianism, it's the need to manipulate through deceit, duplicity or another type of craftiness. Along with this, the unsub will show signs of narcissism, charged by the need to maintain power or control."

"And you're sure this is not the work of a terrorist group of any kind."

"Not in the traditional sense, Captain. The unsub may have recruited subcontractors: Professor Landrosky, the Georgia Tech researcher, Angela Hightower—I believe she planted the bombs—and a few goons here and there, but it's not a real group."

"I'm sorry, Doc, but you're gonna have to explain why you're so sure of your findings."

"Well, Captain, I see none of the signs here that are normally seen in terrorist groups: externalization, splitting, rhetorical self-justification, etcetera."

"Sounds to me that you don't think the unsub is a terrorist at all."

"I consider the unsub more of an opportunist, but the psychologies aren't that different. In fact, the bombings, I believe, are diversions."

The captain's hands shot to his hips. "...Diversions from what?"

"From the real crime."

"Which is?"

"I'm still working on that, sir."

The door to the room opened; James stepped through and made her way over to the captain. She whispered something to him. Captain Franklin followed her out of the room.

"What about physical characteristics?" Marmaduke asked.

"You're looking for a white male—"

"Male you say...in light of recent developments?"

"Yes. The unsub, I believe, employs contractors. But for the sake of discussion, we will keep the profile gender neutral, Detective." Marmaduke nodded in agreement. "He or she is possibly between the ages of thirty and sixty-five."

"Isn't that older than the typical terrorist?"

"Your unsub does not have the psychology of a terrorist. He or she just does terroristic things." Marmaduke nodded as if he understood. Zones continued, "The unsub is well-educated, probably went to college, may even have an advanced degree and is extremely intelligent. He or she lives a middle or upper-middle-income lifestyle. He or she probably has access to a large amount of money. I would also expect he or she might have a military background, Special Forces even. The unsub may be employed with a military contractor or by a university that does military research. He or she is single or, if married, has a job that allows for extensive travel."

"One last thing, Doc, will this continue?"

"It will continue until his or her motive is satisfied."

Right after that, the meeting ended. The room emptied out, but Zones, Marmaduke and Detective Rome remained behind.

"What's the matter?" Detective Rome asked. "You didn't tell them about your swarm theory?"

Marmaduke perked up. "Swarm theory, what's that?"

"He thinks there's a link between the bombings and the crimes that occurred nearby."

"Linked how?"

"Go on, babe...I mean...Dr. Zones, tell him." Detective Rome nudged him.

Zones paused, he knew that his theory would seem strange to Marmaduke. "You remember how I said most people who carry out such crimes make their motives known?"

"Yeah, but you said this unsub didn't."

"Well, that may not be *entirely* true."

"I don't follow you, Doc. Either the unsub did or he-she didn't."

"It's a form of semiotics where—"

"Is this going to be another one of your three-drink conversations?"

"Simply, Detective, I believe your unsub left a message, and it's hidden within the ancillary crimes around the bombings."

"And that's your swarm theory?"

"I believe so."

"What're you gonna need to prove it?"

"I need to find out what swarm is first."

"Then let's go."

Marmaduke led them from the room and headed down the hall where they passed by the captain's office.

"Dr. Zones," someone called out. He turned to see Captain Franklin sitting at his desk. He waved him in. "Marmaduke, you and Detective Rome come in as well." They piled inside his office. "Have a seat." The captain pulled a folder from his drawer. He rifled through a few papers, shuffled them and then tossed them across his desk in front of Zones.

"What's this?"

"That's evidence the Feds collected from Angela Hightower's condominium. The first couple of pages are offshore accounts. They traced them to a bank in the Middle East." The captain tapped his keyboard. "Banco Arabia," he read from his computer screen. "Guess who the signatory on all those accounts is?"

"I'm sure you're going to tell me."

"Nebu Atal."

"That white girl and Atal?"

"Now look at the next section." Zones flipped through the pages. "Those are wire transfers from Banco Arabia to an account at a U.S. branch registered to Ms. Hightower."

"Shit."

"Oh, it gets better, Doctor. Flip to the last section. These are transactions in Ms. Hightower's account. She made a series of withdrawals over the past couple of months. Now look at the last page. These are the accounts of Dr. El-Arabi and Muhammad El-Arabi. You will note that deposits into both their accounts match the day and the amounts of withdrawals from Ms. Hightower's account."

Zones flipped back and forth between the papers. He didn't believe what he was seeing. Nothing in his profile suggested that Islamists were responsible for these bombings. He could not, however, refute the evidence.

"When did you get this?"

"Just now. They faxed them over."

"So, what happens next?"

"The DA is gonna move forward and have Dr. El-Arabi charged."

"I see." Zones felt the air leaking slowly out of his theory. He felt foolish having expounded on his profile minutes earlier, one that contradicted this new evidence. Embarrassed, he struggled to face anyone. "Are we through here?" Captain Franklin nodded. Zones shuffled the papers, tapped them on the edge of the desk and held them out to the captain.

"You keep them." Zones followed Marmaduke and Detective Rome to the door. "And, Doctor," he turned back to the captain, "tell your old man to get himself some representation."

"What do we do now, Doc?" Marmaduke asked as they stepped from Captain Franklin's office. "That evidence just blew your whole profile to shit."

"I need to find Nebu Atal, and you need to stop a murder."

FORTY-FOUR
Brother Nebu

THE NIGHT CLOTHED LUXOR in a dark mourning suit, but the city still had life. This modern-day Thebes had grown from the banks of the Nile. It dipped into its rising tide and bound its rushing stream. Lush fields bracketed the city and swept back desert sands. It stretched forth its hand to lap from the river's cool waters and chase the sandy grit away.

The moon cast a sharp light that split the city in two. The dark side settled over the Oum Koulsoum Coffee Shop that overlooked the market. Bulbs dangled from cords, spraying light into the space. A bamboo screen, some parts now porous thanks to fingers poking holes through it, ran along the breadth of the shop while the other side stayed open. Zones and Detective Rome sat at a table with a clear view of the *souk*—the market. They sipped cups of espresso while people watched. They hoped to catch a glimpse of Nebu Atal.

"Damn, it's hotter than a pubescent virgin in this place," Detective Rome whispered. She took a sip from her cup and fiddled with the scarf covering her hair. "And hasn't anyone here ever heard of taking a bath? Shit, they've got a fucking river running through the town."

"You didn't have to come; I told you I got this."

"And miss the party?" She tapped Zones on the hand. "Besides, if you want to eat the pudding, you've got to pound the poi." Zones turned to her, puzzled. "I used to date this Hawaiian surfer dude..."

"I'm happy for you."

"Look at you, getting all snarky. You think Atal will show?"

"I don't know."

"I think that merchant pulled your leg to get you to buy that ugly-ass outfit."

"It's called blending in."

"It's called bad fashion. You can tell that's some Arab shit because brothers would never design something that god-awful."

Zones shook his head and went back to watching the crowd. Men filled the other tables around the shop. They puffed on pipes and blew hookah smoke into the air. Saidi music irritated Zones' ears but drowned out their conversation. Piles of stuff packed the market. Rugs hung from poles like flags. Highly ornate pots, vases and bowls littered the ground and crept up the sides of walls. They teetered, always on the verge of collapse but never did. Barterers shouted and harassed tourists who tried not to make eye contact. They chased them along the footpath but only walking as far as they could before losing sight of their wares.

"Do you still have that photo?"

Detective Rome pulled out her phone. "I saved it." She held it up to his face. "How do you know this isn't a setup? You can't just go around asking these people about their local terrorist."

"What did you want me to do, look him up in the al-Qaida terrorist yellow pages?"

"Or call the Egyptian police."

"And say what? Help me find a terrorist who I don't believe is a terrorist? They'd laugh me out of here. Besides, they've got their hands full already."

A waiter approached. "More coffee, sir?" Zones shook his head. "Madam?"

"Yes, please."

The waiter poured the strong, black libation from a white ceramic kettle that matched his uniform. He filled her cup almost to the brim.

Steam rose and brushed against her face. She fanned herself with her hand and expelled air from her lungs.

"Drinking more of that stuff won't cool you down."

"If I'm going to work a stakeout, I need this mud." She took a sip. "Say, if your profile is correct, what do you make of the evidence found in the dead girl's apartment?"

"Someone went through an awful lot of trouble to make Dr. El-Arabi and his son look guilty."

"Any guesses who that might be?"

"...Someone with a lot of money at stake."

"That rules out...ninety-nine percent of the population. Me, I got my money on this Nebu Atal character. Just because the crime doesn't fit into your nice, little box of what a terrorist should do, doesn't mean it can't be so."

"So that's why you're here; your mind is already made up."

"Well—"

"Hold it. That's him."

"You're sure?"

"Yeah, let's go."

Zones counted out twenty dollars and dropped the bills on the table. They left the shop and followed a man dressed all in white; he was wandering around the market. When he stopped, they stopped and pretended to be interested in some trinket or garment. The man rounded a corner. Zones and Detective Rome raced to the end of the long aisle. They looked but did not see him.

"This way," Detective Rome said.

Zones turned to see the man in white leaving the market. He was walking quickly to an awaiting van.

"Hey!" Zones yelled. They ran after him. The van sped away. Another van pulled up beside them. The doors slid open and men jumped out, waving guns at them and screaming in Arabic. Zones threw up his hands. He tried to respond. One of the men slipped a sack over his head, shoved him inside the van and bound his hands with tape.

The van traveled for some time. The drive turned rough and the van rattle as it drove over the pothole-filled road. The clash and clatter of the city faded into a desolate quiet, replaced by a hum from the radio as it lost its signal.

"Olga," Zones whispered.

"I'm here."

He felt a shove, and someone shouted at him. The van slowed to a stop, and the door slid open. Zones was yanked from his seat and out of the vehicle. He stumbled forward, feeling another shove from behind. His feet sank up to his ankles and his shoes filled with sand.

The temperature seemed cooler since the drive and a chill lingered in the air. Zones heard howling in the distance and the sound of cattle. A bell chimed a muffled tone as if striking the inside of an empty can. The loose ground beneath his feet changed to a firm, hard surface. Zones moved forward a short way before a hand grabbed his shoulder. He heard a door opening. Another shove and he knew he was inside a dwelling. They pushed him down in a chair and yanked the hood up and over his head. His eyes adjusted to the meager light. A single bulb hung low from the ceiling and dangled in front of him. Slowly, Detective Rome came into view. She was sitting in a chair to his right. They said nothing to each other.

Another door opened off the room. A man walked in, but darkness hid his face. He pulled a chair over toward them and eased himself into it. Zones could see from the man's waist down to his feet. He crossed his legs. Flame from a struck match lit up the darkness, but it went out quickly. The smell of scented tobacco filled the room. The man leaned forward and into the light. It was Nebu Atal.

"You are American—FBI, CIA, NSA?" Zones and Detective Rome said nothing. "Don't answer. It doesn't matter to me. Whoever you are, I'm afraid your employer has left you without many options." His phone rang, sporting a Gil Scott-Heron's "*Home Is Where the Hatred Is*" ringtone. He rose to leave. "Take them out into the desert and slit their throats." Men who stood nearby grabbed them as Atal walked away. A light flicked on and he sat at a desk where a teletype machine rested. The keys rattled as he punched at them.

"Wait," Zones said. He wrestled with the men.

Atal turned in his chair. "Do you have something to say?"

"I'm with the FBI."

"That's just as I figured, and what about her?"

"She's not important."

"Not important," Rome cut in. "I'm with the DeKalb County, Georgia Sherriff's Office." Zones stared at her.

"DeKalb County," Atal said. "You're a little out of your jurisdiction, aren't you?"

"When you set off bombs in my county, jurisdiction or not, we're gonna come looking for you."

"I see, and they sent you?"

"So, you are involved," Zones said.

"My blessings are with anyone who wounds the beast."

"Is that a no? Because, if not, you sure do have my father fooled."

"And who is your father?"

Zones paused, "Thelonious Zones, you know him as—"

"Brother Jabil. Yeah, now I see the resemblance. How is he?"

"... He's still locked up. Now, about your involvement in these bombings, the FBI knows about the accounts you kept overseas. They found them in Angela Hightower's apartment after the bomb blew her up, the one your guys planted. But of course, you already know that."

"Now they've linked your father to me, and like the dutiful son, you're here to what, to convince me to turn myself in?"

"Whatever your conscience tells you."

Atal leaned back in his chair as darkness swallowed his upper half once again. He uncrossed his legs, stood and spoke to his men. They grabbed hold of them.

"I'll decide what to do with you both in the morning."

The men forced the cloth bag back over Zones' head. They snatched him from the chair and dragged him back outside. He felt the sand beneath his feet. He heard the same ringtone from within the house, followed by the sound of keys being depressed. Within minutes, they forced him to the ground, rolled him over and tied his hands to a post that was located behind him. They ripped the sack off from around his head, placed food and water at his feet and left.

"I can't eat with my hands tied," Zones shouted. He looked around the darkened space. The only light came from one eerie moonbeam that sliced through gaps in the door and clerestory window openings. Noises from snorting animals sounded all around him. He lay on a bed of hay. A strong stench wafted through the space. Zones tried to expel it from his nostrils, but the smell lingered.

The door flew open and Detective Rome was yanked inside, escorted by the same men. They pushed her to the ground and tied one of her hands to the same post, right next to Zones. They pulled the sack from her head and she saw Zones sitting next to her.

Detective Rome grabbed the bowl of water from the floor and lifted it to Zones' mouth. He drank his fill. She snatched the other bowl; it was filled with what looked to be rice and beans mixed with salsa. She put it back down as soon as she realized he could not eat from the bowl. With her free hand, she scooped the food up and fed it to him.

"You just had to tell him you were law enforcement," Zones said once his mouth was empty.

"I didn't need your condescending protection."

"I was trying to save your life."

"In case you haven't noticed, we're both tied to this post. Besides, I'm *nobody's* damsel in distress."

"It's called working with a partner."

"Yeah, well, that's why I don't have one. Now, are you gonna use that mouth to eat or to keep popping off?" Detective Rome grabbed another handful. She held it to his mouth.

Zones stared at her hand filled with sticky, slimy mush. He flashed his eyes at her. "Water?"

She frowned and shook the food from her hand. "Shit."

"At least we know he had nothing to do with the bombings."

"Why, because he didn't know that the white girl had been shot, not blown up? Don't be too sure. This guy is slick and probably realized an out when he heard one."

"I don't think so. But we'll know by tomorrow, if we still have our heads attached."

FORTY-FIVE

"...the nourisher of children."

THE SOUND OF NICKERING horses woke Zones from his sleep. Now that the day had broken, he could see the rundown barn. Leftover food lay at his feet, covered in flies. The barn door eased open. A flood of light smacked his eyes as he squeezed them closed.

Detective Rome stirred next to him. "What's going on?"

"I don't know; I can't see."

Zones opened his eyes just enough to make out a figure moving in his direction. Someone cut him from the post, lifted him from the ground and hauled him from the barn. His head was left uncovered as he was once again escorted by two men; the second man had been waiting outside the door. His eyes adjusted to the light as he opened them wider. Tall stalks of wheat were waving in the breeze. Goats grazed on lush grass off in the distance. Men were riding horses for sport or to corral a herd of cattle. The juxtaposition of lifeless desert to lush grass fields spoke to the nature of these people—harsh and forgiving.

Zones was pushed roughly toward a house. Music blared from within. It sounded more of someone playing an instrument than the irritating Saidi music they often played. One of the men threw open a door and dropped Zones hard to the floor. He moaned.

"Careful." Zones raised his head to see Atal admonishing the men. He held a trumpet in his hand and stood in front of a black stand. "Help him up." The men lifted Zones from the floor and placed him in a chair. "Untie him and go get the girl." Zones slumped in his seat. "Your rest wasn't too uncomfortable, I hope. Space is pretty tight in the house…you understand." Atal blew a few notes on the trumpet. "You know, your old man knew how to blow a tenor sax. He loved calling himself a saxophonist. I think he felt it made him sound important, like a psychiatrist or pharmacist or some other –ist professional." He moved the trumpet back to his lips and pressed its valves. "You play?" Zones said nothing. "Yeah, you play. I bet you play the sax, like your old man. You got chops just like him." Atal's phone rang. "Give me a minute." He sat his trumpet down and disappeared behind a door. The sound of frantic typing filtered out from behind it. Atal returned with a saxophone and a big smile on his face. "Here you go." He held it out to Zones, "And it's got a brand new reed."

Zones straightened up. "I don't want to play."

The smile left Atal's face. "Who said you had a choice." Zones took the instrument. Atal sauntered back to his trumpet and held it up as before. "What should we play? How about…'Caravan'? I'll play the lead. You jump in where you fit in." As he was about to play, the door opened. The same men pushed Rome inside. "Great, now we have an audience." Atal shouted to the men in Arabic. One ran over to stand next to a set of conga drums; the other stood next to a tambourine and a pair of maracas.

The conga drummer led in with a solo riff while the maracas rattled and the tambourine jingled. Atal sounded his trumpet as his jowls puffed out. He cajoled Zones to join in and he did, raising the sax to his mouth and playing. A melodious sound filled the small room. Zones and Atal competed note for note, battling and negotiating musically for their release. When it ended, sweat flowed down their faces. Atal was breathing hard. His eyes did not leave Zones. They put their instruments down and caught their breaths.

"Boy, you play just like your old man: mean and hard. I don't get to jam like that very often."

"You're not too bad yourself, for a terrorist."

Atal laughed, "I'm a man of many skills."

"Is bomb making one of them?" Detective Rome asked.

The room quieted. Atal turned to the other men and gestured. They left the room and returned with a woman completely covered in clothes. Only her owl-like eyes showed.

"This is Harrah. She will attend to your needs, Detective." The woman and one of the guards led her away. Atal walked to the door and turned to Zones. "Please join me, Dr. Zones."

Zones followed Atal outside. They walked around the grounds along with one of the guards. Atal's phone rang constantly, but he didn't answer it.

"How did you know I was a doctor?"

"Your father was very proud of you. Said you were one of the best things he had done in his life."

"Well, he didn't have much to do with that, sperm donation is all."

"Your father is a very different man than he was twenty years ago. The system entangled a lot of brothers."

"The system?" Zones chuckled. "Is that what you believe got him doing time, not the alcohol or the abuse?"

"You're too young to understand."

"Understand *what*?" Zones raised his voice. "That America, the white man, the devil or whatever boogiemen you can come up with is the cause of his incarceration? And that Allah is the answer to that?" The guard moved toward them. Atal threw up his hand; the guard stopped.

"It took your father some time to see the truth of the Quran and his prophet, peace be upon him."

"Is that why you launder money for terrorist groups who kill innocent people?"

They came to a pen where goats were kept. A man entered it. He slipped a rope around one of the beasts and led it over to a pit. The goat was laid on its side. It kicked and bleated loudly as if it knew what was to come. The man, already covered in blood, lifted a knife from a chopping block and ran it across the neck of the goat. Blood drained into the pit. The goat's legs flailed until its life ceased. He skinned it, cut it up and left it hanging in the sun.

"The meat from that goat will feed many people," Atal said. "It will sustain their lives, feed and nourish their children, help them bring new life into the world. Would you not agree?"

"…If you say so."

"Oh, I do, but what about the butcher?"

"What about him? He's a butcher."

"Unlike the West, Dr. Zones, the people here get to see the messiness and brutality of life and death. It's not just some supermarket product all neatly wrapped and presented with no blood, no horror. The work I do helps to cure America of this. It helps to bring closer to home the same terror and horror we experience every day with your drones, your army and your politics. We're the butchers that give nourishment to your children and your children's children."

"Is that what you see yourself as, a…nourisher of children?"

"…In part."

"Tell me something, did your religious revelation come to you before or after your imprisonment?"

"The light that is the word of Allah and his prophet, peace be upon him, was revealed to me when the darkness was greatest."

"You were Leroy Brown, a Bible-toting Christian."

"A white man's name and a white man's religion, used to oppress the black man for many years."

"And Islam didn't enslave and change names?"

"If it was Allah's will."

Zones sucked up a lungful of hot air. He soon regretted it; the smell abused his nose. The taste of it sank deep into his tongue. The stench clung to the roof of his mouth. He looked around the farm. People worked the fields. Animals grazed. The wind and sand danced in the distance.

"There is a saying," Zones turned his attention back to Atal, "if two men looked at a rose, one would see the flower and the other would see the thorns. I'm afraid that is what we have here."

"No, what we have, Doctor, is a war."

"One you can't possibly win."

"By the will of Allah, we will."

"By the U.S. military, you won't."

Atal smiled; it unfurled slowly across his face. "Many years ago, Dr. Zones, a small army of four thousand Muslim fighters crossed into Egypt from Palestine. Now, we have all of North Africa. Islam is the natural course of the black man. This was taken from our ancestors…from us by the enslavers, as it served them. We will change that."

"I don't understand. Are the bombings about some anti-American jihad or about a black power agenda?"

"Why can't it be both?"

"I guess it wouldn't do any good to tell you that the vast majority of slaves were animist and Hebrews."

"…Hebrews? Get the fuck."

Atal led Zones back to the house. He took a seat. A door opened on the other side of the room. Detective Rome, the female escort and a guard walked in. They sat the detective across from Zones.

"What now?" Detective Rome asked. She got no answer. "If you're going to kill us, I wish you'd get it over with."

Atal shouted to the guards. Both rushed Zones, retied his hands and placed the sack back over his head. They carried him from the house, loaded him into a vehicle and drove off. As before, the ride grew rough. Zones assumed this was the end. He would lose his head for sure. *But why wait until daylight? The night would've hidden the deed.*

The vehicle stopped. They opened the door and forced Zones out, removed the sack from his head, untied his hands and waited. The big, sumo wrestler-sized men leaned against the van with their arms folded. Zones surveyed the area, nothing but desert from all sides. Another vehicle pulled beside them. More men got out. They forced Detective Rome from the van and shoved her next to Zones. They removed her head covering and untied her hands as well.

Nebu Atal, dressed in white and wearing a kufi, emerged from the second vehicle. A thin beard framed his face. He smiled, and the sun reflected off a gold, front tooth cap with a star cut into it. He walked over to them.

"What now?" Zones asked.

"My mind tells me to kill you both, but I have much love for your old man. Tell him we're even for that solid he did me back in the day. Also, you're not a bad musician." One of the men brought Atal a small, cloth sack. "About twenty-five miles that way," he pointed, "is Luxor, could be more, could be less." He handed Zones the sack. "That's water and bread, enough to last you a few hours in this heat. If you don't get lost or wander around too long, you have a chance to make it. Whether you do or don't is in Allah's hand." Atal and his men piled back inside the vehicles. They headed in the opposite direction. A trail of sand kicked up behind them.

"Well, Doctor," Detective Rome said, "we're not gonna get there by standing around."

"...Twenty-five miles in this heat."

"Just think cool thoughts." She grabbed the sack from Zones, cracked open a bottle of water and drank.

"Don't you think we should ration that?"

"For what? There're two of them."

"Yeah, there's one for you and one for me."

Detective Rome snuggled up next to Zones. She wrapped her arms around his neck and pressed her face close to his. "The odds of us making it out of this desert are slim to none." She kissed his neck and lips. "Now, Doctor, would you want your last day on this Earth to be spent with your mouth full of sand or your cock full of my wet, squishy pussy?" Zones reached into the sack and handed her the other water. She shook her head and took it. "...Men."

The two of them walked toward a distant crest; their feet sank deep into the sand. The sun beat down and sweat poured from their faces. One would stumble then the other. They struggled to their feet and continued, reaching the crest and looking over it. More sand awaited them.

Detective Rome fell to the desert floor; she did not get up. "I need to rest."

Zones opened the second bottle. "Here, drink it."

"No, that's yours."

He grabbed her head and forced the bottle to her lips. "Drink, I said. I want that pussy nice and wet." She smiled and sipped the water. "We gotta keep going."

"I can't walk another step. You go." She touched his lips. Her hand fell to the sand and her eyes closed."

Zones doused Detective Rome's face with water. "Wake up, baby. Wake up." Her eyes sprang open. "Tell me something about UFOs."

She smiled. In a raspy voice she said, "I thought you didn't believe in ET's."

"Humor me."

Detective Rome cleared her throat. Zones lifted the water bottle to her lips. She sipped until she satisfied her thirst. He pulled the bottle away, and she began her lecture.

"In the eighteenth dynastic period in Thebes, Egypt, the scribes of the House of Life rushed to the palace of Pharaoh Thutmose lll. A circle of fire had appeared in the sky. It had no head as a bird would. It made no sound. A foul odor came from its breath. It danced in the sky. More of the disks appeared, and they shone as bright as the sun. The Pharaoh's army looked to him, but he had no answers. He ordered an investigation of the phenomenon. They burned incense and prayed for peace. Eventually, the orbs rose in the sky until they disappeared."

Detective Rome fell asleep. Zones looked around, hoping to see something or someone nearby, but there was nothing. The sun had climbed higher in the sky. He lifted Rome and carried her in his arms. He prayed, but not as he had done before—without belief. His prayer was in earnest and filled with the faith of a prophet. The crest faded behind him. A long, sandy horizon lay ahead. The solitude reminded him of being on the sea. On the sea, he had the breaking of waves against his boat to keep him alert. In this ocean of sand, the only sounds he heard were the quiet screams of his soul crying out for help.

Zones was moving slower than before. He measured his steps carefully to keep from falling. Hours had passed, he thought. *We should have come across something by now.* A faint sound came from the distance. At first, he thought he was hallucinating. He knew isolation could play tricks on the mind. The sound grew stronger the farther he walked. It morphed shortly into the familiar clank of cowbells. Zones walked faster, but his load weighed him down. He sat Detective Rome down on a sandy bed and sprinted toward the bell-clank sounds. The wind picked up. Sand swirled all around him. Through the haze, he saw cattle.

"Hey. Hey!" Zones waved his hands in the air. He ran until he caught up to the herd, approaching a man who shook a stick at the animals. "…English?" Zones rasped.

"Yes." The man held his thumb and index finger apart slightly.

"A little. Okay. I need help." The man left his herd and followed Zones back to Detective Rome. She was not there. He looked around. "Olga!" he called out. She did not answer. He feared he had lost her in the sea of sand. When sailing it was important to keep your bearings or else you'd lose your way. *How could he not have left a marker?* He was an experienced mariner and he knew better, and now Olga may be lost. He continued to shout. His hands formed in to a crude cone, he sang her name. **"Ollllgaaa!"** He stood at the crest of a hill, looking out over the shifting dunes. The wind blew harder, kicking up waves of sand. New mounds formed where there had been valleys. Nothing looked as it once had. Now, Zones could barely see the herdsman standing next to him. He tugged on Zones' arm.

"We go!" He pointed back toward his herd.

"No! We stay! Zones coughed up moistened globs of sand. His shouts turned to screams. His voice crackled. He wasn't leaving, not without Olga dead or alive.

"We go! The herdsman pulled Zones away again. He fought back, pushing the man to the ground. The herdsman stumbled to his feet and scampered off into the distance. Zones chased him. They struggled, falling and rolling around in the sand. The herdsman broke free of him and regained his footing. He gave Zones, still pasted to the ground, a long, hard stare before disappearing into the blinding storm.

"Come back here!" Zones pushed up from the ground, still shouting. He panned the scene. The herdsman was gone. Just as he was stepping away, he felt a tug at his leg. He looked down to see a hand poking up through the sand. Zones dropped to his knees, brushed the sand away and uncovered Detective Rome. He held her saying, "Olga, wake up." She did not respond. "Olga. Can you hear me?" He stroked her face.

"Water," she said in a parched whisper. He had none.

Zones lifted Detective Rome from the ground. He carried her, trudging through ankle-deep sand and heading in no particular direction. The storm had not relented and the wind wielded the sand like a whipped that lashed exposed skin, bruising it. **"Help!"** The desperation sounded in his cries. The limp body he carried reminded him of the stakes. Survival in these conditions was a fleeting thought. **"Help!"** Zones called out again. He could hardly hear his own voice how could he expect anyone else to.

Zones wandered the desert. Exhausted, he dropped to the ground where he placed Detective Rome. The haze-filled air blotted out the sun, giving minimal relief. He rested on his knees, throat dry, vision blurry and no help in sight. The scene spun dizzyingly. Zones felt himself losing consciousness. The ground drew closer and he face-planted the sand.

* * *

Zones' eyes fluttered open to see the herdsman peering down at him. Light twinkled behind his head as it blotted out the sun.

"Where am I? Where is Olga?"

"Here. Here." The herdsman pointed next to Zones. He turned to see Detective Rome lying on the same cart. "We go to town, yes."

"Water." The herdsman pulled a canister from his side and handed it to him. Zones lifted himself up from the cart. He turned to Detective Rome, raising her head and placing the canister to her lips. He parted them, pouring drops of water into her mouth. She coughed, drank, and slowly opened her eyes. Zones pulled the canister away.

"Hi," she said; her voice barely above a whisper.

"Don't talk. Drink some more."

The mule pulled their cart along an unseen trail. Zones continued to nurse Detective Rome, thinking on just how close he came to losing her. She drank and ate, seemingly unaware of the rough ride. Lights shone in the distance and soon the city came in to view. The vacant sounds of the desert gave way to the orchestra of city noises. They were safely back to where they started.

A red light blinked on the hotel room phone; Zones picked it up. He dialed *0* and listened to a voicemail message. Marmaduke's voice sounded back at him. Zones hung up and dialed the front desk.

"May I help you?"

"I need to make an overseas call."

"Certainly, sir, I can assist you." Zones gave him the number. He was soon connected to Marmaduke.

"You must be trying to lose your motherfucking head, Doc," Marmaduke said. "I'll be damned if you don't like fucking with them Arabs."

"What is it, Detective? Have you found a possible murder victim?"

"I'm still working on that. Did you find Atal?"

"He's not the man behind the bombings."

"You sound sure of that."

"I'm willing to bet my head on it."

"What about the FBI? They're all in on Atal."

"I don't know about the money laundering, but they can save their time on the bombings."

"You're there with Detective Rome. They didn't have a room listed in her name. Is she at a different hotel?"

"No."

"So, you two ah—"

"What about Dr. DeGlorious, Detective? Has she found out what the nanoprotein does?"

"Not that I've heard."

"Then what is it, Detective? Why did you call?"

"ATF has finished their analysis of the components ol' girl left at the festival."

"What did they find?"

"Do I look like Urkel? They're gonna brief us on it this week. Captain wants you there."

"I'll be back in two days."

"One more thing, Doc, your office wanted me to give you a message. A Dr. Shrapwa...Shrapwa..."

"Shrapwawineshah."

"Whatever, from the New York City Building Department called your office."

"Did he leave a contact number?"

"Yeah, but it's in India. There's a message as well. They couldn't locate the files you wanted, but the Midong site was purchased by British Petroleum."

"...BP, one of the seven sisters."

FORTY-SIX

The Device

"THIS IS A VOICE-CONTROLLED actuator." Agent Thomas, with the ATF, stood amidst others huddled around him. He talked about the devices recovered from the backpack Angela Hightower left at the festival. Zones dragged himself through the pale, white walls of the CSU lab. His plane had landed hours earlier from North Africa. "It matches fragments recovered from four of the five bomb scenes. This particular device can be programmed to activate based on a word or a phrase." He lifted a bag from the floor and sat it on the table. "We have built a replica based on the components recovered from the backpack. I've programmed the actuator with a phrase." Agent Thomas slipped a paper from his white lab coat. "Will you do the honors, Captain?" He held the paper out to him.

"What do I do?"

"Just read the phrase on the paper."

Captain Franklin took the paper, reached for his glasses inside his shirt pocket and shoved them onto his face. He mouthed some of the words. The captain handed the paper back and gave Agent Thomas a hard stare. "What is this?"

"Please, Captain, it's just a demonstration." The agent gave it back to him.

"I'm…I'm just a girl in love with myself." School girlish giggles spread through the room. The captain gave each of them the evil eye. They quieted.

"Louder, Captain, and move closer." The captain repeated the words. The actuator cranked out sounds. A small cloud of smoke spilled from the device; glitter and confetti flew toward him. Captain Franklin stood there covered in the stuff.

"Was that *really* necessary?"

"Sorry, Captain, that was Dr. Bruno's idea."

The captain snarled. "So this is how the bombs were detonated."

"We believe so."

"But how would the bomber get close enough to activate the bomb without blowing himself up?"

"…A dial-up connection."

"…A phone?"

"Yes, or through any broadcast message, TV, radio…any audio device."

"Can you deactivate it?"

"We're working on a way to jam the signal; that would keep the device from detonating."

"Okay. Now all we need is the S-O-B who's setting these off."

"I thought the FBI said it was Nebu Atal."

"He can't blow shit up and shoot people in the head from across an ocean, Agent. I'll let the Feds worry about Atal. I want his accomplice." The captain shoved the script he had read back at Agent Thomas. "Do you have anything to add, Dr. Zones?"

"Are the components standard issued, or do they require special ordering?"

"You can't get the actuator from Home Depot, but it can be ordered from an electrical components supplier. This other stuff—the wiring, the fuses, and circuit boards—is available in most hobby shops."

"Did the suspect order that one?"

"We traced this to a digital voice-recording manufacturer. They'd had a few break-ins, and this serial number matches one they reported as missing."

"Their records are that detailed?"

"They build black boxes for the airline industry, so they log all parts."

"May I have a closer look at that?"

"Sure." Agent Thomas backed out of the way.

Zones moved closer to the device. He studied it and noticed that the captain was studying him. "How sure are you of the design?"

"It's not exact but…"

"I know that look, Doctor," Captain Franklin said. "What do you see?"

"Your bomb maker distances him or herself but uses a device that allows for controlling the detonation. Why this type of device? Why not use a timer or a wireless radio device?"

"Sounds like you've got more questions than answers."

Zones propped his left arm up with his right. He stroked his goatee. His eyes did not move from the reconstructed bomb. "You said the actuator could be activated through a broadcast, is that right, Agent?"

"…That or an IP device, a phone call."

"There was part of a phone recovered at the primate language center. Was there any information gleaned from it?"

"It was very badly damaged."

"Couldn't you ping calls to the closest tower for the time of the detonation?"

"That would be the toppled tower. The transmitter got damaged in the collapse. AT&T is still trying to recover the information."

Zones turned to Agent Thomas. "How much longer do they need?"

"They couldn't say."

"What about TV and radio?"

"You mean crosscheck all TV and radio signals to the times of the bombings? That's hundreds of channels, if not thousands including cable and satellite. That'll take forever. The ATF doesn't have the resources."

"Neither do we," the captain said. "Let's see what the phone company comes up with first before we go chasing flying dragons. You got anything else, Doctor?"

"Your unsub may have been at each of the bombings."

"How do you figure that? I would think getting caught up in a dragnet isn't exactly on this guy's to-do list."

"He's a predator, a masochist, perhaps, but not sexually. He has to make sure of his kill."

Captain Franklin turned to another detective. "Pull all video and hit up the news stations for theirs."

"That'll do you no good, Captain."

"You're confusing me, Doctor. If he was there then we may have him or her on tape."

"Your unsub is there, but you won't see him or her. It would be like picking out the bad apple, the one that's only rotten from the inside."

"He can't be that damn smart." The captain turned back to the detective. "Pull the tape."

A phone buzzed. "Marmaduke, here—Okay, good work."

"What is it?" Zones asked.

"That was Chennault. I had him search missing persons."

"…For a potential murder victim."

"A pizza delivery driver went missing about two weeks ago."

"Two weeks?"

"That means something?"

"There was a pizza left inside my apartment right before it blew up. I thought I saw a car with a pizza sign on top speed away afterwards."

"You're thinking the pizza guy is our bomber?"

"Probably our victim."

"Whichever, they've tracked his last delivery to an apartment building off Buford Highway."

"Is there anything else, Dr. Zones?" Captain Franklin asked.

"No, Captain." Not unless you want to hear about a murder.

FORTY-SEVEN
Search for Pizza Boy

A ONCE LIGHT SUMMER rain now fell heavier. Dark clouds rolled slowly overhead. They emptied their load liberally onto the Spanish-style apartment buildings that straddled a hump in the earth and sat far back from the road. A torrent of water cascaded along the clay roof tiles, splattered the ground and kicked muddy roux up onto the hard coated-stucco walls. A slurry of soil covered the pavement. It raced down the steep drive and around Zones' black wing-tips as he stepped from Marmaduke's car.

The sign out front read, *La Hacienda.* It was hidden behind an overgrowth of lilacs and French hydrangeas. The architecture was south of the border, and the people spoke a strange mix of southern dialect and rustic Spanish. Some that lived here milled about, even in the pouring rain. Children stomped up and down the breezeway stairs and splashed in puddles of water everywhere. They seemed oblivious to the turmoil that surrounded them.

Zones and Marmaduke raced to Chennault's green Impala. They snatched open doors and hopped inside.

"What do we have?" Marmaduke asked.

"...Other than wet seats?" Chennault dropped his eyes to the rain-soaked trenchcoat Marmaduke wore. "The manager at the Pizza Bar gave this address as the last delivery for his missing driver, a junior at Tech. His fraternity brothers reported him missing after he didn't show for two days of Rush."

"What fraternity?" Zones asked.

"...Zeta Beta Tau. Personally, I didn't know eggheads had time for fun. Anyway, he delivered a large pepperoni, extra cheese with pineapple, no olives to apartment 3E, three floors up, second door from the left—the one with the curtains pulled back and the door propped open."

"Have you questioned the tenants?" Marmaduke asked.

"Was waiting for you, but one of the neighbors said a woman with two small children has lived there for the past five years."

"What do you think, Doc?"

"...Sounds about right, an extra cheese and pineapple pizza, not exactly a grown man's food."

"Perhaps it's a boyfriend," Chennault said.

Marmaduke pulled his weapon from its holster. "There's only one way to find out." He popped the door open. "You coming, Doc?"

"I'll wait here, thank you."

"Suit yourself."

Marmaduke and Chennault tore from the car. They raced across the mud-filled parking lot over to a covered walkway. The children still played there. They stopped and stared at the two men before they broke and ran away. Marmaduke scampered up the two flights of stairs as Chennault followed him. They moved against the wall, guns drawn. Marmaduke poked his head in and out of the open door. He dashed across it and knocked.

"Police!" Chennault stood on the other side. They both entered the apartment.

Zones noticed a tarp draped over what he presumed to be a car. It sat across the parking lot under a large pine tree. He opened the car door and eased from his seat, running through the rain and over to the covered car. Seeds had gathered on top, and water was pooled in the tarp's creases. Zones studied it. He walked from one side to the other and grabbed the front end of the tarp where it clung to the bumper. He flung it back. A rusting, red 1992 Celica GT peeked back at him from underneath. He pulled more of the tarp back and up to the car's roof. A pizza sign sat perched on top. Zones pressed his face to the window but saw nothing unusual inside. As he rolled the tarp back over the car, he heard shouts coming from the apartment. He turned to see a man dive through a window. Marmaduke and Chennault bolted from the apartment and gave chase.

Zones waited and watched from beside the pizza car as all three raced down the stairs, around the building and out of sight. Another door opened, two down from the targeted apartment. A hooded figure walked out. He looked over his shoulder and hunched his six-foot-plus frame as he tried to disappear into the gathering crowd of diminutive Mexicans. The man approached Zones, chin tucked and head bowed. He walked with a familiar gait. The large hood cast a deep shadow over his face. He drew closer. Zones stepped out from between the cars. The man paused and raised his head but not enough to expose his face. He changed direction and walked fast past him.

Zones watched the man as he tried not to draw attention to himself. "Hey, you," he shouted at him, "don't I know you?" The man continued to walk. Zones followed him down the steep drive. "I'm talking to you." He grabbed the man's shoulder. He slowed to a stop and turned back to Zones, his head still bowed and his face still buried underneath the hood. Before he exposed himself fully, he shoved Zones to the ground and ran down Buford Highway.

Zones struggled up from the wet pavement and ran after him. He turned on that 10:05, one hundred meters DeMathis High School speed. The man cut across the road into traffic. Zones gained on him. They dodged in and out between cars as drivers honked and swerved to miss them. The man crossed the street, heading for a large parking lot with every space filled. He ran toward an expansive red and white building, its storefront windows covered with large advertisement banners. Zones followed and continued to gain: thirty yards, twenty. The man glanced over his shoulder. He stopped, turned and fired a concealed weapon. Zones felt the bullet whiz by him and dove behind one of the many parked cars.

From the hard, wet pavement, Zones watched the man dash inside the building. He sprang up from the ground, eased through the glass door and followed him. A jarring resonance of sights and sounds slapped him in the face. The flea market bustled with people, mostly Asians but also sprinkled with Mexicans and others here and there.

Zones moved between the rows of produce and meat stands. Caged, live birds cackled and fluttered. People bartered in strange languages. His gaze moved over the crowd as he worked his way toward the rear of the building. He stepped from behind a rack filled with bottles of juice; one bottle exploded; glass and liquid splashed everywhere. Zones turned in the direction of the shot. The hooded man stood across from him. He pointed his gun and fired again. Zones ducked. People screamed and ran from the market.

Zones followed the hooded man through a door leading to a large storage area filled to its rafters with goods. Very little light beamed in through the skylights cut into the roof overhead. He saw the outline of someone moving amongst the shelves; he worked his way toward the spot where the figure hid. He crept up from behind and wrapped his arms around the person. A loud, high-pitched scream rang out as he wrestled with the person; it was a woman.

"Ma'am, calm down," Zones whispered.

"What's going on?" The woman's thick accent garbled her words.

"Please, ma'am, calm down." He squeezed her tighter. "Did you see a hooded man come through here?" She nodded and pointed down the aisle.

Zones released the woman and moved in that direction. He walked heel to toe on the concrete floor. He looked back, the young girl still crouched on the floor in the corner. He should have been hiding himself with no gun and no backup. No one even knew he was there.

Halfway down the long rack of shelves, a stack of boxes fell on top of him. They knocked him down and pinned him to the floor. He lay there, motionless, bleeding from the head. The wound he had suffered from the car chase in DC days ago had not completely healed. It now gushed with new blood.

Through his semi-consciousness, Zones saw a figure approach. Its shadow crept along the floor ahead of it. The hooded man hovered above him. He blew scented smoke into Zones' face, moved the gun that dangled from his right hand close to Zones' head and pressed it to his right temple. Zones closed his eyes. He knew this was the end. A loud click sounded; it shook him; he heard a piercing scream. His eyes sprang open. The hooded man was not standing over him.

Zones clawed his way from beneath the toppled boxes. He stumbled from the darkness of the storage racks and back out to the front of the store. He pushed through the glass door. The rain had slowed but not the blood that poured from his head.

"Get on your knees, and put your hands in the air," someone shouted from the parking lot.

Zones gathered himself as he looked out over a sea of squad cars. Their lights flashed and sirens blared. He could make out the extended arms of the officers. He knew what that meant. Zones swayed on his feet. His legs grew wobbly; he dropped to one knee and then the other. He brushed the blood away from his eyes and locked his fingers behind his head. Officers rushed him. They cuffed Zones and led him over to an awaiting ambulance.

"Dr. Zones. Wake up, Dr. Zones."

His eyelids rolled up. Marmaduke stared back at him. "Damn."

"What?"

"I guess I didn't make it into heaven."

"Was there any doubt?"

"It's the company I keep. Where am I?"

"In the back of an ambulance."

"An ambulance? How long have I been out?"

"They were rolling you up when we got here. I'll say two minutes. They're about to ship you off to Grady."

"Hell no, not on your life." Zones unbuckled the straps on the gurney.

"Where're you going, Doc?"

"Not to the hospital, that's for damn sure." Zones eased from the back of the ambulance and ripped off his bandages.

"You know that head of yours can't take too many more bumps. What were you doing over there in the first place? We left you in the car."

"While you were chasing El Capitan, some guy slithered out from one of the other apartments. He was headed for the missing pizza guy's car until he saw me."

"You found the car?"

"It was covered with a tarp in the parking lot. I chased him here but lost him in the market."

"Which apartment?"

"Two doors down on the right."

"I'll call it in," Chennault said.

"If you're up for it, Doc, we can head back over and check out this place."

"Let's do that."

Detective Chennault ended his call. "Before we go, we'll need these." He grabbed three HEPA filters from a bin in the ambulance.

FORTY-EIGHT

Pizza Boy Found

THE BLUE STATION WAGON with *DeKalb County Medical Examiner* flanking it sat parked outside the La Hacienda apartments. Zones lumbered up the two flights to the third floor, walking behind Marmaduke and Chennault. They donned protective footwear and entered the unit two doors down from their original search. Officers standing guard pointed them to the bathroom.

"What do we have, Doctor?" Marmaduke asked Dr. DeGlorious. She was kneeling over the tub in the cramped apartment bathroom when he and Zones appeared at the door.

"Detective Marmaduke." She turned to Zones. "What happened to you, Doctor?"

Zones grabbed his head. "Nothing, just a little love tap, Doctor."

"Aaha, you should get that looked at."

"Yeah, I know."

"Is this your case, Detective?"

Marmaduke pressed his mask tight to his face. "It may be tied to our bombings. What can you tell us about our DB?"

"Not much. He's a white male, early twenties. Until I get him on the table, that's about all I have."

"How long has he been here?"

"Hard to say. He's wrapped in dry ice and covered in lye. I should know more at autopsy."

"What about that little business over at Tech?"

"Still working on it, Detective."

"...With all those eggheads?"

"It would help if you could do something about the body count."

"I'm no miracle worker, Doctor."

Detective Chennault appeared at the bathroom door. "Dr. Zones, Marmaduke, you might want to take a look at this." They filed out of the bathroom and followed Chennault to an area just outside the kitchen. A table with electronic components scattered all over it filled the space.

Marmaduke picked up what looked to be a computer motherboard. "These look like the parts recovered from Angela Hightower's sack. Could this be the M in your swarm theory, Doc?"

"Could be, but where's the bomb? It looks like we interrupted his little party with the dead guy in there."

Marmaduke turned to Chennault. "Has ATF swept this place?"

"I haven't seen them on scene."

"Okay, let's clear out of here. Everybody out, now," Marmaduke shouted. "Chennault, call the bomb squad and the fire department. Let's get this place evacuated."

People poured from their apartments and out into a dark, overcast day. The rain had stopped but not for long. Firemen and police went door to door. The people they found inside were escorted away from the building.

The bomb technician wobbled up the stairs in his blast suit and disappeared inside the apartment. Zones had seen something similar at the broker's office. The end result was a building blown up where only little pieces could be found. He hid across the street behind one of the armored vehicles. Minutes ticked by without incident. Zones listened to the radio communication between the technician and those inside the armored van. The radio crackled, and a voice shouted, "All clear."

"Let's go, Doc." Marmaduke trotted across the street and back to the apartment. Zones followed. "Okay, I need the entire place dusted.

This guy made his home here, so DNA shouldn't be a problem. Find out who sells dry ice around here. Look for utility bills with his name on them, and question his neighbors. Someone must know this guy."

"Don't be too sure about that, Detective."

"Why?"

"A white guy living in a predominately Hispanic community…They would've thought he was ICE and avoided him like the plague."

"I'm surprised at you, Doc. Not all Hispanics are illegal."

"The ones you dug out of those apartments are."

Marmaduke smirked, "Let's ask Dr. DeGlorious, shall we?"

Dr. DeGlorious appeared at the door, "Ask me what?"

"About the autopsy," Zones said, "when will you be finished?"

"With this one, give me three days."

Men from the ME's office loaded the body onto a gurney. They wheeled it out to an awaiting van. Dr. DeGlorious followed them.

"Who do you think that is?" Marmaduke asked Zones.

"If the pizza car hidden beneath that tarp is any indication, it's your delivery boy."

"But the ticket order was for the apartment we raided earlier, two doors down. How did he wind up here?"

"Maybe he got the apartment number wrong."

"That's a high price to pay for inattention."

Zones took note of the broken shards of glass outside the door. "What about the cat that dove out of the window?"

"It was like you said; he thought we were ICE. Had him taken down to the station. Let's see what he knows about this guy. By the way, did you get a good look at him during your chase?"

"No, but…"

"…But what, Doc?"

"I know him…his walk, that is."

"…His walk?"

"It's hard to explain."

"Did he give you that shiner?"

"…Ambushed me at the market."

"There were reports of gunfire. Was that you or him?"

"He took a few potshots at me."

"You weren't armed?" Zones shook his head. "If this is the same guy, Doc, he's tried to blow you up, and now he's shooting at you. What gives?"

"Don't know. I'm getting too close, or he or she dislikes good-looking black men."

"You must be an only child."

"Why do you say that?"

"You tend to compliment yourself a lot."

"Is that your fifty cents worth of psychoanalysis?"

"Here's a dollar's worth of detective advice, get yourself some protection."

"I thought that's what you were for."

"Funny. Where's the car?"

"I'll show you."

They filed out of the apartment and headed down the stairs; the car was still covered with the tarp. They watched people trudging across the parking lot, heading for their homes with faces full of distrust and weariness. No answers would come from them any time soon. Any information concerning their suspect would have to be gleaned from the apartment and the car.

"Is this it?" Marmaduke asked. He stopped at the front of the car.

"Grab that other end."

"We should wait for CSU and have a warrant in hand."

"You're not going to find any prints or DNA here or in that apartment. Your unsub is clever. He was prepared for the possibility of us discovering this location. Besides, who's going to object, the dead pizza guy who owns this vehicle?"

"You're trying to tell me he knew we were coming?"

"Not when exactly but eventually."

Marmaduke grabbed the tarp. He and Zones pulled it back. Water cascaded down to the ground. They folded the tarp in on itself and left it on the trunk. Marmaduke pulled a flashlight and a handkerchief from his pocket. He grabbed the door handle, pulled it open and stuck his head inside, shining the light around. The beam of light landed on the glove compartment. He popped the latch. The door dropped open. He pulled out a stack of papers and shuffled through them.

"You know, Doc, have you ever stopped to think you could be wrong about Dr. El-Arabi? He could be calling the shots from the inside, you know, cleaning up any loose ends. That would explain this guy and taking out ol' girl." Marmaduke stopped shuffling papers. He held one up as far as his arms would extend. He chuckled. "Get a load of this. Your DB's name is Lucky Bouye from Lafayette, Louisiana. He's only been in Georgia a little over a month."

"…Any next of kin?"

"There's a co-signatory on the title, a Linda Bouye." Marmaduke handed the paper to Zones. "…Could be his mother."

"She has beautiful penmanship."

"But her choice of names needs work, Lucky Bouye?" Marmaduke's phone rang. "Tell me something good, James—right now I'm ankle deep in mud, processing a crime scene, why?—shit, now?" He took the phone from his ear and stared at it. "Three missed calls," he mumbled. "I'm on my way."

"What is it," Zones asked, "another bomb?"

"No, the DA wants to go over my testimony. He's convening the Grand Jury for your Arab, Nebu Atal, and…your father."

"…My father? He has no evidence that I've seen to implicate him in the bombings. A picture taken of him and Atal together is not a smoking gun."

"Unless you give him something to contradict those bank transactions, he's moving forward."

"…In spite of my analysis?"

"Since two of three suspects are already in custody."

"So is that the new standard, a bird in the hand?"

"You're gumming to the wrong guy, Doc." Marmaduke glanced at his watch. "If I leave now, I'll beat the traffic. Can I drop you anywhere?"

"…The office?"

"Let's go."

* * *

Zones stretched out the tight spots in his body while sitting at his desk. He punched at the keyboard and searched for anything connected to the *SWARM*. His search led to a number of results. Most had to do with insects in motion. He clicked a Wikipedia link labeled *Swarm Intelligence*. He read:

> "…is the discipline that deals with natural and artificial systems composed of many individuals that coordinate using decentralized control and self-organization…the discipline

focuses on the collective behaviors that result from the local interactions of the individuals with each other and with their environment..."

Collective Behaviors, Zones was familiar with Herbert Blumer's theory of elementary collective behavior but wasn't sure if it tied into this swarm intelligence. He rushed to Sam's office.

"What do you know about swarm intelligence?"

"Not a damn thing. Why do you ask?"

"You've studied Blumer's Collective Behavior Theory, right?"

"We're psychologists, not sociologists, Monk. Why do you ask?"

"...Just trying to figure out what swarm means in this context."

"Ah, your swarm theory." Sam rose from his desk and studied the books on the shelf lining his office wall. He took one, flipped it open and thumbed through it. "Here we go." Sam turned the book around.

Zones took the book and read. He flipped it closed. "*Human Nature and Collective Behavior,* Tamotsu Shibutani," he read the title and the author of the book. "Anything in here about swarm theory?"

"Collective Behavior, yes. Swarm theory, no. But do you remember Stats?"

"You mean the geek who helped us out on that Mormon case?"

"And your father's case. I have papers that need to be dropped off. You can run it past him." Sam held out a manila envelope.

Zones grabbed it. "Is he still in the same place?"

"The old cotton mill lofts in Cabbage Town."

"...Still paranoid?"

"More than ever."

FORTY-NINE
The Hack

ZONES STOOD OUTSIDE A large, rolling steel door with *Fuck the Police* scrawled diagonally across it in white, oil-based paint. *That won't fade anytime soon.* He knocked. A tin rattling sound echoed along the dark, vacant hall. The minimal light hid the pockmarked red brick and smoke-stained ceiling of the old cotton mill, now lofts. Stats liked it that way. Daylight eased the anxiety of others; it heightened his.

No one came to the door right away. Zones knocked again. He pressed his ear against the cold steel, hearing voices comingled with other sounds on the other side. He glanced up at the top-left corner of the door where he remembered there was a pin camera.

"Who's there?" someone asked.

"Zones here, open up."

"…T.O.'s boy?"

Zones huffed, "Yeah, crack the door." The door clanked and rolled open. Zones stuck the manila envelope into Stats' gut. "Sam sent this." He pushed past him. The dimness outside seeped inside the voluminous space. Computer monitors and other devices stuffed the loft to its high twelve-foot ceilings. Their glow supplemented the faint light coming from the strip fluorescents overhead. Other people sat at stations. They monitored their screens or typed computer code with blazing speed. "Still hacking?"

Stats groaned, "What do you want?"

"I have a case—"

"...Mormons again?"

"No, I'm working the bombings."

Stats marched to a desk in the rear corner of the space. "I can't help you with that. I'm busy." He plopped in a chair and ripped open the envelope. The papers spilled onto the desk.

"...Too busy, huh." Zones walked to a monitor mounted on a column. "What if I—"

"You can't threaten me by calling the government. They pay me to hack the Chinese."

Zones raised his brow, his leverage gone. "I can't appeal to your sense of civic duty?"

"How much does that pay?"

"I see." Zones spied a photograph hanging on the wall above Stats' desk. "You know Dr. Bruno?"

Stats whipped his head around to the picture. "We're both members of an organization."

"You mean the one where you collect the DNA of other people."

"How did you—"

"No worries, your little freakery is safe with me. What If I told you I could get you Hank Aaron's DNA?"

"Got it already."

"Michael Vick?"

"...Over-traded."

"Gladys Knight?"

"Got hers and got all the Pips."

"What about Tyler Perry?"

"Got his but...can you get me Madea's? She doesn't appear in public."

"They're one in the...absolutely."

Stats cocked his eye. He looked Zones up and down. "No bullshit."

"I got you, baby."

"What do you need?"

"Does *Swarm* mean anything to you?"

"It describes insects in motion."

"I get that. I believe this s-w-a-r-m is for a series of related crimes the unsub committed consciously or subconsciously to spell out the acronym."

"I see." Stats swiveled around to his keyboard. He fired up a computer that sat on the floor next to his desk. Lights flashed off and on. It beeped as it powered up. Stats pecked at the keyboard. "You believe your bomber is messaging through these other crimes."

"That's my theory."

"You have a profile?"

"Yes," Zones told him the details of his analysis.

Stats worked away at his computer. "So far, the only thing showing up for swarm has to do with bugs or particle swarm optimization."

"Particle optimization, what's that?"

"It's an algorithm for artificial intelligence."

"Is that related to swarm intelligence?"

"The algorithm applies to both."

"...Any application there to bomb technology?"

"The algorithm has many applications: logistics, business analysis, manufacturing, you name it."

"Military?"

"Whoa."

"No, whoa, don't go getting all Mr. Rogers on me now, Stats. I need you to summon your inner Guy Fawkes. Now, take a quick peek into their system for anything related to this swarm intelligence."

"You know, if they trace this back to me that means prison."

"A dark, cramped cell with nothing but you and all the computer time you want, you'll feel right at home."

Stats worked away at the computer. "Okay, everyone, we're going dark in five, four, three, two, one." Computers and screens powered off, all except the one Stats worked on.

Zones moved around the desk. The image on the computer screen read, *ADP*. "That's not DOD. I need military, not payroll."

"You think I'm an idiot? Hacking directly into the Defense Department's system would have them banging on my door before Warren Buffett made another million."

"Why ADP?"

"They process payroll for the Wieland Corporation."

"Do I have to rip the details from your mouth?"

"The Wieland Corporation is a mid-size Scandinavian electronics exporter. Most of their products are manufactured by the New China Corporation, a large conglomerate owned by the Chinese government. Wieland ties into their production system. New China links back into the Chinese government's central network that processes other communist front companies. One of these is Xindong Steel.

"Let me guess, they supply steel?"

"...Lots of it, primarily to the construction industry. One of their clients is Bartholomew Construction. They're a primary subcontractor to Beytel Corporation, a major U.S. contractor, including the DOD."

"So you hack ADP to access Wieland's network to New China. From New China you link to the central Chinese government's network. This gives you access to Xindong, from Xindong to Bartholomew, then to Beytel and the DOD."

"They'll all be too busy pointing fingers at each other if the intrusion is detected."

"You've done this before."

"You sound surprised. We're in. We have five minutes." Stats searched the internal DOD database for swarm. He drilled down into its layers but found nothing.

"Two minutes," someone shouted.

"Well?"

"...Nothing."

Zones exhaled. "Does that search include their black projects?"

"Those are kept offline, no outside network access."

"And you haven't found a way inside?"

"Hijacking a dedicated satellite, that's about it."

"Then let's do it." Others turned to them. A low grumble spread through the room. "What?"

"...Nothing." Stats settled himself in his seat. "You see that rack there? Disconnect the red cable and plug it into the router on the other rack, the one marked *port one.*"

Zones unplugged the cable and seated it in the router. "Do you still go through the Chinese?"

"...No, the Brazilians now. They've been hacking U.S. naval satellites since the nineties. I'll sniff for any open channels, exploit their signal and use it to hack the system. They won't be able to trace it back to us."

Lights on the equipment flashed and beeped. The computer chirped and churned. Stats tapped out a rhythm on the keyboard with flashes of "Flight of the Bumblebee" in the background. The room grew quiet as if they had gone silent running. Only the constant buzz of the strip fluorescents overhead could be heard. Zones paced the floor. He bit at his grounded-down nails. If anyone could get him the answers he sought, it was Stats. He had used him on the Mormon case, and his analysis helped bring a killer to justice. He expected no less now.

"Alright, I'm in."

Zones raced back to the desk. "What do you see?"

"Aside from stuff that the Russians and Chinese would kill to get their hands on, nothing…wait…here we go." Stats clicked on a folder, *SWARM.*

Zones leaned close to the monitor. He scanned the other folders on the screen. "What's that?" He pointed. Stats clicked on the folder. Files exploded on the screen. "Can you open one?"

Stats clicked the file. "It's asking for a password."

"I see that. Try something."

"If I guess wrong too many times, it'll lock me out."

"Don't you have some kind of password cracker?"

"First I have to download the file to my system."

"Okay."

Stats created a shared folder on the network drive. He grabbed the files and moved them over to it. A warning popped up on the screen. *Illegal operation,* it read. He tried again. The same warning appeared.

Zones hovered over Stats' shoulder. "What's wrong?"

"The privileges set on the file does not allow it to be moved."

"Can't you change that?"

"Not without administrative rights."

"How do you get those?"

"Not easily." Stats opened a drawer on his desk. He pulled out a case filled with CDs and thumbed through them. He slipped one out and dropped it into the drive.

"What're you doing now?"

Stats' eyes closed to a sliver. The edges of his mouth turned down. His forehead wrinkled. He reached back into the drawer, pulled out a pill bottle and sat it on his desk. The label read, *Loxapine.* Stats twisted off the cap, shook out a pill and popped it into his mouth. He unscrewed the cap to a Coke bottle, took a few swigs, and then another.

"I'm uploading a Trojan Horse onto the system."

"...A Trojan Horse?"

"As the name implies, but in a software sense."

"And this will do what?"

"Hopefully give me the administrative password to Paul Brewer's system."

"Who's that?"

"According to the file's properties, he's its creator."

"Then you could change the privileges to the file for downloading." Stats nodded. "How long, you think?"

"This ain't takeout."

Zones sighed and continued pacing, growing more impatient with each passing second. At least now he knew there was a black operations swarm program being implemented by the military, even though he didn't know what it meant. *Why would the bomber leave such a cryptic clue in the first place? Is the unsub toying with us?* He still wasn't sure if the additional crimes were committed consciously or subconsciously. *What do the bombings have to do with this military program anyway?*

"Shit!" Stats said. He typed frantically on the keyboard.

Zones turned and rushed back to the desk. "What is it?"

"They've discovered the breach, and they're trying to trace it."

"I thought you said they couldn't."

"They're using some type of advanced honeypot." Stats typed even faster. "...Those tricky bastards." He leapt from his seat and ran over to the network rack. He snatched the computer cable from its port and plugged it into the one he had used to hack the other networks. He dashed back to his desk, hit a few more keys and fell limp into his chair. He breathed hard, took a swig of Coke and leaned back.

Zones watched as Stats' hands shook uncontrollably. He rubbed his eyes red and guzzled the Coke down his throat. *I guess the Chinese will take the hit after all.*

FIFTY

NSA No Way

ZONES STEPPED FROM THE shower and wrapped a towel around his waist; his midriff rippled like two knotted ropes. Drops of water raced down his body and he threw the towel off and dried himself. He had taken a bath the night before, but it wasn't enough to rid himself of the stench from the apartment where they discovered the dead pizza delivery driver. He had racked his brain all night, or part of the night, trying to remember where he had recognized the gait of the man he had chased into the bazaar. It had been straight and proper, right out of Emily Post. He knew he had seen that strut before, but where?

The sound of pots and pans rattling came from the kitchen. Detective Rome was preparing breakfast this morning. Tofu bacon sizzled, and the smell of freshly brewed coffee got Zones' attention. His stomach growled. He crept up behind her, threw his arms around her waist and nibbled on her neck. She screamed at first, then she laughed. He turned her around to face him. They kissed. He lifted her on top of the counter. Her caramel colored legs poked from beneath a white, long-tailed men's shirt. Zones ran his hand up her thigh. She stopped its progress at her hip.

"Don't you have a killer to catch?"

"Not according to the DA. He's happy with the suspects he's got." Zones continued groping.

Detective Rome grabbed his head. "What about the creep who gave you that hicky? Didn't you and Marmaduke find bomb components and a body in his apartment?"

"You sure do know how to kill a hard-on."

"So that's all it takes, the mention of dead bodies?"

"…No, the mention of Marmaduke when I'm trying to get busy." They laughed. Zones lifted Detective Rome from the counter.

"My bacon," she ran to the stove and moved the frying pan over to an unlit burner. Smoke rose from it. Looking at the burnt remains, she saw blackened bits of thin strips of tofu. "No, dammit." Her lower lip protruded as she stomped the floor.

"It's okay," Zones held her. "I was actually looking forward to a bowl of Cheerios."

"That's not funny." She pushed him away, plucked two bowls from a shelf and filled them with cereal. "Milk is in the fridge."

"I don't drink milk; I'm lactose intolerant." Zones opened the refrigerator and stuck his head inside. "You got any almond milk, organic preferably?"

"No. Just hemp milk."

"Dry it is."

"You can't blame the DA, given the evidence."

"What, manufactured bank statements?"

"You're saying they're doctored?" Detective Rome grabbed her bowl of cereal and headed for the sofa. Zones followed.

"They're real alright, but they're made to look that way."

Detective Rome stopped chewing. She puckered her lips and stared at him. She raised both eyebrows. "What you talkin 'bout, Willis?"

"I'm glad you're amused."

"No, really, explain."

"If Dr. El-Arabi was part of this, why would he have Angela Hightower killed and still leave incriminating evidence at her condo?"

"Perhaps Atal is the mastermind and he ordered the hit from North Africa. El-Arabi may not have known anything about it. Any evidence incriminating Atal wouldn't matter to him, tucked safely away in the desert."

"That would mean phone calls from Atal to Hightower and the shooter."

"Yes, and?"

"And NSA would have a record."

"You're thinking they may have been listening in?"

"You've been listening to the news, haven't you? If they had ears anywhere, it would be in Egypt. Atal got more phone calls than a five-dollar whore with a half price special when we were there."

"But you know Atal didn't make any phone calls. It rang, but he used that typewriter thingy."

"You know that and I know that."

"So if any transcripts show phone communications between Atal and whoever—"

"We'll know they're not real."

"Good luck getting those records."

"You missed my point. If the FBI suspected Atal of the bombings, why haven't we heard of or seen any phone evidence? The first I heard of him was when the FBI and the *Roman* showed me pictures of him with my old man."

"Huh."

"What?"

"My old man, that's the first time I've heard you call him that. Usually it's T.O. He must be growing on you."

Zones tossed back a handful of cereal. "...If you say so. I say we ask for the records."

"You expect those spooks to just hand over *secret* surveillance records to you?"

Zones tossed the empty bowl onto the coffee table. He picked up the phone receiver and dialed.

"Who're you calling?"

"Detective Marmaduke, this is Zones."

"Doc, why does Detective Rome's home number come up on my phone?"

"I'm at her place."

"At eight o'clock in the morning?"

"Where're you?"

"Currently I am on the porcelain throne. Why?"

"Thanks, I needed that visual."

"You're welcome."

"Meet me in the captain's office in an hour."

"What's going on, Doc?"

"I'll tell you at the station."

Zones dropped the phone back onto the receiver. "Get dressed. We're going to see Captain Franklin."

"…To sell him on trying to get the NSA in bed with you?"

"…With us."

* * *

"Go on in," James said. She sat outside the captain's office at her desk doing her nails. She waved them by.

"Slow day, is it?" Marmaduke asked.

"I can think of one murder that could happen. Now keep stepping."

Zones pushed through the door. Captain Franklin sat at his desk with his head buried in a stack of papers. His eyes shot up as they entered.

"Well, if it ain't the Mod Squad." The captain went back to work. "Make it quick, I got a meeting with the mayor and Congressman Stonewall in an hour."

"Good," Zones said, "because you'll probably need the congressman to pull a few strings."

The captain dropped his pen and looked back up. "What is this about, Doctor?"

"We need a copy of the NSA's wiretapping transcripts from North Africa."

"NSA transcripts? What the hell for?"

"…Nebu Atal."

"I've told you before, Atal is the Fed's problem. We need to stay out of it."

"Listen, Captain," Zones moved closer to his desk, "there is still a shooter out there."

"Good point, that means you're not doing your job."

"If Atal is behind these bombings, the NSA would certainly be listening. They would have evidence of phone calls to the shooter."

"And the egghead from Tech?"

"Exactly, calls to him as well. So, will you ask for the transcripts?"

"Please, you're not fooling me for one second, Dr. Zones. You believe that about as much as you believe Marmaduke is brilliant. You're hoping there are no transcripts of Atal ordering the bombings."

"There won't be because he didn't."

"And what makes you so sure?"

"I asked him."

"Bullshit, Atal is in the wind."

"I found him."

Captain Franklin eased up from his chair. His eyes did not leave Zones. He walked around his desk and leaned in close to him. His breath struck Zones squarely in the face. The captain's hands shot to his hips, his Shar-Pei dog face only inches away.

"What do you mean, you found him?"

"I found Atal. I asked him about the bombings. I'm convinced he had nothing to do with them."

"You went to North Africa?" Zones nodded. The captain looked past Zones to Marmaduke and Detective Rome. "Did you two know anything about this?"

"No," Zones answered. "I went alone."

"Where exactly in North Africa is he?"

"I don't know. We were—"

"…We?"

"I mean me…I was blindfolded. They drove around for hours; we could've been anywhere."

"Where did you fly into?"

"Tel Aviv."

"Then he could be in Egypt." Captain Franklin walked back to his desk. "I'll alert the FBI." He snatched the phone from its hook.

"No, I believe we traveled east."

"…East?" He lowered the phone. "I'm behind on my National Geographic Explorer subscription, Doctor, but east of Israel ain't North Africa."

"I know, but the dialect was definitely North African. Just have them give you all the transcripts from the region for the last two weeks."

"I haven't agreed to do a damn thing."

"But you will. If Dr. El-Arabi isn't the mastermind the DA and *Mr.* Maximus think he is, you still have a problem."

"We'll see. Now if that's all, you three have work to do."

The three of them filed out of the office, past James' desk and around the corner. They stopped short of the elevators. Detective Rome turned to Zones.

"What's up? You lied to the captain about where we landed and the whereabouts of Nebu Atal."

"You saw him. The first mention of Atal and he was on the phone to the FBI. If they find out where he's hiding, they'll send their goon squad in to arrest him or worse, and then they'll wash their hands of this case."

"Your solution to that is lying to the brass?"

"Look who's talking, Miss Search Warrant on Demand."

Detective Rome glanced at Marmaduke then turned back to Zones. "So what, I used a little procedural license to expedite a search. That's a far cry from lying to the captain and the Feds. You may not care about doing prison time, but I do."

Marmaduke stepped between them. "Now, children," he patted Zones on the shoulder, "you're not gonna solve your shortcomings here in the hall. Let's go get a bite to eat. You both look like all you've eaten today is bird food."

Marmaduke punched the elevator button. The bell sounded. The doors slid open. The three of them stepped inside. Zones curled his lip and exchanged sharp glances with Detective Rome on the quiet ride down. They each hugged a corner of the elevator, exchanging side eyes. If tension had mass, it would exceed the twenty-five hundred pound weight limit posted on the wall. The bell sounded again, the doors parted and they filed out of the elevator.

Zones leaned in close to Detective Rome. "We'll finish this later," he whispered.

"Yes, we will."

Marmaduke's phone rang as he pushed through the door to outside. "Marmaduke here—yes, Doctor—when, right now?" He checked his watch. "Ahuh—ahuh—we'll be there in twenty minutes."

"Dr. DeGlorious?" Zones asked.

"She wants to go over the autopsy of pizza boy."

"That was quick; I thought she said three days?"

"Perhaps she had extra motivation."

"Like what?"

"Like the bomb stuffed and sewn up inside the body."

FIFTY-ONE
The Marker

ZONES STUFFED DOWN THE last bites of chicken and egg sandwich and drank the remainder of a large orange juice he had picked up from the Chick-fil-A. He brushed himself off and checked his shirt and pants for any wayward crumbs. He had learned, from their last case together, that Dr. DeGlorious did not like an untidy lab. He placed a hand on one of the double steel doors, ready to push through. His phone rang. He slipped it from his coat pocket.

"…Zones, here."

"Monk, where're you, boy?" Sam's voice blared through the phone.

"I'm at the ME's office about to view an autopsy. What's up?"

"Shapiro called from New York, gave me a name, the person who checked out your father's case evidence file from storage."

"Hold on." Zones pulled a pen and paper from his coat pocket. "Okay, go ahead."

"One Officer Mitch O'Donnell, he walks a beat in Lower Manhattan."

"Did he question him?"

"Shapiro said he clammed up until he threatened to bring charges against him. He said some guy paid him two grand to steal the piece."

"...That particular gun?"

"Here's the thing, according to O'Donnell, he asked for any evidence but not specifically from your father's case."

"When was this?"

"About two weeks ago."

"Around the time of the first bombing, did he give a description?"

"Yeah, said he was green and looked like Benjamin Franklin. Shapiro's still pressing him though."

"That's great. Let me know if there's anything else."

"There's one more thing. Shapiro said he found a key in your mother's things."

"We looked through all those boxes; there was no key."

"He said it was taped to the side of one of the boxes. I told him I didn't know what it was for. He asked if he could run it down. I told him to knock himself out."

"Good enough. I gotta go."

Zones pushed through the door, sniffing the lab's sterile air that left a harsh taste in the back of his throat and definitely ruined his breakfast. He donned a white sterile gown, a mask, a pair of booties and joined Marmaduke and Detective Rome at a table.

"Nice of you to join us, Dr. Zones," Dr. DeGlorious said. "I was just explaining to Detectives Marmaduke and Rome that your victim was exenterated."

Detective Rome turned to Zones. "That means—"

"I know what it means, Detective."

Dr. DeGlorious eyed both of them. She cleared her throat. "As I was saying, the disemboweling of your victim occurred soon after death. This slowed decomposition and reduced the accompanying odor."

"This doesn't look like your typical Y incision," Zones said. "Perhaps the perp was medically trained."

"The ears of the Y are mine. Your perp made these in the abdominal wall. They're not cuts any surgeon would make."

"May I, Doctor?" Detective Rome asked. She grabbed both sides of the flesh and folded them closed. The V-shaped patterns fell into place. "This is a finger splice. The two sides lock together like fingers on your hands when you fold them." She released the folds and locked her gloved fingers together. She held them up for them. "See."

"And what is it used for?" Marmaduke asked.

"Wood jointing, manufacturing, almost anything."

"What about the bomb, Doctor?"

"ATF took it away, said it was similar to the others. It was seated here." Dr. DeGlorious pulled back the fingers on the wound. "Sick bastard even bolted it to his spinal column."

"Was it functional?"

"Fired up and ready to go, just needed the signal. Any idea what he'd planned to do with a body bomb?"

"Not a clue."

"This is the kind of stuff you see in Afghanistan and Iraq."

"A guy couldn't make this kind of mess and not leave any DNA."

"If he had, it would probably be too contaminated to use. Your best hope is prints, Detective."

"Speaking of hope, any progress solving that nano stuff?"

Dr. DeGlorious pulled a sheet over the body. "We're still working on cracking the code for the marker." She slipped her gloves off and tossed them into the biowaste container. She walked over to the counter, opened the door to a large refrigerator and retrieved a jar. "I brought this sample back here to work on in between cases." She sat the jar on top of a stainless steel table near the body.

"So, we're still getting nowhere fast."

"I'm afraid so, Detective."

"Is there anything else, Doctor?"

"I'll call you if I come up with something."

Marmaduke turned to leave. Zones followed. They stopped short of the door to remove their protective clothing. Before she reached the double doors, Detective Rome's phone rang. It chimed out the theme from *Close Encounters of the Third Kind*.

"Hello," she said. No one answered. Detective Rome hung up and headed for the door. Her phone rang again just short of her exiting the lab and with the same tune. "Hello," she answered but still no reply.

"Detective Rome," Dr. DeGlorious called to her.

She turned back, the phone still to her ear, "Yes, Doctor."

The glass jar filled with the nanoprotein was vibrating. Dr. DeGlorious pulled a device from underneath a base cabinet. She plugged it in and worked the controls. The device sent out loud squeals. She continued to adjust the knobs and levers until the squeals mimicked

Detective Rome's ringtone. With each adjustment she made, the pitch grew higher.

"Cover your ears," Dr. DeGlorious said. The sound hammered their ears before completely disappearing. The nanoprotein in the jar glowed bright blue. Detective Rome's eyes locked onto it. She inched closer; the phone dangled from her hand. Zones and Marmaduke turned back as well. They surrounded the jar.

"What's happening?" Zones asked.

"I believe we've found our marker," Dr. DeGlorious said.

FIFTY-TWO

The Diagram

"NOW THAT WE'VE FOUND the marker, how does this help our case?" Zones asked Dr. DeGlorious.

"For one thing, we know for sure it's DOD. They're the only ones who can create a nanoparticle that responds to such a complicated marker sequence."

"What about their contractors?"

"I consider them part of the system."

"But we still don't know what this stuff does or why it's in Saudi Arabia's drinking water."

"Whatever it's for," Marmaduke said, "it was enough to get Muhammad El-Arabi killed."

"May I see his autopsy report, Doctor?" Zones asked. Dr. DeGlorious disappeared behind a door labeled *Office* and returned with a file. She handed it to Zones. He scanned the report; he had read it many times before. "Do you still have his brain specimen?"

Dr. DeGlorious returned to the counter behind her and grabbed another jar from the shelf. She snapped on a set of gloves, unscrewed the lid, removed a section of brain and laid it on a table. "What is it you're looking for, Dr. Zones?"

"How do you illuminate the protein?"

"Let me show you. Detective Marmaduke, grab four goggles from that top drawer." He pulled out four pairs and handed them around. Dr. DeGlorious unhooked a light hanging overhead. "Does everyone have their eye protection on?" She cut the lights. The room went dark. She waved the infrared lamp over the brain specimen. It lit up.

"The nanoproteins concentrate around the frontal lobe," Zones said.

"In particular, the prefrontal cortex. The brain dissections I did on primates for the DOD showed the same concentration."

"So the protein is designed to target this area."

"Could you both let us lower humans in on what you're talking about?" Marmaduke asked.

"A function of the frontal lobe is to control behavior," Zones explained. "There's a possibility that's what these nanoproteins are designed to do."

"Alter behavior? That sounds like Twilight Zone hocus-pocus."

"You'd be surprised, Detective. Finding a way to control human behavior has been a goal of world governments for many years. Some have claimed to have advanced the science but nothing ever materialized. This may be the closest anyone has ever come to succeeding."

"So are you suggesting the U.S. Government developed this for the Saudis to use on their people?"

"It would seem so." Zones thought for a minute. "Do you have a whiteboard?" he asked Dr. DeGlorious.

"We have two. Give me a hand, Detective?" She and Marmaduke rolled two large whiteboards in from an adjacent room. They placed them side-by-side. "You'll need some markers." She handed three to Zones.

"This is what we know and how the nanoprotein may play a part in this case. Muhammad El-Arabi visited Saudi Arabia after joining an environmental group made up mostly of George Washington University students." Zones wrote, *ME Joined GW Environ Gp,* on the board. He drew a box around it. Next to it, he wrote, *ME visit SA.* He drew a box around it as well. An arrow was drawn from the first box to the second. "Muhammad collected water samples in the town of Qatif, I suspect, to test it for petrochemical contamination and expose the poor drilling practices of Euro-Arabia Oil."

"And you know this how?" Dr. DeGlorious asked.

"I went to the town to confirm it." Zones continued to diagram his process. "Muhammad returned to the states with the samples. He gave them to his father to analyze, not knowing they contained the nanoprotein. He drank the water while visiting Qatif. That's how the nanoprotein got into his system. His behavior changed. He changed his appearance. His father—Dr. Amal El-Arabi, a nanoscience researcher at Tech—discovered the nanoprotein in the water sample. He asked his boss and lab director, Professor Uza Landrosky, to confirm his findings."

"Unbeknownst to Dr. El-Arabi," Detective Rome said, "Professor Landrosky was a well-paid consultant for Euro-Arabia. We found invoices at his home office that confirmed this."

"Exactly, and being the golden goose protector that he was, Landrosky passed El-Arabi's findings on to someone at Euro-Arabia. For his efforts, he was handsomely rewarded with a bullet to the head. This brings us to our bombings. I believe they are meant to implicate Dr. El-Arabi in terrorist activities to discredit him, should he choose to go public with his findings about the nanoprotein."

"Why not just have him killed, Doc?" Marmaduke asked. "It's a hell of a lot less complicated."

"A father and son both dead, that would raise more suspicion and narrow the police investigation. A terrorist plot by Saudi nationals, however, would widen the investigation. It'll have everybody twisting in the wind, like we are now, chasing drug dealers, environmentalists, animal rights groups and Muslim terrorists. We see what we have been conditioned to see."

"Your Gestalt."

"Exactly, Detective."

"What about Angela Hightower?"

"She was a contractor, just like Landrosky."

"What makes you so sure of all this?"

"I visited a clinic in Riyadh, Saudi Arabia that claimed to have a program that reduced the crime rate to virtually zero."

"And you believe this?"

"At first, no, the program seemed to be a joke. Now I believe they're using this nanotechnology to achieve those rates, to curtail the unrest."

Zones paused; he rested one arm on the other and stroked his goatee. His teeth and bottom lip wrestled with each other. He turned to the two whiteboards, now covered in black diagrams of the case. He followed the arrows that connected each box and read the details in each. When he reached the end, he started over.

"What is it, Doc?" Marmaduke asked.

Zones said nothing. He stood back and continued to study both boards. He uncapped a marker, approached one board and wrote, *Swarm*. He drew an arrow and wrote, *Blumer's Collective Behavior*. He drew another arrow and wrote *Middle East unrest*. Zones added *Nanoprotein*, *Oil*, and USA, all separated with arrows. He snatched the cap off another marker and ended the flow chart with *House Bill HR 150* printed in red.

FIFTY-THREE

Butlers and Homos

ZONES STEPPED BACK FROM the whiteboards again. He felt good about his analysis. For the first time, he saw the complete scheme, from the opening act to the motive. The only things missing were the main and bit players.

"You plan on telling us what that means, Doc, or do we have to stand here looking stupid?" Marmaduke asked.

"This, Detective, is motive."

"Explain, please."

Zones walked back to the board. "*Swarm* is a clue left by the unsub. It's an acronym formed from the ancillary crimes the unsub committed at the bomb sites: Sexual assault, Weapons violation, Arson, Robbery and Murder. The murder was your pizza guy. We interrupted the detonation of his body bomb."

"Why would the bomber leave this clue knowing it could get him caught?"

"Your unsub is a riddler, Detective. His psychosis compels him to test his own sense of superiority and superior intellect against those blocking his objectives."

"And that's this swarm thing."

Zones nodded, "It has to do with *Collective Behavior*, this box." He pointed with the marker. "Controlling the behavior of the masses is the goal. Ground zero for this program was the Middle East, more specifically, Qatif, Saudi Arabia, a state with little to no international oversight. To carry this out, a nanoprotein developed by the Pentagon was introduced into the population through the public water system. It attached to the frontal lobe of the brain, somehow affecting behavior. Unrest was essentially eradicated in Qatif, the site of a major oil field and a hotbed of protest by Shia Muslims. The objective was to insure the uninterrupted flow of oil from the Kingdom to the USA."

"Hold up, Doc." Marmaduke approached the whiteboards. "That would never, never happen. Not when you got Bush walking hand in hand with King Farooki, or whatever his name is, like they're homos." He turned to Detective Rome. "No offense. We have Obama bowing to his ass like he's his butler, or something, about to serve him tea. We're wedded to them motherfuckas and their oil. I'll tell you, it's just like we told the Indians when we came to this land. We ain't going nowhere, absolutely nowhere. Your land is now our land. Their oil *is* our oil."

"Perhaps you're right, Detective. But right now it's being jeopardized by House Bill HR 150, which will restrict the import of oil from countries experiencing civil unrest, war or any other conflict."

"Supposing your analysis is correct, where do we go from here?"

"...Perhaps a conversation with Euro-Arabia is in order, and we need to find out a little more about this bill. I've got a call in to Congressman Bulwark's office already. He's the sponsor of the bill. I'm just waiting to hear back from them."

"Detective Rome and I have already spoken to the head of Euro-Arabia, a Mr. al-Saud."

"When did that happen?"

"Last week. His plane stopped over at Hartsfield-Jackson on its way to DC."

"...From where?"

"Texas, I believe."

"Figures."

"Why do you say that, Doc?"

"Congressman Bulwark is from Texas. If I had to guess, al-Saud was probably there attempting to influence this bill. Did you get anything?"

"We met at his lawyers' office, the Brooks Brothers kind, with a limited vocabulary. We didn't get anything incriminating. That'll take a subpoena."

"Then let's go get one."

Marmaduke sighed and shook his head. "I won't even ask."

Zones lagged behind Marmaduke and Detective Rome as they left the lab. He waited for them to push through the double doors ahead of him, and he turned back and ran over to where Dr. DeGlorious was returning the jar of nanoprotein to the refrigerator.

"Dr. DeGlorious," Zones called to her.

She turned around. "Oh, Dr. Zones, I thought you had left."

"Sorry if I startled you."

"What can I do for you?"

"Tell me about Paul Brewer."

The blood drained from her face. "I don't know the name." She turned back, rearranging jars on the shelves.

"He worked in black projects at the Pentagon. You sure you don't know him?"

"Certain names are classified; how would you know he works black projects?"

"You said works, present tense. So he's still there."

Dr. DeGlorious dropped a jar onto the counter; a muffled sound could be heard throughout the lab. She turned to Zones, eyes squinted and jaws tensed. "Listen, I've already stuck my neck out much too far on this case, far more than any of you. I see that look in your eyes, Dr. Zones. Going after these guys is something to prove for you, just like those Mormons. Well, guess what, these guys ain't some robe-wearing Bible thumpers with a reputation to maintain. They call them black projects for a reason. You won't even see them coming, unless they want you to. By that time, the knife is in your throat, the bullet is in your head or the bomb has blown your ass into fish chum. Do all of us a favor, Dr. Zones; stay on the yellow brick road. Don't go peeking into dark places. I can't help you anymore."

Dr. DeGlorious stormed from the lab, her high heels clip-clopped across the tile floor. Her white lab coat flared out from the air trapped beneath it. Zones stared in disbelief. *Why doesn't she want to help?* He bolted for the door and raced down the hall out into the parking lot. Marmaduke popped nicotine gum as he and Detective Rome stood next to his car.

"What the fuck happened to you?" Marmaduke asked Zones as he approached.

"What do you know about Dr. DeGlorious' time at the DOD?"

"Nothing. She's been pretty hush-mouthed about her work with them. All I know is that she performed autopsies on monkeys."

"Necropsies, you mean."

"Whatever. Why do you ask?"

"She left there and went straight to the ME's office. Any military in her background?"

"Those are all good questions for human resources. What is this about, Doc?"

"She's a suspect," Detective Rome said.

"*What?*" Marmaduke's voice spiked. He looked back toward the door of the ME's office. "What the hell happened between the end of our meeting and now?" Zones said nothing. "Listen, Doc, you can't go around suspecting your teammates of being criminals." Zones folded his arms, cocked his head and smirked. "What? So now I'm a suspect as well?"

Zones' phone rang. He fished it out of his coat as he watched Marmaduke scratch his head and spin on his heels. "...Zones, here."

"Doctor, this is James. The captain is back from his meeting. He wants to see you."

"Did he get the phone transcripts from the NSA for North Africa?"

"He didn't say, just said for you to get your fine ass in here. I added the fine."

"I'm relieved." Zones hung up. "The captain is back from his meeting with Congressman Stonewall and the mayor."

"Let's go." Marmaduke snatched open his car door. "I want to hear you try to explain to the captain why you think the DeKalb County medical examiner is now a suspect in these bombings."

FIFTY-FOUR

"What have you been smoking?"

"WHAT?" CAPTAIN FRANKLIN SHOUTED. He slammed his fist down on his desk and turned a shade darker. He rubbed his clean-shaven head, paced the floor and rattled the Callaway Big Bertha he practiced golf swings with. "What do you mean you want search warrants for Euro-Arabia offices? Do they even have an office here? Last time I checked, there's no oil in Georgia."

"We can start with their DC and Houston offices," Zones said.

"And what brought this all about?"

"I've uncovered evidence they may have something to do with these bombings."

"Shit, Doctor, one Arab isn't good enough; now you have to go and implicate a whole goddamn corporation full of them? What is this evidence anyway?"

"It's more of a theory."

"A theory. You want me to have the DA exercise his subpoena power based on a theory? You would've been better off coming in here with one of Marmaduke's cockamamie hunches." Captain Franklin returned to his chair. "Okay, let's hear it."

Zones peeked over his shoulder at Marmaduke and Detective Rome. They stood far away, one near the door the other in a corner where the captain kept his Taylors, their heads turned from him, their eyes shifted to the floor, the wall or the ceiling. A "*You're on your own partner*" kind of feeling came over him. Zones turned back to the captain, who was rocking in his chair. He spun his Big Bertha on the tips of his fingers and sucked on a toothpick trapped between lips that seemed anxious to say no.

Zones explained his theory and the nexus between the events that led him to his beliefs. He studied the captain and looked for any sign of support or agreement. Captain Franklin looked past him. His eyes slid across his face to the right, then to the left. He got up from his chair like an old, arthritic man and walked to a bag of golf clubs propped against the wall in the corner. He lowered the oversized driver into its proper place, as if he were handling nuclear material. The captain walked back to his desk. He had that old-school gait. A pimp walk as they called it in the hood—the feet glided across the floor and the hips dipped. He returned to his seat, hung his feet across his desk, leaned back and asked,

"*What* have you been smoking?"

"What do you mean?"

"It has got to be a psychotropic drug making you hallucinate and believe the U.S. Government and the Saudis are involved in mind control."

"It's more like behavior modification."

"Who gives a fuck what it's called, Doctor? The point is, I'm not going to cause an international incident based on a theory that sounds like something Charles Manson cooked up. End of story."

"What about Dr. El-Arabi?"

"What about him? He's about to go to the grand jury."

"But he's innocent."

"That's for twelve low-paid citizens of this great county to decide, Doctor."

"So that's it; this investigation ends here?"

"Do you know who killed that pizza guy and stuffed him with a bomb?" Zones shook his head. "Then the investigation ain't over. On second thought, Marmaduke and Detective Rome can handle that."

The captain picked up the phone and dialed. "James, get in here." He dropped the receiver down.

Moments later, James pushed through the door. "Yes, Captain."

"Settle up Dr. Zones' account." Captain Franklin dropped his feet to the floor. "We won't be needing his services any longer." He slid his glasses on and shuffled through a stack of papers piled on his desk. "...Anything else, Doctor? If not, I got work to do."

"What about the NSA transcripts from North Africa?"

"Not that it matters to you, but, the NSA has recordings of Atal plotting with some unknown person in Yemen to plant bombs here."

"May I see the transcripts?"

"There are no transcripts."

"Then how do you know?"

"How do I know?" He slipped off his reading glasses. "Okay, Dr. Zones, I'll entertain your nonsense for the last time. Congressman Stonewall's aide made a call to someone on the Security Council."

"Then I'll go see him."

"Don't you dare. You two got history. Besides, he's on his way back to DC."

"Only a phone call and that was good enough for you?"

"Unlike you, Doctor, I don't go looking for conspiracies. Now, if that's all?"

"...For now." Zones headed out the door. He stopped short and turned back. "One more thing, Captain, Dr. DeGlorious should be considered a suspect."

"What?" Zones bolted from the office. Marmaduke and Detective Rome followed. "Not you two," the captain shouted. Zones turned to see them stop short of the door. "What in the *hell* did he mean by that?"

Zones mingled with cars and trucks on his way to the Kensington MARTA Station. He needed to think. The walk and the morsels of fresh air siphoned through the smell of car exhaust helped to focus his mind. The captain was back to his old, slothful self again. He didn't want to piss off the suits in Washington by going after the petro-pusher, Euro-Arabia. He had crossed this bridge before, much like the one he was crossing now over Interstate 285. The captain operated in the political realm more than he did in law enforcement. He was getting too bogged down in the minutia of budgets and stagecraft. He always tried to position himself for that next command promotion or recognition by the higher-ups. Captain Franklin's nose was browner than a puppy smelling its own shit. That was okay. Zones knew that his gumption was about as weak as his bladder. He policed like a lazy dog. He wouldn't move unless poked. He needed a stick of the right length and thickness to get him to go hunting.

Zones was muddling his options when his phone rang. "Zones, here," he answered.

"I'm sorry. I must have the wrong number," the woman on the other end said. "I was trying to reach Mr. Saleh. Sorry for bothering you. Good-bye."

Zones stopped, gritted his teeth and said, "No, hold on one moment." He covered the phone and held it from his ear. He cleared his throat, swallowed and pressed the phone back tight to his ear. "This is Makkada Saleh." His voice had changed to a deeper, more Barry White, tone.

"Mr. Saleh, I'm calling from Congressman Bulwark's office."

"Yes, is the congressman available to speak with me?"

"The congressman has an opening tomorrow at one o'clock."

"I'll be there."

"He can only give you thirty minutes."

"I'll come prepared."

"I'll let the congressman know you're coming."

Zones hung up. The call from Washington was just what he needed. Captain Franklin may have kicked him off the case, but that didn't mean he couldn't finish what he'd started.

FIFTY-FIVE

Commies, The Bill and Fine Kentucky Bourbon

THE BANANA-COLORED DC CAB pulled onto Independence Avenue, which ran parallel to Constitution, its twin. The two streets stretched long and broad; they cut through the congressional campus like two cleared paths in a cornfield. Trees dotted the open spaces. They greened-up the white, flat facades that sat like teeth sunk into a spinach salad. Zones passed the Capitol's East Front. The building anchored the campus in a permanence that was as rooted in the country's foundation as the Virginia sandstone that covered it.

The cab stopped in front of the Rayburn House Office Building. Zones leapt out and darted up the stairs. He meandered through the vacant, pale halls, coming to the office of Texas Congressman Bulwark. A placard hung on the wall; it read, *Office of the Thirty-fourth Congressional District of Texas.* Zones knocked. He waited for an answer, none came. He pushed through the wood-paneled double doors and entered.

"Yes, may I help you?" a woman with big, brown eyes hidden behind a pair of black, pearl-framed glasses asked. She lowered her head, staring over the top of her glasses.

"I'm Makkada Saleh; I'm here to see Congressman Bulwark."

She glanced at her wrist watch. "You're early. Have a seat; the congressman will be with you shortly."

Zones took a seat. He spied the Ram's head and pictures of oil fields mounted on deep-warm, mahogany-paneled walls. The rustic décor on this side of the doors pushed back against the cold, heavily-veined, marble floors and walls on the other side of them.

The phone rang without ceasing. The woman answered it when not pecking away at her computer keyboard. Her desk nameplate read, *Barbara Snyder*. She was well-passed her prime in the face, but she showcased two freshly casted bulbous bows as breasts; that was her *job security*.

A clock on the wall read half past one.

"Can you let the congressman know that I'm waiting?"

Barbara flicked her eyes at him. She continued to type. "The congressman knows, sir."

Zones slung one leg over the other. He grabbed a magazine from the end table next to his chair, the *Oil Times*. A heading caught his attention. *What if: U.S. oil imports from the Middle East fell by...*He read on. The article outlined various scenarios for the country if foreign oil imports decreased by percentages over twenty years. It cited House Bill HR 150 specifically as the first step in oil import reduction. As Zones read, a door off to the side was flung open. Four men stepped out, bolted for the double doors and disappeared into the hall.

Barbara pushed her platinum blonde hair back, "Good day, y'all." Moments later, the phone rang. "Yes, sir," Barbara said as she answered it. She eased the receiver back on its hook. "The congressman will see you now. Walk right through that door," she pointed.

Zones cracked open the door and entered. The same décor carried through from the waiting area. Sitting behind a large, presidential-style desk, Congressman Bulwark looked up from behind a newspaper. His bushy brows clung to his face like Spanish moss above his droopy eyes.

"Come in and have a seat." He reached into a humidor sitting atop the desk and pulled out a guillotine and a stogie. He snipped the end and fired it up. "You don't mind, do you?"

"Well—"

"Good." He took a few puffs. "The commies made the whole goddamn building non-smoking. Never seen people so hell-bent on taking all the fun out of life." Bulwark pushed up from his chair, grabbed his cane and hobbled over to a bar across the room. His three-piece pinstriped suit dangled from his gaunt frame; it swallowed him. He pulled two glasses from a shelf and dropped ice into them. "But I'm from Texas, so I say fuck'um." He poured some brown liquid into each one and marched back to his desk. He dropped back down in his seat and slid one of the glasses across the desk to Zones. The congressman raised his glass. "Here's to people who *kill* fun and *will* die like the rest of us." They struck glasses. Congressman Bulwark slurped. "Aahh, that's good. This is my first drink all day. I just met with some sheik from a Saudi oil company. They don't like it when you drink alcohol in front of them. I don't like it when you don't. Hell, I wish they would extend the same courtesy to me when I visit them." He took another slurp. "This here is fine Kentucky bourbon. How do you like it?"

Zones gasped, "Good stuff."

"Yeah, it is. I won it from congressman *dumb nutsacks* when he bet his Wildcats against my Aggies. But that's another story. What can I do for you Mr., ah…"

"Saleh, Makkada Saleh with Black Enterprise Magazine."

"Black Enterprise, you say. That's an oxymoron." Zones gave him a sharp stare. "Aw, don't go gettin your panties in a bunch. No need to call Al Charlatan. I ain't prejudice. I just got my preferences, same as you." He leaned back in his cushioned chair. Puffs of smoke swirled around his face. "For some reason, I thought you were a female." He stared at Zones. "Oh well, what do you need?"

"I have questions about your bill, HR 150."

"What about it?"

"Some say it's designed to completely eradicate Mid East oil."

"Yeah, what's wrong with that?" The office door opened. Zones turned. "This is my chief of staff, Miles Collins. This is Mr., ah…"

"Saleh." Zones stood, shook Miles' outstretched hand and returned to his seat.

"Mr. Saleh here wants to know about your troublemaking bill. Miles, you see, wrote most of it. He can answer all your questions."

Miles walked to a far corner of the spacious office. "Yes, I spoke to you earlier." He flipped a switch on the wall. A vacuum of air sucked in the cigar smoke across the room. "You know you're not supposed to smoke in here, Congressman."

Bulwark leaned across the desk to Zones, "Commie," he whispered.

"What exactly do you want to know?" Miles asked.

"First of all, this bill can't be that popular with the oil companies."

"Not with OPEC. U.S. companies know this bill will be a win-win for them."

"How so?"

"Temporary shortages will drive prices higher. The government will expand domestic drilling rights. The cost and risk of doing business in unstable countries will drastically decrease. More jobs will be created at home, et cetera, et cetera."

"But the oil producing nations don't like the bill because it will reduce their demand."

"And remove the grip they hold over our foreign policy decisions."

"...Any adversaries in particular?"

"OPEC related: Saudi Arabia, UAE, Qatar, all of them really."

"Is that who you met with earlier?"

"What do you mean?"

"The congressman mentioned a meeting with a Saudi oil company head."

Miles turned to Congressman Bulwark, at ease from his fill of liquor. "Yes, I met with Taufic al-Saud. He runs Euro-Arabia USA."

"That was al-Saud?"

"...Yes, why do you ask?"

Zones ignored him. "I understand the bill has a good chance of passing in the House."

"We're close."

"You don't sound too confident."

"There're a few holdouts, but we're working them."

"Mind telling me who they are?"

"...Off the record?" Zones nodded. Miles pulled a file from a stack piled on top of the congressman's desk. He slipped out a sheet. "This should give you what you're looking for."

Zones took the paper and scanned it. His finger stopped on one name. "Congressman Stonewall? He's the only republican holdout, rants about Islamic terrorists all the time. I would think he would be the first to sign."

Congressman Bulwark perked up. "Don't you worry about ol' Stoney. He's just doing a little horse trading. We'll have him on board soon."

"Congressman Stonewall has existing legislation stalled in the House," Miles said.

Zones took a sip from his glass. "…Legislation on what?"

"Immigration, terrorism, you name it, seems that's his thing."

"What about al-Saud? Is he lobbying you to massage or drop the bill?"

"We had a conversation with Mr. al-Saud. Euro-Arabia is a major employer in Texas."

"But the bill will virtually kill their U.S. business."

"Only if there's unrest, terrorism or war in their country."

"We're talking the Middle East here."

"We're talking about taking back control of this country's energy future." Miles pulled up a chair. He sat next to Congressman Bulwark. "Is there anything else, Mr. Saleh?"

"Just one more thing, what can you tell me about the defense department's swarm program?"

Congressman Bulwark's head snapped up, and Miles squirmed in his chair. His eyes seemed to glaze over. Zones knew he had their full attention. He watched as the two men traded glances.

"I don't know what you mean," Miles said.

"The congressman is on the security council, is he not? Swarm is a DOD black project. What can you tell me about it?"

"Where did you hear about that?"

"I have a source."

"Then you must also know that we can't discuss the existence or non-existence of any classified projects. And any release of information on suspected projects by the press could subject them to federal prosecution for revealing state secrets."

"So you have no comment."

Miles stood, fastened his coat, walked to the door and opened it. "Good day, Mr. Saleh."

Zones got up from his chair and straightened his coat. "Congressman, Mr. Collins." He walked through the open door, stopped at the end table by the chair and placed the paper containing the voting for Bill HR 150 on it. He turned to the receptionist. "Can you call me a cab, please?" Zones lifted the paper from the table, along with the *Oil Times* magazine.

The congressman and his chief of staff were hush-mouthed about any knowledge of a black project called swarm. They either wouldn't say or didn't know. This was to be expected. *Military secrets are the only kept secrets in this town—but not for long.*

FIFTY-SIX

al-Saud

Zones stared through the storefront window of McCormick and Schmick's. He sipped on a cosmopolitan and popped firecracker shrimp into his mouth. It was early happy hour. The lunch crowd had sunk back into their paper-shuffling and influence peddling. He missed the horse trading of politics and business that was unique to the district. It corrupted the place, stunk it up even. The smell was like smoke before the fire: You knew something was about to go up in flames.

The Washington, D.C. office of Euro-Arabia occupied a space across the street from the restaurant at 17th and K. Zones finished off the last of his meal and his drink. He pulled out his phone and dialed.

"Euro-Arabia Services, how may I help you?"

"Taufic al-Saud, please."

"Certainly, please hold." Elevator music played over the phone. Seconds later, another voice answered.

"Mr. al-Saud's office, how may I help you?"

"Yes, I'm a reporter with the Oil Times, and I would like to get Mr. al-Saud's opinion on my article in this month's edition. I'm preparing a follow-up article."

"Hold, please." Music played.

A waitress approached Zones. "Will there be anything else? Another drink, perhaps?" He shook his head. "I'll clear this out of your way." She collected the plate of shrimp scraps and the empty liquor glasses.

"Sir," the woman on the phone piped back, "what did you say your name is?"

Zones flipped open the Oil Times magazine. He riffled through the pages to the end of the article. "Peter Grae, that's G-R-A-E."

"And you say you're with Oil Times?"

"I wrote an article on what effect limiting Middle East oil would have on the country. Tell Mr. al-Saud I was there when he met with Congressman Bulwark earlier today. And in light of the congressman's bill, HR 150, I would think it wise for Mr. al-Saud to express his opinion."

"Hold, please." More music was piped through the phone. Seconds later, she returned, "Mr. Grae."

"I'm here."

"Mr. al-Saud will meet with you for thirty minutes, but only if you can be here in ten."

"I'll be right there."

Zones pulled twenty dollars from his wallet. He dropped it onto the table and ran from the restaurant. Minutes later, he was riding the elevator to the twelfth floor of the K street building. The doors parted. He stepped out and two men dressed in black suits met him.

"You're Peter Grae?" one of them asked.

"Yes."

"Hold your hands up, please."

"What is this all about?"

"Your hands, please."

Zones raised his hands as one patted him down. He reached inside Zones' coat and pulled out a notepad and his wallet. *Shit, my ID.* Zones snatched the wallet from him. "I don't think I can hide a weapon in there, do you?"

The two men locked eyes. "Okay, you're good. Come this way."

Zones shoved his wallet back inside his coat pocket. He followed the men down a long corridor; its walls were packed with images of oil fields and refineries. A set of double doors lay ahead of them.

"Welcome, Mr. Grae." A young woman greeted him. "Right this way, please." She led Zones through another set of doors. "Mr. al-Saud, Mr. Grae is here." He waved Zones over.

The office consumed half the floor, it seemed. The sun's rays poured in from two sides, illuminating the reminders of Islamic culture fashioned into ornate furniture and tapestries.

Al-Saud stood, as did the two men sitting at the desk. He pledged with his right hand. "As-salaam alaikum," he said and stuck his hand out.

"Alaikum salaam," Zones replied.

"This is Mr. Ben-Jarvis and Mr. Ellis."

"...Gentlemen."

"Please, have a seat, Mr. Grae;" al-Saud brushed back the sides of his hair. A seven-inch wide part ran down the middle of it. His strong cologne was more imposing than his cartoon-sized frame. He sank deep into the oversized desk chair and leaned back. His hairy arms draped over the sides. He seemed to be holding court like some Caesar or sheik, and he dressed for the part. Gold dripped from everywhere, like a Hindu bride on her wedding day. His silk tie glistened; streaks of the precious metal crisscrossed its front. Zones expected to see a visible gold tooth. Al-Saud smiled, all white. "Now, what is it you would like to know?"

"You're aware of the oil bill Congressman Bulwark has sponsored." Zones pulled a notepad and pen from his coat. "What're your thoughts?"

"My thoughts, Mr. Grae, are that the passage of this bill will not be in the best interest of the American people."

"As I've outlined in my article, a reduction in foreign oil would be a positive thing for the country. Why do you believe in the contrary?"

"I have read your article. What you have failed to consider is the negative impact the bill could have on the global stage. If the U.S. goes from fifty percent oil imports to zero, it would be catastrophic to the world economy."

"You believe it would be good in the short-term but disastrous in the long-term."

"That is correct."

"...Even with the growth of China?"

"China is a future market for sure. But no one consumes energy like Americans."

Zones scribbled in the pad. "The bill will punish countries wherein unrest, terrorism and war are a problem. Given the recent unrest in Qatif, this could impact your exports to the U.S."

"That is why we, the Kingdom of Saudi Arabia, have implemented a crime reduction program that has been very successful."

"The Prince Mohammed bin Nayef Center for Counseling and Care?"

"How do you—"

"I have a friend, a criminal psychologist, who attended a conference in Riyadh at the center."

"I see."

"He reviewed the Qatif report but couldn't quite understand how such drastic crime reduction percentages were obtained. Could the working papers be made available for peer review?"

"I'm afraid that is not my department, Mr. Grae. I am only a businessman."

"Can you tell me about your conversation with Congressman Bulwark? I take it, it was about the bill."

"I am expressing the same sentiments to you that I talked to the congressman about."

"And his reaction was?"

"He listened but wasn't particularly swayed by my argument."

"Now, with this new crime program, the passage of the bill is moot."

"We argued on behalf of less fortunate countries."

"That's no problem. All you have to do is spike their water with the same Pentagon provided, mind-controlling nanoprotein you used on your own people."

The quiet room got quieter. He eyed al-Saud. His black eyes stared back like a jackal hunting prey. Zones had his attention and knew he was angry. Zones turned to the two men flanking him. *If these are his man-handlers, they sure aren't saying much—they didn't know, that's why.* Zones turned back to al-Saud; he had risen from his seat and walked to a counter.

"Tea, Mr. Grae?" al-Saud asked, stirring his drink.

"I'd like to know about your government's involvement in the DOD's swarm project."

Al-Saud walked back to his desk with four cups on a tray. "Here you go, gentlemen." He slid one cup and then another across the desk. "This is Darjeeling Oolong tea from my country."

"Is this Euro-Arabia's way around Congressman Bulwark's bill? Does this scheme stop with the Kingdom, or is every country in OPEC in on it? First you drug the Shia in Qatif, then the FARC in Latin America or the Boko Haram and FLEC-FAC in Nigeria and Angola."

Just as Ben-Jarvis and Ellis moved the cups of tea up to their lips, before they could take a sip, al-Saud said, "Will you gentlemen excuse us?"

They paused. "Are you—"

Al-Saud threw up his hand. "Mr. Grae and I have some things to clear up." The men got up with their cups in hand. They headed for the door, eased it open and out they went. "Where are you getting this information from, Mr. Grae?"

"Do you deny it?"

"Now, you listen to me and listen carefully. You are making very dangerous accusations; I hope you are not prepared to publish them."

"But I have proof."

"If you had proof, you would not be here making inquiries of me."

"No proof, huh? What if I told you there were vials of water samples collected from Qatif stored in a police crime lab in Georgia and that the behavior altering nanoprotein had been discovered and had contributed to the death of a young Saudi national?"

"And where did you get such proof?"

"My sources are not important. What is important is that you tell me who is involved in this and who is setting off bombs down in Georgia."

Al-Saud jumped to his feet. "I'm afraid this interview is over, Mr. Grae." He pressed a button on the phone. Zones heard the sound of the office door opening. "Please show Mr. Grae out." Zones turned to see the same men who greeted him at the elevator. He pushed up from the chair and headed toward them. "And Mr. Grae, I would be very careful about printing such stories about exploding bombs and tainted water. They have a way of biting the teller."

The men led Zones back down the corridor and over to an awaiting elevator. He rode it down to the lobby and stopped by the security desk.

"Can you call me a cab, please?"

"...Certainly." The guard dialed. Zones walked to the storefront and waited. He eyed the rush of people moving along the sidewalks. "...Sir?" Zones turned to the guard. "Your cab will be here shortly. You may wait for it out front, if you wish."

"Thank you."

The guard grabbed a radio from the desk. "Station one, station one, roll Mr. al-Saud's car. Over."

"Roger that, rolling al-Saud," a voice piped through the radio.

"One more thing," Zones asked, "where's the garage exit?"

"...At the end of the building on 17th Street."

Zones tore through the door. He ran up the street to the end of the building and waited behind a column with a clear line of site to the parking exit. Soon, a car carrying al-Saud emerged from the garage and pulled into traffic. Zones looked around for the cab. He ran to the corner, looked down K Street, then back down 17th Street. He ran back to where al-Saud's car inched along, stuck in the cavalcade of cars. He followed them on foot, just out of sight. The pace of traffic picked up. Zones' walk turned into a steady trot. Soon, he found himself at a full sprint. With each stride he took, the car got farther away.

A cab pulled into traffic ahead of Zones. He ran alongside it, beat on the window and shouted, "Stop." He yanked open the rear passenger door and dove inside.

The driver turned in his seat. "What are you doing?"

Zones picked himself up. "Follow that car."

"Brother, can't you read? The sign says, *Off Duty.*"

Zones grabbed a bill from his wallet. "I got a hundred that says you aren't." He held the money up.

"For me to miss lunch with my momma, it's gonna cost you at least two of those."

"Shit." Zones pulled another hundred from his wallet and handed them to the driver.

"Hold on."

"Don't get too close."

"Brother, you ain't my first rodeo. I've been tailing cheating husbands, dirty congressmen, diplomats who were spies and spies who were diplomats in this town before you could say goo-goo daa-daa. Someone is always watching someone else in the capital city. Us cabbies, we watch 'um all. You never know when you'll need that ticket waved or that DUI to disappear. Besides, that looks like al-Saud's car. What's today, Wednesday? He's probably going to his usual."

"Where's that?"

"…The Chowdog."

"…In Anacostia?"

"You know the place?"

"I got ptomaine there back in the day."

"It's still on the menu."

"What's Wall Street doing in the hood?"

"He meets with this cat from military intelligence every Wednesday."

"Military intelligence? He meets with him in full dress?"

"No, in street clothes, trying to blend in."

"Then how do you know he's MI?"

"I know a spook when I see one, son. Spent years in the jungles of Southeast Asia, Army, ninth infantry. The Old Reliables they called us. These guys would always show up in camp with their faulty info about what the enemy was doing. If you followed their shit, you got a gut bag for life, or worse. Besides, I tailed him back to the Puzzle Palace one day after meeting with your Arab friend."

"You know his name?"

The driver scratched his head and gritted his teeth. "I'm Amos, by the way." He reached over the dashboard, grabbed a bush comb and raked it through his salt-and-pepper hair.

"Zones."

"Is that your first or last?"

"Last, first name is Thelonious."

Amos adjusted his rearview mirror. Zones' reflection appeared in it. "As in Monk?"

Zones nodded. "He's taking a left."

"Yeah, yeah, I got him."

"His name, you know it?"

"Yeah, Casper. Come on, man, you don't get that kind of Intel on these cats. If they found out that I knew this much, my life would look a whole lot different, my face too." He rubbed his scruffy beard and loosened his paisley tie; it was pinching the skin on his neck. "So what are you—FBI, CIA, NSA?"

"You're the spook specialist, you tell me." Zones' attention drifted to the other cars that jostled for position in the growing traffic.

Amos stared at Zones through the mirror. "I think you're unaffiliated, a lone wolf, probably not supposed to even be here doing this."

Zones' attention snapped back to the front. "We're not far away, from what I remember."

"Not too far at all."

They crossed the 11th Street Bridge, going over the Anacostia River. A spaghetti junction of overpasses, connectors and turnoffs greeted them on the other side. The water reeked. It was in much need of a river keeper. The buildings grew blighted, but their paint jobs looked fresh, like a butt-ugly woman covered in thick makeup.

The cab twisted through the neighborhood, past grown men with their pants on the ground. They played in their hair like little school girls with nothing else better to do. They smoked thin cigars and sported gold teeth. They planted themselves at corners like weeds overgrowing the sidewalks. The area had a reputation, one that said, *don't be caught over here after dark.*

"Why are all MLK Streets in poor black neighborhoods?" Amos asked.

"Al-Saud's car pulled into that parking lot on the right."

"...Like I said, The Chowdog."

Amos followed the black Crown Victoria. He parked at the far corner of the lot. Al-Saud got out of the car and disappeared behind the doors of the Chowdog.

"How much longer before your spook shows up?"

"He's already in there. Never caught him coming in, only leaving."

"You know what he looks like?"

"He wears this large hoodie, no matter the weather."

"Large hoodie, you say."

"Covers his whole face."

"How long do they meet?"

"Not long, ten...fifteen minutes at the most."

"What time do you have?"

"...Five fifteen."

Zones popped open the rear driver-side door. "Wait for me."

"Where're you going?"

Zones scampered across the parking lot. He eased past the driver of the Crown Vic and up to the door of The Chowdog. He cracked the door, peeked into the darkened space and slipped inside. He took a seat at the bar and looked around for al-Saud and the hooded man. He noticed they were seated at a table in the far corner.

"What can I get'cha?" the barkeeper asked.

"…Courvoisier."

She locked her hips, crossed her arms and puckered her lips, "This ain't the Ritz."

"What do you have?"

"We got gut rot."

"What's that?"

"…Thunderbird."

"Give me a beer, whatever you have."

The barkeep pulled a forty-ounce can of Schlitz Malt from under the counter. She popped the top, shoved ice in a glass and filled it up. "Six dollars even." She stuck out her hand.

Zones pulled a crisp ten from his wallet. "No cold draft, huh?" She rolled her eyes. "Keep the change."

She grabbed the bill. Zones squeezed down on it. "What the fuck."

"A four dollar tip for a six dollar drink. Come on girl, you know I need something."

She sucked her teeth. Her brow rose. "What you want? 'Cause head gonna cost you more than four."

"Maybe later, girl. Playa in the hoodie, you know him?"

"You five-o? 'Cause I ain't no snitch." She turned to leave.

What is it with these people and snitching? Zones grabbed her hand. "Hold on, sweet thang. What's your name, girl?"

"…LaQuanda."

"LQ, is that DC tang still fat and wet?"

A huge smile covered her face. She batted her big, false lash-wearing eyes and brushed back the weave that flowed over her shoulder. "Why don't you find out?"

"…Where?"

"Depends on what you want."

"I tell you what," Zones slipped the pad and pen from his coat, "write your number here and I'll hit you up later."

Zones sipped on the taste bud jarring beer. He kept an eye on al-Saud and his conversation buddy. He saw their shadowy outline move beneath a dim light. The Chowdog was a juke-joint with aspirations of becoming a restaurant. He couldn't make out much about the place in the darkness. Its walnut paneling was peeling like dead skin from the walls. Neon signs blazed streaks of light into dark crevices. The ice machine mixed his drink as it churned and rattled the bar.

Zones shoved a twenty dollar bill at LaQuanda.

"Thank you, sweetie," she leaned across the counter.

"Now, what about playa?"

"He been coming in here every Wednesday with the other guy. They don't eat. They don't drink. They just talk, but they always leave a tip."

"You know him?"

"No."

"You know what he looks like?"

"He always wears that hoodie but..."

"But what?"

She leaned in closer. "I heard them speaking funny once."

"You mean with an accent?"

"No...funny, like in a different language."

"Oh."

"Look, he's leaving."

Zones ducked his head and raised his hand to his face. Al-Saud stayed seated. The hooded man walked past them on the other side of the bar. Zones got up and followed him through the front door. The sun had begun to set. The parking lot had cleared out. His cab was still parked at the far corner; al-Saud's car and a few others were still there.

Zones stopped just outside the door. "Hey, you," he called to the man as he continued to walk. "Pot-na, I'm talking to you." He ignored Zones. "Now you're planting bombs here too?" The hooded man stopped. Zones inched toward him. "I recognize that walk. You're in this with al-Saud. Both of you are going down for the bombings, at least you are. Al Saud will probably get off on some diplomatic immunity bullshit. You have a needle waiting for you, or worse. Folk don't take too kindly to terrorists coming over here blowing up our shit, not even the cons." The man spun around. He drew down on Zones and fired. Zones dove between two cars. "Shit." Tires screeched from across the parking lot. The black Crown Vic whipped through the faded lines of parking spaces and slammed to a stop in front of the Chowdog. Al-Saud yanked the rear passenger door open and hopped inside. The car sped away out of sight.

Zones peeked through the window of a parked car but saw no one. He eased up a bit more to scan the area, then duck-walked from between the vehicles. He stopped just before clearing them and stood halfway up. The cracking of gunfire sounded. Bullets peppered cars around him. Zones hit the asphalt hard, damn near kissing the ground. More tires screeched.

"Get in." Zones looked up. Amos was sitting inside his yellow cab as he fired a large gun out of the window. The rear driver-side door swung wide open. "Come on, man." Zones pushed up from the pavement and flew inside the cab as bullets pelted the outside. They sped off as the door slammed shut. The hooded man continued to fire at them until they drove out of sight. "Brother, somebody is trying to kill you."

"And now I know who."

FIFTY-SEVEN
The Double Back

"YOU THINK AL-SAUD IS trying to kill you?" Amos asked. He barreled down MLK Street, back toward downtown.

"That was his guy doing the shooting back there."

"Who are you exactly and what is this all about?"

"The less you know the better."

"Somehow I doubt that…Where to now?"

Zones sniffed himself. "I need a shower—the Howard Hotel." He slumped in his seat, threw back his head and closed his eyes. He exhaled as if he had just surfaced from a deep dive. *Euro-Arabia, I knew the motive was profit. I knew it. Those motherfuckas would pluck the wings off angels if they got in the way of them making money. Now I need to find the bomber. That should be easy.* He was confident that, once pressed, al-Saud would give up the ghost quicker than a newborn gives up sour milk. That is, unless he skips town first. "Shit." Zones popped up. He ripped his phone from his coat pocket and dialed. "Marmaduke, this is Zones."

"Dr. Zones, I wondered where you had landed after the captain booted you off the case."

"Listen, you questioned al-Saud, didn't you?"

"…If you want to call it that, why?"

"I need you to get the captain to call his counterpart at the Third here in DC."

"…For what?"

"I'm trying to tell you, Detective. I believe al-Saud is going to skip the country. I need him stopped. He's behind the bombings."

"Two questions, Doc. Why are you in DC and what have you been smoking? That ain't happening. The captain ain't looking to arrest any more Arabs, especially one that's connected to the royal family."

"He will once he knows al-Saud has met with the bomber."

"What the fuck are you talking about, Doc? After he met with us, al-Saud couldn't wait to get out of Georgia."

"He met with him here, in DC."

"And you know this how?"

"I was just there. The asshole tried to send me back to my ancestors."

"…Back to Harlem?"

"I'm serious, Detective; al-Saud could be boarding a plane as we speak."

"You know, it's afterhours. The captain is probably deep in it."

"Pull his ass out."

"That's easy for you to say. By the way, is Detective Rome there with you?"

"Why would she be?"

"Don't give me that shit; you both spent a couple of days in Egypt together."

"No, Detective, she's not with me. Why?"

"She missed a meeting this morning."

"That's not like her. Have you tried calling her home?"

"Concierge said he hadn't seen her since yesterday morning. We checked her condo…nothing."

"She probably forgot and took off. She'll bust your balls for going through her things when she gets back."

"…Yeah, probably will."

Zones hung up. He shoved the phone inside his coat pocket and stared out of the side window. They crossed over the 11th Street Bridge back into downtown traffic. From past experience, Zones knew he couldn't trust Captain Franklin to call up the cavalry. He needed a backup plan.

"On second thought, drop me off at Seventeenth and V."

"...The Third?"

"You're familiar with it?"

"I know a few of the guys. They're okay...when they're not writing tickets."

The traffic eased as the cab raced through the streets. Zones kept a keen eye out. The last time he rode through Adams-Morgan, armed men had chased him. But he knew who and why, or so he thought. Al-Saud had the goons and the money. But someone had tipped him off to Zones' first visit. He couldn't worry about that now. He had to keep al-Saud from leaving the country.

The cab slowed to a stop in front of the Third Precinct.

"What I owe you?" Zones asked.

Amos glanced at the meter, "One ten."

Zones pulled two one hundred-dollar bills from his wallet. He held them out to Amos. "Keep the change. Good looking out."

"Shit, anytime." Amos stuffed the bills inside a money sack. "If it's okay by you, I'd rather be left out of that little dustup back there. I got time left on my probation. I'm riding dirty, if you know what I mean."

Zones pushed the curbside door open, hopped from the cab, marched up the sidewalk and into the station. An officer sat in front, secured behind a wall with a sliding window. He slid it open.

"May I help you?"

"Here to see Detective Baker."

"...Your name?"

"Zones."

The officer picked up the phone. Moments later, a door off the hall opened. Two officers stepped out and approached him.

"Dr. Zones?"

"Is Detective Baker here?"

"Turn around, please. Put your hands behind your back."

"What?"

"Turn around and put your hands—"

"I heard you the first time. What is this all about? Where's Detective Baker?" The officers grabbed Zones, turned him around and shoved him against the wall. He struggled, other officers joined in.

They held his hands behind his back and cuffed him. "Get me Detective Baker!" They dragged him down the hall and locked him in a cell.

* * *

The cell door made a loud clank. An early morning sun beamed through a slither of glass in the wall. Zones struggled to get up. His ass did not make it off the steel cot; it had bruised him like a good whipping. He planted his elbows against his knees and buried his face in his hands. He rubbed the sleepy away with his palms, but the message had not reached his brain.

"Dr. Zones, you're up. Good." Detective Baker stood at the door of the cell. "I hope that pile of nuts and bolts didn't beat you up too bad. It's not the Ritz, but you can't beat the price."

"If that's to make me feel better about my false imprisonment, you're not even close. What gives with the inhospitable welcome?"

"Your captain called."

"He's not my captain."

"Okay, anyway, he told the brass here to arrest you for interfering in an investigation. This isn't about your bombing case, is it? I thought you were the lead consultant."

"It looks like they've decided to go a different direction and let the real rat get away with the cheese."

"Al-Saud?"

"He's probably halfway to Mecca by now." Zones kicked a wastebasket across the cell floor. "Shit."

"My old man used to say, 'You can't put shackles on money.' And al-Saud's got plenty of it. Best thing for you, Doc, is to round up the minions."

"That seems to be the sentiment of the day. Can I go now, or do these accommodations have a two-night minimum?"

"You can go, but I've been instructed to make sure you're on the next thing smoking back to Georgia."

"Figures, let's go, Kevin Costner." Zones grabbed his coat, slipped it on and followed Detective Baker from the building.

"Here're your things." The detective handed Zones a plastic bag. He took it and unpacked them.

Zones counted his money. "…Looks like my room wasn't free after all."

"What do you mean?"

"Nothing, let's go."

Zones piled into Detective Baker's black Mercedes convertible—the old kind, built like a tank. He strapped himself in. The car cranked. The diesel puttered like a baby's rattle. They headed west down Florida toward the airport. The morning sun was baking the back of his head. He inhaled the district's first offerings of air before cars and trucks fouled it with fumes and smog. Zones surveyed the car's interior. He ran his hand along its leather finishes and polished metals.

"DC Metro pays well, I see."

"Don't let the bling fool you. I married well."

"Damn well. This baby is a classic."

"She's a beauty."

"And not a scratch on her."

"Came close though. The other week some fools chased a cab down near Dupont Circle. Shot the place up something good. She damn near took one in the side."

"Oh really?"

"I don't normally bring her out during a weekday. That day my work vehicle was in the shop, like today. I almost lost her." Detective Baker sniffed. He grabbed a handkerchief from inside his coat. "…The bastards."

"Did you find out who it was?"

"We found the cab driver, some immigrant from East Africa. But aren't they all." He turned to Zones, smiled and winked. "Couldn't get much out of him though; he was scared to fucking death. You would think that with all the shit going on in the motherland, the motherfucka would've been a little braver."

"What about the shooters, their nationality?"

"Don't know, but we found the car abandoned in some projects over in Anacostia."

"…Anacostia?"

"Yeah."

"Was it a black, four-door Crown Vic, no whitewalls on the tires, dark tinted windows?"

"How did you—"

"You get anything from it?"

"Clean, it was registered to a limousine company. They reported it stolen a week before."

"…A week?"

"Yeah, why?"

"Never heard of shooters stealing a car a week before a hit, one…two days…three days max, but not a week."

"Who said there was more than one shooter? Who said this was a hit? And why are you so interested in a bunch of DC thugs bangin in the streets? You don't have a big enough caseload with gangsters back in Atlanta? Aren't T.I. and Geechie Mane from there?"

"Just conversation, Detective. You did say fools, plural, chased the car. Hit was just a figure of speech."

Detective Baker gave Zones a distrusting look. "I got a keen nose for trouble, Doctor."

"We're on our way to the airport, aren't we? Any trouble I make will be far away from here."

"Famous last words from the chickens before they came home to roost."

"So what did you say the name of that limo service was?"

"I didn't and I won't."

Detective Baker wheeled the black 280SL onto the access road. Several planes flew low overhead. The air trembled. The engines' thrust sounded like a thousand whistles. The foiled wings sliced through the sky and flapped against the stress of the wind until the planes landed.

The car pulled to the curb, and Zones hopped out first. Detective Baker popped his door open, eased up from his seat and rounded the rear of the car. A uniformed officer approached him. He flashed his badge. The officer stopped and waved him on.

Zones collected himself. "Thanks for the ride, Detective."

Detective Baker joined him on the sidewalk and pulled a piece of paper from his coat. "Here's your plane ticket." He shoved it at Zones and followed him inside the terminal.

"I think I got it from here."

"Orders are to make sure you get on the plane."

"Suit yourself."

Zones took off across the terminal. The empty space seemed cavernous. It echoed; sounds bounced off the spit-shined floors; they glistened like a boot camp latrine. A convex roof hovered above the expansive space. Light streamed in through sheets of glass stretched between slanted columns that stuck up from the ground like bones on a carcass. They rode the escalator to the mezzanine. The security checkpoint line stretched through the terminal. People stood in queue to have their asses patted and subatomic particles blasted through their bodies. They boarded a train that whisked them to B terminal. Zones glanced at his ticket. The gate number read *B-76*.

"That little dust up in the streets, it was your case, wasn't it?" Zones asked Detective Baker as they hurried along the concourse.

"I was first on scene."

"You're not going to find the shooters."

"What makes you so sure of that?"

"Because where they're hiding, you're afraid to look." They reached the gate. The attendant called for final boarding. Zones hurried toward her with ticket in hand. "Our cases are connected." He handed the ticket to the attendant.

"How do you know that?"

"I was in that cab."

Detective Baker stood blanked-faced. Zones walked through the opened door and disappeared around the corner of the jetway. The door slammed shut behind him. He hid inside the jetway and waited for the plane door to close. It slammed shut, and the plane backed away from the gate.

Zones walked back to the door of the terminal and cracked it open; he poked his head out and scanned the growing crowd of people racing along the concourse. *Good, no Detective Baker and no attendant.* He pushed through the door and into the seating area. He cut through lines of chairs and headed for the wide swath of tile floor dividing the sides of the concourse. Zones continued to survey the crowd for Detective Baker but didn't see him. He made his way to ground transportation, hailed a cab to the Howard Hotel and checked in.

* * *

The day was still early. Zones paced the floor, recalling all the evidence in his head, everything from finding the body of Muhammad El-Arabi at the first crime scene to al-Saud's meeting with the bomber. He had followed up all leads, except one. Zones pulled his phone out and dialed.

"Stats, this is Zones."

"…T.O.'s boy?"

"Yes, T.O.'s boy. You remember our little business?"

"I appreciate the discretion."

"The name on that file, you remember it?"

"I have a hyperthymestic memory, T.O.'s boy."

"Great, I need his phone numbers, work and home." Zones heard rapid typing through the phone.

"Both are classified."

"That's why I called you."

"Got them."

"How'd you do that so fast?'

"Netflix, he has poor taste in movies."

"Can you text that to me?"

"I'll encrypt it. The key is my favorite hobby."

The call went dead. Seconds later, Zones' phone beeped and he pulled up the text message. It asked for the code. He typed, *DNA Collecting* and the phone numbers popped up on his screen. He raced downstairs to the front desk with his phone in hand and worried the concierge for a burner and one-hour dry cleaning. The young man pointed the way to a convenience store and instructed Zones on getting his clothes cleaned.

After buying a phone, Zones returned to his room. He stripped, shoved his soiled clothes inside a plastic laundry bag, hung it outside his door and called the front desk. After showering, he opened one of the disposable phones and charged it. He took his iPhone, logged onto the Apple store and searched for ringtones. Zones scrolled down a list. His finger stopped on *Close Encounters of the Third Kind.* He hit download and installed the application.

From the disposable phone, Zones dialed one of the numbers Stats had given him.

"Hello," a voice answered.

"Paul Brewer?"

"Who is this?" Zones played the Close Encounters ringtone. "Who is this?"

Zones hung up, waited and dialed again. This time, he timed the call. He played the ringtone. "We must meet."

"Who is this and how did you get this number?"

The second hand on the clock reached fifteen. Zones hung up. He waited again and called back. "…The Lincoln Monument in two hours. Bring a Washington Post. Turn the sports page out."

"I'm not meeting with you unless you tell me who you are and what this is about."

"You know what this is about. If you don't show, I'm going to the press. Lincoln Monument, east side, in two hours. Come alone."

Zones hung up for the final time. He tossed the phone on the bed next to him and sank deep into the pillow. Seconds later, the phone rang. He snapped to it. The display read *Private*. He ignored the ringing, closed his eyes and drifted off to sleep.

A knock came.

"…Concierge."

Zones woke from his sleep and rolled from the bed. He collected his dry cleaning and dressed. He stuffed the list he got from Congressman Bulwark in his pocket and left to see the man with the final piece of the puzzle, the last piece of information he needed to solve this case—or so he hoped.

FIFTY-EIGHT
The Spook

THE NATIONAL MALL CUT through the heart of the District like an Indy drag strip. It was the country's Greek Acropolis—an aggrandizement to itself. This day the plaza overflowed with people. They milled about the monuments and buildings that stood like granite pieces on a board game. They graced the mall with all the pomp and pageantry afforded a nation in love with itself.

Zones watched it all from the top step of the Lincoln Memorial. He roamed around the giant homage to the sixteenth President of the United States, snapping fake pictures with his phone and joining a group of sightseers to blend in with the crowd. He checked the time; it was two o'clock. *You should be here by now. Where are you, Mr. Brewer?* He scanned the crowd closer as a man trotted up the steps with a newspaper in his hand, folded to the sports section. Zones took off and headed down the rear steps of the monument, walking to the cemetery. He was more than halfway there before he dialed Brewer's phone.

"I'm here. Where're you?" Brewer answered.

"Go to the rear of the monument, cross Arlington Memorial Bridge to the Women in Military Memorial. Wait there for further instructions. You have ten minutes."

"That's over a mile away."

"Then you better get going."

Zones continued to walk and take fake pictures. He drew closer to the memorial where several people were gathered. They knelt, prayed or stood in quiet silence around a pool. The sound of feet pounding the ground in rapid succession grew louder. Brewer ran past. He was sucking up air. Sweat poured from his face and drenched his clothes. He collapsed on one of the bollards that roped off the grassy areas. Zones focused his eyes down the long stretch of walk. No one seemed to have followed him.

Zones pulled his phone and dialed again. "…Brewer."

"Where're you?" He huffed.

"In two minutes, a black man wearing slacks and a crisp white shirt will walk past you snapping pictures. Follow him."

"No, I'm not taking another step. That run almost killed me."

"I don't care about your lack of conditioning. Follow the man snapping pictures. I will find you."

Zones pointed and clicked his phone as he walked. He stopped and pretended to read from a sign mounted on the wall of a kiosk, hidden behind a row of trees. Brewer struggled to his feet and followed Zones. He walked closer.

"ID," Zones said.

"What?"

Zones grabbed Brewer, turned him around and jacked him against the wall. "I said, let me see some ID." He patted Brewer down, pulled a wallet from his back pocket, ripped out a Virginia driver's license and read it. "Okay, Mr. Brewer, turn around." Zones shoved the wallet back at him.

"Are you crazy?"

"Are you alone?"

"What is this about?"

"I'm not playing games, Mr. Brewer. Are you alone?"

"I'm sure you know that I am. That's the reason for this goose chase isn't it?" He scratched at his stringy, salt-and-pepper beard.

"Don't do that."

"Do what?"

"Keep your hands down." Zones looked over his shoulder. "I don't have time for bullshit, so I'm only gonna ask you once. Tell me about the swarm project."

Brewer's eyes grew wide behind his frameless glasses. He turned white beneath his reddened skin. "That's classified."

"It can't be. I know about it, and others will too if you don't start talking."

"Who're you—KGB, NSB, MI6, which one?"

"Right now, I'm the only one standing between the world media and the Pentagon having to explain why a behavior altering engineered protein is in the drinking water of Saudi Arabia, courtesy of the DOD."

"I didn't have anything to do with the way it was deployed."

"Deployed? Is that what you call it? Quite the military word. Good thing for you I know that. What I don't know is who authorized sharing this technology with the Saudis for them to…deploy."

"I don't know."

"…Wrong answer." Zones pounded the wall with the flat of his hand and stuck his face closer to Brewer's.

"Listen, only someone high-up in the government could've okayed it."

"Who're you talking about—the President, Vice-President?"

"They wouldn't risk the blow back."

"I don't want to play twenty-one guesses."

Brewer gulped a lungful of air. It seeped out through two flared nostrils. "Before the brass ordered me to share the technology with the Saudis—"

"Al-Saud?"

"Yeah, they met secretly with some suit in government."

"Some suit, you mean a senator or congressman?"

"I don't know which."

"How do you know that?"

"I gave them a presentation on the program."

"Who were they?"

"Some military brass and this suit."

"Would you recognize him again if you saw him?"

"I would but I won't help you, not until I get some answers."

"What would you like to know?"

"Who are you and what is this about, to start with?"

Out of nowhere, a light summer rain began to fall—no thunder, no lightening, just a fine mist to help squelch the heat. They ducked beneath the kiosk, out of the rain.

"Have you heard about the bombings in Atlanta?"

"Sure, it's all over the news."

"I'm a consultant for the FBI on that case. Whoever authorized this program with the Saudis is behind the bombings."

"But I thought they arrested some Arab scientist."

"A little too convenient, don't you think?" Zones fished the voting list on House Bill HR 150 and his iPhone from his pocket. He unfurled the list and scrolled through it. With his iPhone, he logged onto the *House.gov* website. He pulled up a picture of every congressperson who voted against the bill. "Check out these headshots?" Zones showed Brewer every image.

"No, that guy is too young."

Zones clicked to the next image. "What about him?" Brewer shook his head. Zones held up the next one.

"That's my congressman."

They went through the list, nearing the end, Zones pulled up the picture of Congressman Stonewall.

"That's him!" Brewer tapped the screen. "That's the man I met with."

"He's on the security council. How come you didn't know him?"

"I work in black projects. Outside of the executive office, these guys rarely know what we do. I do remember his loud cologne though."

Zones turned the phone around and studied the image. "You're sure, right?"

Brewer nodded. "I have to get back before they get suspicious." Zones gestured for him to leave. Brewer stepped from under the kiosk and turned back. "I'm not going to hear from you again, am I?"

"No—you won't."

Zones caught the Metro back to his hotel room. *How was I going to tell Captain Franklin about this new suspect?* This thought kept running around in his head on his way back to the hotel. If the captain didn't want to hear about al-Saud's involvement in these bombings, he'd cut off his ears before listening to him implicate a U.S. congressman. Stonewall had been a staunch anti-terrorism supporter. To say that he masterminded the bombings in Atlanta would be antithetical.

Walking back to his hotel room from the Metro station, Zones' phone rang.

"Yes, Detective Marmaduke."

"Where're you, Doc? Captain said you were supposed to arrive back in Atlanta hours ago."

"Tell the captain I decided to find better accommodations."

"You need to get back here now."

"What's going on?"

"Detective Rome is still missing."

"I'm on my way."

FIFTY-NINE

Rome is Burning

"WHAT'RE *YOU* DOING HERE?" Captain Franklin asked Zones as he burst through the door of the conference room.

"I asked him to come," Marmaduke said. "We need all the help we can get."

The captain turned, rubbed his head and paced. "Alright, but don't you so much as take a whiz without asking me first. I got enough shit going on. First, these damn bombings and now I've got a detective missing. Go on Marmaduke."

"Okay everyone, we all know Detective Rome. Here is a stack of her Atlanta cases from the past seven years. Take one. Go through it. We're looking for anything that'll help us find her. Crosscheck all convictions with release dates. Run them down and haul their asses in. I don't care how long ago it has been since their lockup. If you find anything hot, let me know immediately. I don't have to tell you time is of the essence."

"How can I help, Detective?" Zones asked.

"Do what you do best, profile this bastard."

"Let me see, she had a foot up that Jamaican's ass."

"Mr. Dixon? We're rounding up his crew now."

"What about that cat at the pawnshop and that body tagger?"

"We got Skinner in five. We can't find the scratcher."

"That's all I have for now."

"Shit, that's not much."

"What was Detective Rome doing prior to her going missing?"

"Captain sent her to Dr. DeGlorious' office to question her after your little conspiracy revelation."

"What did she say?"

"Nothing, Dr. DeGlorious said she never showed up."

"So she went missing between leaving here and going to the ME's office. Are there any cameras along that route?"

"Chennault is working on that."

"What about phone records?"

"Got that covered. Listen, Doc, I know how to run an investigation, but who should I be looking for in terms of a suspect?"

"To take down Detective Rome, it would have to be someone young, strong and athletic, for sure, unless she knew him or her and felt comfortable enough to let down her guard."

"Hell, that could be anyone, Doc."

"But it wouldn't be someone she had put away. Detective Rome would never be caught that off guard."

"Are you saying that this was someone she knew?"

"Why wait until now to go after her, even if someone did keep a grudge? She's been in sex crimes how long, five...six years?"

"Something like that, why?"

"Those guys might be creeps, but they're not that stupid. They must know they'd be the first you'd suspect."

"All I'm hearing is a lot of conjecture, Doc. You got any facts in all this theorizing?"

Zones stroked his goatee and bit down on his lip. He hadn't anticipated this. How can Olga be missing? An ex-con's revenge doesn't make sense, neither does a friend; she doesn't have many of those.

"I'm afraid that's all I have for now, Detective."

"That ain't much."

"How about this, you know she was into aliens and UFOs and shit, right?"

"You think she was abducted by little green men?"

"Real funny, but there's a convention of them in town right now."

"You mean Dragon Con?"

"You're familiar with it?"

"Pulled duty down at the convention center a few times. Plus Detective Rome mentioned it in one of her UFO rants. They're a strange bunch but harmless."

"Lead the way, Detective."

* * *

Marmaduke parked close to Peachtree Street. People were packed both sides, waiting for the parade to start. Police had blocked off traffic. The street, void of cars, was desolate until a lone figure, dressed as a Star Wars stormtrooper, marched up the street carrying a white flag. Lights flashed in the distance. Soon, police on motorcycles rode toward them. A solo bagpiper—dressed in a kilt and a ruffled, white shirt—marched close behind and played "Scotland the Brave." Behind him, a pirate and a wizard carried a sign emblazoned with the words *Dragon Con*. The crowd cheered as the procession of aliens, wizards, soldiers and other strange creatures passed them.

Zones caught Marmaduke marveling at the spectacle. "You look right at home, Detective."

"...Just appreciating the diversity of the human mind, Doc."

"You're beginning to sound like me."

"I would think you would've thought that was a good thing."

"It's just strange coming from your mouth." Marmaduke shrugged. "If she's here, we'll never find her in this crowd."

"Perhaps we should split up." Marmaduke stretched his neck above the crowd. He looked left and right. "I'll go south. You go that way. We'll crossover and meet back in the middle. If I see her, I'll hit you up on the phone. You do the same."

Zones headed north. He pushed through the crowd—noticing every tall, slender black woman with a natural hairstyle, and hoping that one of them was Detective Rome. The procession continued down the street. Convertibles carried celebrities, some washed up, some still on the scene. They waved to the crowd. The parade's cast of characters grew, and the crowds roared. Some of the parade participants dressed in drag wearing nine-inch heels with claw-like nails, clown makeup and big hair. Others pranced around like Lady Gaga or Cher. Zombies seemed to be the favorite. They drooled and limped their scarred bodies down the street to the delight of the crowd.

Ahead of Zones, a young woman caught his eye. She was quickly walking away from him. "Olga!" he called to her. She did not turn or stop. "Olga!" he called again. He picked up his pace, amping into a full trot. Zones dodged onlookers who wandered into his path. Some he couldn't avoid, and he barreled into them. He approached the woman quickly and grabbed her by the shoulder. She turned; a shocked look covered her face. "I'm sorry, ma'am." Zones continued to the end of the parade line at Courtland Street. He crossed to the other side and made his way back to where he had started.

Zones rounded Baker Street and headed back to Peachtree when a large float, pulled by a team of horses clad in black armor, rolled toward him. On the float, a woman was standing at the top of a hill, chained between two petrified trees. She was struggling to free herself as devil-like creatures clawed their way to her. A black mask covered her face. She did not scream; she only moaned. A white Angmar overdress flowed from beneath a black Katie corset that squeezed her tight at the waist, and her long, flowing hair swung all over the place. The scene, something out of a horror movie, ignited the crowd. Zones watched the float roll by. His gaze seemed to lock on to the chained woman until the float turned the corner.

The crowd spilled into the road. Zones neared the spot where he and Marmaduke had separated. They joined up at the corner of Ellis and Peachtree.

"…Anything?" Marmaduke asked.

"A whole lot of freakery but that's about it."

"…Same here. If she's in one of these getups, we wouldn't recognize her anyway."

"…Where to now?"

"Right here, the Convention Center at AmericasMart. They're gathering here after the parade."

They followed a group of women inside the building, strutting ahead of them and dressed in fishnet stockings, high heels and booty shorts. Vendor booths stretched across the massive space. It opened into a curved atrium that rose as high as the building. People wandered about. They sampled various goods and services the vendors offered. A large stage with a curtain backdrop stood at the head of the exhibit inside the atrium. A vampire paced back and forth on stage. The curtain parted. A wall of monitors lit up. The credits to a movie scrolled up the screens as a clip played. The monitors flickered. Another image replaced the first; a woman lay bound and gagged with a bomb vest strapped to her. A clock counted down from five hours. Zones looked closer at the hair, the mask and the dress. It was the girl he had seen earlier, the one chained between the trees on the float in the parade. He figured it was all a part of the convention theatrics. People scurried about as if something had gone wrong.

Zones turned to Marmaduke. "…Terrible timing."

"…Nerds."

"You mean geeks."

"Huh?"

"They prefer to be called geeks. Nerd might be offensive."

"What's the difference? I see Pee-wee Herman written all over them. Besides, since when did you become such an expert?"

Zones ignored him. "This is a huge place. We're gonna need some help."

"We're it, Doc. Everyone else is bird-dogging the last seven years of Detective Rome's life."

"We start up and work our way down?"

"Elevators are over there."

The glass-clad elevator whisked them to the top floor of the atrium. They peered down onto the crowd. Nothing seemed out of place, if you overlooked the dread-hair Predator and Superman sharing a fruit smoothie. The door slid open and they stepped from the elevator. Marmaduke spied the signs attached to the wall.

"Okay, Doc, do you want prom and bridal or social occasions?"

"You're the one with children and three ex-wives."

"I'll meet you at the bottom."

Zones meandered through shops filled with display racks jammed to their edges with gowns, dresses and other items. *Girly, definitely not her style.* He wound his way back to where they had started. Detective Marmaduke was waiting near the elevators.

"…Anything?" Zones asked.

"Saw a dress for wife number four," Marmaduke quipped. "You?"

"Nothing."

"One down, eleven more to go, Doc."

Zones tapped his foot as they waited for the elevator to arrive. He peeked over the rail and out onto the atrium. The wall of monitors still showed the image of the woman tied down with a fake bomb strapped to her. Thirty minutes had ticked off from the timer.

"Shit, I'm taking the stairs."

"Suit yourself; these bones are too old." Marmaduke's phone rang. He pulled it from his pant pocket. "Marmaduke, here—where? Fourteenth and Northside Drive—Is Atlanta P.D. on scene?—cordon off the area for two blocks. I'm on my way."

"What is it?" Zones asked.

"They found her car."

"What about Detective Rome?"

Marmaduke shook his head. They raced back to the car and headed through town to Fourteenth Street in Midtown. Yellow tape was stretched across a wide swath of space. Sirens blared and lights flashed. People scampered about, some in uniform, others not. In the distance, the black Corvette sat parked askew in the lot of a Krystal burger joint. Bystanders, lined along the perimeter, pointed and gawked. Some sipped on drinks or scarfed down bite-size burgers or carried bags with the joint's name printed in red.

Marmaduke flashed his badge to an officer guarding the site. Zones and he ducked beneath the police tape and approached the vehicle.

"What the fuck, Marmaduke?" Detective DuBoise charged toward him. "We loan you one of our best detectives and she goes missing."

"Dr. Zones, you remember Detective DuBoise," Marmaduke said. "For the record, Detective Rome asked to work this case."

"And that's supposed to make her disappearance better?"

"I didn't say...what did you get from her car?"

"Nothing so far. We're about to tow it to the crime lab."

"...Any idea how it got here?"

"Obviously, it was driven. Rome lives in Midtown, straight up Fourteenth. She could've been getting something to eat. We're pulling the tapes from the Krystal's security cameras."

"No," Zones said.

"What was that, Doctor?" Detective DuBoise asked.

"Detective Rome wouldn't eat there. She's a vegan."

"Then how do you explain her car?"

Zones scanned the surroundings: *Burger joint, Used-car lot, Gas station.* "You have a map, Detective DuBoise?"

"I got a city map in my car." He headed for his vehicle.

"What gives, Doc?" Marmaduke asked.

"I'm not sure."

Detective DuBoise spread the map over the hood of his car. He smoothed out the creases. "Here you go, Dr. Zones."

"This is Fourteenth and Northside, correct?" Zones asked.

"Yes, right here." Detective DuBoise pulled a pen from his coat and marked the map.

"Detective Rome's condo is here." He ran his finger along the map. "Georgia Tech is here. The Fourteenth Street Mosque is here."

"You're not thinking what I think you're thinking, are you?" Marmaduke asked.

"I don't know, Detective. I don't even know what I'm thinking yet."

Another detective ran over to them. "DB, the video is ready."

Detective DuBoise marched toward the entrance of the Krystal. Zones and Marmaduke followed. They pushed through the door, wound their way past cooktops and deep fryers and came to a cramped office in the back of the kitchen.

"We've reset the video to the time when the car was left there," the detective said. He pushed play on the monitor. The video rolled.

Marmaduke thrust his finger at the screen. "There's the car. Is that Detective Rome? I can't see her face."

"No. That's not her," Zones said. "And that's not a she."

"How can you tell underneath all those baggy clothes?"

"For one thing, look at the wrist. That's a man's watch. Second, at five-nine, Rome's Vette hits her here." Zones touched his chest with the side of his hand. "That guy's at least six-two. Third, it's the wrong color."

"What's the wrong color, Doc?"

Zones pulled out his phone. He opened his calendar. "When did we first run into Detective Rome?"

"Three...maybe four weeks ago."

"No, I need the exact week."

"Let's see, the bombings were one, two, three...This would be the fourth week."

"You're sure?"

"Yeah, *goddamn it*, four weeks!"

"Black, red, black, red, she should've been in the red Vette, not the black one. She alternates weeks."

"You're thinking whoever has her took the other car?"

"The driver walked off in that direction."

"…East on Fourteenth."

"Isn't the mosque in that direction?"

"You're thinking exactly what I thought you were thinking."

"I'll get a team over to her place," Detective DuBoise said, "and see who took the red Corvette."

Marmaduke turned to Zones. "I guess we've got a date with the imam."

SIXTY

Holy Men and Cannon Cockers

AN UNMARKED VAN HUGGED a curb across from the Fourteenth Street Mosque. Marmaduke snatched open the rear cargo door and hopped inside.

"Damn, Marmaduke." The FBI agent jumped in his skin. "You're gonna get your ass shot pulling that shit."

"Calm down, Agent."

"Calm down, my ass. You and your entourage need to get the hell out of here before you blow our cover."

"Your cover was blown the minute you mixed stripes with polka dots." The agent checked his clothes. "I need the tape from yesterday."

"I haven't seen any paperwork authorizing that."

Marmaduke leaned in close to him. "There's a detective missing," he said in a whisper but loud enough for Zones to hear. "Her kidnapper is possibly on tape going into the mosque, could even be inside there right now. I got a pack of rabid detectives outside chomping at the bit. Do you want me to tell them I can't find her because some bureaucrat didn't issue you the paperwork?"

The agent looked past Marmaduke to the other detectives pacing about. He rolled his eyes, slid on headphones and worked the controls of the recording equipment.

"You said yesterday?"

"Start from late evening." Marmaduke turned to Zones. "Doc, we're on."

Zones stepped inside the van. He squeezed into a space between Marmaduke and the agent. The video fast forwarded to ten o'clock, showing a lone, hooded figure scurrying across the sidewalk and approaching the side entrance of the mosque.

"Freeze that," Marmaduke said. "Print me a picture."

"What're you going to do with it?"

"Show it to the imam in case he denies this person coming here."

"Can't do that; he'll know we're watching, despite what you think."

"Hell. Give me something, man."

The agent glanced over Marmaduke's shoulder again. His eyes slid from one corner to the other. They stopped at Zones. "Okay, but you didn't get this from me."

"Yeah, okay, whatever."

"Grab those." He pointed to a set of headphones hanging on a hook. Marmaduke slipped them over his ears. "This is a recording from the time your hooded man entered the mosque."

The agent pressed a button. Marmaduke listened. His expression grew intense. He pressed the headphones tight to his ears, as if to stop what he listened to from leaking out. He slipped the headphones off.

"What do you make of this, Doc?"

Zones took the agent's headphones. He pressed one against his ear and listened. "One of these men is al-Saud. I thought he'd left the country."

"You're sure? 'Cause all of them sound alike to me. What about the other guy?"

Zones continued to listen. "Hard to say, sounds like he's trying to disguise his voice as if…"

"He knows they're being recorded."

"…Exactly."

"Who knows you've got ears in there?" Marmaduke asked the agent.

"The usual, AG, State Department—"

"National Security Council?" Zones asked.

"…Yeah."

"What're you thinking, Doc?"

"…Nothing." Zones pressed the headphones back to his ear. "Al-Saud said he gave a lot to support his campaign. Any idea what he meant by that, Agent?"

"No idea."

The recording ended. "Is that it?" Zones handed the headphones back to the agent.

"…For now."

"Let's get in there."

Marmaduke hopped from the van. Zones followed, darting across the street to the mosque. A horde of detectives swarmed around it. Marmaduke pounded on the mosque's door. It opened to a man blocking the entrance with his wide frame.

"Imam Khalid," Marmaduke said.

"The imam is not available." He shuffled backward. The door swung to close.

Marmaduke jammed his foot between the door and the frame. He shoved it open and stepped inside. "That wasn't a request." The man stood frozen, his large frame puffed up like a snowman. "Take me to the imam, big boy." Marmaduke pointed. "Let's go."

The man led Marmaduke and Zones down a long hall. Detectives piled in after them. Another man stepped from behind a door.

The large man stopped. "Imam," he said.

"Brother, who are these men?"

"I'm Detective Marmaduke. This is Dr. Zones. Are you Imam Khalid?" He looked past Marmaduke to the other detectives lined up behind him. "Don't mind them. Is there somewhere we can talk, Imam?"

"What is this about, Detective?"

"We can talk about it in your office or down at the station."

The imam's eyes lowered to Marmaduke's feet. "…Your shoes."

"Yeah, what of 'em?"

"Please remove them. All of you."

"Why?"

"It is our custom, Detective. My office is this way."

Zones and Marmaduke kicked off their shoes and followed the imam up a flight of stairs. The space stood quiet, except for the melodic recitation of a quiet prayer. They came to a door. The imam pushed through it.

"In here, gentlemen." They entered, scanned the spacious office and followed the imam over to a small conference table. "Please, have a seat." Imam Khalid pulled out a chair and sat. "Now, what is this about?"

"There is a detective missing. We found her car up the street at the Krystal. Canines tracked her or her abductor's scent here."

"Here, to the mosque?"

"Yeah."

"You must be mistaken, Detective. No one here would be involved in a kidnapping, especially of a law enforcement officer."

"How do you explain—"

"Who was al-Saud meeting with here yesterday?" Zones asked.

"What?"

"Taufic al-Saud, the head of Euro-Arabia's U.S. operations, who did he meet with at the mosque the other night?"

"I know who he is, Dr. Zones. Brother Taufic is a supporter of Al-Farooq Masjid."

"Yeah, I got that. Who did he meet with?"

"He met with leaders of the masjid. We are building a community center, and he is assisting us."

"Financially?"

"Yes. Why are you asking about Brother Taufic? I thought this was about your missing colleague."

"Do you have a list of your leadership?"

"Is this really necessary?"

"You got something to hide, Imam?"

"Of course not." Imam Khalid pushed back from the table, reached into a desk drawer, pulled out a slip of paper and handed it to Zones. "Whatever you're looking for, Doctor, is in here."

Zones scanned the list. "What political campaigns does al-Saud contribute to?"

"Political? I would not know about his business relationships."

"What about the masjid? Do you?"

"We do not support one candidate over another, although we do express our concerns."

"Is that what al-Saud was doing here, expressing his concerns?" The imam said nothing. Zones whipped out his phone. He logged onto Detective Rome's Facebook page. "Have you seen this woman around here?" He thrust the phone at Imam Khalid.

"No."

"Look at the fucking picture."

"I will not have you speak to me in that way. You are not in some bar or night club."

"Look at the picture!" Zones moved the phone closer to him.

"I do not have to look at the picture, Doctor, because she was not here."

"What makes you so sure, Imam?" Marmaduke asked.

He took a deep breath and released it. "Since 9-11, I've made it a practice to review every security tape from the day before. She was not in any of the recordings from this week."

"Then you wouldn't mind if we searched the place."

"You do not have a warrant. I do not have to do that."

"No, we don't and you don't. But it would go a long way to calm that cavalry downstairs."

Imam Khalid pushed his frameless glasses back up on his face. His dark eyes swung between Marmaduke and Zones like windshield blades. He raked his hand across the salt-and-pepper, Chin Loofah goatee that framed his mouth. Through the window, a ray of light struck the heavily embroidered prayer cap the imam wore. It shimmered like a rainbow halo around his head. He plucked it off and brushed back the mop of spiny hair that matched his goatee.

"Okay, Detective, conduct your search but no shoes." He eased the cap back atop his head.

Marmaduke pulled his phone out and dialed. "DuBois, you got the go ahead but no shoes."

"What about the video?" Zones asked Imam Khalid.

"What about it?"

"We want to see the security video from yesterday."

"You are pushing your luck, Doctor."

"Tell me something I don't know, Imam, the security video please."

Imam Khalid walked to a bookcase that lined an office wall. He slid a plastic container from a shelf and thumbed through a rack of CDs. He slipped one out, walked over to his desk and loaded it into a computer. Zones and Marmaduke gathered around a monitor that sat near the edge of the desk. The imam worked the software that controlled the recording.

Zones pointed to the screen. "Start there." He locked in on the images of people arriving at the mosque. "That's al-Saud." More people filed in.

"That is the last of the board members."

"Fast forward to after your meeting." The imam clicked the mouse. Images raced past them on the screen. "There. Who's that?"

"I do not know."

"How can you not know? He's going into your mosque."

"First of all, Dr. Zones, it is not my mosque; it's Allah's. He mumbled something in Arabic. "Second, I do not know every member of the masjid. Does your pastor know every member of his church?"

"I don't have a pastor, and this isn't about me. Now, pull the video from inside."

"There is no surveillance of the interior."

"Don't bullshit me, man."

"Contrary to what you may believe, Dr. Zones, this is a house of prayer. We do not pry into one's time with Allah."

Marmaduke's phone rang. "What do you have, DuBois?"

Zones listened. He hoped their search of the mosque had turned up something. Imam Khalid was keeping a death mask face. He showed his true emotions only when the mosque was mentioned. Every other time, Zones had been staring into a Medusa head.

"Okay." Marmaduke hung up. He shook his head at Zones who fell back in his seat. "Thank you, Imam. We'll let you get back to your work. Sorry for the intrusion."

Zones followed Marmaduke back down the stairs. They filed from the mosque, going back outside. More cars had filled the parking lot. Worshipers drifted in and out, walking past the detectives as they stood around.

"Perhaps it was a coincidence, Doc," Marmaduke said, "that the dogs tracked the scent to the mosque."

"I don't believe in coincidences, Detective. Synchronicity or acausal parallelisms, I believe in them. Coincidence, or better yet, the remarkable occurrence of events or ideas at the same time…happenstance…is actually an archetype of the collective unconscious."

Marmaduke's phone rang again. "Thank goodness." He wrestled the phone from his coat pocket. "Yes, sir—the canine unit tracked the scent to the Fourteenth Street mosque—we swept the place, found nothing—okay, on our way."

"The captain?" Zones asked.

"He wants us back at the station."

"Shouldn't we be out here breaking legs?"

"That's what those guys are for." Marmaduke nodded at the other detectives. "Don't worry, Doc, they have good orthopedists in Atlanta."

* * *

Zones and Marmaduke headed for the entrance to the precinct. The media was swarming the area. Word of Detective Rome's disappearance had gotten out. It wasn't every day that a member of law enforcement went missing. Reporters hurled questions. Zones and Marmaduke tucked in their chins, pressed through the scrum and scurried up the steps.

"Do you really think the dogs tracked the scent to the mosque by chance alone?" Zones asked.

"I thought you didn't believe in coincidences."

"I don't."

"Then, tell me what you're really thinking."

"I think Rome's disappearance is connected to the bombings."

"Damn, Doc, that's a swing for the bleachers."

"It's the only explanation."

"No, I can think of a few others."

"Consider this, Detective. We interrupted this guy's plans for pizza boy when we stormed his lair in little Mexico."

"Is this the *M* for murder in your swarm theory again?"

"He may have snatched Detective Rome to complete his scheme."

"You said Rome wouldn't let some stranger get the drop on her." Zones folded his arms. He gave Marmaduke a *keep thinking* kind of look. "You believe the bomber is someone she knows?"

"…That we all know."

"Who, and don't say Dr. DeGlorious? She's already threatening to submit a defamation suit if we associate her name with these bombings."

"Well, Detective, if you don't want to hear her name, then you damn sure don't want to hear this one."

Marmaduke spread his legs to steady himself. "You sound as if you're about to say something stupid like…the governor did it."

"That's close."

"What do you mean, that's close?"

"Congressman Stonewall, he's behind the bombings, or he knows who is."

Marmaduke grabbed Zones by the arm. He allowed himself to be led from the area in front of James' desk. "What the fuck is wrong with you, Doc? First, it was al-Saud; now you've got the hots for a U.S. congressman. Who's next, the President?"

"I just came from DC; I spoke to the Pentagon egghead who developed the stuff that killed Muhammad El-Arabi. Guess who pushed for deploying that shit in Saudi Arabia?"

"Maybe Stonewall was behind that, so what? What does that prove?"

"What would you do to cover up an illegal program that infects the brains of people with a mind-controlling substance?"

"I'm not buying it."

"It isn't like they're not capable: Tuskegee, Third Chance, and MKUltra."

"Look, Doc, if you want to bite from that big-ass apple, go right ahead, but you're on your own. I'm not taking that to the captain; that's for damn sure."

"Taking what to me?" Zones and Marmaduke turned to see Captain Franklin standing behind them.

"…Nothing, Captain."

"Don't give me that *nothing captain* bullshit, Marmaduke. It must be something for you to be huddled in a corner, whispering like two school girls."

"Dr. Zones would like to have an audience with Congressman Stonewall."

"I don't understand, Detective." The captain folded his arms. "We're supposed to be focusing on finding Detective Rome. What does the congressman have to do with that?"

"If I may, Captain," Zones said, "I believe Detective Rome's disappearance has something to do with the bombings."

"Come again?"

"It's a long story, but I need to question Congressman Stonewall."

"What does he have to do with this?"

"He sits on the National Security Council. The bombings may have something to do with his work on it."

"What about Detective Rome?"

"She was taken by the bomber."

The captain's jaw tightened. His puckered lips swung from one side of his face to the other. "And you think the congressman may have information that will help us find her?"

"I do."

"Okay, here's how we're going to play this. Marmaduke, run down every suspect and every lead, shake all the trees. If nothing falls out, then—and only then—take a black and white and go pick up the congressman."

"And if he asks what this is about? Connecting him to these bombings and a missing detective may spook him."

"I don't know; make something up. Congressman or not, one of ours is missing. If he has information we *need* to find her, we'll haul the whole goddamn House of Representatives in here." The captain stomped back to his office. "Call me when you're back with the congressman."

"Wow, that was weird," Marmaduke said.

"What, you've never seen the captain with a backbone?"

"Honestly, no."

"Where do we find the congressman?"

"Where all those fucks are this time of year, some campaign fundraiser or a whorehouse."

"Can we stop by my office first?" Marmaduke nodded.

* * *

Marmaduke wheeled the Deuce onto the grounds of a plantation-style mansion in the heart of Buckhead. The house sat on a knoll between two large, majestic oaks. Only remnants remained of the sprawling cotton fields that signaled its glorious past. Newer, more modern homes populated the subdivided site.

The car wove along a serpentine drive, flanked by fresh plantings of lilacs and calla lilies. A patrol car followed. The place dripped with money, but not just any money, it was old money. This kind of wealth scoffed and turned up its nose at the new dotcom invaders—those who made their riches by manipulating ones and zeros on a computer, not by the sweat of the brow.

Valets parked cars ahead as Marmaduke pulled up to the house. He and Zones hopped out. A young man rushed over to them.

"We won't be long," Marmaduke said. He shoved his keys inside his pocket. They trotted up the granite steps, past towering fluted columns and onto the wraparound porch. A set of double doors stood in front of them. Marmaduke knocked. The door parted and an old black man, dressed like a penguin, greeted them.

"Yes?" he asked in a long drawl.

"Detective Marmaduke," he whipped out his badge, "this is Dr. Zones. "We're here to see Congressman Stonewall." The man stepped back from the door and flung it wide open. They stepped in and followed him to the entrance of a large room full of people.

"Wait here." The old man disappeared into the crowd. Music played. It seemed live. Zones gawked at the crystal chandeliers, the flowery wallpaper and grandmotherly furnishings.

"What's the matter, Doc, not to your taste?"

"Not to anyone's taste, so I thought. Is this the best décor slave money can buy in the South?"

"If you had given us a couple hundred more years, perhaps we could've done better."

"You're full of it, Detective."

"And looking for more."

"How may I help you, gentlemen?"

Zones and Marmaduke turned to see Byrnes Maximus, Congressman Stonewall's aide, standing at the entry to the room.

"Where's the congressman?" Marmaduke asked.

"Congressman Stonewall is busy enjoying the hospitality of his host. Perhaps I can help you."

"Unfortunately, this is something only the congressman can help us with."

"What's this about, Detective?"

"It's about *you* going back in there and telling your boss to get out here, or I'll have to come in there and accessorize that Brooks Brothers with some jewelry." Marmaduke pulled handcuffs from his pocket.

Byrnes Maximus stared at the cuffs. His gaze shifted back to Marmaduke. "Okay, Detective." He headed back inside the room.

"Risking that pension of yours, aren't you, Detective?"

"I got three exes, won't see any of it anyway."

"What do you think he rakes in at one of these?"

"A million, maybe two."

"So much for God and country. Here he comes with his lap dog."

"Detective Marmaduke," Congressman Stonewall extended his hand. "To what do I owe this visit?"

"Sorry for the intrusion, sir." He shook his hand. "We tried your home first. Your wife was gracious enough to direct us here."

"No problem, Detective, anything for a fellow public servant."

Zones cleared his throat partly for attention but more from the congressman's strong cologne.

"You remember Dr. Zones? He worked with us on the bombings." Zones nodded. "Congressman, we need to speak with you."

"Go ahead, Detective."

"Down at the station, sir."

"I can't leave now. We're conducting very important business here."

"That's funny 'cause it looks like a bunch of rich white folk sipping on five-hundred-dollar bottles of wine and eating caviar."

The congressman tilted his head back. He looked down his nose at Marmaduke. "You know, I could have you busted back to the streets, chasing down crackheads, pimps and whores, don't you, Detective Marmaduke?"

"That may be so, sir, the company will still be better than those here."

"What Detective Marmaduke is trying to say, Congressman," Zones said, "is that a detective is missing, and we believe it has something to do with the bombings. We were hoping you could answer a few questions."

"I'm sorry, Doctor, but I don't see what this has to do with me. I wish you luck in finding your colleague though. Now, if you'll excuse me, I've ignored my host long enough." Congressman Stonewall walked back into the room.

"I guess we'll just have to go to the media about the Pentagon's secret swarm project," Zones shouted.

The congressman stopped midstride. The crowd quieted. All eyes were focused on Zones and Congressman Stonewall. He eased back over to the doorway. A nervous smile crept across his face. Byrnes Maximus followed him, as usual.

"How do you know about the swarm project?" Congressman Stonewall asked in a whisper.

"That's not important. The fact is that I do. Got your attention now, Congressman?"

"I'll meet you in your captain's office in one hour."

* * *

Congressman Stonewall pushed through the door of the interrogation room. Byrnes Maximus followed close behind, along with attorneys Ben-Jarvis and Ellis. Zones hugged the corner of a small conference table, the captain to his left and Marmaduke to his right.

Captain Franklin sprang to his feet. "Welcome, sir." He met the congressman as he entered.

"Let's make this quick, Captain. There's a largemouth bass waiting for me to cast my bait and hook."

"Please, have a seat."

"We were hoping this wouldn't require a sit down, Captain," Ben-Jarvis said.

"And you are?"

"My attorneys, Ben-Jarvis and Ellis," Congressman Stonewall answered.

"I didn't know this required any attorneys."

"That makes us even, Captain," Ben-Jarvis said. "We didn't know it required a reporter either."

"What do you mean?"

"Mr. Grae." He pointed.

The captain turned, "Dr. Zones?"

"He introduced himself as a reporter when he met with my client in DC."

"You must be mistaken; Dr. Zones is a consultant with the FBI."

"That's it; we're out of here. Let's go, Congressman." They turned to leave.

"If you walk through that door," Zones said, "I'll make sure the world knows what's going on in Qatif."

"What're you talking about? You can't blackmail a United States congressman, Mr. Grae or Dr. Zones, whatever your name is."

"It's not blackmail. It's a promise."

Congressman Stonewall turned back to Zones. "Leave us."

"Congressman, I advise against that."

"Don't worry, you'll still get your retainer. Now go. You too, Max."

"Are you sure, Congressman?" Byrnes Maximus asked. "Dr. Zones has a motive for wanting to divert this case."

"I'm good. Now go."

The three of them left the room. Congressman Stonewall pulled a chair from the table, unbuttoned his coat and eased into it. He brushed back his silvery salt-and-pepper mane, crossed his legs and stared straight at Zones.

"Okay, Doctor Zones, what is it you would like to know?"

Zones reached across the table, grabbed a glass, turned it upright and poured water and ice into it. The ice cubes rattled around, clinking against the glass' edge before they buoyed to the top. He pushed it across the table to the congressman and turned over another glass.

"To start, Congressman, does the thought of ruling the world frighten the hell out of you?"

"What is this, Captain, some game? I thought this was about a missing detective?"

"Doctor Zones…Detective Rome?" Captain Franklin said.

"Okay, Congressman, where is she?"

"How should I know?"

"Hah," Zones chuckled. "How would you know?"

"If you're accusing me of having something to do with this detective's disappearance, this conversation is over." Congressman Stonewall got up to leave.

"Hold on, Congressman," Captain Franklin said. "Dr. Zones is just going over some routine questions. We can move on." He stroked the air. "Isn't that right, Doctor?"

"Tell me about Qatif," Zones said.

"Apparently you already know."

"But not why."

"Why not? Better them than us."

"You really believe that."

"Is this conversation off the record, Captain?" He nodded. Congressman Stonewall turned to Zones. "Don't you get all sanctimonious, Doctor. You and your liberal ilk want to live in the promised land, but you don't want to cross the ocean of a cesspool to get there. Do you know what the success of this project could mean? It could mean the end to all wars and civil unrest."

"…Using mind control."

"It ain't like they aren't already brainwashed by their religion. We're just replacing one elixir for another. Don't you see? This could mean real peace on Earth."

"And more profits for Euro-Arabia and a quick work around for them if H.R. Bill 150 is passed."

"…By-products."

"Is that why you killed Muhammad El-Arabi and detonated the bombs?"

"Slow down there, Tonto. I ain't killed nobody or blew up anything."

"Were you in DC the other day?"

"Yeah, why do you ask?"

"Who did you meet with?"

"My staff and Congressman Bulwark."

"Not al-Saud?"

"No."

"Do you own a gun, Congressman?"

"Does RuPaul own high heels? I'm southern, boy. Of course I do."

"Here or in DC?"

"Crime don't end at the state line."

"You mind if we take a look at it?"

"There's more than one; go right ahead."

"Congressman Bulwark said you were against H.R. Bill 150."

"I was and I was against the swarm project too."

"Against it? What changed your mind, oil money from the Saudis dried up? Or was it that once the swarm project was up and working, they could easily qualify for oil imports into the country?"

"Neither, Dr. Zones, I was shown the error of my ways."

"How so?"

"These bombings, for one. We're financing our own demise by importing their oil. They use the money to make bombs and hijack planes. It's time we shut off the spigot."

"What about the Saudis?"

"They're allies. Besides, if Abdullah starts to smell himself, we'll see to it that he parts this world sooner than later. Now, are we finished?"

The captain turned to Zones. "Outside." He snatched open the door. Zones and Marmaduke followed him into the hall. "Okay,

Doctor, you wanted out of the bullpen. You're on the mound, but I don't see no strikes."

"He's lying."

"Saying it doesn't prove it." The captain turned to Marmaduke. "You got anything to connect the congressman to the bombings or to Detective Rome?"

"…Nothing."

"Cut him loose."

"Wait, Captain." Zones looked past him to James sitting at her desk. "The bombs, they were voice activated, right?"

"You saw the one Agent Thomas made. Why?"

"Marmaduke, do you still have the bomb parts from the backpack Angela Hightower left at the music festival?"

"I'm sure we do."

"Get one. Have Agent Thomas rig it up, but don't change the settings on the voice actuator." Zones charged down the hall. "James."

She turned in her chair, "Yeah, baby?"

"I need Congressman Stonewall's itinerary for the past month and recordings of his speeches."

"Stonewall? You're going mighty deep, Doctor. Has the captain approved this?"

"Does it matter?"

James looked toward the captain; he still stood with Marmaduke down the hall. "You want his wife's too. I've seen her on TV with her big hair and big implants. Probably crooked, just like her husband."

"The congressman's info will do for now."

Zones headed back to the interrogation room. Captain Franklin followed him inside. Congressman Stonewall was staring out a window that overlooked the interstate. The faint sound of cars honking seeped through the building's walls. He tucked his hands inside his pockets. The tailored suit he wore draped his body like a humid day. He turned. Zones and Captain Franklin took their seats at the table.

"Are we through here, Captain?" Congressman Stonewall asked.

"Just a minute more, sir. Dr. Zones has a few more questions."

The congressman sighed. "Okay." He pulled a chair from the table. "Let's get this over with."

Zones leaned back in his chair. He crossed his legs and relaxed his posture. "You serve on the National Security Council, right, Congressman?"

"You know I do."

"Did you know the FBI wiretapped the Fourteenth Street mosque?"

"We don't keep track of every bug the bureau plants, Doctor. For all I know, they could be listening to us right now."

"Do you know Imam Khalid?"

"I know *of* him."

"What do you mean?"

"After 9-11, all these guys came looking for something, mostly protection from what they thought was gonna be a massive ass kicking by some good ol' boys."

"And did *you* provide protection?"

"No more than for any other American."

"Then why did your office request a beefed up police presence at Fourteenth Street and the Islamic Center in DC?"

"I'm a public servant. That was a public service."

"But they're not even in your district."

"I am a United States congressman, Doctor. I serve the people of this country as well as my district. Besides, it didn't cost the taxpayers one red cent extra."

"Al-Saud and Euro-Arabia picked up the tab?"

"And well they should have, considering."

"Is that when they paid you to hold up the bill?"

"I won't even dignify that with an answer."

Through the glass cutout in the door, Zones saw James wave him outside. Without saying a word, he pushed up from the table and walked to the door.

"What did you find?"

"Here's the congressman's itinerary from the last month." James handed him a folder. "I downloaded files from four speeches he gave as well. I sent them to your phone." A tone sounded. "That should be them now. Oh, and this too." She handed him another folder.

"What is this?"

"The congressman's bio. Thought you may want to mind-meld him or whatever it is you do."

"Good job."

"You're telling me? Tell him." She gestured toward the captain. "I need a raise."

Zones ducked back inside the interrogation room. He sat back down into his chair and flipped open the file. He read. "I see you were in the military, Congressman—in Nam."

"First Marine. What of it?"

"Sniper unit, no less." Congressman Stonewall stared. "How many kills?"

"It's been a long time. I don't remember."

"That's funny," Captain Franklin said, "every cannon cocker I served with could remember their kills down to the number of fingers and toes."

Congressman Stonewall thought for a moment. "Ninety-five...okay, now are we finished?"

"Ninety-five?" The captain leaned over the table. "So, you're a pretty good shot. You keep your skills up?"

"...As they say, Captain, once a ghost, always a ghost."

"What's your pookie?"

"...M40 standard-issued with a Premier Reticle Heritage Tactical scope. I can take a bump off a gnat's ass at eight hundred."

"M40. That holds a .30 caliber, doesn't it?"

"...Yeah."

Captain Franklin looked to Zones who knew, like he did, that the bullets taken from Professor Landrosky and Angela Hightower's bodies were .30 calibers. The door to the room flung open. Marmaduke walked in with Agent Thomas carrying the replication of a bomb.

Congressman Stonewall jumped to his feet. "What the hell is that?" He backed away from the table and plastered himself against a wall on the opposite side of the room.

"It's a bomb," Zones said.

"I can see that. What's it doing here?"

"Relax, Congressman. It's perfectly harmless."

Agent Thomas eased the bomb onto the table. He pulled wires and slid levers. "Ready, Captain."

"Dr. Zones, this is your show."

Zones pulled his phone out. "Do you have input-output cables, Agent Thomas?" He reached inside a box and handed him the cables. Zones plugged one end into his phone and handed the other end to Agent Thomas who plugged it into a component on the bomb. "You haven't modified the actuator, have you, Agent?"

"No, it's the same as when we collected it from the scene."

Zones opened one of the speech files that James had given him. He played it. There was no sound, just quiet. Time ticked by; nothing happened.

"How much longer, Doctor?" Zones said nothing. Captain Franklin drummed his fingers on the table, waiting.

Ten minutes into the experiment, Zones got up and pulled the cable from the bomb and the phone. Congressman Stonewall's voice blared from the phone, spilling over into the room.

"That's me." He peeled himself from the wall. "That's my speech. What're you doing with it?"

"Demonstrating how you detonated the bombs."

"You think I had something to do with these bombings? I'm a U.S. congressman, for God's sake."

Zones pulled a slip of paper from one of the folders. "You gave speeches on the twenty-fifth, the twenty-sixth, the twenty-ninth and the thirtieth of this month. Each coincided with the date of an explosion. You were also in Washington on the day the bomber met with al-Saud at the Chowdog in Anacostia. Perhaps these are just coincidences, Congressman?"

"Y'all have gone too far now. I'll have all your badges." Congressman Stonewall turned and stormed to the door. He grabbed the handle and yanked it. The door rattled but did not open. "Am I under arrest, Captain?"

Captain Franklin turned to Zones and gave him a funny look, one that Zones had never seen before. "Marmaduke, unlock the door for the congressman." Marmaduke jiggled the handle the opposite way and cracked open the door.

"I'll be sure to let the governor know how you all are using state funds."

Congressman Stonewall flung open the door. The actuator on the bomb cranked out sounds. A small cloud of smoke spilled from the device, along with glitter and confetti. Captain Franklin sat there covered in the stuff as before. Everyone turned to the bomb sitting on the table.

"What triggered that?" Captain Franklin asked.

Zones rewound part of the recording. He hit play. The congressman's speechifying continued. *God bless you. God bless the United States of America*, it ended. The bomb cranked up as before.

"It seems to happen only at the end of a speech."

"How many of those do you have, Doctor?"

"Four."

"Do they all end like that?"

"I can check."

"No need," Congressman Stonewall said, "they do."

"How do you explain that, Congressman?" Captain Franklin asked.

"Explain what?"

"That the last words to your speeches activate the bombs."

"Many people use that ending, even the President. Are you gonna accuse him too?"

"Not with your voice. That's how these bombs work. They use a voice signature."

"What makes you think I could even build such a thing?"

Zones snatched a slip of paper from the folder. "Says here you graduated from Tech. What was your major?"

"…Engineering, so what?"

"Electrical engineering, to be precise."

"Does that paper also tell you that I flunked every course and changed my major to economics?"

"I flunked music theory, but I can still play a mean tenor sax."

"I think I've said enough."

Zones scanned through the pages. "I see that you run a very successful investment banking business too." He paused for a reply. None came. "I've always wondered why just being rich was never enough for people like you. You have to also run our lives as well."

"I told you I have nothing more to say."

Captain Franklin pushed up from the table to his feet. "No need to continue; you're under arrest."

Zones' eyes lit up. "At least tell us where Detective Rome is."

"Go fuck yourself!"

Marmaduke pulled a set of handcuffs from his pants belt loop. "Turn around, Congressman." He slipped the cuffs over his wrists and led him from the room.

Zones stood in silence along with Captain Franklin and Agent Thomas. He had just witnessed the arrest of a United States congressman. This was sure to hit the news in a big way. Something about his arrest didn't quite feel right. Congressman Stonewall didn't meet Zones' personality profile; he had diagnosed the bomber as a narcissist. He wouldn't have admitted to ninety-five sniper kills. It would have been three times that. A true narcissist would have tried to control their conversation, with him at the center of it. The congressman seemed to fit the bill as the perpetrator of the bombings. All the evidence pointed to him. He seemed like a prime candidate to orchestrate these crimes, but he didn't fit the profile.

Captain Franklin leaned in close to Zones, whispering, "For what it's worth, keep an eye on the mouthpiece. I hear they're playing footsies with both sides."

"What do you mean?"

"I mean, when politics and money are involved, these cats switch sides more often than Anne Heche."

"Is that what a little birdie told you when you met with the congressman's challenger? Arresting Stonewall wouldn't have anything to do with the election, would it, Captain?"

"I learned one very important lesson about survival in Southeast Asia, Doctor, one you would be wise to heed."

"And what is that?"

"White tigers die first in a green jungle."

SIXTY-ONE

A Clown, a Witch, ET and a Victorian Frock

MARMADUKE FLUNG OPEN THE door to Captain Franklin's office. He grabbed a chair next to Zones. The captain reclined in his new leather high-back; it had chrome rhinestones encircling it. He looked at ease, but this case kept him on edge. His conversation concerned the possibility of blowback from arresting Congressman Stonewall. Zones was flabbergasted the captain had taken such aggressive action. He knew the arrest of a high-profile political figure had been a huge risk to the captain's career, a risk he would only take if there was a bigger reward.

Captain Franklin twirled a toothpick between his lips. "How's the congressman enjoying his new digs, Marmaduke?"

"James put him in with the skins to make him feel at home."

The captain leaned forward. "Dr. Zones seems to have cold feet. He is questioning our hasty decision to arrest the congressman."

"Why, Doc?"

"I wondered how much his arrest had to do with his guilt and how much it had to do with doing a solid for the captain's friend, the guy who's running for Stonewall's seat."

Captain Franklin eased from his chair. "Listen, despite all the evidence to the contrary, let's assume the congressman is innocent. What's the worst that can happen? He gets a little muddy." He walked to a corner of his office and plucked a putter from a golf bag. "That's why these guys have cleaners."

"And while you play politics, Detective Rome is still missing."

"That's because you're in here gumming it up with me instead of being out there kicking ass and taking names." He took a swing with the putter.

Marmaduke's phone rang. "Hello—where?—any sign of Detective Rome?—I'll be right there." He stuffed the phone back inside his pocket. He carried it that way, like a first-grader. "They found the red Corvette."

"Where is it?" Captain Franklin asked.

"…North Atlanta, near the stables."

"What's her connection to that area?"

"…None that I know of." Marmaduke looked to Zones. He shrugged.

"You two better get out there."

Zones followed Marmaduke through the office door. He pulled it shut behind him and zipped past James without saying a word.

"Listen, Marmaduke," Zones grabbed him by the arm, "why don't you take this one alone?"

"You're sure? The car color thing was your call."

"Yeah, I…got something I want to follow up on."

"What gives, Doc? It's not like you to give up the hunt."

"You go get 'em. I'll listen for the shot."

"Suit yourself."

Marmaduke disappeared down the hall. Zones raced back to James' desk. "Where's Congressman Stonewall?"

"Locked up, why?"

"What block?"

"You can't speak to him. He lawyered up."

"That's for the police. I ain't one."

"You do know the concept of agency, don't you, Dr. Zones?"

"Is that like when you round me up all the good-looking sisters in Atlanta and then weed out the ones with weaves?"

"First of all, that number would start and end with me, because I'm the finest thing you'll ever see on two feet. Second, this is all natural." She raked her fingers through her hair. "I figured you for a mane lover."

"There you go again, getting me excited below the waist."

"You're full of shit," she chuckled. "...C block. Tread lightly."

"...C block? Marmaduke said he was in with the skins."

"I told the Honorable Congressman that if he didn't stop popping off about what he was gonna do to us, I would put him in with the SS boys. That didn't get his attention, so I stashed him in with the lady-boys."

Zones headed for the elevator, riding it to the fifth floor. The jailer ushered him past the maze of doors that lined the halls. A chorus of catcalls and whistles rang through the place. Men pressed their faces to the glass windows in their doors. They gawked, blew kisses and styled themselves, as if they were awaiting a suitor.

The guard stopped by the front of a door. "...Right here." He shoved a key into the lock, turned it, slid open the door and called out, "Visitor."

Congressman Stonewall lay stretched out along a steel cot mounted against the wall. He turned to see Zones standing at the door and looked away, his eyes glued to the ceiling. "If you've come to apologize, it's too late. Y'all will be out of a job before the day is over."

Zones stepped inside the cell. The guard shut the door with a loud clank. "That might be so, Congressman, but job security is a little overrated anyway, if you ask me. Since I'm already on the outs, you mind if I ask you–"

"What don't you understand about the Sixth Amendment, Doctor?"

"Not about the bombings or Detective Rome, it's about the government's swarm project."

"I'm not telling you shit about classified projects."

"It could help prove you're innocent. Charges like these could drag on well past the primaries. It'll be hard to run a successful re-election campaign fighting terrorism and murder charges at the same time."

Congressman Stonewall whipped his head toward Zones. He sat up. "I'm listening."

"Whose idea was it to share the nanotechnology with the Saudis?"

"...Beats the hell out of me."

"You mean you didn't know?"

"If those fucks had come to me in the beginning pitching that shit, I would've hauled their asses before a congressional hearing just for suggesting it."

"So, what won you over?"

"I told you before, the bombings."

"…And money from al-Saud."

"You say that with more than a tinge of righteous indignation, Dr. Zones." Congressman Stonewall stood, walked to the door and fixed his hair in the reflection from the glass. "The world is not perfect, Doctor. You should know that more than anyone—with the crazies you see. No one scripted this shit out. We're all just bit players trying to hit our marks and say our lines the best we can. You idealists think this government, *Runs on the will of the people*," he mocked. "If the money dried up and the people's will was in abundance, this country would come to a screeching halt. So yes, I took his money *after* the program had already been in place. I just held up the passing of HR 150 long enough for the science to be perfected. Now that it has been, I'll support the bill." Congressman Stonewall turned to Zones. "How does that look? Not good, I know. Note to self: use money from firings to put mirrors in each cell." He plopped down on his cot. "Does that answer your question, Dr. Zones?"

"…Almost. Who else knew about this?"

"…Other than black projects, no one."

"Not even the NSC?"

"That's filled with flower children, especially not those fucks. The media would've known about the project before the piss hit the splash pan."

"How did you find out about it?"

"The generals wanted to cover their asses in case shit blew up. They wanted me to cosign the program."

"I see." Zones knew this to be true. He had gotten the same story from Paul Brewer, the developer of the nanoprotein. Zones pounded on the cell door. "Thank you, Congressman."

"What about the charges?"

"I'll speak with Captain Franklin."

The door swung open.

"One more thing, Dr. Zones, how did you find out about the swarm program?"

"The bomber is a riddler. The acronym, S-W-A-R-M, was encoded into secondary crimes he or she committed with the bombings."

"Huh, and you figured that out?"

"…With some luck."

"Good thing they went with the name change."

"What do you mean?"

"The program they pitched to me was initially called Dragon Con."

"You're sure?"

He nodded, "Don't know why they changed it though."

"I got one more for you, Congressman. What can you tell me about Jack Burroughs?"

"The lobbyist? He's a liberal prick from New York. He used to run the building inspection department. Now he's heavily tied-in to developers. Why?"

"Another case I'm working." Zones followed the guard back down the long hall to the elevator.

"Tell the captain to move me in with the skinheads," Congressman Stonewall shouted. "I can't take these fairies any longer."

* * *

Zones stepped from the elevator and rounded the corner to Captain Franklin's office. James was shuffling papers at her desk.

"The congressman settled in okay?"

"He likes his women with a little more testosterone. He wants to bunk with his people." Zones scanned the space. "Where's his crew—the Roman and his attorneys?"

"Your Roman is in room two. The attorneys went to arrange bail for the congressman."

"I see. Hey, can you get more information on him?"

"What do you want, family?"

"And colleagues, army buddies, girlfriends, the works."

"You think we missed something?"

"Don't know. He holds the key to these bombings and Detective Rome's whereabouts."

"I'll dig up something within the hour."

"Thanks. Marmaduke still at the stables?"

"They're processing the scene."

His phone rang, "Zones, here."

"Dr. Zones, Stan Shapiro here."

"I was hoping to hear from you."

"I got a sketch for you."

"Of the person who paid for the gun?"

"Took me a while to tie down Officer O'Donnell. He got no jail time, but they booted him out of the NYPD. You got a number I can fax this to?"

Zones slipped a business card from a holder on James' desk. He called out the number.

"I'm sending it now."

The fax next to James' desk rang a familiar tune of gurgles and pings. Paper crawled from between dark slits and furled onto the holding stand. An image emerged, a face. It printed, chin first. Zones watched as it formed on the page. The fax stopped and James stretched the drawing out on her desk. She held it down with a stapler and a tape dispenser. They studied the drawing: weak jaw, protruding eyes, pronounced nosed and coifed hair.

"Hey, that looks like—" James turned to Zones. He raced down the hall toward interrogation room two.

Zones pushed open the door to an empty room. He checked the others. They were empty as well. He slammed his fist on one of the doors. "Shit." Running down another hall, he saw Ben-Jarvis and Ellis, Congressman Stonewall's attorneys, standing at the elevator. Zones sprinted toward them. The door to the elevator opened. The attorneys stepped inside. "Hold that elevator," he shouted. He reached it just as the door slid closed, shoving his hand between the sliver of an opening, and springing the door open. Zones stood in the doorway. "Where is he?"

"Who?"

"Byrnes Maximus." A bell began to sound and the door pushed against his foot and his hand.

"He left."

"Where did he go?"

"I don't know."

Zones reached inside the elevator and grabbed a handful of Ben-Jarvis' shirt, pulling him close. "You better use that Harvard-trained brain of yours to think of some places he could be, or I'm gonna smash your face against this door."

"How am I supposed to know where he is?" Ben-Jarvis stuttered. "He's not my client." Zones pressed his face forcefully against the jamb of the elevator door.

Ellis stood wallpapered against the elevator wall in fright as his partner screamed, "I overheard him discussing the return of a costume."

"A costume? That's it?"

"That's all he said."

Zones gave Ben-Jarvis a shove. He fell to the back wall of the elevator and held the side of his head. Zones stepped away from the door and he hurried back to James' desk. "Is your car here?"

"Oh, no, not after what you did to my baby last time." James snatched the phone receiver from its hook.

"Who're you calling?"

"...A cab, for you."

"I'll wait out front."

"Where should I tell them you're going?"

"Downtown, Atlanta Convention Center."

* * *

Zones snaked his way once again through the costume-dressed crowd of the convention center. He wondered if Dragon Con, the prior name of the DOD's swarm project, had anything to do with this gathering of science fiction fanatics. It could be coincidence, the rumination of a fellow devotee. Once again, his training rebuked coincidence.

A crowd gathered around the stage, the same one where a wall of monitors gave backdrop and carried the image of a damsel in distress. This time the monitors were dormant. A man, dressed as Darth Vader, paced back and forth on the stage. Zones circled around it to the rear. A mesh of cables and wires lay entwined along the floor. A man worked at them, pulling one and tucking in another.

"What happened to the image you had up there before?"

"...Wasn't our feed."

"Whose was it?"

"Don't know. They sent me here to check it out. I couldn't find out where the signal was coming from, so I shut down the whole thing."

"You should've asked the float driver. It was his display."

"I don't know who that is." The man continued working.

Zones' phone rang. "Tell me something good, James."

"You know it ain't easy to track down a costume rental when you've got a freak show in town, Doctor."

"Being the genius you are, I know you did it anyway."

"Lucky for you, I found five rental returns for today."

"Give them to me."

"…A clown, a witch, some kind of E.T. thingy, a Victorian frock—"

"What's that?"

"Do I look like Andre Leon Talley? Hold on. I'll Google it…It's just some ugly-ass men's costume. I'm sending you a pic."

Seconds later, Zones' phone sounded. He pressed on the thumbnail image. A picture popped open; it was a costume he had seen before—the coachman.

"What shop was this rented from?"

"The Boo Factory in North Atlanta."

"…Near the stables."

"I'll call Marmaduke."

"Get him a picture of the Roman. Have him show it to the clerk." Zones slipped the phone inside his coat. He turned back to the man working with the cables. "I need you to reconnect that signal."

"I've just about gotten this mess figured out."

"Unfigure it." Zones whipped out his FBI badge. The man reconnected the cables. A loud sigh filled the atrium. Zones rushed to the front of the stage. The image of the woman reappeared. She was still struggling against her restraints. The time clock steadily ticked down. Two hours remained. Zones studied the image for any clue that would lead him to the source of the video. He rushed back to the rear. "Have any idea where this video is coming from?"

"Beats the hell out of me. They've patched into the network some kind of way. The engineers are up in the computer room. Maybe they know."

"Take me there."

The man led Zones through the crowd, up flights of stairs to a room packed with computer servers and routers. People hovering around a desk in the corner turned as they entered.

"Have you gotten those wires straightened out downstairs?" one asked the man escorting Zones.

"He made me put them back."

"And who are you?"

"I'm with the FBI," Zones said. "That image downstairs might be the real thing. Can you trace that feed?"

"This guy back-doored our system. The only way to shut him down is to physically disconnect him. What does this have to do with the FBI?"

"No time to explain. Do not disconnect him." Zones pulled out his phone and dialed. "Stats, this is Zones."

"Hello, T.O's boy."

"I need a video feed traced?"

"Does this have to do with our little trip to Washington from China and Brazil? Because I think they're trying to read my mind. I wrapped everything in foil, except for one spot. The store ran out."

"Damn, off his meds," Zones mumbled. He hung up and dialed James. "Anything from Detective Marmaduke?"

"The clerk ID'ed Byrnes Maximus as the one who rented the costume."

"How did he pay?"

"...Credit card. I got the address from American Express. Marmaduke is taking a team by there now. What about you? You find anything?"

"Not sure." Zones took a deep breath. "Let me know what they find. One more thing, ask Congressman Stonewall if there's any place his aide would hideout."

"Can't, he made bail and told the captain to submit any further questions to his lawyers in writing. But I did run a background on Mr. Maximus. Not much there. A real boy scout, it seems."

"You're sure? A prick like that has gotta have a bone or two beneath his bed."

"He graduated from The Citadel—"

"The military academy? That's why the captain called him a cadet. Did he see any action?"

"Desk duty in Desert Storm is all I see."

"Shit, James, give me something."

"Marmaduke is checking out the stables, the costume shop and his home. What more do you want? It's like this guy has disappeared off the face of the Earth."

"He's gotta be somewhere." Zones mulled over his options. He had no concrete evidence that the bound woman on the screen was

Detective Rome. It was merely a hunch. Resources were already spread thin. He didn't want the captain to pull men from their search elsewhere to run down an image on a screen. "What do you know about fishing?"

"You're talking to a real southern girl, Dr. Zones, not one of these dainties you see struggling to open a bubble gum wrapper. I can fish and hunt with the best of them. Why?"

"Where's the best fishing for largemouth bass?"

"That's a no-brainer, the Oconee."

"Where's that?"

"Putnam and Greene Counties. East of Atlanta."

"Got anything on Congressman Stonewall in those areas?"

"There's a cabin registered to him."

"How far away is the lake?"

"…This time of day, about 2.5 hours."

"That might be too long. Call the locals. Have someone check out the cabin. We might get lucky; perhaps our Roman is hiding out there. Call me first thing you know something." Zones turned to the engineers. "I have to go. Who has a phone?" One of the men raised his hand. "Let me see it." He handed Zones his phone. He dialed and his phone rang. "I have your number. If you get a call from me, pick up." Zone turned to leave. "And do not disconnect that feed."

* * *

Zones hopped from a cab parked outside of the Cotton Mill Lofts in Cabbage Town. He shot through a closing door as someone exited the building. He raced up the stairs and pounded on the steel door of Stats' loft apartment.

"Go away," Stats shouted through the door.

"Stats, it's me, Zones, T.O.'s boy."

The door cracked open. One large eye poked through.

"…You alone?"

"Yeah." Zones stuck his hand through the crack and forced the door wide open. The space was pitch black. Not even the computers and monitors that filled the room gave off their familiar glow. Zones felt for the light switch. He flipped it on. The space glistened as light bounced off the aluminum foil that covered almost every inch of it.

"No light. No light!" Stats covered his head with the long, white robe he wore.

"Where're your meds?" Zones ripped away the foil from Stats' desk and rummaged through drawers looking for boxes or whatever else could hold his medications. He found a bottle of expired pills. The label read, *Loxapine take one twice daily.* He shook the bottle. It rattled. Zones twisted the cap, popped it open and shook one pill into his hand. He looked over to see Stats bouncing off the corner of the walls. He shook out two more pills. He filled a glass with water from the kitchen and marched it and the medication over to Stats. "Here, take these."

Stats squatted on the floor. He rocked back and forth and shook his head. "I don't want to take those." He buried his face into the wall.

Zones knelt beside him on the floor. "Look at me," he said, his voice calm and monotone. Stats turned but looked straight ahead. "You know that Mormon case you helped me with?" He nodded. "Thanks to you, two young women's lives were saved. You're a hero. Now, they will live to be mothers, wives, or whatever they chose to be." Stats glanced at him. "These bombings have caused a lot of damage and have hurt a lot of people. Another young woman needs your help. She needs saving. The only person who can do that right now is you." Zones held out the pills. Stats took them from his hand, tossed them back and gulped down the entire glass of water. Thirty minutes later, he was sitting at his desk. Zones ripped the foil from the windows. Light poured in. Computers cranked and beeped.

"Okay," Stats adjusted his seat, "what do you have?"

"There's a video being fed into the Atlanta Convention Center at AmericasMart. I need it traced. I'll call and tell them to turn off their firewall."

Stats pecked at the keyboard. "No need, I'm in. There're multiple signals. Which one you want?"

"Can you pull them up?" Ten boxed videos popped on the screen. "There." Zones pointed. Stats typed. The videos disappeared except for the one of the woman tied down with a bomb strapped to her. The timer read one hour. "Can you trace it?"

"I'll capture a packet to analyze the payload; they're using RTP on top of UDP." Zones scowled. "Real-time Transport Protocol over User Datagram Protocol. This shouldn't have gotten past the firewall. Let's investigate...Ah, they used a sophisticated roll-over technique, exploiting an open port—tricky bastards. I'll run a reverse DNS lookup of the IP address for the domain name—shit."

"What's wrong?"

"They've spoofed it. They forged the source of the IP address."

"Can you trace it?"

Stats pushed up from the desk. "I can, but it won't be easy." He yanked a file drawer open and pulled out a CD. He pushed the open button, slipped the disk inside and closed it. "I'll let them know I'm rerouting the video to my network."

"Then what?"

"I'll map the network the data traveled over and try to pinpoint the source."

"How long will that take?"

"Depends on where it's coming from. If it's in the next county, it'll take no time at all. If it's in the next country, count on a long time."

"Can we speed that up?" Stats shook his head. "Do what you can." Zones' phone rang. "James, did they find anything at the cabin?"

"...The Roman."

"Are you sure?"

"The officer laid eyes himself, spoke to him even, told him it was a routine check."

"And what about Detective Rome?"

"Said he saw only the Roman. They're sitting on the cabin just in case."

"You say it's a two hour drive?"

"Approximately, where are you?"

"Near downtown Atlanta."

"If you can get to DeKalb-Peachtree Airport, I've got a chopper waiting for Marmaduke."

"I'm on my way."

"T.O.'s boy," Stats called to Zones. "Let me see your phone." Zones handed it to him. He plugged a cable into it, pressed on the display and handed it back.

"What did you do?"

"Made us more connected."

SIXTY-TWO

One Down, One to Go

THE HELICOPTER LANDED. THE blades twirled as the high grasses that carpeted the distant field yielded with the wind. Zones and Marmaduke hopped down from the fuselage with their heads low and boarded an awaiting cruiser. Within minutes, they pulled up next to an assault team that had gathered, dressed in their military-style gear. Zones followed Marmaduke from the cruiser and over to the command station. Agent Thomas joined them.

"Commander, this is Detective Marmaduke with DeKalb County and this is Dr. Zones."

"What's your plan, Commander?" Marmaduke asked.

He unfurled a map over the hood of the police cruiser. "This is the targeted cabin, right here." He pointed to a spot circled in red ink. "We have men stationed here, here and here. As soon as we get the go ahead, we'll take it."

"Have you seen anyone else?" Zones asked.

"Just the one guy."

"How do you plan to raid the place?"

"Agent Thomas said there may be explosives; best thing is to take him by surprise."

"You have binoculars?"

"…Right here." The Commander handed them to Zones. "The cabin is straight through there." He pointed across the lake.

Zones peered through the lenses, looking through a window. "Yeah, that's the Roman alright." He turned to the Commander. "And you're sure no one else is in there?"

"We've been sitting on this place since we got the call. The only one we've seen is that Roman guy you refer to."

"What Dr. Zones is trying to say," Marmaduke said, "is that there could be a detective held hostage in there, so be careful. Now, when do we go in?"

"If it's a kidnapping, the FBI makes the call."

"The closest thing we've got to that is you, Dr. Zones," Marmaduke said.

"Me? Why not the sheriff like last time at Brown's farm?"

"No kidnapping there, Doc. The alternative is to wait for the FBI to get here. That would be another hour or so. No telling what could happen before then."

Zones gazed across the lake to the distant cabin. He didn't like making life or death decisions. He preferred to be unencumbered, taking responsibility only for himself. He turned back to Marmaduke. "You're sure it's my call?"

"Yeah, it's your call, Doc."

Zones sighed, "Then let's do it."

The commander grabbed his radio. "On my word, move in and take it."

"Copy that," a voice crackled over the radio.

They all piled into an armored van and drove around the lake, stopping just short of the driveway to the cabin. The rear door flew open as they filed out. The Commander led the way.

Marmaduke turned to see Zones following. "Where're you going?" He stiff-armed him in the shoulder.

"…To the cabin."

"This is as far as you go, Doc. Remember that Mormon case and your fat friend in the farmhouse?"

"Move in," the commander ordered over the radio.

447

Zones watched through the binoculars as the SWAT team fired tear gas and concussive devices into the cabin. The blast split the air and shook leaves from trees. Smoke billowed from openings made by the assault. Men stormed the structure, barking orders and shouting demands. A radio had been left in the van. Someone announced, "Suspect in custody. All clear." Zones grabbed a gas mask and raced to the cabin. He rounded a line of trees to the driveway, anxious to reach the cabin and hopefully Detective Rome. If his hunch was correct, little time remained. The literal clock was ticking. He made his way up the winding drive. The tree canopy blocked out most of the sun, except what little light seeped through openings between the still falling leaves. Members of the SWAT team raced past Zones toward the cabin. He lowered his eyes, looking ahead of him as a powerful, blinding light flashed. The cabin erupted into flames. The blast knocked him off his feet and sent him crashing to the hard ground. Objects rained from the sky and struck the earth in a shower of deadly debris.

"No!" Zones' cry echoed through the once placid lakeside retreat. He struggled to his feet and ran closer to where the cabin once stood. He searched for a way into the wreckage, but the heat of the flames barred him from going farther. He moved to another position, finding an opening. He prepared to enter, holding his hands up to shield himself from the heat. As he stepped forward, hands grabbed hold of him and he was pulled a distance away from the burning building. **"Let go of me!"** He fought with the commandos who held him.

"Calm down, Dr. Zones," one said. "There's nothing you can do for them now. Getting yourself killed won't help."

"But she...they could still be...shit!" Zones stood helpless before the flames, forced to accept the cruel reality of the moment. He surveyed the ground around him. Large pieces of burnt wood stuck up from the earth, half smoldering, half consumed with fire. Stones, papers, bodies and body parts also littered the ground. The commandos unhanded Zones and he staggered back down the street, toward the armored van. He climbed inside and slumped into a chair. He pulled out his phone and clumsily punched at the keys.

"Stats, this is Zones. Did you lose the signal?"

"How did you know?" The phone fell from Zones' hand onto the floor. "Hello?" Stats continued to call to him. He got no response.

The sound of sirens blaring in the distance brought Zones back to reality. He waited, half-conscious, until they arrived. Soon, the lakefront site was crawling with police. They cordoned off the area as dogs scoured large swaths of land. Zones heard a familiar voice. He struggled to his feet, stumbled from the van and braced himself against the rear bumper.

"Dr. Zones," Captain Franklin charged toward him, "are you okay?"

"…Yeah."

"And Marmaduke?" Zones shook his head. "Shit. What the hell happened?"

"I don't know. They assaulted the cabin…secured it…the next thing I knew, it exploded."

"Was Byrnes Maximus in there?"

"…Detective Rome as well, I think."

"You think? So there has been no confirmation of the death toll?"

"No, but, Captain—"

"Then there's hope for Marmaduke and Detective Rome."

Zones said nothing as Captain Franklin paced the road, rubbing his face and head, clearing away the sweat. He turned to Zones. "Where was ATF?"

"Agent Thomas? He waited for them to clear the cabin. He might be over near the rubble."

The Captain sighed. "It's the FBI's investigation now…Shit! I hope Marmaduke didn't go and get his ass killed and leave me to deal with it just to fuck with me." He continued to pace, stopping long enough to nervously ask Zones, "you're sure you don't need a doctor?"

"I'm sure."

Minutes later, Agent Thomas rounded the drive and over to the command van.

"How bad is it?" the captain asked.

"It's pretty bad, Captain."

"…Marmaduke and Detective Rome?"

"I'm sorry."

"So that fuck just decided to take them all out with him…Shit!…Shit!" Captain Franklin stared off into the distance, a grimace on his face. "Where was ATF?"

"I waited for them to—"

"AARGH!" He threw up his hands and continued to pace. Agent Thomas turned and walked back toward the smoldering cabin.

Zones waited with Captain Franklin, as night consumed the day. The scene was a blur, as if the *fast forward* button had been pressed to speed it up. He wished he could find one that read r*ewind* and have this day to never have happened. Zones' thoughts drifted to the time he and Detective Rome spent in the desert in Luxor and to the bombing at his apartment. He almost lost her both times. If this was fate, it was cruel.

Agent Thomas returned carrying a brown bag. "We found this, Captain." He pulled out a badge and held it up.

"It's Marmaduke's."

"What about Detective Rome?" Zones asked.

"Nothing so far."

"Then she could be okay."

"We don't anticipate finding any survivors."

"Come on Dr. Zones...no...have they taken your statement?" Zones shook his head. "Fuck 'um. I'll leave word where they can find you...Shit!...I gotta go make the notifications. Come on, we can catch a ride back in the chopper."

Zones grabbed his phone and followed the captain over to an awaiting car. He could not bring himself to glance back at the smoldering pile of fallen timbers; he had just lost two colleagues. *I should have seen this coming. Nothing in the profile indicated this would happen—a suicide mission.*

* * *

Zones threw back a few at Mama's. It was Marmaduke's old haunt before he got back on the wagon. He ordered a shot of Johnny Lightning in his honor but could only stomach a sip. He drew a line at gut rot when commemorating a friend.

"Too bad about Marmaduke," the barkeep said. "We've missed him around here ever since he...you know...tried to dry out." Zones nodded. "Anyway, let me know if you need anything. The next one's on the house."

A TV hanging from a wall behind the bar showed news of the explosion. All eyes stayed glued to it and others mounted throughout the room. Pictures of officers covered the walls. Bagpipe music of old Irish drinking songs filled the air, competing with the stench of cheap cigars. It wasn't Zones' type of place. He preferred the melodic riffs of jazz oozing from the bell of a tenor saxophone and the sweet aroma of well-cured cognac as it crossed his lips. Nevertheless, it was the least he could do for a fallen colleague and friend.

"Barkeep, if that offer is still good, I'll take a rum and Coke."

"Sure thing." He mixed the drink. "Here y' go."

Zones sipped the stinging libation. He was numbing up, exactly the intended purpose. Just when he felt at ease, his phone rang.

"Zones, here."

"Is this T.O.'s boy?"

"Hey, Stats, what's up?"

"Where've you been? I've been trying to reach you since you hung up on me."

"Be nice to me, Stats. I almost died today."

"Are you drunk?"

"Not as much as I want to be."

"Did you get my message? I got the video feed back."

"Huh? What do you mean you got the video back? The place blew up. There is nothing else to video. Are you fucking with me, Stats? 'Cause it ain't nice to fuck with a drunk."

"No, I'm not. I'm sending you a map of the location now."

Zones' phone beeped. An arrow appeared on the screen. It moved on its own to the text icon and pressed it.

"Hey, how did you do that?"

Stats ignored him as he controlled Zones' phone remotely. "I mapped the network used to transmit the video." Images appeared as he explained. "The sender used a proxy server and onion routers worldwide to hide the origin of the video."

"Where's the proxy server located?"

"…East of Atlanta, Greene County."

"You're sure about this?"

"I'm a hero; you said so. Of course I'm sure."

"Yes, you are. Now tell me how you hacked my phone."

"Good-bye, T.O.'s boy."

Zones hung up. "Barkeep."

"Another rum and Coke?"

"No, give me some coffee, make it black and strong."

Zones dipped his lips into the steaming cup and slurped. The black libation burned, but he did not care. He grabbed a lid from behind the bar, shoved it over the mouth of the cup and dashed to the door. He stepped out into the early night. Lights from the city sparkled like fireflies in the distance. Zones raced to his car, snatched the door open and hopped inside. One, two more sips of coffee and he perked up. His phone beeped again. He plucked it from his inside coat pocket and opened the map Stats had sent him. He studied it.

"Fourteenth Street?" he said. Zones called up his keypad and dialed. "Stats, this is Zones. Are you sure about the location of the video transmission?"

"I told you I was sure."

"Can you double-check?"

A loud, breathy sigh shot through the phone's speaker. Words were replaced by the sound of fingers pecking away at a keyboard. Zones waited as he drummed a tune on the steering wheel. If Fourteenth Street was correct, it could be only one place—the mosque. The wait seemed long. He glanced down at the time on the clock. More than five minutes had passed.

"Stats, are you still there?"

"I retraced the network. This time I sent a packet with an error checking payload. The location is good."

"Zones hung up and dialed again. "Captain, do the Feds still have eyes and ears on the Fourteenth Street Mosque?"

"Dr. Zones, what the fuck...why aren't you out somewhere getting drunk or laid, or both?"

"The *mosque,* Captain?"

"As a matter of fact, they pulled the detail earlier today."

"How'd that happen?"

"Seems someone raised a big enough stink."

"Someone, like al-Saud?"

"Don't know. Atlanta's not my jurisdiction."

"How'd you know then?"

"Got a call from Agent Rose. He was looking for a place to farm out the van. What's this all about? I hope you're not thinking what I think you're thinking. We've been told to back the fuck down, Doctor."

"I'll let you know if I find anything."

"Doctor!"

Zones shoved the phone inside his coat pocket. He fired up the car's engine and raced through the emptying streets. Soon, the Fourteenth Street Mosque loomed in the distance. A single minaret rose above the subtle cream facade and glistening golden domes. Zones pulled off to the shoulder, just short of the mosque's parking. He glanced over to where the FBI surveillance van should have been. The space was empty. He grabbed a flashlight from the glove compartment, pushed the door open and followed the sidewalk through the parking lot to a side entrance—the same door they had stormed earlier that day. He yanked on the door handle; it was locked, of course. He circled around back, scanned the facade—nothing, except for a small window at eye level. Zones grabbed a brick lying on the ground and smashed it against the window, shattering it. He cleared away the shards, crawled inside, flicked on the flashlight and shined it along the walls of the room. A door lay straight ahead. He grabbed the knob, turned it and the door opened a little. A sliver of light pushed through. Zones shoved his face up to the door and peered through the crack but saw nothing. He swung the door open and stepped from the room. The volume of the sanctuary swallowed him. A single, large chandelier that hung from the ceiling cast light over the whole space. Zones eased up a flight of stairs, the same one he and Marmaduke had ascended earlier while heading to the imam's office. The second floor lay in darkness. He shined his light and listened—it was as quiet as a Lawrence Welk concert held in Harlem.

A noise sounded from above. Zones flicked his light to the stairs leading upward. He followed them, no floor, only more steps. He realized he was climbing to the top of the minaret. The sound, a muffled scream, grew louder, followed by pounding. The stairs ended at a closed door. Zones passed the light over it, grabbing hold of the knob and turning it. It was locked. He took two steps back, raised his foot and thrust it into the door. It rattled but did not budge. The noise startled a flock of pigeons. They fluttered above his head and revealed an opening above the door.

"Hello? Who's in there?" No one answered, just more moaning.

Zones looked around for anything to aid him. He scurried back down the stairs to the second floor and into an office. It was the same office where he and Marmaduke had met with the imam. He grabbed a chair, dashed up the stairs and shoved it against the door. He stuck the penlight between his teeth, hopped on top the chair, climbed the wall to the opening and pulled himself up. Zones straddled the wall above the door. He shined the light down onto the floor. A woman was there spread-eagled. She was struggling against her restraints.

Zones spat the flashlight from his mouth. It made a loud thwack as it hit the floor but did not break. "Hold on. I'm coming." He swung his other leg over the wall and lowered himself to the floor. He ran to her, knelt and pulled the black mask from over her eyes. "Olga." Her eyes stretched wide. She shouted through the gag that muffled her cries. Zones pulled it from her mouth and dug his fingers into the knots of her restraints.

"What the fuck took you so long?" she shouted.

"You're welcome." Zones continued to work at the rope.

"For what, getting yourself blown into chum with me?"

"This knot is too tight." Zones looked at the bomb and timer strapped to her. "Shit."

"No time for soliloquies, Doctor. How much time we got?"

"Thirty minutes. I'll try to disarm it."

"What, with pails of water? No thank you. Get ATF on the phone."

"They won't get here in time."

"No, but they can talk you through it. Call that agent who reconstructed that bomb in the lab."

"…Agent Thomas? Good idea." Zones whipped out his phone and dialed. He watched the digits on the timer tick down. The phone rang.

"What's the holdup?" Detective Rome asked. "We don't have all day."

"No one's answering."

"No one's answering? He's ATF, for shit's sake." Zones hung up and dialed again. "Who're you calling?"

Zones said nothing. "Hello, Captain."

"Doctor, this better be 9-11 important for you to—"

"Captain, I found Detective Rome."

"She's alive…where…is she okay?"

"Yeah…I mean…no."

"What the fuck are you saying, Doctor?"

"She's alive but she has a bomb strapped to her."

"Have you called the bomb squad?"

"Agent Thomas isn't answering."

"He's in DC attending some conference. I'll call our boys. Where're you?"

"Fourteenth Street Mosque, but they won't get here in time. We have less than thirty minutes before…you know." Zones glanced at Detective Rome.

"Hold tight. I'll have a tech call you and walk you through it."

"Okay. Hurry up though." Zones shoved the phone back inside his coat pocket. He ran his hand over the vest; it was crisscrossed with wires.

Detective Rome lifted her head. "What're you doing?"

"I'm getting my bearings now so I'll be ready when the bomb squad calls."

"DeKalb is gonna walk you through this?"

"Captain's giving them a call now. Why?"

"…Call Dr. Bruno."

"That nut? He's not a bomb guy."

"He'll know more about this one than DeKalb." Zones' eyes focused on the timer. It read *15:25*. "You stare at that thing any longer and they'll be peeling your balls off the ceiling. Call Bruno now!"

Zones pulled out his phone again, "I don't have his number."

"DNA DUDE, 404"

Zones huffed. "Figures." He dialed and the phone rang. Voicemail came on. *One if by land two if by sea.* "What? One if by—"

"Press two," Detective Rome said.

Zones hit the two on his phone. *I'm not in. Please leave a message.*

"This is Zones. I found Detective Rome. She has some kind of bomb vest strapped to her. I need you to help me disarm it. I'm sending you pics. Call me back." Zones snapped pictures of the vest. His phone beeped. "Dr. Bruno, did you get the pictures?"

"This is Agent Thomas."

"I thought you were in DC."

"I am, but the captain called and said there's another bomb."

"It's strapped to Detective Rome."

"Tell me what you got."

"Looks like a vest bomb with wires."

"Describe them."

"They're black, green, red and blue."

"I mean, can you see where they lead?"

"Beneath her, but I can't see where."

"Do you see the actuator?"

"That voice thingy, no."

"Are you sure, Doctor? Feel along the vest."

"You mean touch it?"

"Yes, but be careful."

"Okay, I'm putting you on speaker." Zones sat the phone on the floor next to Detective Rome. He pressed his fingers along the vest. The flashlight helped guide his way. "I don't feel anything."

"What about beneath her? Ask Detective Rome if she feels anything hard."

"Besides this floor," Detective Rome said, "no."

"Okay, do you have something to cut with, Doctor?"

Zones shined the light over the floor. A bottle lay in the corner. He ran over to it, grabbed it and smashed it against the wall. The bottle shattered, and the loud noise bounced off the walls. He scooped a shard from the floor and raced back to Detective Rome.

"Dr. Zones, what was that?" Agent Thomas asked.

"Nothing, now which wire do I cut first?"

"Let's start with the black one."

"Okay, cutting the black one."

"No, No, No, first I need for you to follow it with your hand. Roll Detective Rome on her side if you must."

"Is that safe…moving her, I mean?"

"Nothing is safe, Doctor. Detective, Can you hear me?"

"Yes."

"Have you been struggling to free yourself?"

"…Ever since I woke up."

"Then there probably aren't any pressure sensors to set off the device. Trace each wire to where they terminate, and tell me what you see."

Zones felt along the black wire for as far as he could until it disappeared beneath Detective Rome. He tossed back the layered garment, slipped his hands beneath her and rolled her as far as the restraints allowed.

"All the wires terminate into the back of the vest."

"Terminate into what?"

"Can't see what it is."

"Okay, is there a timer?"

"Yes, and with only seven minutes left."

"We need to find the power source. Trace the wire from the timer."

Zones followed the black and red wires to a pocket sewn into the dress. "I think I found something." He felt around for an opening. "It's sewn shut. I'm cutting it open."

"Be careful and watch out for wires."

Zones sawed at the stitching with the glass shard. The threads frayed and the pocket opened. "There's a battery in here."

"Okay, that must be the power source. Are there any other wires?"

"Not that I can see." Zones glanced at the timer. "Can we speed this up, Agent? Time ain't in abundance."

"Go back to the timer and find another set of wires that lead to the detonator."

Zones scanned the timer. "I don't see any other wires."

"Are you sure, Doctor? Please, look again."

Zones pulled a pen from his pocket and shoved it beneath the timer. He inched it up from the dress. "I see them."

"Can you disconnect them?"

"Not without opening the timer. But I may be able to cut them." Zones sliced a hole in the dress around the timer and exposed more of the wires. He grabbed them and sawed at the plastic jacket protecting the copper. Detective Rome struggled to sit up. "I got this."

"For both our sakes, I hope you do."

"If it makes you feel any better, the Roman is dead."

"Why would that please me?"

"Isn't he the one who put you spread-eagled in a minaret?"

"I don't know who put me here. One moment, I was digging through a pile of dirty laundry in a frat house. The next thing I knew, I was in a cart being pulled down Peachtree Street, strapped between two poles."

"...A frat house?"

"The pizza delivery driver was a student at Tech and a member of—"

"...Zeta Beta Tau. Yeah, I know. You're sure you didn't get a look at this guy?"

"Don't even know if it was a guy."

Zones continued to cut at the wires. His phone sounded.

"What's that, Doctor?" Agent Thomas shouted through the phone. "Is everything okay?"

"Nothing, it's just another call." The phone stopped ringing. It beeped again. A message flashed on the screen. *Don't cut the wires.* "Shit." Zones stopped cutting.

"What is it?" Detective Rome and Agent Thomas asked at the same time.

"A text from Dr. Bruno. He says not to cut the wires."

"You get those wires cut, Doctor," Agent Thomas demanded. "You don't have much time."

Zones locked eyes with Detective Rome. He grabbed the phone. "Hold on, Agent." He dialed. The phone rang once. "I've got you on three-way, Dr. Bruno."

"Dr. Zones, good, you're still alive. I thought it was too late."

"Almost, now tell me why I should not cut the wires because ATF is telling me just the opposite. Talk fast. We only have a few minutes left."

"The pictures you sent, there're too many wires."

"What do you mean? I didn't know there was a wire limit on bombs. You know what he's talking about, Agent Thomas?"

"Yeah, a hero bait bomb."

"...A what?"

"It's a bomb with a false detonation timer meant to trick bomb technicians into self-detonating a bomb."

"By cutting the wrong wire, you mean?"

"By cutting any wire, Dr. Zones."

"I have less than a minute. What do you want me to do?"

"If Dr. Bruno is right, do nothing."

"You want me to just sit here and wait to see if the bomb gods are on our side? I don't think so." Zones turned Detective Rome over and felt along the back of the corset.

"What're you doing?"

"...Looking for a way to get this thing off you."

"Are you deaf? They said don't do anything."

"You're kidding, right?"

"Look, if you want to go, then go...Wouldn't be the first time."

"What's that supposed to mean, the desert in Luxor?"

"You're feeling guilty?"

"I saved your life."

"It was the least you could do."

The space grew quiet. The time ticked down. To Zones, the numbers sounded like a noon day train as they tumbled backward to zero. *Ten...nine...eight,* his gaze cut to Detective Rome. Her eyes were squeezed tight. Her torso rose and fell, breathing heavy. *Seven...six...five, tears* leaked from beneath her eyelids. They streamed down the sides of her face. This was the first time he had seen her cry. *The hand of death must have that effect on you. Four...three...two,* Zones braced himself. He felt as he had when he had flown in airplanes—helpless. He didn't like it then, and he didn't like it now. He grabbed hold of Detective Rome's hand, squeezed it tight, bent down and kissed her. *If this is the end, I am going to go the second best way I know how. One…*zero, an alarm sounded. Zones relinquished his kiss. Lights on the vest flashed and lit up. The numbers on the timer raced around the dial and stopped, the time read *8:00:00.* It ticked down from there. Lights on the vest faded and all was quiet.

"Is everything okay?" Dr. Bruno asked. He got no immediate answer. "Dr. Zones, are you and Detective Rome okay?"

"Yeah—we're okay. What now?"

"Now, you wait. The captain has ATF and Atlanta P.D. on the way."

Sirens blared in the distance.

"I hear them. I'll go let them in."

Zones jumped to his feet and snatched open the door. Detective Rome still lay with her eyes shut tight. She seemed to be praying or perhaps was in shock. He had never seen her so shaken. Zones slipped through the door and raced down the stairs to meet the agents. *A hero bait bomb. That Roman was a sick motherfucka. First he blew up himself, Marmaduke and a team of tactical agents, and then he left a trap like this.* He recalled his profile of the bomber—*a riddler.* What riddle was he leaving behind?

SIXTY-THREE
Frat Brothers

CAPTAIN FRANKLIN PUSHED THROUGH the door of Detective Rome's hospital room. He kicked Zones' outstretched legs as he slouched asleep on a couch.

"How is she?"

Zones sat up, massaged the back of his neck and worked a cramp from his leg. He glanced over at Detective Rome. "She's still asleep."

"I'm surprised she could sleep at all with your hog-calling. Need to get that checked out, could be a heart problem."

"What're you doing here?"

"I came to check on my detective. What else?"

"She's not yours."

The captain patted Zones on the thigh. "Scoot over." He sat next to him. "Now, I don't know how it works with you PhD types, but for those of us who hold the line between you and the next bombing or the next bullet, this is a brotherhood."

"...A brotherhood?"

"And if you weren't so consumed with your own issues, you'd know that. But I guess it's no longer an issue for you, now that this case is over."

"Is it over?"

"Of course it is. One dead psycho bomber and the safe return of Detective Rome, I call that over any day of the week."

"The Roman may have been many things, but I never saw him as suicidal."

"You mean your profile of the bomber didn't account for a suicidal maniac. Don't worry, Doc. We all get it wrong every now and then. Your check is still in the mail." Detective Rome stirred. "How long has she been out?"

"Since she got here. The doctor gave her something."

"Does she know about Marmaduke?"

"I thought it best for her not to, given her condition."

"And what condition is that?" Detective Rome turned to them, moaning.

"Olga," Zones said. The captain cut him a look. "I mean...Detective. You're awake."

"What else am I supposed to be, dead?"

"Good to see you're okay, Detective."

Detective Rome grabbed the rails of her bed and pulled herself up but got stuck midway.

"What're you doing?" Zones asked.

"Waiting for a little help." Zones raced to her bedside, wrapped an arm around her back and eased her up.

"Are you sure that's a good idea, Detective?" Captain Franklin asked. "The doctor hasn't cleared your release."

"If I relied on doctors to tell me when to come and go, Captain, I wouldn't have been born a preemie." Detective Rome ripped the IV from her arm, grabbed Zones' hand and pressed it over the needle prick. "Here, push on this." She leaned over the rail, grabbed a bandage from the cart next to the bed, ripped it open and slapped it on her arm. "Now, what about Marmaduke? I'm surprised he's not here blabbing about how I'm Title Nining my hospital stay. Where is he, out in the hall?" Her gaze whipped between Zones and the captain.

Captain Franklin raised his arm to look at the time. "I'm late for a meeting." He sprung to his feet, pulled an envelope from his coat and shoved it at Zones. "Here you go, Doctor. I'll let you two catch up." He turned and bolted through the door.

"Why's he so jumpy? You'd think he was trying to avoid having a conversation. He ain't fooling nobody. I know what that little meeting is he's in such a hurry to make, probably a midday booty call. Did you know his wife is damn near younger than me? He must've been there to catch her just as she slipped through the fucking slit, dirty old man. If his ass doesn't show up for work one morning, you'll know why. A heart attack on the down stroke, I tell you—"

"Marmaduke is dead," Zones interrupted.

"What?"

"He was blown up at the cabin with—"

"Hold up." Detective Rome stared Zones straight in the eye. She didn't blink, didn't divert her gaze. "Marmaduke is dead?" Zones nodded. "Shit, he's got babies too." Again Zones nodded. She stared off into the distance, quiet, seemingly lost for words for the first time since she awoke. "We have to do something for the babies."

"The captain is seeing to that."

"Shit, I ain't talking about some flag and a funeral. They're going to need shit. You know, kids' stuff."

"I see."

"And you're sure your Roman is good for it...for Marmaduke, me and all the bombings?"

"That's what it looks like."

"But..."

"But our bomber wasn't suicidal. Narcissistic, yes, but suicidal, I don't think so."

"What does the captain say?"

"Dead suspect, case closed."

"I'm not surprised. Captain Franklin might be many things, but he's no ghost chaser. So what's your next move?"

Zones raised the envelope the captain gave him. "Cash my check and head to Harlem."

"...Just like that."

"...Just like that. You're coming, I hope?"

"I don't have the luxury. What if you're right? By now the real bomber knows I'm alive and that I could possibly ID him or her."

"But I thought you didn't see who snatched you."

"The bomber doesn't know that. I'm sure he, she or they had no intention of leaving me alive in that mosque."

"That's all the more reason to let me take you out of town."

"...For how long? I can't be gone forever, unless you're balling like that." Zones looked away. "I thought not. You can't take me anywhere but home, Doctor."

* * *

Zones shoved clothes into a soft-shelled, black, leather Tumi bag. The TV played in the background; it was tuned to the news. Hot water was boiling on the stovetop for his coffee. It was the instant kind with the name of a cheap hotel stamped on the outside of the box. Sam didn't bother with name brand anything. He preferred to pilfer instead. The whistle from the kettle sounded. Zones ignored it. He continued to stuff his luggage with what few clothes he had left from the bombing of his apartment. He still hadn't gotten over that. If Byrnes Maximus was in fact the bomber, he regretted not having the opportunity to punch him in the fucking mouth for the second time.

Sam charged down the stairs. "You deaf, boy?" He shouted and stomped into the kitchen. Steam billowed into the air. It filled the kitchen and spilled out into the family room. "You got it looking like a Chinese sweatshop in here." Sam snatched the kettle from the burner and turned it off. He poured a cup. "You still like it black?"

"Like I like my women."

Sam peeked toward the stairs. "You see, that's your problem," he whispered. Always limiting yourself. That's why you're having relations with your right hand instead of with a real woman."

Zones took the cup and sipped. The hot libation stung. "Don't start."

"You're headed back to Harlem?"

"Case is closed. I got paid. I'm out."

"...For how long?"

"Until I get answers."

"There're plenty more cases, Monk. We're leaving a lot of money on the table."

"I gave you one; now it's over and I'm out."

"Well, I be damned."

"I guess you're just gonna have to be. My plane leaves in two hours."

"What? No...I mean...isn't that your Arab?" Sam pointed to the TV.

Zones turned to see al-Saud on CNN. He stood in the background as another man addressed the media. The caption read, *Saudi Arabian U.S. Embassy.*

"Turn that up."

> *"...this donation will benefit the much needed medical research of NIH from which the whole world benefits. So we are honored to participate through this small gesture given on behalf of His Royal Majesty, King Abdullah, and the people of Saudi Arabia."*
>
> *"A billion dollars is a lot of money, Mr. Ambassador. How will such a large donation be managed? Will the donation be given to the U.S. treasury?"* a reporter asked.
>
> *"No. It will be managed from a trust,"* the Ambassador said.

"Now, why would those motherfuckas give that kind of money away?" Sam asked.

"I don't know and I don't care."

"If you ask me, this smells of quid pro quo. You watch; gas is gonna go up, or we're gonna have to send them a boatload of ice or blonde white women."

"Blonde white women? Where do you get this stuff?"

"It's a fact. Those Arabs love blonde white women more than O.J."

"Whatever, man."

Sam moved toward the stairs. "You're gonna say good-bye to your aunt, aren't you?"

"...In a minute." Zones watched Sam as he slumped up the stairs, coffee cup in hand. His checkered night robe hung from his frame like wet laundry thrown over the line in haste. He turned back to the TV. Al-Saud still lingered in the background, behind the Saudi Ambassador. He had not left the country. *Some balls, hiding behind that fake-ass diplomatic immunity.* Zones listened closely.

> *"Mr. Ambassador, what is your response to critics who say this is a ploy to deflect attention from your government's crackdown on Shia Muslims in Qatif?"*

*"I'm afraid you are mistaken. There is no crackdown, as
you say, of any citizens of my country."*

*"How then do you explain the sudden disappearance of
all protest in the area?"*

*"If we address the grievances of our citizens, why is this
considered a bad thing? Now, please excuse me."*

Zones watched the media scatter like ants whose mound had been
disturbed. Al-Saud followed the ambassador as he slipped between the
polished doors of the granite-clad embassy facade. Zones shoved the
last few items of clothing inside the bag and zipped it closed. He slung
the carrying strap over his shoulder and headed for the front door,
stopping short of opening it. He turned back to the stairs and looked
up. Each step reminded him of the ones he'd sat perched upon as a
toddler on the night he lost his mother. He strained to remember her.
The image in his mind always morphed into that of his Aunt Sheila, the
only mother he had ever known.

Zones walked to the stairs. "Auntie, I'm leaving." His Aunt Sheila
scampered down the steps. One hand patted her hair; it was wrapped
around large, multicolored hair rollers. With the other hand, she raised
her floral nightgown modestly above her feet and made sure to land
every step. She threw her arms around his neck and squeezed him tight.

"You stay safe, baby, okay?"

"Sheila," Sam shouted from the top of the stairs, "the boy's just
going to Harlem; he's not going to boot camp."

"You hush." She flicked her hand at Sam. "Don't pay your uncle no
mind; you call as soon as you get there."

Sam stomped down the stairs, a pipe tucked between his lips. "If
you heard how he talked about your cooking, you wouldn't think he was
the second coming."

"I told you to hush and get out of here with that pipe...It's smelling
up my house."

"Oh, so this is *your* house."

"That's the opinion of at least five very good, high-priced divorce
attorneys."

"Now, baby, why you wanna go and talk like that? You know I
love—"

"I'll call you when I get there," Zones said. He kissed his Aunt
Sheila and headed for the door.

"Hold on, Monk. I'll walk you out." Sam squeezed past Sheila's big hips. He followed Zones out the door to the front stoop. "Your Aunt Sheila, she worries about you," he told Zones.

"Yeah, I know. Listen, Unc, you still got money with that investment banker?"

"Why, you running short?"

"Nothing like that. How much does he charge?"

"...To manage my money? Too damn much. Those bastards can charge anywhere from one to five percent. Why you ask? You come into some money I don't know about?"

"Just a little quid pro quo."

"What?"

"...Just in case I hit the lottery."

"Shit, you do that and your ugly ass will be the best looking thing to every honey in Atlanta."

"True that."

"You take care."

"You take care of *her.*"

"Motherfucka, do I look like I need instructions on how to handle mine? I was holding this down when you were still burping up Similac."

"Alright, old man, peace."

Zones hailed a yellow cab at the corner of Cascade and Danforth.

"Where to?" the driver asked.

"Airport...no...make that Georgia Tech."

* * *

The cab's brakes squealed to a halt in front of the Zeta Beta Tau fraternity house. The Letters *ZBT* were emblazoned across the red brick facade in white. It was the last place Detective Rome remembered being before her abduction. It was also the fraternity of Lucky Bouyé, the dead pizza delivery driver. Zones didn't believe in coincidence, so he wanted to follow-up on a possible connection. He stepped from the cab into a light mist. Angel tears, they called it down south.

"I won't be long," Zones told the driver. He hurried out of the rain, rushing to a door beneath a long, flat roof. Dark clouds settled over the city. Light spilled through windows from behind closed shades. Shadowy, blank silhouettes moved between the solids and voids in the wall. Zones approached the door. Music played as the sharp-edged notes from electric guitars beat against vibrating windows. He knocked and no one answered. He tried the knob. The door eased open, and he pushed through it into a darkened room. "Hello, is anybody here?" Zones ran his hand along the wall next to the door. He flipped a switch and the space lit up. Photographs lined every inch of wall. Zones studied them. The images covered pledgees from many generations, it seemed.

"Dude." Zones turned to see a young man standing at the opening to the room. "What're you doing?"

"You live here?"

"Why are you in our house?"

Zones slipped his phone from his side. "This detective was here several days ago." He showed him a picture of Detective Rome. "You remember her?"

"Whoa, you're five-o?" Others appeared behind the young man. "Don't you need a warrant or something?" The others joined in, jeering and demanding a warrant.

Zones sniffed the air. "Either the Mexicans have gone haute couture or that's one hundred percent Oaxaca Eldorado." They quieted and smelled each other. Their eyes shifted. "You still want that warrant?"

"She was here," the young man said. "Said she was investigating who killed Turd...I mean Lucky."

"What did you tell her?"

"Nothing, didn't know nothing."

"You have a basement?"

"Yeah, but she already checked down there."

"Show me."

"It's a little messy."

"This ain't a Good Housekeeping visit."

Zones followed him through a gap in the crowd. They descended stairs hidden behind a closed door. The old steps creaked. Years of foot pounding had aged them. They led to a space dominated by a large pool table, the old Irish pub type. Zones scanned the room. Like the one upstairs, photographs dominated every wall. One in particular drew his attention, a black and white image of men dressed in blazers. A familiar face from forty years in the past jumped out at him. He lifted the picture from the wall.

"What's your name?"

"Jordan...sir"

Zones turned the picture to him. "You know these people?"

"That's my father, the one on the far right." He pointed.

"And this guy, you know him?"

"That's Brother Stonewall."

"You mean Congressman Stonewall." Jordan nodded. "Was he here when the detective came by?"

"He was on campus, over at the nanoscience lab."

"Why?"

"His pet projects that he funnels money to."

"...For how long?"

"For as long as the director has been here."

"You mean Professor Landrosky?"

"He and Brother Landrosky," Jordan pointed to the picture, "were good friends, until...you know."

Zones studied the photograph and hung it back on the wall. Another picture grabbed his attention. "...Dragon Con?" Zones pointed to the image.

"That's a Halloween party."

"Here?"

"Law firm downtown, Brothers Green, Ben-Jarvis and Ellis. That's one of them wearing that waiter's suit."

"It's a Victorian frock."

Zones dashed back up the stairs and pushed through the front door out into a torrent. He snatched out his phone and dialed.

"This better be damn important," James said. Her voice cracked, hoarse and raspy.

"You see that news conference with al-Saud and the U.S. Saudi Ambassador?"

"Giving away a billion dollars, who didn't?"

"Any idea who's managing the trust?"

"Is that a question or a request?"

"Tell your man it's break time."

"The hell you say, it ain't easy cranking an old car once the engine's gone cold. Good thing for you I know how to keep it idling."

"TMI."

"Shit, you called me."

Zones ducked inside the cab. The wipers sounded like croaking frogs as they rubbed against the windshield. His phone went silent. "Hello...James?"

"Hold your horses, child. I'm getting to my computer. Let's see…according to papers filed with the SEC, an investment bank, Capitol Securities…hey…isn't that Congressman Stonewall's firm? It was in the report I gave you."

"One and the same, who was the filing attorney?"

"…Ben-Jarvis, Green and Ellis, aren't they—"

"The slick licks that represented the congressman? Yeah, and I just found out that one of them is behind the bombings and Detective Rome's kidnapping."

"How do you know?"

"One of them has a penchant for Victorian frocks."

"What?"

"Still not up on your fashion?"

"I know I shouldn't, but I'm gonna ask. Why are you still sniffing around this case? You got your money."

"Can't explain right now, but send me the congressman's address."

"Stonewall's home…this time of night…you sure?"

"Sure as I'll ever be."

"Okay, you know white folk still shoot niggas at night. It's your black ass."

Seconds later, Zones' phone beeped.

"Where to?" the cab driver asked.

Zones opened the text message, "Decatur."

* * *

The cab stopped outside a stately home with large white columns and steep gabled roofs. A veranda hugged the front and the sides like arms around a waist. Zones leapt from the cab. The rain continued to beat down as he raced up four brick steps to the protection of the covered porch. Two large, white doors stood closed beneath a single bright light. He grabbed onto a golden lion's head knocker; it filled his hand. Zones slammed it against the door. He turned to see the cab still idling. The rain pelted it severely. He turned back to hear the chink of locks opening. The door cracked.

"May I help you?" a twangy voice, no louder than a kitten's meow, asked.

"Yes, ma'am, I was looking for Congressman Stonewall."

"Are you with the police too?"

"…Yes, ma'am, the FBI actually. Is the congressman here?"

The door eased open. Her blonde coif and pencil-thin frame blocked the entrance. "I told the other detective that I hadn't seen him all day."

"…The other detective?"

"Yes, a black gal with bushy hair. I can't remember her name though."

"How long ago was that?"

"About two hours. Is there something wrong? Is Stoney okay? He hasn't returned any of my calls."

"Everything is fine, Mrs. Stonewall. Did the detective say where she was going?"

"No, but I told her Stoney might be working late with his attorneys at the office."

"Where's that?"

"Downtown Atlanta." She squinted and her face tightened. "Oh, I can't remember the address. It's that pyramid building—"

Zones tore from the porch. He skipped two steps as he raced back to the cab.

"SunTrust Plaza, downtown Atlanta." He slid into the backseat of the cab and slammed the door closed. "And I got an extra C-note if you get me there in fifteen minutes."

The cab's engine revved, and the rear tires licked the wet pavement many times before finding their grip. They sped away down the street toward downtown Atlanta, zipping along the slick, wet roads. The driver dodged machine and pedestrian in a race with time and money.

"I didn't say you should kill someone to get me there."

The driver pulled up to SunTrust Plaza. Zones shoved one hundred and thirty dollars at him, hopped from the cab and hurried inside the lobby.

"May I help you?" someone shouted.

Zones turned to see a man in uniform approaching him. *Shit.* He wasn't sure how he would talk himself past the guard. "Yes, officer," he said, knowing the man was not an officer. "I'm here to pick up papers from my attorneys."

"It's after-hours; the building's closed."

"I know, officer…you see…I have this child support hearing in the morning and…you know…ol' girl is trying to break a brother down. She won't let me see my kids but she wants—"

"To get paid," the guard said. "Bro, I feel you. That's why I'm on third shift now, trying to pay her ass."

"This is her." Zones slipped his phone from his pocket. He showed the guard a picture of Detective Rome. "Have you seen her? She came through earlier."

"My shift just started. But I tell you what, give me the name of the law firm."

"...Ben-Jarvis, Green and Ellis."

"Wait here, I'll give them a call."

The guard made his way to a large desk and plucked the phone receiver from its hook. Zones eased out of sight, over to a bank of elevators and pressed the call button. The door slid open, and before stepping inside he studied a large directory mounted on the wall. *BGE twenty-third floor.* He stepped inside the elevator, pushed twenty-three and waited. The door did not close, and the elevator did not move. He pressed the button again, still no response. Zones exited the elevator. He noticed a closed door labeled *stairs and* shook the handle. *Locked.*

"Sir, sir," the guard called. He rounded the corner. "There you are. I called but didn't get an answer. Sorry about that."

"He must've left the papers upstairs, or he could be taking a dump or something. I got to get those papers tonight, or the judge is gonna lock my black ass up."

"Tell you what, Bro," he pulled a card from his side pocket and swiped the access reader, "you go up, get your shit and come straight back down here."

"Thanks, officer."

Zones rode the elevator up to the twenty-third floor. He stepped out into dead quiet. Two large double doors stood closed tight. He yanked on the knob, but the doors did not open. He checked another set on the opposite end of the hall. They were locked as well. A sign above a door read, *Exit.* Zones stepped through it and into the stairwell. He scurried up one flight to the next floor and followed the row of locked doors off the hall to one labeled, *Capitol Securities.* He turned the knob. The door opened onto a dimly lighted reception area. He followed the faint sound of voices to a closed door at the rear of the office, pressing his ear against it and recognizing Congressman Stonewall's voice. He listened but could not quite hear all they said.

Zones burst through the door. All heads swung to him.

"Dr. Zones, what're you doing here?" Congressman Stonewall asked. "This is a private meeting."

"Whatever you're about to sign, Congressman, don't sign it."

"…Why not?"

"Because one of these men is a murderer."

SIXTY-FOUR

"…I am a riddler."

"WHAT'RE YOU TALKING ABOUT, Doctor?" Congressman Stonewall said. "You know these are my attorneys."

"Yes and one of them, if not all three, is behind the bombings, the kidnapping of Detective Rome and the murder of Professor Landrosky and Angela Hightower."

"The hell you say." Attorney Ben-Jarvis leapt to his feet. "Byrnes Maximus has already been found guilty of those crimes."

"Convenient how he got blown to shit and couldn't be questioned. But that's just the kind of de facto proof the bomber hoped for."

"And what proof do you have?"

"For one, I know that your firm stood to lose out on millions of dollars in fees if H.R. 150 passed in Congress. It would have derailed the money train you had going by representing the Saudis and other OPEC countries."

"That's pure bullshit."

"Is that a legal objection, Counsel?"

"Is that all you got? 'Cause if it is, I must ask you to leave."

"What's he talking about, Robert?" Congressman Stonewall asked. "You've been double-dipping with the Saudis and OPEC?"

"Don't listen to him, Stoney."

"Are you representing me and then lobbying for the ragheads? Fuck man, you know how that could look. My political opponents would rake me over the coals if they found that out."

Ben-Jarvis turned to Zones. "I must ask you to go, Doctor."

"Last time I looked, the name on the door said Capitol Securities, not BGE."

"You need to get rid of him, Stoney, so we can decide what's next."

"Yeah, tell us, what's next, Stoney," Zones mocked him.

"That's Congressman Stonewall to both of you. And my next move is to get new legal representation. You three assholes," he pointed to his attorneys, "are on your own. Now get the fuck out of here!"

"One more question," Zones said. "The Halloween party last year, which one of you wore the Victorian frock?"

"I did, why?" Ben-Jarvis asked.

Zones said nothing. He smiled, turned and walked through the door. The others, including Congressman Stonewall, followed. They walked a short way down a hall until they heard a loud noise.

Zones stopped and turned in the direction of the sound. "What was that?"

"I didn't hear anything," Congressman Stonewall said.

"Bullshit, I heard it too," Ben-Jarvis said. "Sounded like it came from there." He pointed at a door.

"That was nothing…probably some boxes fell down. I stacked them in their earlier."

"Do boxes also moan?" Ben-Jarvis snatched open the door. "What is this?"

Zones rushed to the door and pushed Ben-Jarvis aside. "Olga!" She lay bound and gagged beneath a pile of cleaning supplies on the floor of a storage closet. He cleared the bottles and boxes away from her when shots rang out. Blood splattered him and stained the packages strewn over the floor. Zones turned to see three bloodied bodies lying there like mats tossed down carelessly. He looked over to see Congressman Stonewall squared-off, his hand outstretched. At the end of it was a smoldering gun. Zones wiped blood from his neck. "So, it was you after all."

"Surprised, Doctor?"

"Not really, just wondering how you beat parts of my profile."

"Your captain was kind enough to copy me on your analysis, so I knew what you were looking for."

"Then you knew I said the unsub was highly organized. How will you explain this mess?"

"Easy, you came in...confronted Robert...he pulled out a gun...shot you, Detective Rome, poor ol' Joe and Ben here and me. I survived, the only one, of course."

"What happens when the resulting investigation reveals your lawyers' connection to the Saudis? They won't stop there."

"You just let me worry about that. Now get up."

Zones eased up from the floor, hands raised. "What now?"

"Pick her up."

"Just shoot me right here and carry around your own dead weight."

"How about I shoot her first and you watch her die."

Congressman Stonewall moved the gun away from Zones and pointed it at Detective Rome. Zones lifted her from the floor, still bound, not fully conscious. The congressman marched him back to the conference room that overlooked the now quiet Peachtree Street.

"If you're thinking of jumping," Congressman Stonewall said, "a bullet to the head is a lot less painful...and a lot less messy. Put her down."

Zones lowered Detective Rome's limp body onto the table. She moaned.

"What did you give her?"

"Just coffee—with a special little...how do you people say it...somethin, somethin."

"Why? She can't identify you."

"When Detective Rome showed up at my office today, I thought she may have remembered some small thing. I was right. It seems that my love for expensive, exotic colognes betrayed me. I could see her piecing it all together with her probing questions. By the time she realized that I knew what she knew, it was too late for her, of course."

"And Muhammad El-Arabi?"

"Who? Oh, of course, your dead Muslim. He couldn't mind his own business. Never heard of a tree-hugging terrorist before. He should have been out blowing up shit like any self-respecting raghead instead of meddling in United States foreign policy."

"So you killed him, left him inside the animal shelter and detonated a bomb to cover it up."

"Only I didn't; the ME's report said he died from a brain infection."

"One caused by drinking water contaminated with your little mind control concoction."

"We lost astronauts during the race to the moon and countless others in drug trials. Look at it as a casualty for the advancement of science."

"A pawn, just like all the others."

"You're talking about Angela, right? Considering that I saved her from a life of pimps and twenty-five dollar johns she met in dark back alleys, it's the least she could've done."

"...And don't forget Professor Landrosky."

"Uza was paid good money for his work, and he delivered. His loyalty...well...that's another story. He got his payment for that as well. You, Doctor, on the other hand, weren't that easy to kill."

"...Your goons in DC?"

"And my little bed massager. How did you get out of that?"

Zones did not answer. Again, he glanced down onto the street below. "Why go through with the bombings? You could've carried out your plans without the...*carnage.*"

"Where's the fun in that? Besides, the bombings were Uza's idea. He had hoped they would be tied to Dr. El-Arabi."

"To discredit him in case he went public with the nanoscience experiments in Qatif."

"I must admit, it wasn't the most original idea."

"And what about the other crimes?"

"Ingenious, weren't they? I was quite impressed that you figured out the acronym."

"Again, why the theatrics?"

"It's as you've said, Doctor. I am a riddler. Plus, it kept the authorities busy."

"Why sacrifice your accomplice, your aide, Byrnes Maximus?"

"Dear Byrnes was not an accomplice; he was a pawn like all the others. Sure, he helped me acquire that gun from the NYPD and plant it at the language center. He didn't specifically target the weapon from your mother's case, of course; it just happened that way."

"Still doesn't explain blowing him up."

"Byrnes got a little greedy."

"…The trust money from al-Saud?"

"Somehow, he got it in his mind we were partners. It was a godsend when he had you booted from the case. But too bad for you, you couldn't leave well enough alone."

"So I've been told." Zones turned to Detective Rome. She still lay unconscious on the table. He stroked her hand and feared that he had run out of chances or time to save her. He turned back to Congressman Stonewall, gun in hand. "Now what?"

"Now, I finish what I started." The congressman opened a drawer to a large cabinet. He reached inside and pulled out a bomb vest, like the one he had fashioned earlier for Detective Rome. "Put this on her." He slid the vest across the table and dipped his hand back inside the cabinet, pulling out one more. "Don't worry, Dr. Zones. This one goes with me. It's the convincer, my George W. Bush, if you will." He shoved the other vest into a briefcase.

"That's the decider."

"Whatever, put it on her."

"Do it yourself." The congressman's armed hand tightened up. "You're gonna have to shoot me."

"With pleasure."

A flash and a loud bang filled the room. Glass shattered and sprayed the air. Zones crashed to the floor. A sharp pain rushed through him; it felt like a fat woman in high heels dancing on every nerve. Blood gushed out from a hole in his right shoulder. He jammed his finger into it. The rush slowed.

"You shot me, you fuck!"

Congressman Stonewall hurried to dress Detective Rome in the bomb vest. "I figure you've got thirty minutes before you bleed out, about as much time as she has before she becomes a puzzle—literally." He secured her in the vest and pulled the phone from the wall jack. He searched Zones and ripped his phone from his pocket. "I'll take that." He tossed it into his briefcase. The congressman flipped up the lid of a laptop and worked at it. Shortly, words poured from its speakers—one of his speeches. "Change of plans. I probably shouldn't get wounded. Preferably, I will be far away from here when you two…kiss the sky."

"It won't be long before the FBI figures out you were behind all this."

"By that time, I'll be somewhere tropical with a billion dollars in my possession." He raised his pinky finger to the corner of his lip, like Dr.

Evil, and laughed. "I've always wanted to do that. It's nothing but good times from here on, Dr. Zones. Too bad your time, good or otherwise, is about to end forever. Don't worry; I'll tip my wing to you on the flyover."

"So it was about the trust money."

"That, my friend, was a bonus. Those sand jockeys were paying me a pittance for the risk I was taking. They won't miss it."

"You won't get away with this."

"I have so far. And there won't be much left of you or this place in a few minutes. Now, shut up!" Congressman Stonewall slammed his foot into the side of Zones' head.

* * *

Zones awoke to a pounding headache and blurred vision. The room spun like a top losing its momentum. Blood, some wet, some dry, drenched and sealed him to the floor like half cured paint. He sat up, struggled to his feet and managed to walk over to the conference table where Detective Rome still lay. There was no bomb vest. Zones raked his hand over his bloody coat, pulling back its flap. The bomb vest was strapped to him and the timer on it was counting down. The recording of the congressman's speech continued to play. Zones ripped the computer from the power outlet and flung it through the shattered window. Five minutes remained on the timer. He ran his hand along the many wires that crisscrossed the vest.

"What the hell is going on here?" someone shouted. Zones looked up. The guard from earlier stood in the doorway of the conference room. "Man, what happened to you? I've been looking for you all over. Then I saw the broken window on my rounds and—"

"We've got to get this off me," Zones said, his voice raspy.

"Man, do you know you're bleeding? I don't want to get AIDS."

"That'll be the least of your worries if this bomb goes off."

"Bomb!" His voice shot up an octave or two. "They don't pay me enough to be fucking with no bomb." He turned and bolted from the room.

"I'm FBI, motherfucka. If you leave, I'll make sure your child support gets tripled."

The guard returned. "Tripled, really?"

"Tripled, motherfucka, you heard me. You'd be working so many jobs they'll have to issue you Jamaican, Mexican and Nigerian passports."

"Damn, man. What do you want me to do?"

"You got a phone?"

"…Right here."

Zones dialed. "Dr. Bruno, I got you on speaker. There's another bomb, like the one before."

"Dr. Zones? What do you mean another bomb?"

"Another vest bomb, only this time it's not a hero bomb."

"A Hero Bait Bomb, are you sure?"

"Listen, I got less than five minutes on the timer."

"Then I suggest you not do anything as before, Doctor. It would seem that this guy really likes jerking your chain. Who's he got on a string this time?"

"Me."

"I see. It seems this guy loves playing mind games with you, Dr. Zones. Just wait it out as before."

"That's not an option." Zones slammed the phone on the table. He turned to the guard. "Find me something sharp, a knife or scissors."

"You heard the man. He said to wait." Zones gave him a hard stare. "There's a kitchen down the hall."

"Go. Go!"

Zones placed his back to a large mirror hanging on the wall and felt along the vest. A fine seam, one he had seen before in the first vest, ran vertically the length of its rear. He saw no wires in this one, however. Zones shuffled around the room; he was faint and tired. His blood loss had weakened him, but it had slowed. He braced his good arm against the table to steady himself.

The guard returned but paused at the door. "Did you know there were dead bodies out in the hall?"

"You got something to cut with?"

"I found this knife."

Zones waved him over. "You see this timer right there?" The guard nodded. "What does it say?"

"Three minutes and thirty seconds."

"That's how much time is left before all your baby momma drama is over for good." The guard's eyes grew wide. "Now, give me your hand."

Zones wrapped his bloody palm around the guard's hand. He moved it over the back of the vest. "You feel that seam?"

"…Yeah."

"Take that knife, cut along this seam and don't stray one bit."

The guard sliced the vest along a line he could only feel, slow and deliberate, as if he was cutting sushi. He rent it in two as Zones glanced at the timer. Less than two minutes remained.

"Now what?"

"What's your name, Brother?"

"Luquicious Jackson."

"Luquicious?"

"My mother wanted a girl. My friends call me Luke."

"Okay, Luke, gently remove the vest." He eased the vest from around Zones.

"What do you want me to do with it?"

"Toss it out the window."

"Can't, I got guys down there cleaning up glass."

"Shit. Sit it down and grab her."

"We won't make it. There's only a minute and thirty seconds left, and you can barely stand up."

"Don't worry about me, just grab her. And don't stop or touch anything, no matter what."

They ran from the room. The guard tore down the hall with Detective Rome slung over his shoulder. Zones labored close behind. He dragged himself over the three dead bodies rotting in the hall, rounding a corner only to see Detective Rome lying on the floor. *What the hell?* Zones staggered over to her.

"Luke," he called out. No one answered. Zones moved to the doorway of a room and saw Luke standing at an open safe. "What're you doing?"

"Man, there's got to be a hundred thousand dollars in here."

"We gotta go."

"And leave all this bread? Are you crazy?" Luke stuffed his pockets with bricks of cash.

Zones grabbed him to pull him away. "Let's go. That bomb is about to blow." Luke fought him off. Zones hurried back to Detective Rome, and with his uninjured arm, he grabbed her shirt collar and dragged her toward the elevators. His pain grew, but he fought against it. The door to one elevator stood open. He stumbled into it and leaned Detective

Rome against a nearby wall. The lighted numbers on the call display were blurred. He raked his hand across the panel of buttons, but the door did not close. Zones pounded them, but the door remained open. He slumped to the floor. Through his haze, he saw Luke charging toward him. There was a bright flash and a loud roar. Luke no longer charged; he flew through the air and landed inside the cab of the elevator. It shook terribly from the shock of the blast. A ball of fire, burning bright amber, roared toward them. Zones ripped the access card from Luke's pant pocket. He swiped it over the reader and pressed a button on the floor call panel. The doors closed, though it seemed like they took forever, and the elevator descended. A short ride later, the doors sprung open.

Luke, his pockets bulging with cash, lifted Detective Rome from the wall. He carried her to a lounge area in the lobby and laid her onto a sofa. Sirens blared in the distance. Soon the place was crawling with fire and rescue personnel. They wheeled Zones and Detective Rome to awaiting ambulances.

"What're you doing?" Zones asked a paramedic.

"You've lost an awful lot of blood, sir. We have to get you to the hospital."

"I'm not going to the hospital; patch me up right here."

"You've been shot, sir." Zones struggled to throw off his caregiver and free himself from the gurney. The paramedic held him down. "If you don't calm down, I'll have to sedate you." Zones stopped his fight with the paramedic. They loaded him onto the ambulance.

"I got one more," someone shouted.

Luke stepped up into the same ambulance. "We cool, Bro?"

"We're cool. But if you want to keep it that way, get me out of this." Luke wasted no time unstrapping Zones. "You got a car?"

"Yeah, but—"

"Keys?" Luke pulled them from his pant pocket. Zones snatched them. He noticed a little less girth on him. "Where's your money?"

"...In my car."

"Great, what is it and where's it parked?"

"Green Crown Vic on thirty-inch chrome whips, parked on the ground floor of the garage across the street. Don't scratch it."

"Let me have that coat, your hat and your phone."

Zones cracked the cargo doors of the ambulance, peeking out before throwing them open. He stepped from the bed, pulled the cap emblazoned with *Security* down to cover his face and disappeared into the crush of first responders.

* * *

Sparks flew from beneath the Crown Vic as cold steel struck warm asphalt, fishtailing out of the parking deck. He raced down Baker Street and hung a left onto Piedmont Road. He pulled Luke's phone from his pocket and dialed.

"James, it's me."

"...Dr. Zones? Caller ID says Luquicious Jackson. Who's that?"

"Not important. I need to know if Congressman Stonewall owns a plane."

"Listen, Doctor, I don't have time for this. There's been a bombing at some office building in Atlanta, and the captain has me waking up everybody to patrol downtown Decatur."

"I know. I was just there. The congressman was behind the bombings. He tried to blow our asses up in that building."

"Our, meaning whose?"

"Detective Rome and me. I believe he's leaving the country on a private plan. My guess is that he's heading for Cuba."

"I should've known you were mixed up in this somehow. Do you ever get tired of trouble?"

"We can discuss my propensities later. Right now I need—"

"It's a Beechcraft Baron G58 and it's hangered at DeKalb-Peachtree Airport."

"Tell the captain to get some men over there. Don't let him leave. With a billion dollars, the congressman could make the moon disappear."

"What do you—"

Zones hung up. He gunned the Crown Vic, heading down Piedmont Road, through North Atlanta, toward the airport. Soon the control tower lights loomed in the distance, just above DeKald County. A squad of flashing blue lights greeted him. A uniformed officer charged Zones as he approached the airport's entrance. Barricades stretched across the road.

Zones rolled down his window. "FBI." He flashed his badge. "Is Captain Franklin here?"

The officer gawked at the car and then back at him. "You're bleeding."

"Yeah, and it hurts like hell. The captain, is he here?"

"Through the gate and follow this road to the end. The terminal is on the right."

Officers removed the barricades. Zones pulled through the gate and raced down the long, straight road. He hopped from the car and pushed through the terminal door.

"Captain Franklin?" he asked an officer. He pointed to another door. Zones rushed over to it. The captain was standing outside with other officers. They stared into the night's sky. "Captain," he called out weakly, "did you get him?"

"Shit, Doctor, I hope that's red paint."

"Did you stop Congressman Stonewall?"

The captain turned his gaze back toward the sky. "That's him there." He pointed to lights blinking against the black curtain of night. "Sorry, Doctor, looks like we're too late."

"Too late? He's right there. Aren't we near an airbase? Have the military scramble a few MiGs to force him down?"

"You've been watching too much TV. All we can do now is have the FAA track him until he lands."

"I know where he's heading, Cuba."

"Then it's up to the diplomats."

"You think Castro will send back a billion dollars, man? That kind of money will buy him a lot of immunity."

"What're you talking about?" Zones didn't answer. Captain Franklin eyeballed him from head to toe. "You look a mess. I'm calling an ambulance."

Zones watched the plane lights ascend. Congressman Stonewall was right. He had gotten away with everything. But it didn't seem right. The taste of it was worse than the airplane fuel that tickled the back of his throat in an unpleasant way. He knew that after the initial media blitz, this whole thing would fade behind the glare of the next headline. *I need to stop him, but how?* Just then, an officer brushed past him.

"Captain, the controller wants to know when he can have the runway back to land the other planes."

"When I say so, that's when."

"He said he can't keep them up there for much longer."

"Okay, let's pack it up. But tell him to keep tracking that plane. I'll let the suits in DC decide what to do with one of their own."

"Yes sir." The officer darted back inside the terminal.

"That's it," Zones said, almost in a whisper.

"What's it?"

"Was Congressman Stonewall alone?"

"The tower controller said he piloted the plane himself. No mention of any passengers."

"What's the congressman's cell phone number?"

"Hell if I know."

"Let me see your phone." With a distrusting look, Captain Franklin handed it over. Zones dialed. "James, I need Congressman Stonewall's cell phone number." He plucked a pen from the shirt pocket of an officer standing nearby. As James read the phone number to him, he grabbed the captain's hand and penned the number onto his palm. "One more thing, send a copy of Congressman Stonewall's speech to my phone, the closing salutation only." He hung up and dialed again. "Stats, this is Zones."

"T.O.'s boy, why are you calling me from a DeKalb County police captain's phone?"

"Listen, that trick you did with my phone, you know, taking it over. How did you do that?"

"With an emulation app I designed and installed onto your phone. Why, you want to give it to The Man?"

"Tell me how to do it."

"No. It's my program, and the Feds can't have it."

"Shit, Stats, this is no time to be possessive. Look, you still want to be a hero, right?"

"I am a hero."

"Right, you are. Well, there's a bad man who has hurt a lot of people. He's getting away. I can...*we* can stop him, but I need to know how you hacked my phone." There was a long pause. Zones watched as the lights from the plane drifted farther away. The plane would be out of cell phone range soon. Not much could be done after that. "...Stats, you still there?"

"He's a bad guy, huh?"

"...Very, very bad."

"You'll need the passcode." Stats called it out. Zones hung up.

"What's this all about, Doctor?" Captain Franklin asked. "What're you doing? And who's this Stats guy?"

Zones ignored him. He moved the captain's palm toward what little light there was and dialed Congressman Stonewall's number from Luke's cell phone. It rang as he held it in place, trapped between his shoulder and neck.

"Hello," the voice on the other end answered.

"Congressman."

"Well, I see I underestimated you once again, Dr. Zones. How are your shoulder and your face?"

"I'm still good-looking, and my shoulder can support an RPG."

"Touché, Doctor. And I take it that Detective Rome is in one piece?"

"No thanks to you."

"It seems it all worked out well for everyone."

"You know…we won't stop looking for you."

"I wouldn't expect anything less."

Zones used the captain's phone to dial his own cell phone. Congressman Stonewall had tossed it into his briefcase with the vest bomb. The phone rang, and Zones entered the passcode for the emulation app Stats installed. Soon his phone's display appeared on the screen.

"Mind telling us where you're going?"

"I told you, somewhere warm."

"That somewhere wouldn't by chance be Cuba, would it?"

"Tenacious as ever, Dr. Zones. I once tracked a tenacious black rhino across the Serengeti."

"Did it get away from you as well?"

"Let's just say I'm going to miss seeing its head mounted on my library wall. Please tell the captain I'm sorry for all the trouble. It's been fun."

"No talking you into giving yourself up, Congressman? Last chance."

"You know better than I, Dr. Zones, that there're always more chances."

"Not for you."

"Good-bye, Doctor."

"One more thing, Congressman."

"Yes?"

Zones used the emulation app on his phone to open the recording of the congressman's speech. It played.

> *"God bless you. God bless the United States of America."*

Zones hung up.

"What was that all about?" Captain Franklin asked.

Before Zones could answer, the sky lit up; fire rained down far off in the distance. The explosion could be heard for miles. The plane that occupied everyone's attention was no longer ascending. The wreckage plummeted to the ground, streaking the night's sky like burning fireworks. Zones stood and watched. Satisfied and unshaken; he knew what the others did not.

The captain snapped his head around from the scene as he turned back to Zones. "What the hell just happened?"

"Justice just happened."

Zones peeled back the flap of the captain's coat, tucked his phone inside a pocket and, without another word, marched toward the terminal. Shouts from the captain admonished him to be sure and get his wounds looked after. He pushed through the door of the terminal out to where he had parked the Crown Vic. He hopped inside, barreled down the ramrod-straight airport road and through the still barricaded entrance. This case had ended as it had begun: with death and destruction.

SIXTY-FIVE
The Homestead

ZONES SAT ON THE attic floor of his childhood home, Indian style. He pored through boxes of papers and reports. His bandaged shoulder was on the mend, days after being shot by Congressman Stonewall. The doctors wanted to keep him longer, but he wasn't having any of that. They wanted to pretty up his wound a little bit more. The scar reminded him how close he had come to death—for the fourth time. *But who's counting.* For the moment, he was back where he wanted to be. There were still questions to be answered about his mother's death. From what he had found out so far, and from his talk with Belinda, her death seemed connected to her job with the building department. The two cases had intersected at a point almost thirty years apart. One had its resolution, now the other demanded final closure.

"Found anything interesting?" Detective Rome asked. She sat a cup of tea on a box next to Zones and kissed him on his neck.

"Not unless you're into inspection reports and engineering analysis. Want to see?"

"I'll pass."

"Thanks for coming."

"It's the least I could do. Besides, it gives me a chance to see where you grew up."

"Not much to see. I only spent four years here. I barely remember it."

"It's nice, nonetheless." She scanned the room. "Say, did you ever find out what that key was for?"

"Shapiro's still working on that."

Detective Rome took a sip from her cup. She raked her hands through Zones' hair. "How did Stonewall ever think he would get away with this?"

"Hubris."

"And you think his planting the gun connected to your mother's case at one of the bomb sites was purely coincidental?"

"That's what he said."

"But why did Stonewall kill the kid?"

"The pizza delivery guy? Probably because he recognized him from the fraternity. Hard to explain why a U.S. congressman is camping out with the eses."

"And Angela, I can't believe he made her endure a sexual assault just so he could get his kicks."

"Sick bastard, what else can I say?"

"What did the captain say after you told him how the plane was blown up?"

"His guy won Stonewall's congressional seat, so he wasn't all that choked up about it. Any way you can get it, I guess."

"Huh." Detective Rome leaned in to kiss Zones.

"What's that for?"

"Do I need a reason? Drink your tea."

Zones continued to separate papers into stacks on the floor. He shuffled them out like cards in a deck. The case felt concluded and like new. There was a final resolution with Congressman Stonewall. The monies pledged by the Saudis would go to the NIH for disease research and nothing else, thanks to a series of well-placed, anonymous calls to Congress threatening to expose their swarm research. Now he knew he had to move on to a new challenge, something more personal and fraught with more pain.

THE END

Don't miss the next novel in

E.W. SULLIVAN's

Award winning Thelonious Zones trilogy

THE PATH to KRIYA

A MURDER-MYSTERY THRILLER

*9 7 8 0 9 8 8 7 5 8 4 0 7 *